D0976996

Ashes of Gold

Also by J. Elle

THE WINGS OF EBONY DUOLOGY

Wings of Ebony

WINGS OF EBONY

J. ELLE

A DENENE MILLNER BOOK

SIMON & SCHUSTER BFYR

NEW YORK • LONDON • TORONTO • SYDNEY • NEW DELHI

An imprint of Simon & Schuster Children's Publishing Division
1230 Avenue of the Americas, New York, New York 10020

Interior design by Hilary Zarycky
The text for this book was set in Adobe Jensen Pro.
Manufactured in the United States of America
First Edition
2 4 6 8 10 9 7 5 3 1
Library of Congress Cataloging-in-Publication Data
Names: Elle, J., author.
Title: Ashes of gold / J. Elle.
Description: First edition. | New York : Simon & Schuster Books for Young Readers, [2022] | Series: Wings of ebony ; book 2 | "A Denene Millner Book." | Audience: Ages 14 up. | Audience: Grades 10-12. | Summary: Half god and half human, Rue has made a vow to restore the magic that the Chancellor and the Grays have stolen from the Ghizoni and take back their land; she has more fully embraced her identity among the people of Yiyo Peak, but she is also from East Row in Houston, and girls from East Row do not give in to oppressors.
Identifiers: LCCN 2021008409 (print) | LCCN 2021008410 (ebook) | ISBN 9781534470705 (hardcover) | ISBN 9781534470729 (ebook)
Subjects: LCSH: African American teenagers—Juvenile fiction. | Magic—Juvenile fiction. | Good and evil—Juvenile fiction. | Identity (Psychology)—Juvenile fiction. | Young adult fiction. | CYAC: Magic—Fiction. | Good and evil—Fiction. | Identity—Fiction. | African Americans—Fiction. | LCGFT: Fantasy fiction.
Classification: LCC PZ7.1.E438 As 2022 (print) | LCC PZ7.1.E438 (ebook) | DDC 813.6 [Fic]—dc23
LC record available at https://lccn.loc.gov/2021008409
LC ebook record available at https://lccn.loc.gov/2021008410

To Mommy,
for making me believe
I could do anything,

and,

to Emily,
who held me up
every step of the way.

PROLOGUE

KAELI BERRIES DOT THE morning leaves like dew; usually they sparkle in the sun's rays, winking at me over the edge of the mountain peak.

But this morning there is no sun. No glittering water at the edge of the shore. This morning fog hugs the island like a scarf tied too tight. I squint through the hanging gray clouds, and a chill of air sweeps up my arm every few minutes. I tighten my sleeves around myself and clench my skirt tighter in my fist. The sooner we finish, the sooner we can get out of here.

Mornings like this, when the world is just waking up and the blood bugs are still asleep, Memi and I do our walks to gather. It is much cooler, so we do not return home as itchy. I work a few berries from branches where the leaves have fallen, and salty mountain air gusts my tightly coiled hair, the gold twine wrapped around it coming undone. The berries hide beneath the blooms of the *shiske* flower, a thick red plant with toxic leaves. In their center is a tiny red berry, hiding like a pearl in an oyster.

I dig my fingers around a stubborn one determined to stay attached to its flower. The riper berries are softer, but too ripe and their sticky sweetness sours on the tongue. The blooms that are just opening are the perfect ones. Still hard on the outside, but when pestled are smooth, creamy, and sweet. The foliage on the island is thick with them, a tapestry of bendy black-bark trees dotted with red.

Jpango leaves curl and twist over one another, fighting for sunlight. I pull my shift up around my knees and pluck more red dots, dropping them in the belly of my skirt. I glance over my shoulder at Memi. Sweat drips from the edges of her head wrap. Tufts of salt-and-pepper hair coil up on top of her head like a crown. Her fingers work around the berries, and with one snatch of her wrist, she grabs a fistful to drop in her makeshift bucket. Her eyes flick to mine and her eyebrows jump.

"If you want that lekerae for your ceremony," she says, "you better fill that skirt faster."

A smile tugs at my lips. Memi's threats are as rigid as jpango sap. She is all sticky sweet. She's been stocking up on kaeli for moons. Because tonight when the moon is highest, it will be my turn to dance the l'jyndego to the Ancestors. My turn to be presented to our clan as a woman in her own right. Kaeli lekerae is the first dish a girl eats after she becomes a woman. It is sacred, and to make it takes all day and thousands of berries at the precise sweetness.

I toss one in my mouth and move down the thorny bush, working my fingers between the leaves. I crane for another view of the water, hoping the sun has decided to wake and greet us too. But fog hangs, closer somehow, over stoic waves. An eeriness prickles my spine at the sight of the fog moving in from the ocean, hovering like a ghost. I scoot closer to Memi, picking berries in arm's reach of her.

The Ancestors say the goddess of the sun smiles on us, washing us in her warmth. And her lover, the god of moon, smiles so radiantly at night—so captivated by her beauty that he glows too. But when neither shows their face, it is a foreboding day. A day for wrapping hands in prayer cloths and singing around the fire. The lines in Memi's face say she senses it too, even if she doesn't admit it aloud.

"Very good, then," she says. "Come on. Before it gets too hot out here. You have a full day ahead."

"Ya, Memi." Today, the morning of my ceremony, I'd woken more tired than usual. I was up all night with Tomae picking out which silks and jewels to pair with my sash later today, deciding how to paint my face, and what beads would adorn my hair. Or messing up my hair more like. Little sisters are good at that. Tomae will not turn out for seven more years, so she's wrapped up in furs still, fast asleep, while I'm out here. But I wouldn't have it any other way.

I've waited on this day for as long as I can remember. Since Memi would fold me on her lap and let her rings swallow my fingers. She'd wrap me in her gold robes and kick out her ankles, showing me how to dance in praise to the Ancestors.

It was fun then. I swallow. Now the thought makes my insides wriggle like a bed of worms. What if the Ancestors think me not good enough? What if I dance wrong and when Memi reaches to put the *usapa* around my neck, with its fine jade beads, what if . . .

My breath catches. No, I will not think it. I will turn out beautifully, just like my saisa and Memi and GraMemi and her saisas and every Yakanna before me. I clench my robes in my hand.

The fog is suddenly so blindingly close, I can hardly see the bushes of berries steps in front of me. I shudder.

"Memi, can we get back to the chakusa? The clouds are snoozing far too close to the ground." I touch my hair. It's set in coiled rollers, and the humid air won't be helpful for the style.

She gazes up to the sky and her brows kiss. "Yes, maybe you are right."

Thunder rolls and I knot my skirt, the berries stored there like a sack dangling against my leg. I loop my arm under Memi's and she grabs her walking stick and we turn back for our village. Her fingers hang loose at her side. Somewhere a branch cracks. She nudges me with her elbow and I let my hand hang by my side, tingling, warm, ready.

Ever since the veil was extended over the entire island, we have coexisted with the Grays. Most are friendly enough. They keep to their villages. We trade once each moon. They love our silk dyed robes and they're very adept at metalworking.

But occasionally, a radical or two among the bunch gets beside himself, parched with ambition, envious at us—the "brown-skinned with magic" as they call us—and shoves his way into our village late at night, demanding we share our magic. Demanding we heal their ailing parent or some other reason they deserve to have what the Ancestors gave us: magic. We have rules, lines they cannot cross. When they barge in like that, armed with their sharp blades, with their demands and murder in their eyes, we cut them down. And tighten up our sentry patrols.

Thirteen have gone missing from our village in the past moon. Twenty-two before that. Four washed up on the shore, bloated and open-eyed. All appearing to have drowned. My chest pangs, my jaw tightens. The Grays did it . . . even the village Elders suspect it. But no one could ever prove it.

Memi taps her ears, snatching me from my ruing. *Listen,* I can practically hear her think. Branches crackle against the sound of crashing waves. It's quiet, subtle, but goosebumps skitter up my arm. This part of the island is ours—its rivers, its trees, its kaeli berries. That's the agreement. I bite down. And aside from Trading Meet each moon, no Gray has any reason to be over here. We respect their boundary. They never respect ours.

We buried the four by the Ancestors, next to Yiyo Peak. We pray daily that those gone live on with the Ancestors in eternal peace. Memi gestures for me to get closer to her. I do. Branches scratch my legs, but the cover of leaves isn't one we can risk. If someone is following us, we know this part of the forest better than anyone. Heat tickles my fingers as we creep over branches. I won't be a body washed up on the shore. I have a turning out ceremony today, a life to live, and if I'm to be all that Memi is, a clan to run . . . one day! A sick feeling twists in my gut remembering the faces, and yet so many are still missing. This should be a morning of celebration. *If the Grays come for me . . .* My knees shake, threatening to go out from beneath me. *I-I will defend myself.*

Something burns my leg, but before I can glimpse it, a flicker of movement between the branches catches my eye. I bend instinctively, crouching behind a thick jpango tree, hiding myself in its folds, my heart thumping.

Memi holds out a shaky hand, trying to push me behind her. I touch my burning leg and my fingers are sticky. The thorny branches cloaking us in safety cut me. I shift in my stance to get a better view of my leg and a few berries spill out of my makeshift bucket. *The ceremony!* I reach for them, not wanting to lose even one.

Memi gestures for me to be still, and I notice the fire rolling in her hand. I peer harder between the branches. There is a lone man, young from the looks of it. Skinny, with thin sharp features, a prominent nose, a well-defined jaw. He's one of the well-to-do Grays. The ones with the larger plots of land. The leathers he wears and silver buckle at his waist both confirm his standing. He comes from a name, a family. Which means he knows the rules—well. But I guess he doesn't think they apply to him.

He crouches at the edge of a muddy patch of water. He angles his back to us, and I tiptoe. But his shoulder blocks my view from seeing what he's doing. He leans over the water like he's taking a drink and fiddles with his pockets. I move a branch and step up on a rock for a better view, but my foot slips. Twigs snap under my feet. Memi cuts me an iron stare and I still.

The man is still hunched over the water; thankfully, he didn't hear it. I study Memi to glean some meaning of what she thinks is going on. Why he is on our side of the island. To drink from our river? He has servants that fetch things like that for him, I'm sure. He stands up, dusting off his pants. His skin's as red as a kaeli berry when he stares at the tree line again. His mouth thins and he pulls a blade I hadn't even noticed lying flat in the dirt beside him. It's longer than his arm. I gulp and I swear he looks through the branches right at us.

I gasp. And Memi's thick fingers clamp across my face. Blood pools in my ears. I summon magic to my fingertips and fire erupts in my palm. I squeeze my hand closed and the fireball shrinks. I can't risk him seeing the light. *I don't want to fight this man. But I will. . . . I will defend myself, my people, if I have to.* I think of

Memi's jade and gold armor that she'd left by her bed. Because why would she need to be armed picking berries with her daughter on the morning of her turning out?

The man still stares and tears sting my eyes, panic climbing like bile in my throat. Memi hasn't moved, but terror is etched in her wrinkled expression. Her hand loosens over my mouth. He sees us. I just know it. He knows we're here. The swollen bodies we buried just days ago flicker through my memory. I swallow hard, letting the fire in my hand swell. I've never fought anyone before. I haven't even been fitted for armor. That doesn't happen for three more years after turning out.

Memi mouths the word "stay." I grip her wrist, my nails digging in. *Wait, don't leave me here,* I want to scream, but a word right now could be a knife at both our throats. She unlooses the knot in her dress, and the bunch of berries, hours of labor, spill out like blood on the soil. I tug on my knot tighter, willing mine to stay put.

"I know you're there," the Gray says. He holds open his empty hand and stabs his blade in the dirt. "There. I'm friendly. See? Just needed a drink is all. Long day of walking."

"You've broken the territory agreement," Memi says, stepping out. "Why are you here?"

"A thirst is all."

A thirst? But I don't see a canteen.

"You need a blade that large to get a drink? You have your own rivers to drink from. Trespassing is a punishable offense. But I'm merciful. Get out of here." She lets the fire in her hand go out and shoves the air. A gust of wind obeys Memi's command, shoving the Gray off his feet. The trees behind him tip over. He stumbles up but doesn't flee like I think Memi hoped he would.

I let the fire simmer in my shaky hand and duck down lower. *I will be ready if she needs me.*

She raises her fist and pulls it back down. The sky darkens and thunder claps answering to the call of her magic. Lightning touching down behind him.

The Gray flinches, his nostrils flaring.

"You think me stupid?" she asks. "Why are you here?" She peers at the water closely.

"To get *water*." His lips are a thin line somewhere between anger and scared as he gets up, dusting his pants. "That is all. I was taking a hike." He pats his pockets and pulls out a container, something like a canteen, and hands it to Memi.

"See for yourself. It's very refreshing."

"No!" I step out of the foliage. "Don't drink that, Memi. He never filled that canteen from the river, I was watching!"

She turns her back to him to face me, her expression wide with fear.

I go cold all over as I realize my mistake.

A blur of metal flashes behind her and Memi grunts in pain, falling to her knees. Red. So much red. I'm frozen, my legs locked in place with terror. *Your magic! Do something.* But I only manage to blink.

"You should have stayed hidden in the forest, girl," the Gray says, blade slick and red, held high. Memi is on the ground and she does not move. A cry dies in my throat as I turn to run. I rush through the forest, thorns scratching my legs. *My magic.* I try to summon it, but fear overcomes whatever bravery I'd thought I'd had and my feet fly across the familiar passageways. The trails I've walked with Memi and Tomae year after year. A patch of sunlight peeks through the trees up ahead and my heart flutters.

He won't catch me. He won't.

Leaves patter behind me. The Gray's breath is heavy, louder, closer as he gains on me. My knotted shift catches on a jagged branch, yanking me to a halt. He's so close I can smell him. I tug and pull, snatching the fabric tethering me to the tree. It rips. Metal overhead blots out the ray of sun.

Berries from my makeshift sack spill, painting the forest floor red.

CHAPTER ONE

THE ENEMY LIES IN wait to bleed my people.

To litter the homeland with our bones.

To bury its secrets.

But first he has to go through me.

I crouch in the brush surrounding Yiyo Peak for a better view of the Chancellor and his men. The sun washes Ghizon in shades of evening. Bleak wasteland stretches before me, scorched and burning. Blackened jpango trees are claws raised in sacrifice to the Ancestors. An armament of uniformed Patrol stand where there was once a field of lush vegetation and wispy grass, onyx glowing on their wrists.

Pangs churn in me—for justice, for the death of my parents, for the terror the Chancellor has caused my Ghizoni people, for the magic on his wrists that isn't his own. He'd made sure the treachery was scrubbed from the island's textbooks. But bones whisper from their graves if you listen hard enough.

My gilded arms warm instinctively with power, but I blow out a breath. *Easy, Rue.* With my Ghizoni people nearly magicless, it's basically me against thousands of Grays, the Chancellor's men. I have one shot at this and timing is everything.

Yiyo, the home my people have hidden in for years, sits behind us, perched in the middle of the forest. The Ghizoni and I hide in the foliage around it, clad in armor. I duck down lower behind thick waxy leaves to get a better glimpse of the enemy's movement. Everything he and his men have touched in the past three days of this siege has been destroyed. The Chancellor paces so rigidly, I expect to see steam rise off him. As if he'd burn every piece of beauty in the world if it would secure his power.

The destruction out here in the wilderness ends abruptly at a barrier as transparent as glass, which forms a dome over us and the mountain. Bri, in her haste to get me here quickly, said he'd broken through the barrier. Thankfully she was wrong. But he's about to. And it's the only thing keeping them from us.

It glistens, hanging above us. Thin cracks spiderweb on its surface and my heart ticks faster, my fingers twitching. The Chancellor scans the area and I hide myself behind a smooth-barked tree that's as wide as I am. Thousands of Patrol surround him. There's so many of them. So few of us. I swallow and gaze at the trees at my back, but my people are well cloaked, tucked into nooks of branches and wide leaves, in pockets of shadow, waiting, watching. The lines written into their faces are more determination than fear.

The Chancellor's nostrils flare and he shouts. Because of the barrier, I can't hear it. But his men raise their arms in unison. I clench, my muscles tightening in angst as I watch them aim magic at the barrier. The cracks on its glossy surface spread. Their arms lower. He yells and they fire again. It's been going on like this for days. But each "aim and fire" twists the corkscrew in my chest. That dome breaks, then what? I clench my fist.

I fight.

Outnumbered and all. I picture Moms's face. There's no other way. The General's demise must have reached the Chancellor's ears while I was in East Row. He is always poised, pensive, stoic. Three days ago, when they started this siege, they were collected, organized. But now, his reddened complexion, his corded throat, say the orders he's shouting are rooted in exhaustion and frustration, not control. Which I intend to exploit.

I wish I could have seen his face when he learned that hundreds of my people still exist. That some actually got away when he showed up to unify the tribes under him. And that they've been hiding inside Yiyo for generations, their magic fractured, a wisp of what it used to be. But even still, resiliently hopeful, strong, and ready.

A twig snaps behind me and I turn to find Jhamal pressing in beside me. He's no more than a breath away, a wall at my back. The siege glows orange in his ebony eyes.

"They won't break through," he says.

They will. I'm sure of it. But I swallow the words. I don't want his hope to falter. Hope is its own kind of magic. But Jhamal studies my eyes and finds the truth. The lines deepen on his face and I squeeze his hand in reassurance.

He gestures for everyone to come together and hundreds in shining gold armor emerge from the shadows. They surround us, eyes flicking between the two of us.

"It appears the barrier will break today," Jhamal says, broadening his shoulders, forlorn shadowing his expression.

"It will," I say. "But we can exploit the Chancellor at his most vulnerable point."

"The island is our home," says a Ghizoni clad in armor with bear-claw insignia perched on his shoulders. "We know these paths better than anyone. We should take cover in the thickest leaves and let them come to us. Ambush them." He tightens his grip on his curved blade.

"So we line up here," a girl with a braided topknot says, digging the tip of her shield into the ground, drawing a picture of the plan.

I glance for another view of the Chancellor. The barrier's thinning with every attack, magic sizzling its dulled surface. Rage is burned onto the Chancellor's skin. *I'm the true threat. The opposition to his power.* What if . . .

"I'm the carrot. Dangle me."

Their expressions twist in confusion.

I stand. "Listen, we don't have time to strategize. For three days we've been hunkered down in this forest with no clear consensus of a plan, watching his movements, studying him. I've got to get out there. Before it's too late."

"We've learned a lot about his movements these past two days," the Ghizoni says.

Crack. I suck in a breath, glancing at the barrier. The spiderweb of cracks I'd just seen has doubled in size. "I'm not trying to minimize that and I'm sorry if it came out that way. I'm just saying, the Chancellor wants *me*." I hold out my golden arms. "These. And they outnumber us greatly. I'ma fight him one-on-one. That's our chance. Our only chance."

Heads turn in silent conversation with one another.

"Jelani," Jhamal starts. "Don't do this. What is the full plan? Lay it out."

All eyes on me.

I step back. "To get out there. To fight." They're wasting time. I leave the huddle and creep closer to the task at hand.

My Ghizoni people are like collateral damage to the Chancellor. He's razing the land where our Ancestors grew their food, the chakusas where my father's father raised his family and buried our dead, where aunties and their daughters picked kaeli berries for their turning out ceremonies. Anger moves through me in a rush of heat. I don't want to sit and talk about a plan for another minute. That barrier is going to fall. And I need to be in position to end him.

"And what would you have us do while you're out there?" someone shouts at my back. I don't know. I just know they can't die for this. They've suffered enough at the hand of the Chancellor. The Ancestors gave me this magic. My parents died so I'd have it. So I could do this. So I could fight.

Crack.

I summon heat to my fingertips, keeping to the edge of the tree line so I can see him, but he can't see me. A flicker of hope thuds in my chest mangled with fear. *I can do this. I have to do this.*

My people call for me, but I jet off. The Chancellor's narrowed eyes search for me at the edge of the trees. Patrol snaps to attention. Magic flies through the air, slamming into the glass dome overhead. It shutters.

I can't stop them from shattering the barrier, but I can be ready when they do. The second before the barriers opens up wide enough for him to step through, I'm going to reveal my position and fire at him before he can fire at me. I'm counting on catching him off guard. I blow out a breath. It's gon' work.

A crack cuts through the air and the protective dome above us cracks like an egg. I summon that familiar heat; magic swirls in my hands.

"Jelani," Jhamal says, his clammy hands curling around my wrist. As if the sweat on his palms is just as much about me as what we're all up against. The last time we were together, my lips were pressed to his. Aching churns in me for the simplicity of that moment again. The moment of peace and comfort it gave me. Especially amidst so much loss.

I rub his hand on mine and his eyes soften. But the moment is interrupted when a glassy chunk of the barrier falls from the sky like a jagged piece of hail. A rip slides down the side of the barrier, its glass splitting in two.

"It's going to fall in any moment."

The Chancellor practically salivates, a crack widening right in front of him. It's time.

"I have to," I say, tugging my hand from Jhamal.

"I'll come with you," he says.

He doesn't have magic. He can play defense only.

"No," I say. "Not if you don't have to."

He tucks his lip and nods. I hold on to his fingers as long as I can before letting go and leaving him there.

I step from the clustered jpango, and the Chancellor's eyes snap to me like a magnet, the cracking glass splintering the image of his face. The gap in the barrier widens, its edges being chiseled away by Patrol's magic. Delight curls his lips and my fingers twinge with heat.

Minutes. I have minutes.

I picture my magic slicing through him, ripping his stolen power from his bare hands. I close an eye to gauge my vantage point, the split second I'll have.

Crack.

I straighten. I just need one clean shot. One. I swallow. Magic pools in my wrists as the Chancellor holds a hand at the ready, waiting to signal his men. Bits of glass fall to the ground like snow.

The crack widens.

My heart beats in my throat.

Magic jitters through me and I tremble for fear I might burst. Everything my father died for, my mother was sacrificed for, amounts to this moment. This man.

Crack.

The final pieces of the barrier fall, shattering like glass. A cloud of dust surrounds us from the impact. I cough, lifting my hands. Weapon and shield in hand, Jhamal suddenly frees himself from the brush, armored in a gold breastplate lined with bits of fur, and sticks to my heels.

No! Dammit, Jhamal.

With no time to yell at him I turn back to the task at hand.

"Aim," I say, squeezing an eye shut, the Chancellor's head in my sights.

His men's arms raise in unison, all pointed at me.

I root my feet, hold in a breath. "And *fire*." My magic flies straight for his face. His eyes widen in anticipation and he shifts aside at the last second. My magic darts past, grazing his face, leaving his cheek red-streaked.

Close, so close. *We could win this.* I raise my shaky hands, suck in a breath for fear if I breathe too deeply, the pressure will shatter me in a million pieces. Patrol fires back and a cloud of crackling energy streams at me overhead. I retreat back into the cover of the trees. Their magic slams into the blackened wood, lighting up the edge of the forest like a firework display.

I zip through the branches, over a stump, and book it to the farther end of the forest so I can attack them on their flank. I find the perfect spot and aim at the sides of their faces. Glass rains around us, my sliver of an advantage buckling like a dam as magic barrels from my fingertips toward the Chancellor. Hope swells in me like a balloon. I clench my fists as streaks of light zip past the trees, through the air, and slams into them like dominoes.

A few falter, their heads turning my way, now aware of my new position. The Chancellor fumes, reforming his men up. I aim for him again and heat tugs through me like live wire. I bite my lip until I taste copper, watching my magic fly through the air straight toward him. Yes, yes, that's it. I bite into my knuckle.

"Raise," he shouts, and Patrol raises their arms. "And fi—"

His expression widens with fear when he spots my magic barreling toward him. He jerks the man beside him in front of him as a shield. My magic slams into the man squarely in the face. The Chancellor tosses him out of the way, his jaw mean. He points in my direction, shouting at his men. The small advantage I'd had is disappearing like fresh rain on dry soil.

"Ahhh!" Desperation rips through me as I urge my magic to burn through me, firing in succession as fast as I can. I manage to hit a few Patrol who fall over and don't move.

"Charge!" The Chancellor orders his men and their ranks break, running toward me. The cloud of dust thickens under their stampede. I blink but the haze of dust stings my eyes. The glass has stopped raining, but panic has a hold of me.

I look for a target, something to fire at, but it's harder to see. Something sharp grazes my back and I turn to find flames flying through the air at me. *Run!* I take off toward the tree line, skimming for anything to use as a shield. The sound of glass crunching underfoot crushes my confidence. A fireball pummels through the air and I jump sideways, its heat warming my face. I spot Jhamal dodging fuzzy strands of magic behind his shield.

"Jhamal!" But he doesn't turn in my direction. Can he even hear me over all the screaming? More Ghizoni emerge from the forest, vengeance rooted in heartbreak behind their battle cry. *No, they have to go back!* Another blow flies at me and I dodge, covering my head. Jhamal runs toward me and a swirl of magic chases him.

"Get down!" I charge his way, push him down, and kick off the ground. Up. Up. Air whips beneath me and my wrists connect with the magic midair. It sizzles then fizzles out. I land hard.

"Jhamal, you okay?" I ask, panting.

He nods, gripping my hand and I tug him up to his feet. He falls in behind me, back-to-back.

"You need a shield!"

A burst of magic flies toward us. He pulls us aside, this time, dodging the blow. The Patrolman stumbles in shock at his miss. Jhamal takes advantage of the moment, slamming his knuckles into the Patrolman's face.Violence erupts in explosions in every direction. I aim and fire toward them, heat pulling through me like a rope tethered to my chest. Magic flies from my hands slamming into someone with a Ghizoni in a headlock. Jhamal and I rotate. I aim and fire. Aim and fire again, until my wrists ache from the recoil.

Something slams into me and the world goes sideways. I stagger. Pain pinches my knees as they slam the ground. The world goes black.

Silence.

I'm a fragment, a feeling, a thought. I am air.

Smoke stings my nose.

Boom.

"Ahhh!" Shouts blare in my head.

For several moments the world is silent. Death is all I hear.

I blink and the sky is a blur. I blink again and sounds swell around me. Magic sizzling armor, groans, screams. The battle rages.

"Up, Jelani," someone says, pulling me up by my arms. "Can you hear me?"

I cup the Ghizoni's face expecting to see Jhamal, but it's not him. My hand is warm and sticky. "Th-thank you . . ." I gesture for his name, blinking his blurry face into focus.

"It's Rahk."

"Thank you, Rahk."

"You were out for some time."

"I-I was?"

"They ambushed us," he say. I take in the scene around me when an explosion pops overhead. We tuck our heads and run, skirting around fallen bodies, crumpled armor tangled around bleeding Patrolmen.

The battle has turned.

And not in our favor.

What have I done? Why didn't I tell them to stay in the forest? Or take cover somewhere or . . . something. My eyes sting. I try to blink the shame away and look for Jhamal.

I-I did not think this through. There are too many of them.

Panic grips my throat. Magic zips past in a streak of light and I halt, stumbling backward. I turn but there's magic coming from that direction, too. Cornered, bodies barrel into me. I hold my wound with one hand and fire darts of magic at the shooters.

Jhamal sprints toward us. His arm is streaked with red and he holds his elbow.

"Rahk." Jhamal greets him with some special handshake.

"All the others I was with have fallen," Rahk says to no one in particular, but his stare is fixed on me. "What should we do?"

Jhamal throws his blade; it swivels and whistles over my shoulder. Somewhere behind me someone groans before hitting the ground. Rahk covers himself with his shield, the ferocity in his eyes dimming. The ground is a sea of carnage and ash on both sides.

"What should we do?" Rahk asks again, his gaze darting between us. Jhamal looks at me too.

"I—" I break out into cold sweat.

"Jelani?"

"I, uh—" My heart races. "Go back through the forest. We need cover. You all do. Get inside Yiyo Peak. Bar the door shut. I'll finish them off out here."

"What?" Jhamal cuts in, but Rahk doesn't wait to hear. He runs off to grab the others.

"Jhamal, go with them. Defense isn't enough. Without you all armed with magic, it's— I missed the moment I needed. Having you out here now is too big of a risk."

"No." His jaw flinches and he deepens his stance, his mug mean.

"You have to listen to me!" I grip his arms. "You will die out here, you hear me? GO!" I shove his chest. "Listen to me, dammit!"

His nostrils flare.

"Please."

He doesn't move for several moments. We cut down three others, back-to-back, before he pulls me to him, presses his lips to mine, and retreats into the forest.

I sense the Chancellor before I see him.

"It's finally just you and me then, Jelani." His eyes flick to my gleaming wrists and I swear he licks his lips. I raise my arms, summoning my magic. A ball of light glows brighter between my shaky hands.

Magic flickers on his fingers, but I react first.

"Ah!" I fire at him.

But the world goes lopsided.

My head is wet and sticky, my fingers red. I blink. Someone pulls me. *No,* I try to say, but the words only play in my head. I spot Jhamal, running faster than the wind toward me, fury in his eyes. His javelin flies from his fingers and someone holding me lets go. But others grab hold of me. I can't move. I can't breathe.

"No!" Jhamal roars, fighting through the army of them growing around me. Their prize. The prey they've hunted for so long. Captured. I look for someone, anyone, to help. But all I smell is the mountain where I sent my people—burning.

CHAPTER TWO

METAL CLANGS AS I come to. Something tickles my throat, but I can't seem to cough. Jhamal's hands work carefully over me, sewing something. His brow is slick with sweat, worry kneaded there too. He pulls a bandage, tearing it with his teeth.

"Help me! It's too much blood, please!" he says to someone, and I squint but the world is hazy. Where am I? The surface beneath me is cold at my back. It's hard, like a floor. Stone walls and a row of iron bars form the cell around us. We're imprisoned? My breath catches and I try to sit up, but pain shoots up my back. I lie back down, pain rippling through me. Everything hurts.

A woman hobbling by shoves a needle and thread through the bars at Jhamal.

"All I could manage," she says before limping off.

"Thanks." He takes it.

I'm sprawled out on the ground. Something stings and the wrinkles in Jhamal's brow soften. He presses down on my leg and works the needle in and out. My skin tugs. Stitches? He's sewing the flesh back together where my gold cuffs meet my arms. It's only then I notice scrapes all over my body. I see them, but I feel nothing.

I close my eyes, running my fingers across the wounds, trying to remember.

"What did they do to me?" I try to say, but it comes out like a cough.

Jhamal's head doesn't lift, his focus as rigid as the iron holding us in this cell. How long have we been in here? How long have I been out? Questions are a cloud in my mind, but my tongue is heavy. My head lulls sideways and there are other faces peering through their own cell bars, heads tilted in curiosity. I try to speak, but my throat is a useless lump. The world ripples like water and I am heavy. So much heavier than before.

"The Ancestors have not brought you this far to leave you here, my Queen." Tears pour down his cheeks. "Stay with me."

I reach for his hand, but mine is clumsy on his. His skin is warm and I relish its closeness. The world is a haze, but at least I'm not in here alone. *I'm here,* I try to say, but the world fades away.

Drips from the rocky ceiling of my cell are cold on my nose. *Where am I? Where is everyone?* I listen for sounds of the battle but hear only the plop of water. Jhamal sewing my wounds back together, my hand touching his, people shoving food through the bars . . . wisps of memories nudge me.

The battle was a long time ago.

I close my eyes and see an unfamiliar face with long eyelashes hovering over me. I search for more meaning, what happened, when and how exactly I got in here, but find nothing. Last I remember, I was fighting the Chancellor and then I wasn't. I blink and see long eyelashes again, but the image is void of any meaning I can latch on to.

I blink again, and try to make more sense of my surroundings.

Thick lead bars hold us in the craggy cell and fire torches bob just outside. I know we're beneath the Central District because of the smell, the walls, and the people who bring us food wear the Chancellor's pin with his profile in the center, Yiyo, sunrays, and a jpango tree etched around the design. I'd know the symbol anywhere. It's minted on the money, emblazoned on the buildings, carved into the naked cover of every book. The Chancellor stamped his seal on everything in Ghizon like a dog marking a tree.

How long have we been in here? I tug at the fuzzy purple strand on my neck, its charm still missing. Tasha. She's probably worried sick. I try again to sit up on shaky elbows, but my insides feel like they've been smashed with a hammer. A smooth hand caresses my cheek and I flinch.

Jhamal's face solidifies in focus, his brows knit.

"What have they done to me?" I try to say, but it comes out a wheezing rasp.

"My Queen," he says. "Can you hear me?"

"I can," I try to say, but again, nothing, so I nod instead.

"You can hear me! I'm here." He reaches for my hand, but I run my fingers across my stitches, searching for some meaning, a better sense of what happened between the battle and here.

"Thank you." That time it comes out raspy but audible. I try to lift my arms, but the familiar weight of the armor is as heavy as lead.

"*Eaaasy.*" Jhamal's arm is sturdy under me, helping me sit upright. He's wrapped in a dingy set of robes. He holds a bowl to my lips and warm garlicky liquid fills me. The warmth coats my insides and they twist in a cramp. I hurl over and he holds my hair back. The bile is salty when it comes out and I spit until I can hardly catch my breath.

I press against the cold wall, panting. Weak. Why am I so weak?

"What have they done to me?" I mutter.

"They tried to remove your cuffs, my Queen."

I gasp and the puffy skin around where my cuffs meet my skin makes sense. But why can't I remember? The walls of our cage suddenly feel smaller. My pulse ticks faster. "We're in prison, so the Chancellor, he—"

But the blood rushing through me so suddenly makes the world swim.

He swipes cold sweat from my clammy forehead before making me drink more. It gurgles right back up, but I gulp it down. Bile and all.

I grunt. He holds the bowl to my lips again.

"More. For strength. Come on, you need it."

I take another sip and this one goes down. But my words trail off. Eating soup has completely exhausted me.

"Rest," he says, laying me back on my pallet on the hard cell floor. I'm cold all over, hugging around myself, and he scoots closer to me. Under his warmth my eyes are as heavy as my gilded arms. Sleep tugs at me.

I give in.

"Up." Jhamal tugs me and my body cooperates. The wall of our confinement cell is at my back. The tiny strings between puckered spots on my arms are gone, and only slightly swollen skin remains. How long has it been? I blink and see the same unfamiliar face with long eyelashes in my head.

Questions are a haze in my mind, but as I try to form them on my lips, a woman with a limpy gait slides a tray between the grates of our prison cell. I recognize her face. She's one of the ones who brings us meals. The same one who gave Jhamal the needle and thread.

She always comes this time of day. I blow out a breath in relief that at least some of my memories are coming back to me. I search for more. Jhamal holding stone bowls to my lips, clanging metal bars, the slap of the food tray on the cold stone floor. And sleep. Lots of sleep. I still can't remember being brought in here.

"Food," the woman says.

Jhamal thanks her and I do too . . . in my head, my tongue still chalky. She glances over her shoulder before pulling a book from under her robe. "Remember, the matches. Burn it if they come back before I do."

Books . . . for what? I turn to look for Jhamal and my neck doesn't ache as much as it once did. I scoop a bite from my tray and am able to sit up a little more. The more I chew, the more bits of the world makes sense.

"H-how did . . ." I clear my throat.

Jhamal folds open the book and his fingers slide down the page. "Drink more, it'll help."

I take the cup in my hands and they shake less. "How did we get in here?" I manage.

He squeezes my hand. "We have to hurry, while your strength allows. Your memory has been so spotty and you were hardly awake for a blink yesterday." His cheeks push up under his eyes. "Come on, repeat after me," he says, checking the book. "Ya, lindz."

"Y-ya lindz," I say.

He unfolds my hand, stretching and massaging my fingers. "Keep them loose."

I flex and unflex.

"Good, there we go. Next one, fee-yel."

"Feey'l."

"That one's for shifting energy or conjuring fire. Now, griska, mwepah, ya giz ya giz. Come on." He turns the page and my mind clicks into the familiar cadence, more of it coming back.

"Griska, mwepah, ya giz ya giz. For twisting fire into, uh-uhm, static energy?"

"That's it! You're remembering." His brow beads with sweat.

The drills continue until my head dangles from my neck. My legs ache and the cuts on my arms burn. Down, down. Then sideways. The world swims. Jhamal whispers something, but I don't hear it. A heavy fog sets in. . . . I drift off to sleep.

I wake with Jhamal's hand cupped around mine, his eyes glazed with something I can't place.

"We ready for today's rehearsing?" he says when he spots me studying him. I sit up and he reaches to help me, but I push his hands away and do it myself.

Guilt turns in me like a corkscrew. I straighten, the prison cell wall at my back, and sift through the collection of memories in my mind for any more hints. Meaning. They come back in a rush.

I remember waiting to gain an edge on the Chancellor when the dome fell. I remember smoke plumes from Yiyo. I can almost taste the bitter smoke in the air, screams scratch my ears. I blink and see long eyelashes.

What have I done?

"Ah!" I claw my hands through my hair, trying to push the images from my mind, but they take over. I can't look away, vivid memories of the battle consuming me in a rush.

Yiyo burning.

"Rahk . . ."

Screams.

Piles of bloodied armor folded over fallen Patrolmen. I tug harder at my roots, trying to tear the haunted memories out of my head. Jhamal's hand is warm around mine. He tugs gently on my wrist, trying to unlatch my hands from my hair.

"Jelani," he says, and his words are soft as silk. But I don't deserve to be wrapped in their comfort.

What happened to everyone? I sent them to the mountain. They couldn't have all made it into Yiyo that fast, but still. How many survived? Are they still out there? How long have we been in here?

I grip Jhamal's shirt. "Tell me what happened!" I don't mean for it to come out like a yell but it does. He startles, biting his lip.

"I'm sorry for yelling."

He sighs. "You—" The clang of our breakfast tray slapping the stone and sliding underneath the bars to our cell steals our attention. Breakfast Lady hovers a moment, eyes darting between us, before slipping a book out from her robes. She slides it between the grates. Jhamal hands back two hiding in a shadowed corner of our cell. She's out of sight without a word to me.

"We should use this time to practice, my Queen, not dwell on things we can't change." He reaches for my fingers. His are warm and I remember how he worked over my wounds, put me back together, helped me heal. But I tug my fingers away, curling into myself. I need to get up, walk around. I wiggle my fingers, reaching for my magic, but only puffs of air float up from my fingers. What's wrong with me? I hate this feeling. I hate feeling weak.

"It won't work in here." He runs his fingers across the bars of our prison cell. "These lead bars sedate magic. I overheard a guard say."

Great, so I'm in prison, without the ability to use my magic, and I can't quite remember how I even got in here?! I try to stand but my knees buckle. Jhamal catches me, and for a moment I let him be a wall around me. A wall against the storm raging through me. But even that sears after a moment.

"Thanks," I say, pulling away from him and steadying myself on the wall. "I got it."

I can't even stand on my own two feet? *I did this. I got us in here.* Or I let the Chancellor do this? I-I should have fought harder or been smarter or listened to the Ghizoni in the forest when they wanted to think out a plan. But no, no, I had to storm out there and take him on myself. The guilt chokes and I slide down the wall to the floor, hugging my knees. Tears sting my cheeks, shredding everything inside me that used to beat with hope. I've saved one home but lost the other one.

Jhamal sits next to me, tucking his lip in understanding. His warmth soothes, but I can't look at him. Not after what I've done.

"Jelani, I forgive you. You could not have known—"

"Stop!" *Excuses.* I won't listen to it. They looked to me to protect them out there, to make decisions, and I failed. That's the truth of it. And I won't let him water it down. I'd pace, but my body feels like it's barely glued together. If I even breathe too hard, I might break. I gaze at his chin on his chest and shame burns my cheeks. He doesn't deserve this. He's done nothing but mend me.

"I'm sorry," I mutter.

His gaze meets mine. "It's okay. I hate that you even—" His shoulders slump next to me and for a moment I let my head lie on his shoulder.

"My people. They need me," I breathe, and I'm not even sure

Jhamal hears it until he turns to me. Everything kind and warm hangs in his ebony eyes.

"We will not think of these things. Right now, getting you strong is the focus. It has to be."

My eyes sting. "I'm the only one with magic a-and they're just out there. Without me."

"Jelani." He caresses my jaw with his thumb. But the flutter I feel is buried in memories of Yiyo, Rahk, a battlefield full of blood, until it's an ember smothered in the ash of my failure.

"You should eat. It usually helps."

I nod begrudgingly as he sets out the tray. I blow out a breath, trying to keep quiet the panic tugging at me. The angst to feel like not only a prisoner of the Chancellor but a prisoner in my own body. The meal is some sort of oats and purple berries with a peanut-buttery aftertaste. Once we're done eating, the world is heavy, like I used up every bit of energy I had with anger and have none left for practice. Jhamal warned me of that. But I hold my eyes open as best I can, focusing on Jhamal as he feeds me spells. I repeat and recite until every other syllable is a yawn.

"Sticky spell," he says, the first one open.

"Surpizah."

"Fireball."

"Feey'laska."

"Cord of light."

"Prim."

"You're remembering so well."

"I just want to know why I don't remember." I touch a spot on my forehead and it's rough with a scab. "Ow."

Eyelashes.

"Breathe, it's going to be okay. Maybe that's enough for today." He lays a leg over mine. "What is it you call it, again?"

"Pretzel legs." A smile tugs at my lips, but the wail of dying people is a ghost in my ears. I untangle my legs from his. Jhamal must sense the question in my pained expression.

"You are remembering, Jelani. That is what matters."

"How long have we been doing this?"

"Too long. Moons? I don't know. Every time you wake, we have good progress though. You're going to be so strong, so good at your magic by the time we get out of here."

I close my eyes again, reaching for a memory of getting in this cell. For what happened after the Chancellor captured us. But find only a burning battlefield.

My breath hitches, my pulse picking up. *What have I done? And what about Tasha . . . Ms. Leola . . . they need to know I'm okay. I—*

"Breathe."

My strength falters, my hands shake. But his eyes find mine and they urge me to listen.

I inhale, then let it out. *Five . . . four . . . three . . . two . . . one.*

His hand closes around mine.

"Wh-what did they do to me?"

He rubs the inside of my palm, stretching my fingers, and I scoot closer to him, to comfort, understanding. His nails massage circles on my hairline, and my shoulders sink."

"It doesn't matter. What matters is what you do next."

"I will get stronger. I'm going to get us out of here."

"I know you will, my Queen."

CHAPTER THREE

Six Months Later

SMOKE, PUNGENT, SALTY, HEAVY, burning with the stench of rotting flesh, curls my nose. I bat my eyes open and my cell surrounds me. I sniff again but the smell is gone.

Drip. Drop.

Clammy air sticks to me and I smooth droplets from underneath my eyes.

A dream, it was just a dream.

The rocky ceiling sharpens in focus, rows of rails on the peripheral. Every inch of me is cold except my left side, where Jhamal sleeps.

"One hundred seventy-one . . . one hundred seventy-two . . . one hundred seventy-three . . . ," I whisper, running my fingers in the familiar divots I've carved into the floor. My body might be in a cage, but my mind doesn't have to be.

"One hundred seventy-six . . . seventy-seven . . . seventy-eight." It's been one hundred seventy-eight days since I told Jhamal I'd get us out of here. And today's going to be that day. I reach for my magic out of habit. A spark of something coils in my hand then dissolves like dust.

I sleep next to the bars of the cell so I can always keep an eye down the corridor. Not too close, touching them makes my insides feel like a squeeze bottle. I rotate my head, careful not to wake Jhamal, and peer into the dark hallway. Nothing. No one.

I hug around myself, lying there on the ground, setting my mind on what I need to do today. What I've thought about doing every minute of every day between hauntings of my failure on the battlefield—getting out of here.

I need to get back to those who managed to survive. I swallow. Wherever they are. Once I survey the damage, I'll figure out a way to fight the Chancellor again. But this time, win.

I gulp down the nerves welling in my throat and blink. The familiar sights, smells and sounds of my failure taunt me. But the air doesn't get caught in my throat anymore when I know they're coming. I focus on my breath, easing it out, and shove the images of bloody armor, chaos outside Yiyo, the crumbling barrier, far, far away.

I push and they fade.

I blink.

Eyelashes.

His face, I can't seem to shake. I close my eyes hard, pushing them farther, but the face with long eyelashes comes firmer in view and new glimpses of the past slither their way around my throat.

Something sharp digs into my arms. Bright lights bob over me in a room with all-white walls and a metal table in the center, chilly at my back. I'm weighed down and covered in a thin shift. I strain for the sights and sounds of magic but hear only the scrape of metal. Stale air curls in my nose and I blink.

"Where am I?" I ask, trying to sit up, but I'm heavy all over, tethered

to a table with straps. Panic claws at me. "Jhamal?" But only my echo answers.

A woman in a lab coat presses me down to the chilly table at my back. "She's awake. Give her more."

I gasp and sit up fully.

"You okay?" Jhamal asks.

I blink and the images disappear. "Yes."

I still can't remember how I got in here or fully grasp why there's a person with long eyelashes haunting me like a ghost in my memory. His curly smile, his touch. Blips of the foggy memory have returned over the months, but in bits, a wisp. That's been my life for however many months. Sleep, eat, practice, and fight off broken pieces of memories.

My stomach hovers in the back of my throat. *Up, I have to get up*. But my brooding pins me to the ground like a weighted blanket. How is guilt like that? So heavy you can almost *actually* feel it.

Focus, Rue. But my father's dying stutter rings in my head. I grab the metal bars I sleep beside and shake them to drown out the sound. Metal rattles down the orb-lit passageway between cells.

"Let me out of here," I want to scream, but no one ever answers. The bars are cold and heavy and I'm woozy for a second, holding the actual lead in my hands, against my skin. I let go and the light-headedness lifts. The cells around us have all emptied. I shudder to think of where they've gone.

"Morning, sunshine." Jhamal stands, his warmth sweeping away. And just like that I'm cold all over.

I turn to him and he smiles. I smile back. At least I'm not in here alone. At least he's been by my side. For all of it.

The familiar knot in the back of my neck, from sleeping on a bed as soft as rocks for months, aches. A clanging rattle and muffled footsteps somewhere above us urge me to my feet. We have minutes, no more.

Breakfast Lady drops food at the same time every day. The sun twinkles through a fissure in the cavernous ceiling. The lunch and dinner meals come heavily provisioned, flanked with armed Patrol on either side. But she's always alone and never armed from what I can tell. Still, she's nice and all, letting us borrow books. But today she's my ticket to freedom. If I can take her unawares and convince her to give me the key to this cell, we're out of here.

My fingers reach almost instinctively for the blade I fashioned from a fork the Breakfast Lady gave me weeks ago. I had to swear I'd never received one. I thought for sure a guard or the Chancellor himself would come cut off my head right then. But she believed me. And turns out, rubbing it back and forth against rock works well to sharpen it.

I scurry up and press into a wall of the cell so that she won't be able to see me right away.

"Over here, hurry." I wave at Jhamal. "Before she comes."

"Jelani." He pinches the bridge of his nose.

"Shut up." I'd told him this plan last night before we fell asleep. He laughed then and I see his opinion of it hasn't changed.

Black moons hang beneath his naturally sculpted brows. So beautiful they put mine to shame. His cheekbones push up, his lips purse in a smile. "We will not get out of here this way."

"It's going to work."

"It will not. The server is not as naive as you think, Jelani. She might sneak us a spell book or two, but she won't let us out of here. I—"

"I thought I was your Queen?" A joke. I'm no one's royalty.

"You are." He sighs, pressing into the shadow behind me. He's a wall at my back.

"Mhmm," I say, turning backward to look at him, and he does this thing with his lips and something below my navel twinges, but I shove it away. We've been close. Together. Alone. Relying on each other in this destitute cell for months. He sleeps next to me, his smiles start each of my days, and we rehearse my magic. I've watched lines hug his eyes that were never there before. His frame is leaner than it was months ago. His hair has grown out. But what's grown the most is the longing in his eyes. We are all we've had . . . for so long.

He leans into my ear as I strain to hear how close the server is. "You should kiss me every morning, you know," he says. "We could die in here."

I laugh nervously. I can't pretend I don't remember how I shuddered with passion when my lips were pressed to his forever ago. But now the space where I'd carved out something for him is flooded with grief and shame. I can't. I just can't be that person to him. Not right now. Not after what I've done. Not with so many unknowns of what lies ahead. I gaze down at my feet, unable to meet his eyes, before turning back around. As much as Jhamal is comfort, help—the one who put me back together—he is also a reminder of how I failed.

I step forward to put a little more distance between us to keep my mind clear. I can't let him cloud my focus. We're getting out of here today.

He clears his throat and I know that are-you-serious-look he's making. That same look when I'd had the idea to dig our way out.

"There's a hole in the ceiling. If we could just . . . ," I'd began.

He'd actually laughed at that one. And I mean, sure, it was ridiculous. Not one of my best ideas, but I hadn't eaten in long while, and, well, I'd seen it on some old movie. I turn and sure enough his lips are pushed sideways.

"You think I'm joking?" I shove him off. "This plan will work."

"Fine, I'll go along. But—" He taps his cheek.

I roll my eyes and his hint of a smile dissolves.

"The mind is not above our tricks," he says.

"We must go through the motions, keep living as much as we can every day, to maintain soundness of mind. To keep a firm grip on our sanity."

His proposition to kiss me *might* be about soundness of mind like he says, but it's equally about . . . kissing me. I ain't dumb. This is his way of holding on. We eat, recite spells, tell stories, then sleep. Every day it's the same thing. And Jhamal doesn't get nightmares like I do, but he does have this faraway stare each morning. And he makes sure I fall asleep first. When I wake every morning, his gaze is always already glued to the ceiling. But when our eyes meet, he's all warmth and optimism.

He's starting to think we might really die here.

He just doesn't want me to think it too.

"They are just fattening us up for slaughter," I say. "I'm not sitting here waiting for it." What else explains why no one has seen us but the people who bring us meals? A draft moves from the hole overhead, and I run my fingers across the stone. Solid rock all around us.

"I do not know what they want, my Queen, but it makes no sense to capture us and keep us prisoner, feed us well, keep us alive. That is not the Ghizoni way. It is most honorable to end a life you intend to take with swiftness, or bring the Ancestors'—"

". . . wrath down upon you. I know." Jhamal's storytelling has been a much welcomed sleeping aid the past couple of months. Honor and warrior ethos is apparently very important to my people here. I told him we have a code back home, too: ride or die. That's what we call it.

"If the Chancellor wanted to kill us, we'd be dead. He wants us alive."

"All I'm sure of is that he wants my cuffs, and I'm not sitting around any longer for him to decide to try to take them off me again." I have a weapon, finally. This is our chance. I press deeper into the shadow. "I saw—"

But the words escape me, images rushing at me too fast to catch them.

Smoke.

Ash.

Death.

My father's smile flickers in my memory. The joy stamped in his eyes even once their light had faded. Breathe, Rue. I shove out the air through gritted teeth, determined to grab my lucidity firmly with both hands. *Five . . . four . . . three . . . two . . . one.*

The images flee.

I clench my fist. The Chancellor is going to pay for what he's done.

"So, what exactly are we going to do to her?" he whispers.

"We're just going to scare her," I say. "Convince her to give us her keys. We won't hurt her."

Jhamal sighs, but he falls in line beside me. When she comes down the hall, she won't see the shadowed corner we're in until she's within arm's reach.

We press against the wall, listening. I press a finger to the fork's tip. Out pops a bubble of red. I suck my finger and dig my nails into my palm, clenching the weapon. Anticipation coils in me like a snake.

"Je—"

"Quiet," I say. "She won't even see it coming."

"Outwit your enemy by convincing them they are your friend."

Here he goes again.

"Feed the enemy until he eats from your hand, so when you lace it with poison . . ."

". . . he will take it without question. I know your little warrior-isms, Mal."

"Juh-mal."

"I like Mal."

"It is Juh-mal."

"If I'm your Queen, shouldn't I say it the way—"

Clang.

He clamps a hand over my mouth. Footsteps grow louder, and I tighten my grip on my weapon. She's here. The *clack clack* of her feet drums faster, echoed by heavy breaths as if . . . Is she running? Jhamal's and my quizzical stares match.

I spot her garment before her, a flutter of fabric denting my vision, and I reach between the bars to grab some piece of her. I snag the edge of her robe and yank her toward me. She grunts.

"Sssh," I say. "I'm not gonna hurt—"

But when she faces me, her eyes bulge and a dagger tip bursts from her neck.

I yelp, holding her tighter as she goes limp.

"I-I—" she sputters. "I-I'm so-sorry. I-I didn't know. She—" She lets out a gush of air with her last word and her weight doubles in my arms. Red flows like a river over her robes, soaking my arms.

"I—" Words are tar in my throat. This woman did nothing to me but feed me, greet me with a smile each day. I didn't hurt her, but somehow her blood is on my hands. Like so many others'. Her glassy stare stills and I swear I see smoke plumes rising from Yiyo in them. I blink and hear screams. *No* . . . I bite my lip to stay in the present and turn, expecting to find Jhamal shocked, but instead his brows kiss as he reaches for the tip of the gold point protruding from the woman's throat.

"This is—"

"Ghizoni gold."

I don't recognize the voice, but it's brittle, with a smirk lurking behind each syllable. The girl who comes around the corner shoves a long weapon into a strap latched to her thigh. She's tall with broad shoulders, a narrow waist, and even broader hips. Gold armor covers all but her right shoulder, rippling off her like waves. Light from the floating orbs reflect like diamonds off her velvety brown skin. Her head's shaved low on the sides, and a thick braid down the center of her head is wound up in a high bun. Jhamal looks like he's seen a ghost.

"You don't look happy to see me, coquella."

"Brother?" Jhamal scoffs. "Friendly, are we now?"

She steps over the woman whom I'm struggling to keep up. I ease her to the ground and press her lids closed when this friend of Jhamal's sticks out a hand.

"I'm Kai. I didn't get to meet you before."

"Rue." I blink, half confused and half relieved to see the face of one of my people. Hope blossoms in my chest. For a second the air is thick with silence as we stand behind bars waiting for this Ghizoni warrior to let us out of this cage. She plucks a card-shaped key from the woman slumped on the ground and slips it into the cell door. The bars glow and clank open.

I take a step but Jhamal stills me with the slightest touch. "Why are you here, Kai?"

"Don't be ridiculous. To rescue you, of course."

Silence.

"Don't be silly. We were kids. I harbor no ill will to the boy who dumped me. I'm here to free you, Jhamal, and the Ancestors' Chosen." She smirks, turning to me. "Have you been stuck in here with this arrogance this entire time?"

I scrub the surprise off my face and resist laughing because Jhamal probably wouldn't appreciate it and I don't know this girl like that.

We step out of our cell into the dimly lit hallway. A chill washes over me like I've stepped through an icy waterfall, and something that was on my chest like deadweight lifts. My fingers titillate with warmth. I whisper a spell and my magic answers, flames dancing on my fingers. A smile tugs at my lips.

"I'd missed this. My magic. Thank you," I say. "For coming and finding us. I'm sure it was no easy task breaking in here alone."

"Oh, never alone." She dips her chin when I walk past. "My girls are clearing the exit point. Never enter and exit the same way. Misdirection is its own magic."

Jhamal side-eyes her on the sly, but I don't miss it.

"We should go," I say, fragments of broken memories playing in my head like a pile of puzzle pieces calling to me. I need to see the state of things aboveground, figure out where the Chancellor and my people are, decide what's next to take him down.

"After you." Jhamal gestures for her to lead the way, and she stares at him for a second, stuck at my side. If the childhood crush was nothing, what's this awkwardness between them? I don't have time for the bullshit. Jhamal's only got eyes for me, I know she sees that. Without another word, Kai takes off, and we stick close to her heels.

The tunnels wind in every direction and my legs throb. Sleeping in such confined quarters and on such a hard surface for so long has made me weak. My muscles cry with each step, and my eyes burn from the flames dancing in orbs overhead.

"The Web, underground tunnels, runs from Yiyo to the Capital and all across the island. That's how we found our way in." Kai hangs a left and Jhamal and I keep pace, my hands dangling at my side, fingers loose. Ready for anything. She's so close, I can smell her, a mix of jpango wood and something acrid like burnt rubber.

She glances at me over her shoulder before hanging a right around the next corner. "And you're welcome, Jelani. It's no problem. After everything you've been through, it's the least we could do. We tried to get in sooner, but security has been tight. With our numbers cut in half . . ."

Numbers.

Cut.

In.

Half?

Guilt is an invisible hand wrapped around my throat.

". . . Yiyo desecrated," she goes on, "we had to find somewhere secure to hole up before we could even think about an extraction plan."

I came back to Ghizon to save our people, not destroy our home. "I'm sorry." The guilt squeezes. "I had hoped I could take him down. One-on-one, I had hoped—"

She stops. "Hope is not enough. Not anymore. Not for you, not for anyone."

"I—"

"You tried to save us, Rue. And you failed."

CHAPTER FOUR

KAI STORMS AHEAD AND her words echo in my mind like a gong as memories pull at me faster than I can fight them off.

I'm on the battlefield, the shield is broken, there are Patrol soldiers everywhere. Magic zips past in a streak of light, and I stumble back.

My pulse tick-tick-ticks faster. *Five . . . uhm . . . four . . .* I try to count away the panic. I don't want to see it again, I don't. I bite down and taste copper.

"All the others I was with have fallen," Rahk says to no one in particular, but his stare is fixed on me. "What should we do?"

"I, uh—" My heart races. Wails of dying scratch my ears. Blood pools in my ears and I rake my hands through my hair, the stink of burning flesh swimming around me.

"Go," I say. "Back through the forest. We need cover. You all do. Go inside Yiyo. Bar the door shut. I'll finish them off out here."

I stagger, gutted by seeing it all again, hearing it play in my head.

Dead. So many. Because of me.

My knees threaten to buckle, and I catch myself on the wall beside me, the horror of what I've done slicing through me. The smoke from Yiyo. Images of it crumbling and burning prick me, the ghosts of my past, a tether.

"I-I sent them to their deaths," I say, words bubbling out of my throat unbidden. "I-I . . ."

Every time I stare in a Ghizoni's face or see a wound, mark, or maim, will it knock the wind out of me? Will I ever be free? *You don't deserve to,* my conscious whispers.

"Rue!" Jhamal's voice cuts through my fog of panic.

"Rahk," I mutter, and Kai's eyes snap to me. "The others."

"Rahk is dead," she says, her nostrils flaring.

He sighs. Kai turns up her nose.

"Rue," he says. "We focus on the forward. We all make mistakes we regret. I—"

A hollow wail sails through the air, and the hair on my arms stands tall.

"It's the past," he says, darting a glance around. "Let it be in the past, *please.*"

I nod to appease him, but I can't. I can't just let it go. My people looked to me for answers of what to do, a plan that would work.

They trusted me to lead them.

And I sent them to their deaths.

I try to fight the tears that come as we fly up a flight of stairs cut into the wall. The wails grow louder. I sniff, trying to shove off the weight, the guilt, the shame, but it's a stain I could never erase. How many of them survived? Kai, her girls . . . but who else? I want to ask her. But how do I even word that without it sounding insensitive? Why would she even tell me? I put some space between us, guilt worming its way deeper into me. I just need to see for myself.

We hurry down the hall, past cells, toward the exit. I look for a familiar face. Bri? More Ghizoni? But the cells are all empty. My insides twist. *Bri . . . where are you?*

Magic tingles my fingers, waiting and ready, as we slip past a window. The room is empty, but I freeze, my father's dying stare flickering in my mind like a candle that won't blow out. The hope and promise he saw in me grating against the sallow, thin, weak person who stares back in the glass. This is not what he died for. For me to fail our people like this.

"Jelani, let's move," Jhamal says.

I tear myself from the quicksand of my guilt as we spill out into a dimly lit corridor where a Patrolman is standing sentry. His gray skin is a sickly yellow in the hall light. I recognize him; he's one of the ones who escorts the server who brings us our midday meal. He glances at a door at his back when another wave of wails ripple through the air. I blink and see smoke. *Away.* I blink again, and thank god the image is gone. *Focus, Rue.*

"There should be more guards," I say under my breath. Jhamal nods in agreement.

With endless time on my hands, noting the rotation of the guards in our cell corridor became a hobby. They operate with a particular decorum, even just standing duty. They stick together in groups of five, always. One in front, two in back, and one on each flank. The onyx stones fused to their wrists glow, as if they're hungry to strike anyone who might buck up against them. And one of the rear guards usually carries a blade.

But this guy's all alone.

"We need to go this way," Kai says, unsheathing a spear tip from a sack at her back. Its point is gilded, like the one that poked through Breakfast Lady's throat. "There's just one of them. Sit tight, I'll take care of him."

I hesitate a moment. "N-no." I grab her wrist, and a flicker of something in her eyes makes me let go. "Something is off."

"I know what I'm doing." She slips the pointed head into a gadget that pulls back. It springs into a place with a click. The guard's head swivels in our direction. *Shit.*

He strikes first and Kai sends a dagger in his direction. But he's fast. He twists out of the way and shoots magic back at us. I dodge and tug at the warmth gushing through me and let my magic rip through my hands. It burns through me, rekindling a part of me that I feared had all but burned out. This I know. This I can do. I fight. My magic blasts like a torch, the hallway glowing blue in the light. Jhamal is beside me, slashing a blade he got from Kai.

More Patrol slink from the shadows and we're surrounded. Jhamal tries to charge past me, but like a reflex I shove him back. I aim and fire, dodging Patrol's shots. But this time I miss and the wall above them explodes in a cloud of dust. I fire again, coughing. Aim. Fire. And again. Aim. Fire. My wrists are numb from the intense heat. I can't tell if any shots are landing. I can hardly see. But I'm just so glad to feel *something* besides shame.

Someone moves on my right. I whip around to face them, fire erupting in my hands, and find myself nose to nose with Jhamal. The someone is behind him, magic sizzling through the air toward us both.

"Down!"

He ducks and I fling my wrists forward, pummeling a fireball at Patrol rushing up behind him. The fire catches the Patrol's robes. He stumbles into a group of guards behind him and they all topple like dominoes.

Jhamal's back up and we're back-to-back, circling. His heart pounds against my back with rage and iron-willed determination. He, like me, sees the light at the end of the tunnel. He finally sees that *today* we could smell the briny Ghizoni air, feel the sun on our faces. And he, like me, would die before letting that chance go.

I pivot and he moves with me, in sync as if he can predict my steps, hear my thoughts. A strike barrels toward us. His nostrils flare and his rage intoxicates me. In the best possible way.

"There," I shout, pointing. We shift sideways as one and the streak of magic whirs past. Our eyes meet. When we're together like this, fighting for our people, shoulder to shoulder, I am a part of him. In a way I couldn't be part of anyone else. He gets why we have to win, why we have to survive this. It sets his jaw. And courses through him like fuel now.

Dust and bits of stone make it hazy. I squint for Kai, but all I see is a blur of gold, shifting and thrusting, followed by grunts and clangs.

"Help her. I'll be fine," I tell him.

Jhamal's nostrils flare. "Not leaving your side." The months might have slimmed his frame, but a lion still lives behind those eyes, and the ember for him that I buried begs for life.

But I deny it air.

I can't. He doesn't deserve the shell of a person I am. I can't even look at myself in the mirror. How could he see me any differently? Magic dents my periphery.

"Jham—" Before I can get the words out, Patrol pops up through the smoke clearing and fires right at me. Magic whistles through the air.

"Yo'kuse," I say, flinging my arms forward. A clear substance oozes from my fingertips and hardens into a barrier between us and them. Their magic slams into the wall and fizzles out with a *hissss*.

Where there were just a handful of guards, now there are at least a dozen. One sneers, his buddy joining him. They keep coming, two, no, three of them, firing at me. Their magic sails through the air like a thousand arrows loosed at once, and the barrier between us shatters in a shower of chimes. *Shit. Shit. Shit.* I throw my arms up, blocking as best I can. Bits of their magic and glass burn my skin, raining from overhead.

I dig deep and thrust. The air ripples, knocking them off their feet, and for a second I can almost catch my breath.

"Jhamal! Kai!" Everything is chaos around me.

Dead ahead, Patrol's back on their feet and . . .

They. Keep. Coming. Bodies, ten, maybe more, are charging in my direction. We knock them down, but more keep spilling into the hall from connecting corridors. I zig and zag, blocking blows. Fire streaks past and I cover my face. Magic ricochets off my gilded wrists like bullets. More Patrol flood the hallway. Gooseprickles spread on my arms, memories tugging at me. Dread weighs on me like lead.

We can't win this.

We need to get out of here.

I reach behind me, expecting to feel Jhamal, but there's no one there. A cough claws its way up my throat, and I spot the door Patrol was guarding earlier. The exit—he was guarding the way out of this death trap. It's wide open. I catch a glimpse of Jhamal and dart in that direction. Something hot sears my arm and it's warm and runny to the touch. I try to look back, but the hall is a cloud of dust, bits and pieces of walls crumbling. Jhamal has a Patrolman in a headlock, arms twisted behind his back, and he's using him as a shield. Kai is steps away, pulling her dagger out of someone's throat.

"Through there, the exit is that way, let's go!" I point at the open door and signal for them to go behind me. "I'll try to buy us a few minutes."

Jhamal pulls Kai off another Patrolman and they disappear at my back. The words . . . It's been so long. Spells are like recipes, if you haven't used them in a while they get foggy.

"C-co . . . cokenzae . . ." *Shit, how does this one go?* "Co . . . quinzae . . ." Magic buzzes through me, hot, ready to burst, waiting for the command to dictate its form. "Coquinzayea a'yi!"

Droplets of fire swirl in one hand and a transparent ball of gas in the other. I slam them together and thrust. The hallway explodes. I fly backward through the doorway.

"P-pwas . . . ," I say, sliding my palm down the splintered wood, trying to remember. "Pwas . . . pwastomee!"

The door shudders before turning to stone, locking the guards in the hallway with the flames and smoke. I stumble up and run.

The exit is actually a long corridor that empties into a domed room with a glass ceiling. Like a large foyer off the main street aboveground. The quiet says we've outrun them for the time being. They can't get through an enchanted stone wall easily. Even with magic.

In the center of the domed foyer is a stage of some sort with seating around the perimeter. Safe for the moment, Kai is there wrapping her leg. She pours a liquid on top of the bandaged wound and bites down, flinching.

"Are you okay?" I ask.

"I am." She gestures over her shoulder. "Jhamal is checking the halls that lead to this room. Are *you* alright?" She skims me up and down and it's only then I notice I'm bleeding heavily from my arm.

"I think so."

"Let me." She lifts the edge of her breastplate and rips the fabric underneath. "Dipped goatskin. We wear it under our armor. Very porous and the substance we dip it in is made from garlic. Helps leech out any infectants." She wraps it around my arm tight. "I did not mean to come off rude earlier, if I did. For the past several months, I'm the one who's been making the decisions, looking out for us."

"It's all good."

She tucks the edge of the wrap so it stays put.

"And thanks for the goatskin or whatever it's called."

"Of course." She holds a deeper gash lower on my arm close to her nose.

"What's that?" I ask, pointing to the liquid she's now holding.

"Oh, this is wine. Made from vineyards beside Yiyo." She unstoppers it. "This one is going to sting."

She pours it down my arm and I see red.

"FUCK! That hurts."

She smiles. "I know, but it'll help."

"Thank you."

"What remains of my tribe, my saisas, should be here soon." She presses a coiled shape insignia on her armor, and it glows. My brows cinch.

"Geolocation. It's a spell woven into the forging of our armor. . . .

When our people had a forge and magic to imbue armor back in Yiyo. Now we only have what we inherited."

A sore spot somewhere inside me churns with pain or shame or a mix of both, I don't know. I did this to them. It's my fault.

"About the thing I—uhm, did . . . I'm very sorry. I never meant—" Wails of pain ripple through the air. "Do you hear something?"

She finishes cleaning up the wound and turns to a barred doorway on the far side of the dome.

"Rue, Kai . . . in here!" Jhamal's voice, laced with urgency, shouts from the doorway. We hurry his way. Groans of pain echo off the walls in the closet-like chamber where we find Jhamal. He's bent over a table with straps, and scrawny pale legs are dangling off its edge.

"She's still breathing. Help me get her up." He grunts, helping the familiar pale-faced blond sit up. Her cheeks are sunken, dark circles around her eyes, and her hair is a matted mess.

"Bri?" I rush to his side and help hoist up my best friend. Her eyes bat open and my heart skips a beat. "You're going to be okay."

I'd feared the worst. When Jhamal said they had her, but I didn't see her in the cells. I . . . My chin hits my chest. White powder lines her mouth and her hands are covered in pricks. *What did they do to her?* I want to ask, but the words are a lump in my throat.

Jhamal and I throw one arm over each shoulder, and Bri stumbles as we help her stand.

"Rue." Her voice is raspy and her lips tug sideways in a smile. "I knew . . ." She's breathless. "Y-you'd come. I knew. Ri-ride or death . . . right?"

"Right. Right. I got you, always." I blink away the stinging in my eyes. She reaches, gesturing at a bag or something across the room, and it's then I notice Kai, leaning in the doorway, arms folded.

"Can you grab that?" I ask her.

She scoops up the bag with a grunt and shoulders it without a word. But her grimace says it all. Glass clinks against metal as Bri sifts through the bag with clumsy hands. I hold on to her as firmly as I can to keep her up.

"It's in here somewhere. . . . There's . . ." She pants. "Glass . . . blue liquid." She rears back in pain and Jhamal chews his lip. I fumble through the bag, and my hands close around cold glass with a shimmery blue liquid in it. Bri opens her mouth and I pour it in. She lies on my chest panting as her breathing levels out.

"I-I'm going to be okay. They just gave me a lot of Extractor." She takes the rest of the potion herself and her sickly pallor perks up a bit. She sits up on her own. "Thanks."

"What did they do to you?" Jhamal's expression is riddled with lines.

Probably the same thing they did to me. "Do you remember?" I ask her.

"I remember everything." Her lips are thin, eyes sullen.

Not the same, then. She's not weak like I was. I could hardly walk for months.

"They poisoned me, basically," Bri goes on. "Well, first they wanted me to help them crack Rue. Apparently, they'd tried coaxing information about the cuffs out of you?"

The memory of a grinding sound of metal instruments pinching my skin claws at me. I bite my lip to bring me back to the present. "Th-they did? I don't remember much of it, to be honest."

Bri wrinkles her brows and Kai's eyes flick to me. My cheeks burn. She already sees me as a screwup. Will they all see me that way? Is that what I am, then?

Burning.

Smoke.

Screams.

I suck in a breath to stuff down the panic.

"I told them to show me to their labs," Bri goes on. "And I'd brew up a potion that would essentially knock you unconscious. So they could do whatever they wanted to you." She pulls another vial from her bag as she talks, her countenance growing more lucid. This one has a minty paste inside, and she rubs it on the scratches on her arms. "They're idiots, of course, and had no idea what I was actually doing. What I made instead was a Defense Boost that would fight off anything they gave to me. I hid away as much as I could. But after a while they realized I was just buying time and started poking me with needles and making me take stuff to pry the truth out of me. They told me they'd stop if I agreed to do something for them. Something to you, Rue."

Chills run down my arms.

"But when I refused, they decided to try to extract any and everything I knew about your magic from my memory synapses. Your cuffs . . . well, arms now, I guess. They're determined to get them off in one piece, as long as it takes. That's why they haven't killed you."

Jhamal and I glance at each other. *He was right.*

I take the paste from her and dab it on her face, under her eyes, too. The swelling there deflates like a balloon.

"They gave me potion after potion, but my Defense Boost kept me holding on. And joke's on them because while I had access to their lab, I made all sorts of stuff we can use. Ha! I knew you'd come for me eventually."

I press my forehead to hers, grinning. "Oh my god, you're such a badass. WHO ARE YOU? Did I do this to you?"

"Yes, I credit you for this metamorphosis." She smirks and throws an arm around my shoulders. And for a moment one thing in all this mess feels right. Bri's going to be okay.

"I'm just so glad you're alright. Before they captured you, when we got separated during the fighting, I realized you didn't have your watch. . . ."

I cup my arm. *Julius*. I left it with him . . . when I told him I would bring him here once things got settled. It's been months. He's probably worried as shit. And my sister, Ms. Leola. They're all probably freaked out.

". . . I couldn't reach you and I freaked. So, I followed them. But they caught me."

"If this reunion is over, we really should be going," Kai says with a group of armored girls at her back. They all wear their hair in the same way, braided up in a bun. But the sides are not shaved. And where Kai's armor is solid gold, theirs are painted with patterns in shades of jade. One, a thicker girl, with a hoop nose ring, holds a javelin as tall as the doorway. Her eyes flick from Kai to me and back to Kai.

"You may follow this corridor out," Kai says to Bri. "My girls have cleared it."

"She's going with us," I say.

"She will do no such thing," Kai says. "I do not mean any disrespect to your father, may he rest in power . . . yoo t'cuzi maska—"

"Yoo t'cuzi maska," her girls echo under their breath in unison.

"But," Kai goes on, "we do not welcome her. She is a thief like the rest of them."

"Kai," Jhamal says. "Bri does not—"

"And no disrespect, but I'm not asking," I say. "Bri's coming."

Bri looks between us and the girl with the nose ring clenches her grip on her weapon.

Jhamal holds out Bri's wrist. "Do not make an issue where there is none, Kai. She is not a perpetrator anymore. Master Bati did the ritual himself."

"Agh," she scoffs. "Bati is old. Too forgiving. How do we even know what she says is true? That she did not agree to help them?"

The girl with the nose ring lays a hand on Kai. "We must go, saisa."

"I-I just want to say," Bri says. "I-I hate them as much as you do. We—"

I elbow her to shut up and she does. "You heard your sister," I say. "Lead the way."

CHAPTER FIVE

THE WEB, THE TUNNELS Kai'd mentioned that run under the island, stink with rot. We snake through the maze, a hollow of dirt tunnels and dusky light. Our hurrying kicks up more dust and the lights pinned to the walls are dim, like headlights in fog. The underground air is chilly, and every few moments rattling shakes the world around us, loosing bits of dust from overhead.

Kai and her girls lead the way, sticking tight together. I push, one foot in front of the other, but my knees are heavy. My feet, too. Air is ragged in my lungs. It's been so long since I've fought like this.

"I saw you out there, by the way," Kai says, beside me. "You fight like you have Yakanna in your blood." She smirks.

"Yo kan who?"

"Yakanna." She laughs to herself. "The Ghizoni were not always one, Jelani. When this land was united under the Chancellor, our people fled into hiding in Yiyo. Our individual clans had become secondary to just surviving. But do not be mistaken. I am of the blood of Moi Ike Yakanna, warrior goddess of Ghizon."

I had no idea the Ghizoni I met weren't just one big group. It makes sense that there were clans within the tribe and that much of those delineations of their heritage dissolved over the years under the sheer stress of trying to survive.

I picture my father's pencil locs and deep brown skin, the child he must've been, the way he met my mother, imagining a long life was ahead of him. Did he dream life outside the mountain could ever really happen again? Did he let his mind go there, or did reality bleed him of hope, whittle him down to the instinct to just survive? Did he pretend to be brave so I would be? Did he worry I'd fail? I have so many questions . . . that will never be answered.

Kai's arm brushes mine as she directs us around a corner. "The exit up to the ground is just this way." The next leg of the tunnel has a higher ceiling but is much less dusty, the floor a mix of hard pavement and dirt.

"You know," she says to me. "My mother's mother told me as she died that when she was a girl, she actually met Yakanna's half sister." Her cheeks push up under her olive-green eyes, sparkling with longing. "What a day that was, I cannot imagine."

"I wish I could have met her. Mother Yakanna." I wish I could have met lots of my father's people. Known them, their stories. So much of my connection with my people here is instinctive. The Ancestors chose me to wield their magic . . . but what were they like? What stories did they gather 'round and tell on holidays? Did they go to they Grandma's a certain day of the week like I grew up doing at Ms. Leola's?

I study Kai's arched brow and beautifully wide nose, my feet sliding over the patches of pavement. Her lips are full and her teeth, perfectly white. I don't know if it's her armor that makes her stand the way she does. But her shoulders are back, which almost forces her chin up. Even her gait oozes pride. The Ancestors probably look down on her with such joy.

I'll never understand why they chose me.

I straighten my posture and try to imagine I could be like that, make them proud in the same way, but the only picture I can conjure in my mind is plumes of smoke rising from Yiyo.

Kai points and speeds up to a light jog. "It's just there."

I slow my pace to walk beside Bri, my mind still tarrying over Kai and her saisas. The way they moved in there, as a unit. Each having the other's back. Their strength is in their togetherness, their unity.

"You okay?" Bri asks, but I can't meet her eyes.

"I'm fine." Not the entire truth, but once I'm out of here I can focus on what I came back to do—take down the Chancellor. *Somehow.* I try to swallow but my throat is raw.

The problem with my whole plan in the first place is I lack what the Yakanna had. They broke into the Chancellor's own building and broke me out. *Together.*

"It's just . . . I'm . . ." I hold up my wrists, and despite the dim underground light, they gleam in the orb light. "There's only one of me."

Maybe if . . .

Oh my god, that's it!

"Bri, I need to find a spell to restore the Ancestors' magic." Thinking I could take on the Chancellor myself was . . . stupid. Shortsighted. We need to fight him together.

"Oh, wow. You really think that's possible?"

"There's got to be a spell somewhere about magic messing up and needing to be restored. That only makes sense, right?"

"Uhmm." Bri's eyebrows cinch in skepticism but she keeps her mouth shut, which I appreciate. I have a world of doubt on my shoulders; I need this ray of hope.

"There *has* to be a way, Bri. And I'm going to find it. I'm fighting beside my people against him next time."

"I'll help, however I can, of course."

I shake her shoulder in excitement, light budding in the shadows where I hide my fears. "When we get there, we need to find Bati. He'll know where their spell books are."

"Shouldn't we try to figure out what the Chancellor's been up to since we've been locked up?"

"Yes, that too. But magic is the key. Trust me."

She nods and we walk the next few minutes in silence, my mind working over any remnant of information I've ever even seen on magic restoration. Maybe it takes magic to restore magic, and that's why they haven't done it?

Kai leads us through the winding corridors. My calves ache like we've been running forever. The tunnel converges with several others. There are ten or more directions we could go, and each looks exactly the same: dusty pavement, stone archway, and floating orbs lining the way. But Kai and her girls don't hesitate and lead us down the third one on the left.

We follow the twisty tunnel. The orbs are fewer and more spaced apart. By the time we stop, I can hardly make out my hand in front of my face. A door in the ceiling attached to a set of stairs that pull down like a ladder is barely a sliver in the dark. Finally.

Kai grunts and light splits the ceiling wide open, hinges groaning as she opens a steel door above us.

"This will put us closer to the Chancellor's building than I like, but it is the shortest route to where we've been hiding."

"Where have you been hiding?" I ask.

"Underground. The Web. Just the other side. The entire island is full of tunnels. But they don't all connect." How does she know all this? I want to ask, but they've been searching for a way to break us out for months, she said, so it makes sense.

Kai nods at the girl with the nose ring. "Be vigilant. It's a war zone."

"Zora," the girl with the nose ring says, introducing herself.

"Rue."

"Pleasure." She gestures for me to go first.

Last I remember, the Central District was under fire, buildings toppling, burning, chaos when the General's betrayal was aired on screens everywhere, thanks to me. Half the people were enraged by his lies and betrayal, ripping the City to shreds, while the other half fought against them in the name of treason.

Then, my people had a chance. Then, I was free. I take the rung on the ladder and climb, my stomach twisting in anticipation of what I will see. The salty, humid air slaps. I pull myself out of the tunnel. The world aboveground is a pile of rubble. The others pull themselves out of the hole behind me. The door in the ground we came through is sectioned off with barbed wire in an alleyway near an abandoned warehouse. If you were to drive by, the clutter and trash would completely camouflage it like a sewage drain back in East Row.

We emerge from the alley and most buildings in the Central District—or what's left of them—are half collapsed. The Chancellor's tower looms a mile or so away, a pillar of alabaster stone. Its windows are broken on the bottom floors and TRAITOR is painted across its facade in big red letters. We keep moving through the narrow block, careful to stick in the shade.

"I'm going to have your head," I say under my breath before turning my back on his stone tower. We hurry through the main artery of the island, which is like a mini downtown. Where stores and screens once were on every corner with bewitched storefronts trying to lure you in, sits rubbish, piles of broken concrete. Storefronts are boarded up or burnt. Some of this is new. It was sort of like this when I left, but the destruction must have continued. New buildings are burned, way more than before. The Chancellor's own people have turned on him; shattered glass and spray-painted messages scream of the unrest. Goose bumps skitter up my arm, mixed with a bubble of pride. The demand for justice hasn't dulled; it's amplified.

"It's a disaster up here," I say, and Kai nods.

"Who's responsible, you think?" I ask Bri.

"Dwegini . . . probably," she says, a flicker of something shading her expression. That assumption is more rooted in pride than anything else. Her family has been Zruki for as long as the faction existed. Blame for destroying her home doesn't quite sit right with her, I guess. . . . If it did, would her answer have been different?

Kai shrugs. "All I know is this place is torn in half. Grays fighting other Grays."

"Yeah," I say. "And neither is backing down, from the looks of it."

Jhamal's jaw clenches.

"Zruki, we lived in entirely different worlds from Dwegini. I just can't imagine us doing anything like this. Dwegini have always had that air of arrogance about them because of the way the Chancellor favors them. Their glittery homes on the mountainside, their fancy research jobs and social gatherings. The way they—they just move through this place like they own it because the Chancellor's decided they aren't suited for mine work." Bri spits the words. "If anyone is tearing this place apart, it's probably them. They have no respect for anything."

Respect? I don't respect this place either. Does she?

She sighs, apparently reading my expression. "I hate him. Don't misunderstand me. I just—" As we pass what looks like it used to be a trinket shop, she runs her fingers along the brick facade and her eyes turn down. "'Respect' wasn't the right word. The Chancellor should burn for what he's done. I just . . . I don't know."

I study her pinched expression, the lines written into her forehead, as we skirt another corner, pass another crumbled block that used to ring with life. It was her home, and as messed up as the Chancellor is, she still has an affection for the place. Memories. It's been her entire life.

"What was that place?" I say, pointing to the store we just passed.

"Trixy's Fine Trinkets." She turns a silver ring on her finger. "Dad gave it to me when I turned sixteen. My Binding present. Took him my entire childhood to save up for it."

I rub her hand. "Hey, we will win. And then, rebuild."

She nods.

The Chancellor's tower still watches despite being farther in the distance. It's so tall, even from Yiyo it can be seen like a dot in the distance. A watchtower. His dais. On the uppermost deck of the Chancellor's tower is a room fenced in windows with a wide balcony, the jewel-on-top stone somehow untouched by the carnage. Curtains flutter behind the glass, and the hair on my neck stands. I squint, but whatever lurked there is gone.

"I don't like this," I say. "We need to get off the street. Back underground."

"And we will," Kai says. "But we have to get there first."

"There's a whole web of tunnels underground," I say. "You said yourself. You *sure* none of those lead where we're going?"

Kai turns, a flicker of something in her expression. "What are you suggesting, Jelani?"

"Just that coming outside, being exposed in the open, might not be . . . a necessary risk."

"Oh, and you'd know?"

"Enough." Jhamal steps between us.

It stings. She's right to question me after what I've done. But I have good fighting instincts and I'd bet money we're being watched.

"You will not speak this way to the Ancestors' Chosen," Jhamal says. "Kainese, you dishonor the gods with your loose tongue."

Kai sucks her teeth with a hiss. But she says nothing else, just leads the way.

"You don't have to do that," I say to him out of Kai's earshot. But he says nothing, just holds his chin up.

"I can handle mine, really." I step away from him so he knows I mean it.

His adoration and protection of me is kind, sweet. But it's his love for the Ancestors, for his people, crown jewels of Ghizoni pride, that sets his shoulders square—makes him puff out his chest. After my mistake, I don't deserve a spot on that list.

CHAPTER SIX

WE HURRY ACROSS ANOTHER street and the quiet is eerie. Broken glass crunches under my feet and trash litters the street. It's an upward incline and my thighs burn. Once we reach the top of the hill, I can see the District fully. Smoke from far off somewhere rises to clouds. The City is a carcass with burned bones. Businesses are dead, no people wander the street. Katsu's is empty where patio chairs used to be teeming with students, their fizzy drinks in hand on a study break this time of day. A screen still hangs from a high-rise that's somehow still standing. But its screen is glitching, black and white lines of static across it.

The truth of the Chancellor's "great" land is bursting through like a boil preparing to pop. I dig my nails into my palm. The memory of his angry mug taunts me, his grimace when he told me I shouldn't exist, the way he let the General play his games, killing my people back in East Row. My wrists warm at the thought and my fingers twitch. When I went up against him . . . what exactly did I do that made things go wrong? I look for the memories of how we started losing, but they're not there.

I glance back at the Chancellor's tower. How can a land be great when it's nailed together with lies and nourished with poison? When it was built on bones, then dressed in half-truths? If he thinks his City is fractured now, wait until I'm done with it.

Ashes will rise.

Blood will boil.

And those stolen from will take.

The Chancellor will pay. For stealing my people's magic, forcing them to live in hiding. What would my father say? Would he be proud? Even if I messed up the first time?

I glance at Zora, then Kai, and can't help but admire her posture. The way she moves. I need the Yakanna, Jhamal, all of us united. But something in Kai's body language, the way she moves, the knowing way she runs everyone around her, tells me that will be easier said than done. I turn to Jhamal, walking close enough to him to feel his warmth.

"You think—" I start, when something dents my peripheral vision. "We're not alone. Quick." I gesture at a lamppost across an intersection. Kai's girls move in one motion, bare shoulder pressed into the back of the girl in front of them. We duck behind a pile of debris as the growing footsteps get louder. The Chancellor's footmen march past, sentries patrolling. We stick tight together and I notice how the Yakanna curve around one another, moving as one unit. Except for Zora, who is stuck to my side. Jhamal's on my other side, wariness written into his brow. He needs food, rest. He's held up the strength of the both of us for so long.

"Left," the Patrolman yells, and his men rotate on their heels. The drum of their footsteps races my pulse. If they even so much as look in our direction, we're caught.

"Halt." The march comes to a standstill, their knotted fingers over their chests, when a siren wails. We scurry backward to tuck farther behind an old rusted communal trash dump, and I swear if that Patrolman listens hard enough, he could hear my thumping chest. A truck rolls to a stop beside them.

"Macazi," the driver says to the sergeant leading the march. "Sixty degrees north of here, looting, another group on the southern quadrant vandalizing government property."

The sergeant nods and more Patrol hop off the back. The truck rolls off and the marching formation breaks into a jog. They disappear around a corner and I step out, motioning for the others to come out too.

"That was close."

He said "Macazi. . . ." Those the Chancellor deems unfit to be bound to magic at the Binding ceremony are cast into community housing, given bare minimum wages. Most die or disappear. Some he keeps and lets his researchers experiment on, I've even heard. I shudder at the thought. You don't treat people like that to no consequence. The tags on the Chancellor's tower, the looting, vandalizing statues . . . it all makes sense. The Chancellor has more than us working against him. When the City started to fall, they probably saw their opportunity to step out against the tyrant who kept them as second-class citizens for so long.

But the Macazi are magicless. . . . How could they even? . . . I shake off the thought and turn my attention back to the fight ahead.

Despite the march being gone, we still press into building sides as we walk. Getting spotted out here isn't ideal. Kai and I scout before we cross each intersection, then motion for the others to come along. We walk for what feels like miles. The sun has dipped low and the mosquitoes, or blood bugs as Jhamal calls them, have picked up like they do in the evenings in this humid place. The scene is desolate, but random pops of revelry ring in the distance.

"That way." Kai points east of Yiyo, its peak half caved in. "We must reach it before sunset."

Bri and I share a look. "What happens when the sun sets?"

"The City is not deserted." Kai's steel stare sends gooseprickles up my arms. "It is asleep. Pochalla e'yuna kessi."

"The cover of darkness is the enemy's greatest friend," Zora whispers to me.

I meet her eyes and she smiles, but her gaze falls, craters denting her cheeks. All of Kai's girls, the Yakanna, have a rigid look about them, but Zora's eyes are soft and her words gentle. She's a bit shy, maybe? But the rest of her, pure steel.

Bri rummages through her bag and pulls out some metal gadget. She presses a button on its top and it glows green. Jhamal shoots her a quizzical glance.

"It senses magic harnessed through onyx. If there's any Patrol or Grays nearby, it should buzz. Look, it's the best I got."

"Your tricks are no use," Kai says. "But for those inside the District, Patrol has almost all gone plain clothed. They've renamed themselves and—"

"BEEP! BEEP!"

The light on Bri's device flashes with a pulsing red. Zora steps in front of me and I almost have to shove her out the way.

"I can handle myself, really."

If she heard me, I can't tell. She crouches low, hand on her weapon, watching, waiting.

"You carry the Ancestors' magic," Kai says. "She is protecting it more than you."

"I—"

"BEEP! BEEP!"

Kai rolls her eyes.

"I trust Bri's gadgets. If it's beeping, someone is definitely nearby."

Jhamal nods in agreement.

"Let's get to higher ground, see what we can see," I say. "We need to know where the enemy is to run from them."

Kai hesitates but nods and takes off. Her girls form an octagon, their backs to one another and weapons out. They crouch, gait loose, bouncing ever so slightly.

"You go that way," I say to Jhamal. His lips are a hard line, but he runs off in the direction I tell him. Bri and I follow the pulsing beeps, they grow louder the closer I get. Her hands are shaking, but her elbows are firm.

"Stay behind me," I say as we peek around a corner near what used to be some sort of art gallery. A statue is overturned in the courtyard outside what used to be a dormitory for first-year Bound students. But other than that, no one else is there. That I can see. A rumbling noise rolls in the distance, and I hold my hands up at the ready. Just in case. Bri wanders around the statue and the device in her hands screeches louder.

"Help me with this," she says, pushing on the crumbling plaster that was the Chancellor's head. "Someone's under here."

"Get back."

Bri scurries backward.

I probe the spells covered in cobwebs in my brain until I sort the one for *destroy*. Hope this works. "Perdch yee'me."

White shards fly through the air as my magic blows the statue into pieces. I jerk us into a huddle. When the dust clears, what's left is a body. Gray skin, long hair, and an open-eyed stare. He's about my age. I lift his sleeves, looking for onyx bubbles protruding from his wrist, but there's nothing. Bri's gadget beeps quieter.

"Magic was used here. Very recently." She bangs the top of her doohickey. "But the whiffs of it are fading. Or this isn't working any-more or something." She shoves it in her bag with a scowl.

That march of Patrolmen . . . they killed him? For tagging a statue?! I can practically hear what Jhamal would say: *There is no such thing as fairness in war.*

His legs and arms are sprawled out like an X. In his right palm is the letter *L* painted in red. His lips are so dry, they're peeling. I trace the letters *M-A-C-A* painted on his forehead in red.

"Maca."

"Short for Macazi," Bri says.

"The magicless bother no one," I say, the injustice of it twisting nerves inside me. "They lived in community housing and those that were released from there are hardly seen by anyone." No telling how bad it's been for them now that the Central District is in pieces. The last time I saw a Macazi, he was no more than five years old. I was running from being captured by Patrol and I'd given him a carcass of meat. I can still remember the way his curly hair bounced as he ran off to take it to his family.

I search the dead man's pockets for weapons. He has light scrapes on him, and his hands are dusty.

Bri sniffs them. "It's the plaster from the statue. He must have toppled it after tagging it."

The stuff underneath his nails says he fought hard against whoever hurt him.

Light footsteps and clanging armor behind me tell me that Jhamal and Kai's search came up empty. Instinctively, I look for the window on the top of the Chancellor's tower, but we're too far away now to see it. I press a palm to the Macazi's forehead. He's cold, so cold, like he's been here like this forever. Like someone wanted this to happen here . . . and for us to find him.

"*Na!*" Kai shouts, and it startles me. "Get away from him." She turns to Jhamal. "Does she know nothing?"

"Rue." Jhamal rushes beside me. "Don't touch—" He scrubs a palm down his face at the sight of my hand laid across the dead Macazi's forehead. "Alright, get him up," he says to the Yakanna hovering nearby, shocked. Zora nods and leads them in lifting the body.

"I don't understand," I say.

Jhamal pulls me aside, cutting a glance over his shoulder. Kai's back there pacing.

"It is of great responsibility to touch the body of an innocent slain. The Ancestors consider honor above all Integrities. Honor is an inescapable duty, Jelani. And there is no honor in the death of an innocent. Whomever they are."

"But I didn't hurt him."

"But you touched him. You are aware innocence was slain. So you are bound by honor to give him a proper burial now."

"I . . . But . . . We don't have time for that. I was just trying to—"

"I understand. But we have to. It is the way. You cannot dishonor the gods when it is their power that flows in your veins."

I study his eyes a moment and the weight of the world hovers in them. This is serious. "Okay. Okay, if that's the Ancestors' way, okay." I nudge my chin in Kai's direction. "And what about her? She looks pissed."

He sighs. "Yakanna are headstrong, rigidly loyal, and full of pride. Honor for the tribe is more valuable than anything, even life itself. You'll never meet a more fierce, ambitious warrior than a Yakanna. But they can be so brittle. . . ."

"That they break."

"Yes."

"And you? You're not Yakanna." He's never mentioned his clan or any clans before.

"Yakanna are matriarchal. They do not partner with men . . . long term, I should say. If they take one on, it's purely in servitude. We were a thing a while ago, but that is not a life I wanted, so I insisted we go our separate ways."

Ah, so she's clearly not over it.

"I am Beerchi." He slaps his chest. "Might, wisdom, the two fiercest weapons. Whether male or female, it does not matter. We are drawn to follow whoever embodies these values best. But, Jelani, those alliances have long since dissolved. We are talking about the loyalties of our parents' parents. Generations ago."

"It doesn't seem like everyone's let them go." I gesture at Kai again, who is apparently in a tense conversation with Zora, and I realize they are not sisters in the traditional sense. "I didn't mean to be disrespectful, really. I just—"

"You didn't know. I understand."

"Division will destroy us."

"Agreed. Send up a chant to the Ancestors that when we return, no other ancient loyalties have reemerged. I can keep Kai in line. But the others . . ."

Before I can ask more, Jhamal jets off and inserts himself in the conversation between Zora and Kai, and Bri walks up.

"Everything cool?" she asks.

"I guess. We have to bury this poor guy." I can't tear my eyes away from Jhamal talking with Kai. A vein pulses at his temple and everyone around them moves away. Bri gazes their way in apparent confusion.

"I just have a sick feeling, Bri, that . . ."

"That what?"

That I'm not cut out for this. That the more I try to help, the more I screw up. The more will die at my hand. The fear in Rahk's eyes when he'd asked what they should do is a torchlight in my memory. The way he ran off without question at my order to retreat to the mountain. How his last breath must've burned. How he probably died with a scream in his throat. I bite down hard. My lip bleeds.

"Rue, that what?"

"Nothing."

CHAPTER SEVEN

THE ACCESS POINT TO the section of the Web where my Ghizoni people are stowed away is between a boarded-up consignment store and what used to be a magical malady shop. Its tin roof is folded like a strong wind took it half off. Kai drags open the door to the hole in the ground, and rungs plummet into darkness. My heart thumps in my chest at the prospect of seeing everyone, how they're doing. Little Titube and her mother, Bati with his knobby walking stick. Those that made it, are they okay? Do I even deserve to ask? Will they even want to see me?

I tug at the end of my shirt. Bri sticks to my side as we descend. Sunlight fades the deeper we go, my pulse ticking faster with each rung. We continue the descent in silence. The door above us slides closed and Jhamal moves next to me, his arm grazing mine.

The ladder deposits us in an underground passageway much like a basement. The walls are close, so close we can only walk two side by side at a time. Stone walls surround us, blue light streaming from fissures in the ceiling. The space is cozy with winding corridors in several directions. I swallow. It's small down here, tight. I suppose the tunnels could lead somewhere grand, robust, like their home in Yiyo. But something tells me when Kai said numbers were cut by half, she did not exaggerate.

"You ready?" he asks, as if he can hear the whisper of my fears. I set my jaw, hoping it masks the angst trying to drown me. But he stares as if he can see right through me. He reaches for my hand, but I shake my head.

"I'm good, really. I want to find Bati."

He huffs out a breath, sensing the push. But he only nods and walks a few steps ahead.

We take the first corridor on the right. This part of the Web is different from the dirt tunnels where we escaped. The floors are more paved and along the walls are actual rooms. Where the Web had stone archways, this has makeshift doors, which are panels of wood perched in front of room openings. We traipse down the long hallway around bins and piles of stained armor.

Bri's at my back, sticking close, arms linked around herself. "Do we even know if Bati . . ." Her words trail off. She's right. I don't know if he survived. But I can't think that way. I have to hope he is.

The hall opens up to a big room with towering beamed ceilings full of people. Water drips through the tiny fissures, making puddles on the ground. Orbs dot the walls and long tables run the perimeter of the space. The light in here is brighter and a mix of earthy spices and something musty swirl in my nose.

Nostalgia blossoms in my chest at the memory of the first time I sat with my people. How we ate and talked and laughed. How I was scared and knew no one, but all they wanted to do was see East Row win.

Seats scrape the floor as people rise when we enter. But many remain seated . . . intentionally. The warmth dissolves and my cheeks flash hot. I peer harder at the expressions on the people's faces.

Lines etched in brows, dry, cracked hands, heavy shoulders, a nod to heavier hearts. What am I going to say to them? What could I say to make any of this better? We walk several more steps in silence.

Five . . . four . . . three . . . two . . . one.

I push out a breath.

Maybe it's not what I say . . . maybe it's what I do?

The Yakanna are steps ahead of me, greeted with hugs and shoulder squeezes. Jhamal is swallowed in embraces. I stand there shuffling on my feet as eyes flick my way. For a moment I wish I was standing next to him, his hand wrapped around mine. But I made this bed, I gotta lie in it alone.

The room is full, but the crowd is a fraction of what I remember. There could be no more than a hundred, maybe two here? Yiyo was home to thousands before. Maybe there's another big room elsewhere? Maybe some are sleeping still? Maybe—

"This is everyone?" I suspect I know the answer before I ask, but desperation makes the words spill from my lips anyway.

Kai doesn't respond, just meets my eyes, and that's answer enough. I feel sick. I glare at my hands and I swear I see red. So many . . . so many lost. My fingers grab at my throat. I force out a breath and blink, but all I see is smoke and Yiyo on the backs of my eyelids. I stagger, gripping a table that we pass, and stares snap to me.

"Rue?" Jhamal says.

"I'm *fine*," I lie, as horrible as that feels. How do I lie to the one person who's been there for me through all of this? It feels so wrong. But I can't be broken to him forever. I can't stand the way he jumps when I move or groan. I need him to see the person I *was* when I look in his eyes, not this shell of a person I am now, struggling to put one foot in front of the other.

Maybe if he sees it . . . I'll see it too.

"Please, don't worry about me." I'm the least of who they should be worried about. He tsks, muttering his disagreement.

Chatter hovers over the room like fog and I scan for Bati, or some familiar face, anyone I know. A place to set my eyes and calm the panic taking flight in me.

We move between the tables and I swallow more courage, forcing myself to stand a little taller. I spot a crowd of men in long robes, twine tied at their waists and rings in their braided hair. They're huddled on the opposite end of the room over a table. One or two look my way, but quickly turn back around.

"Bati might be over there," I tell Jhamal, and he squeezes my arm in sympathy before being pulled away into a conversation with someone I don't recognize. The guy he is talking with is rocking a Harden-style beard and fur sits on his shoulders. He wears armor like Jhamal used to, in the same pattern. A stack of golden rings adorn one ear and a chunky ring with a bear's claw hugs his knuckle. He and Jhamal grip arms in some unusual form of handshake and pull into a hug.

"Come on, Bri."

Bati wasn't on the battlefield. If anyone has the details on what I've missed, he would. Bri and I move through the bodies of people and their cloak of whispers. Walking back in here is like walking through a nightmare. How do I tell them we need to get up and fight when their numbers are cut at least in half because of what I've done? How do I tell them anything? Who am I? *The Chosen*

One, my conscious whispers. Yes, but not chosen to lead . . . chosen to fight.

Bowls of fire sit on the tables. Closer now, I scan the huddled group for white locs and a stocky frame. I spot the back of a man with a round face, holding on to a knobby stick.

"Excuse me," I say, squeezing between the edge of the huddle for a glimpse of his face.

Deep brown eyes I don't recognize greet me. "Hello, how are you, dear?" It's not Bati.

"H-hi. Sorry."

His lips split in a smile. "No, no, it's okay." He turns to face me fully, his braided beard grazing the floor. Blue stripes paint his cheeks.

"I am so pleased to see you are okay, child." The stranger cups my hands. His eyes glisten and he gasps at the sight of my gilded arms.

"Thank you. I-I'm so glad you're okay too." I dig a toe into the ground.

He dips his head, backing away. I bite down, hard, and notice the scab in my palm I've been picking at is actually bleeding. I tug Bri along. Heads turn as we pass. I tuck my head between my shoulders, wishing I had my hoodie.

I plop at a table and Bri sits beside me. Many around us sit absorbed in their conversations, not even the slightest bit interested in me. But some side-eye me with a look that sends cold pricks down my spine. Is he really not here? Could Bati be . . . gone? Guilt shudders through me.

"Your mind is working a million miles a minute," Bri says,

pointing to my hand, which I hadn't realized is pulling loose threads at the bottom of my shirt.

"Excuse me, Jelani?" A familiar little face shrouded in colorful beads speaks. Titube. She's a little taller than the last time I saw her, but still only elbow high on me. I look for her mother, the kind woman who'd made the delicious grub last time I saw her. But she's nowhere to be found. Titube stares up at me.

"My flower girl, Titube!" A smile tugs at my lips that I can't fight off. Parched for some warmth, some joy, I squat and take in Titube's smile, those perfect cheeks, the joy that dances in her eyes. It warms the parts of me frozen with worry.

Bri settles at a table, lost in her bag of gadgets, and I squat, pulling her into me for a hug, hoping she can feel my love, my care. Somehow, we will put this broken world back together. And it will be better, for her. For everyone. I squeeze her hand. "You're literal sunshine, you know that?"

She smiles and I can count each one of her teeth. She curls one hand around the other like she did the first time we met, and this time a flower with gold petals appears. Her magic is fragile, stunted like all of theirs, but she knows this flower trick well. "For you," she says.

"You're so good at that." I pick it up gently, but its crinkled petals turn to dust. A gust of wind steals them, and her smile blows away with it. She sulks away deflated.

"Titu—" But she doesn't turn back.

"Her mother did not make it." Jhamal appears out of nowhere. His words cut like a blade.

I did this.

He strokes my hand and for a moment I let him.

"Did you find Bati?" he asks, massaging the tension out of my hand, like he just knows I'm a ball of stress. There's a sense of longing in his expression. And yet his words come out measured. How is he so calm? How can he look at the size of this crowd, know how his home has been desecrated, and not be furious with me? I'm furious with myself.

"No." There are hundreds of people here, maybe I just haven't found him yet.

"I know it's a lot. You are doing great."

I snatch my hand from his and his expression crinkles.

"How can you say that to me?" My voice is louder than I mean it to be.

"Jelani, I've told you so man—"

"No, how can you look at this place, then look at me and see anything but—" My eyes sting.

Heads turn our way. I sigh.

"You know what, never mind." I won't do this. Not here. I have a plan and it's the only thing keeping me upright on my feet. Even if I can't find Bati, someone knows where the texts are. I will find a spell or some way to restore our magic. I will.

"Rue." He never calls me that unless he feels like he's not getting through to me. He throws an arm over my shoulder, making light of the situation, and the nosy stares we were getting dissolve. He ushers me to a shaded corner of the room. He takes my hands in his and pulls me into a hug. "I'm on your side," he says, sadness shading his expression.

Everything in me wants to push him away. But here in this

corner, with no one looking, when my head and heart feel like they might burst from the pressure of it all, the reality of what I've done, not a memory, but staring me right in my face, I can't even find the strength to do that. He is a wall around me, his chest hard against my face, like he's determined to hold me up, no matter how sure I am my knees might falter.

"You're going to get through this. *Our people* are going to get through this."

A single tear rolls down my cheek, and I turn into him fully and let it. He holds me a moment longer before I smooth my cheek clear and put some space between us. I don't know what's sustaining me at this point, but my next words come out easier.

"Thanks."

His beautiful eyes smile at me. I look away.

"I'm gonna keep looking for Bati. I want to see what he knows and I need to find any spell books they have here." I put even more space between us, finding surer footing.

He peers through the crowd, looking too. He's a good foot taller than me, so I imagine he can see a whole heck of a lot more. His brows dent. Then he waves over someone. A brawny man parts the crowd, carrying a piece of armor. He hands it to Jhamal.

"Thank you, coquella."

They grip arms.

"Shaun, did you ever get to meet Jelani?"

"No. Jelani, good to see you are well." I can't tell if he means it, but I greet him as pleasant as I can. We give each other a nod. I grimace at the icky feeling sloshing through me. I look for some other corner of the room to hide in. I need a moment to myself. If I fall apart here, if guilt erodes me from the inside out, I've only failed *again*. I've only brought more death upon my home.

"Have you seen Bati?" I ask Shaun, and the way he shakes his head tells me he isn't gone. I clutch my chest in relief. "Okay, I'm just gonna go look for him."

I turn to find a line of people waiting to greet me. Some in armor like Shaun's and a few in rippled armor like the Yakanna. Several others in long robes as well. I say hello and apologize to every single person that says hello to me. Most bow, which makes me shift on my feet. So I apologize again. Eventually, they back away, smiling.

The next in line is a man in ivory robes. He talks so fast, I have to focus on his lips to get everything he's saying. He has reddish-brown hair and small ears. He looks so much like . . . Rahk.

Triggered, more snatches of memories come to me. Screams echo in my head. The taste of smoke lingers on my tongue. Sticky. My face is so red. Fragments of images flash before me, familiar pieces and some I've never seen.

I tug at my arms and the strap holding me to this metal table groans. A man with long lashes and kind eyes in a white lab coat joins his side and presses something cold to my lips.

"Where am I?" I ask. "Wh-what are you—"

But the way their lips twist in satisfaction tells me my words aren't making any sense. My eyes grow heavier. I crane for a view of the room. Wires, a metal door, sterile, but the walls are made of stone. I know this place . . . from Binding. Am I in the Central District? Boots walk past a small window high on the wall.

Underground. I'm . . .

I need to get back to them . . . my people . . . they . . .

I blink again and this time the space between the images is longer. Even my breath is heavy somehow. A weight. "Jham—" The words dissolve on my tongue as everything disappears.

I swallow, my shirt balled in my fist. H-he had me strapped down. The one with eyelashes. I-in a lab or somewhere. It looked like the room where I was bound to magic. I close my eyes tight, glimpsing for more but find nothing. Why . . . why did I forget? I run my fingers over the places Jhamal stitched. I shut my eyes, trying to pull at more remnants of the memory, but it's gone as fast as it'd come. The weight of the past several months sits on me like a brick.

Five . . . four . . . three . . . two . . . one.

My grip eases.

Five . . . four . . . three . . . two . . . one.

Focus, Rue. I force out a breath. *You can do this. You can find a way to get everyone fighting again. You can* win.

I blink and the Ghizoni looks at me expectantly. My cheeks burn, realizing I don't know anything he just said. I want him to know he is important to me. Not only in fighting for us but sitting in the little moments too.

"You know what I mean?" he says, smiling warmly, my distractedness going unnoticed, thankfully. "Anyway, it was so nice to meet with you."

"I-it was so nice to meet you, too." I reach for his hand. "Let's talk again soon." He smiles brighter at that, and I smile too, thankful to have done something right.

I spot a crowd of onlookers folded over drinks across the room.

Bati isn't among them. I recognize Kai and her Yakanna at the center of all of them. They are standoffish from everyone else, and something about Kai's expression tells me that's intentional. She's not a fan of me or she doubts me. Of course she does. Why would she feel any other way? But I can show her. I can show all of them.

Another steps up to talk to me when I catch sight of a white head of locs and almost fall out of my seat getting up. "Sorry, if you'll excuse me." I jet off, push between a few pointy elbows, and clamp a hand on the familiar shoulder.

"Bati!" Without thinking, I hug him.

"Jelani!" He lets me go and I straighten his robes, which my eagerness disheveled. He holds my hands. "I'm so, *so* pleased to see you, dear." His voice cracks and the way his lips tighten in a smile, I know he means it. "Why, you're pale as a ghost. What is it?"

"I'm okay," I say, willing myself to hear his voice over the phantom shrieks ringing in my head. *How have you fared?* I want to ask, but I can *see* the answer—not well. "Any word on the Chancellor's whereabouts? What's the last you've heard?"

"Oh, many whispers, Jelani. But it's hard to tell which are worth their weight in jpango sap." He huffs. "Kai had gotten word he was on the outskirts of the island when she and the Yakanna snuck in to rescue you."

"I see." I'd hoped for more helpful information than that. "Would you happen to have any books here? Did those make it?"

"Oh, yes, we guard those very close."

"Could I read them? I'm looking for a spell."

"Whatever you need, Jelani. You're the Ancestors' Chosen. I am at your service."

"No, that's not. That's not what this is about. I'm just looking for something to help us."

"You'll find several just over there. That wooden trunk against the sack of rice."

"Thank you so much." I about-face. By now, the Chancellor knows we've escaped. He has to have people looking for us. We won't get another chance. This time we do it right.

Together.

CHAPTER EIGHT

I PUSH THE RICE SIDEWAYS and it's deceptively heavy.

Inside the trunk, I finger a train of book spines before grabbing an armful. I plant myself at the farthest table in the room. Bri joins me, lugging her metal contraptions. I shove a book her way, but she's distracted with some laser-looking gadget with a suction cup on the end. But by the looks of how her tongue is poking her cheek, whatever she is trying to do must not be going right. She holds it near a firebowl on the table and narrows her eyes. But nothing happens.

"Come on!"

"We okay over there?" I envy her ability to be in her own world right now. For half the stares I'm getting, she's getting ten thousand more, and she doesn't seem to care one bit.

"Yeah, just trying to get this stupid thing to—" She turns a knob on its top and it falls off. "Dammit!" She rumbles through her bag, which sounds like shaking a metal trash can full of rocks. The more noise she makes, the more stares we get.

"You and your bag of gadgets . . . could you be a little quieter?" I flip a few more pages but find no related spells. I set the book aside and grab another one.

"Sorry, I'm just . . . trying . . . to . . . ," she says between grunts as she shoves two ends together, "get this thing to work."

I flip, searching, reading for anything on restoring spells. I turn another few pages and drown out the sounds of chatter, the burning stares I know I'm getting, and focus on the words on the page.

"Come on, help me. There's bound to be something in here about restoring magic."

Skepticism twists her brows.

"Listen, I know . . ."

Bang! A blade slaps a table and heads turn in that direction.

"Mordit'z aka," a man shouts, the body of the fallen Macazi hanging over his shoulder. The burial. I'd almost forgotten. Fists pound the table and a few hands go up. Bri and I glance at each other.

"What's going on?" she whispers to me.

"I don't know," I admit, and bite my lip in shame, the thought that I *should* know needling at me.

"Mordit'z aka!"

"Innocence slain," everyone answers in unison. A few more hands go up, including Zora's, but Kai sits back in her seat.

They're volunteering for something . . . but what?

"Mordit'z aka," he shouts once more, with a growl under his voice this time, and I spot Jhamal nodding in my direction, gesturing for me to raise my hand. *The burial.*

"They're volunteering to help with the burial, I bet," I say to Bri, my hand shooting in the air. It's my fault we even have a man to bury. I have to help. What kind of Ghizoni would I be if I didn't? The spell can wait a moment longer.

I shoot my arm in the air, hoping I'm not too late to help. "Innocence slain!" *Please let me help,* I want to say, but no one else is talking. There are silent hands only, and I want to respect the tradition if that's what it is.

"Rue, this book is a bust too." Bri folds it closed.

"I need a minute. I have to do this with them."

"You do?"

"Yes, I just have to. I can't explain it."

"Keshkech m'bwan!" The Beerchi counts the eleven hands raised. "Ya ya lo nizka. Na lo'misha!" He pounds his staff made of jpango on the ground. "Mordit'z aka!"

"Innocence slain!"

One last hand goes up and he seems satisfied.

"The burial will begin in ten minutes," he says before departing through the doorway. Those with raised hands rush to the door.

"Listen," I say, turning to Bri. "While we're doing the burial, can you flip through the rest of these books and see if they have anything at all about restoring magic? There has to be a way written down somewhere."

"Sure, I'll look. But I've read tons and there's not much on it."

"Bri, you don't know everything, remember."

She blushes. "Yes, sorry."

"There are books here you've never seen."

"Got it. I'll look."

"Thank you. I'll be back." I join Jhamal in the doorway and cool air meets us outside.

"Thanks for the heads-up."

His hand touches the small of my back as he gestures for me to walk in front of him, and my insides twinge with longing.

"I want to help." I'm not even sure what that means. I wish I knew. I wish I knew a lot. If I'd fully understood more about where I come from, our customs, traditions, I'd have known not to touch the body. I'd have known that my people are a tapestry of clans and traditions and cultures.

"I know you do," he says.

"How exactly will the burial ceremony go?"

"Twelve are needed to complete the burial ritual. But helping is not enough. We need to show them you are learning. You are trying to get it."

"Get what exactly?"

He stops me. "Get what it means to *be* Ghizoni."

He keeps walking but I'm stuck where I'm standing. His words hit like a brick. The truth that's been tugging at me, the burning conviction that helping with this burial is as important as finding that spell. The weight of his words takes my breath as we climb out of the underground lair.

Embracing my father's heritage, my people here, is one thing . . . but he's right, understanding what it means to *be* Ghizoni is something different entirely. If I knew more, maybe I wouldn't have failed them on the battlefield. Maybe I would have better understood the plan the others were trying to convince me of in the forest outside Yiyo before everything went to shit. Maybe I wouldn't have been locked up for months if I knew more about our tactics, the ways Kai leads and protects her saisas.

Shame sears through me. Once we get our magic back, why would they fight beside me? Why would they believe I even care if I'm not earnestly trying to understand who I am, *all* of who I am?

And so much of that is here, in Ghizon, which I missed out on for seventeen years.

Maybe my people would be alive if I were Ghizoni in more than name.

If I'm going to be worthy of any of this, any of them—I glance at Jhamal—I have to stop screwing up. I study the ground as we move outside, watching my feet, embarrassment coiling in my gut. Here, in this place, I am home, but . . . I know nothing.

CHAPTER NINE

A SMALL COURTYARD ABOUT A hundred meters from the access point where the Ghizoni are is the closest thing we can get to a proper burial ground, Jhamal had explained. Abandoned buildings are walled around us, backed up by overgrown field. The fur-cloaked guy and a few others who dress just like him follow us outside. Kai and the Yakanna come along with a few other stragglers.

They stand on opposite ends, and I remember what Jhamal mentioned about tribal loyalty. The guy cloaked in fur wears armor similar to Jhamal's: leather straps, the gold plates across half his chest. He is Beerchi, I bet. He and the men at his side must also be part of Jhamal's clan.

Others in long robes tied with gold twine at the waist—huddle together away from everyone else, and it's clearer what's going on here; more than Yakannaian loyalties have reemerged. There are many divisions here.

"Gahlee," Jhamal says, nodding in the white-robed men's direction. "Or scribe, if you prefer the term. But gae-lee is how you would call their clan. Learned, lettered. Scholarly." He means Bati.

I nod. I can totally see it. Two men lug a stone vase, grunting. I peer over its edge and it's full of dirt from what I can tell.

"Let me help." I point and flick my wrist up. "J'meh."

The vase lifts, hovering above the ground. They thank me, but it's me that should be thanking them. This was my mistake. Despite their pinched stares and foot tapping, they are going through with this knowing we don't have the time for it. Because of me. I'm indebted to them.

Apology after apology claws at me.

"It is okay, Jelani," Zora whispers, moving closer to me.

"I feel so bad."

"Sssh." She squeezes my hand and the knot in my chest eases some. "Stand here." She gestures and I move next to her. "Now just copy what everyone does, and when it's your turn, I'll tell you what to do."

I nod.

A drum sounds, signaling the beginning of the ceremony. And it is beautiful. And would only be more so if we could have it properly at the Ancestors' burial ground behind Yiyo. But for now, this dirt patch surrounded by abandoned buildings on the outskirts of the Capital will do.

We stand in a circle around the boy, and two Beerchi in fur cloaks, lay stones over each of his eyes. The next two in line adorn his hands with flowers. The next pair, wearing long white robes, scoop dirt from the vase and cover his feet.

Zora is next in line, then me. She steps forward and the most beautiful hum floats from her lips. Her eyes are closed, her palm on her diaphragm. The song comes out like ebony silk, a wave of emotions. Her voice rises high, touching the stars, and flutters like wings on the wind. She sings of a pain that feels rooted and very real. Each note makes my skin tingle.

The group joins in a low hum, grounding her lilt with heavier notes of sorrow. When their hums stop, all that's left is Zora's voice as high as the clouds, holding a note that would make the gods cry.

Staffs bang the ground, and she smiles at me. "The hole, you must now dig it."

I scan for spells and thanks to Jhamal's drilling me for so long, several cross my mind. I whisper the words under my breath and part my hands. Streams of energy sprout from my hands, parting the dirt like hair. The four remaining volunteers lift the boy and lay him in the divot. Then each of us crouches on the ground and covers him in dirt. Jhamal scoops out the last fistfuls of dirt from the vase and shakes it out over the grave.

"It is from the Ancestors' burial ground. In it their ashes are alive with their spirit. We leave pieces of them here to show our faithfulness to the tradition."

Then dancing breaks out, catching me completely off guard. Jhamal loops his arm in mine and we're spinning. Someone is tapping drums somewhere, and all I can think of is what if someone hears us? But the elation tugs at me, and before I know it, I'm doing my Renegade to the rugged beat. It's a whole remixed bop and I'm feeling it. Zora jigs with me, her eyes brighter than the sun.

"What is this?" I ask.

"We seal the ceremony with joy. Joy, Jelani, is the greatest form of rebellion." Jhamal presses his hands on my hips and I twist and grind. "We cling to it. It is the Ghizoni way."

The revelry is short but refreshing, and I'm still bopping my head as we go inside, a smile still staining my lips.

Inside, Bri is folded over a mountain of books at a corner table.

"Find anything?"

"Sort of." She folds over a chunk of pages. "Look at this."

I squint over the pages, hearing Moms's voice in my head about how badly I need glasses. But before the words solidify in focus, a clanging snatches me around. Kai is standing chin to chin with Shaun, the guy with the fur cloak. Beerchi, like Jhamal, if I had to guess. His nostrils are flared and his fingers hover over a sheath at his hip.

"They're about to take each other's heads off."

"You're not kidding." Bri ducks beneath a book.

About what? I wonder. Jhamal, the peacemaker, is nowhere in sight. So I hop up.

"Strike first and it will be your last breath," Shaun, the Beerchi, says. "You Yakanna, so stubborn, unyielding. You're headstrong and it will be your downfall."

"Tradition is tradition. But the old way of preparing the yupza takes twice as long. The armor is just fine. We don't have telee leaves for every little thing. Look how we are living. Some corners will be cut." Kai scowls, her girls an army at her back. "Back down, coquella!"

"I am not your brother, Kainese. I see through you. You're a disgrace to Moi Ike Yakanna and everyone here."

Kai spits and Zora thrusts her javelin, stopping it as it grazes the hair on his throat. Are they really this angry about breaking tradition? The clench of Shaun's jaw says it's much more than that.

"Put your blade where your arrogance is, Beerchi, and you can meet Mother Moi Ike in person," Kai says.

We need each and every person here for the fighting when the time comes. Not to mention more of our blood spilled is the exact opposite of what we're going for.

"Stop," I say. "Zora, Kai . . . you . . ." All the warmth in the towering Beerchi who greeted me is gone.

"This does not concern you."

"Maybe it doesn't, but still." I'm not sure of a lot right now, but in this I know I'm right. "Kai, listen to me. . . ."

"I do not need your help, Jelani," Kai says without a glance my way.

"This ain't about help. We can't be fighting like this. People out there wanna kill us and you gon' do it for 'em?" Now I'm shouting, my frustration kindled. "Stop, please!"

No one moves.

Neither speaks.

A voice crackles through the air with age. "Shaun, Kai, you will reap cursing on your heads. Stand down!" Bati's voice slices and I exhale, taking down the barrier between them, thankful someone else sees the problem with this and is stepping in to fix it. As fragile as he is, he commands presence. He is wearing white Gahlee robes with gold twine tied at his waist.

"Rue, my dear." His hands cup my face, and a million creases around his eyes greet me. "It is truly so good to have you back here in our midst." He turns to Kai. "Good work, Kainese. Your girls did good getting Jelani out of there."

Shaun sneers at the compliment Bati gives Kai. But neither moves. They breathe heavier than before, staring, practically nose to nose, two hurricanes ready to unleash.

Bati sets a hand on Zora's shoulder. "Please, even Goddess Yakanna held peace in great esteem."

Zora doesn't move.

Bati's words are swallowed by the silence. "Kainese, your mother would . . ."

Shaun shoves the blade away; its blunt side slams into Bati. He stumbles backward into me. Zora swipes with the blunt end of her stick. Kai ducks when Zora strikes and Zora blocks as Shaun does. It's a dance, one Zora and Kai have practiced. One Shaun isn't prepared for.

Kai's next blow lands and his face is bloody. Her girls hiss in delight. Shaun's alone and I remember what Jhamal says about the Beerchi. If he can't hold his own, one of his tribe mates will take his place. I chew my lip, waiting, hoping, wishing someone would jump in and stop this. But the Beerchi stand around arms folded, watching how he handles it. He pummels toward Kai in brute strength. I can't stand and watch this anymore.

"I said, *stop!*" Magic shoots like daggers from my hands, my arms warm all over, pinning Shaun and Kai back from each other. Veins bulge in Shaun's corded throat as he huffs. Kai is more stoic, but the speed of her chest rising and falling says she's anything but calm.

"We *can't* fight like this!"

Bati pulls himself up. "Jelani is right. It is beyond time. We will flounder without proper leadership. Get to your rooms. Make your preparations! Kowana Yechi at High Moon."

Kowana, what?

Everyone stands around, shock written into their faces in lines.

"Now!" Bati yells, and people scatter. Kai cuts a glance at me before leaving. A look that could kill. The same one she gave Jhamal.

CHAPTER TEN

KOWANA YECHI IS THE ritual the Ancestors used to nominate a tribe leader from one of the clans, or at least that's how Jhamal had explained it. They haven't done one since fleeing into Yiyo. The crowd filters down the thin corridors to where I'd guess the sleeping quarters are. The light from the fissures has dimmed. But it's a long way until High Moon. Jhamal snaps his armor around himself.

"They wouldn't . . . no one in their right mind would think of me that way."

"Tribe members have to be present for two years before they can vote or be nominated by their clan," he says, sensing my paranoia.

My face flashes cold, grateful that the weight of the decision making won't feel like it's squarely on my shoulders anymore. I've proven in more ways than one I'm a fighter, not worthy of such responsibility.

"But you do bear the Ancestors' magic. So you should be able to vote, at least."

"Voting is important where I'm from. If I can chime in here, I want to."

"I'll talk to Bati. But I can't imagine it wouldn't go over fine."

A Beerchi, a Yakanna, or a Gahlee will rule. This is good.

"Electing a leader should help with unity," I say.

"I agree."

"I'll see you in your room, later, then," he says, hurrying off before I can ask him more about this Kowana Yechi thing.

The room Bri and I are ushered off to is farthest from the entry we came through, which I don't like. Being near an exit is just a habit. Something I strongly prefer. The damp air reeks of musk, and somewhere in the distance droplets of condensation *plop plop* on the ground. The hallways twist as people duck into rooms out of sight. We follow behind a Gahlee man with kind eyes.

On either side of the corridor, beds protrude from the wall; they are flat pallets of metal wedged into the walls, three or four stacked as tall as the ceiling, like floating bunk beds. As small as our numbers are now, there's still not a ton of room for everyone. Not like their home before, in Yiyo.

"You're in here, Jelani." The robed man bows, and I resist the urge to roll my eyes. I hate when they do that. I don't deserve special treatment. Especially after what I've done.

"Thanks."

The room they give us is a moderate size, dirt walls, paved floor. There's a small bed, which is basically like a raised pallet on the floor with a thin blanket. Outside, the shuffle of footsteps and chatter are constant. Bri and I sit on the thin bedding. I huddle over the stack of books she found during the burial ceremony. And she dives neck deep into her bag of gadgets, immediately trying to fuse two parts together.

I shift in my seat and close a book that looked promising but ended up being about macronomins, a type of magic that converts water to light. I pull another on top of me, but it's apparently full of recipes. I don't even flip past the first page. Another. This one's full of spells, and I run a finger down the gritty page. *Dextrontum.* I flip past a section on the properties of magic that deal with chemical energy. "The Twelve Essential Plants for Potion Making." And again, more pages. "Toxicity in Potions," "Imbuing Inanimate Objects," "Imbuing Living Organisms," "Shifting Time and Space," "Magical Matter and Why It Matters." This book literally has everything. It has to be here somewhere. I turn and turn until my neck aches and my legs go numb under me. I find nothing by the time I reach the end and slap the thick back cover closed.

"Ugh."

I crack my neck and pull open another book. Then another. And another, until the stack of "not it" books is as tall as my head. A yawn scratches my throat, but I refuse to give it space. I don't have time to sleep. Every second we're not working toward getting our magic back is a moment the Chancellor has to root us out and kill us all.

Hours must go by. I look for a glimpse of the sky, but this room doesn't have a single window.

"There has to be a way to restore magic once lost," I say, setting aside the last stack of books I've still yet to open. I grab the next one from the pile, which looks oddly familiar. "I think it takes magic to access magic. That makes sense, right?" I glance at Bri, but she's about to chew her lip off, screwing one side of her Reflecto-whatever she calls it.

"Are you listening?"

A spring bounces from her fingers and she slaps the ground. "Ugh!"

"Bri?"

"I'm listening."

"What's the last thing I said?"

"Last thing you said was 'Bri.'"

I toss a pillow at her head. "Seriously, there has to be something here. Help me."

She sighs and lugs a book onto her lap. I'm almost sure it's one I looked through before, but having her do *something* makes me feel like we're getting somewhere. I read another few pages, careful to sit with each word. Maybe there's something I'm missing? Some underlying meaning or interpretation that's flying over my head? Bri's red frames are pressed to her face and she squints, flipping a page, scanning, then flipping another.

"Are you seriously reading that fast or just looking at the pictures?"

"Is that a joke?"

"I'm just saying, like . . . look carefully . . . you know?"

She folds the cover closed with a huge sigh. "Rue, I've looked through all of these books at least twice." She reaches for her gadget, but I narrow my eyes and she turns her attention back to the book.

"Look, the only helpful thing I've found is there." She points at the pages parted in front of me.

I've flipped through this one ten times at least and keep coming back to the section on Magical Malfunction. That's the closest section on any sort of magic loss.

"This doesn't say anything about losing magic. It's only if it doesn't work."

"Exactly." She smooths down her flyaways and tugs her gadget back in front of her. "I hate to say it, but this looks like a dead end. Best we can hope for is . . ." She grunts. "Me getting this stupid thing to . . ." Another grunt and a blue light flickers on. "YES! Would you look at that?" She holds in my face a metal something that looks like a banana and an iPad had a baby.

"You don't look impressed. Rue, be impressed."

I sigh.

"Rue, this Refractor can trace magic from miles away. Not only that, it works underground *and* it can source where the magic came from like . . . magical fingerprints." Her expression is as bright as the sun. "This is going to help us!"

She wants me to get hyped, but I'm entirely distracted by the fact that none of these books I've managed to look through has what I need or anything close to it. But Bri's proud of her gadget, so to be a good friend, I plaster on my most impressed face and that seems to appease her.

She eases it in her bag ever so carefully and I press my book open wider. I guess I have to figure this out myself. I'm not giving up that easily. I don't believe there's not a single word written anywhere on what happens if magic is lost. They could never do anything about it because they didn't have magic to do magic. But I do.

I pull my knees to my chest and flip a few more pages, then flip several more until my back aches. I switch positions and start at the front of the book again. I'm missing something. I have to be. I flip and flip, practically reciting the words, they're so familiar. And it amounts to nothing. My shoulders sag and Bri scoots closer to me, peering over my shoulder.

"Yeah, I'd hoped in the footnote in this one, maybe there'd be something. I've seen a few of these texts before. But I went through them all again . . . nothing," she says. "I'm sorry, Rue."

"It's like in every instance if magic is lost or not given . . . it's intentional. So they wouldn't need to teach ways to get it back."

"Yep. Because if it *was* given back, that's on the Chancellor. Only *he* has to restore it. Because he gave it."

"Oh my god, Bri. That's it!" If my brain was a light bulb, it would be buzzing. "Magic can only be restored by those who gave it, right?"

"Yep, the Chancellor." She furrows her brow. "How does that help us?"

How did I not see this before? I stand. "The Chancellor *stole* magic. He's not the real magic giver."

Bri's eyes widen and she stands, too.

"The Ancestors," we say at the same time.

It makes perfect sense. If magic can be restored only by the giver because the Chancellor gave the Grays magic, then the Ancestors must be the only ones able to restore Ghizoni magic, since they were the original purveyors of magic.

"Bri, we've been looking up the wrong spells! We need to reach the Ancestors."

"As in raise the dead?"

"Well, when you put it like that . . . it sounds . . . creepy. But yes! That's what we need to do."

"Hmmm." She taps her lip and grazes the spines of a stack of tomes piled in a corner. "Do you remember anything about your time locked up that could help us?"

"There's this weird bit of memories that keeps coming back to me in pieces. I remember prison fairly well, and the battle, of course." My insides slosh. "But . . ."

Eyelashes.

A white lab coat.

Something cold on my lips.

"I think I was . . . I don't know. There are pieces from a lab or something missing and I'm not sure why."

"A lab?" Her lips push sideways. "What do you recall?"

"Not much, Bri, really. Fragments here and there. It's like I've lost a huge chunk. And I don't know why or what caused it." I pull a book from the bottom of the stack and the others topple. I read its title—*Magic Beyond the Grave*—then restack them.

"Do the fragments come back in dreams or flashes?" she asks.

"Yes. Both."

"What about headaches?"

"Nope. None."

She sits back on her heels, studying my face. "Any extreme physical fatigue or overall lethargy?"

"I was really weak at first. That lasted for several months."

"Any scars you don't remember getting?"

I show her the scars at the edge of my cuffs, where Jhamal had sewn stitches forever ago.

She strokes her chin. "Rue, when you woke up, what do you remember about what condition you were in?"

"I'd dreamed of drowning or something. My lips were cracked and peeling. In the cell, I don't remember much. Just that Jhamal was huddled in a corner bawling his eyes out. When he saw me sit up, talking, he calmed down though."

"Any weird smells? Tastes?"

"There was some sort of dry powder on my fingers and on these scratches actually. I distinctly remember a cup of water sitting by the gate to my cell. I didn't drink it though, despite how thirsty I was. I was sure it was poisoned. Oh, and some sort of rancid flowery scent was in the air. It was weird."

"Rue, those are side effects of a memory loss potion."

I stop stacking books. Her smile is gone. She's foreal.

"And those are weird. You can't really control *what* the person forgets. You just sort of give it to them and the most recent memories become spotty." She turns the book in her lap to face me. "Uh-huh, that's what I thought. The most common side effect of a memory loss potion is—"

I lean over the open pages. "Immobility, extreme fatigue, extreme limitations of basic physical function." There it is in the book in black and white. That's why I was weakened. That's why I don't remember.

"Rue, I don't think you forgot those fragments."

She's right. "Whatever happened in that lab . . . he must have not wanted me to know." The thought sends a chill down my spine, my mind swimming with memories of Jhamal stitching me back together, nursing me back to health. "It took forever to get back on my feet again."

"It's a nasty brew too," she says. "Calls for sap from a rare tree that's toxic when measured wrong or heated too much. One misstep or improper ingredient and it could have killed you. Potions are a precise art."

My fingers find my throat and I'm suddenly more aware of how hard my heart beats in my chest. How badly the Chancellor wants to stop it.

"The one good thing about memory potions is they wear off," she says. "It'll come back in pieces . . . eventually. You're probably having random visions now."

I nod. "But why would he want me to forget temporarily? That doesn't make sense."

"Maybe he gave it to you for the side effects? To weaken you. So you couldn't escape?" Her eyes tilt down. "Unless . . ."

"Unless what?"

"Nothing. It's dumb."

"Unless what, Bri?"

She meets my eyes hesitantly. "U-unless, he wanted you to forget because . . . you'll be dead before remembering matters."

A knock at the door startles me, and my pulse slows when I see Jhamal. Bati is with him and the remnants of their conversation stain their expressions.

"Jelani." Bati's smile is warm, but it doesn't quite reach his eyes. The worry dug into his forehead is permanently etched there. And to a degree . . . I did that.

"Bati." I slap his hand and pull him into another hug, hoping at least the appearance of being okay convinces him. And maybe even me. His shoulders shake with laughter and his eyes crease.

"Is that one of those homeboy hugs like you do?"

"Something like that." I usher them inside.

"Speaking of East Row, I have to meet this Ms. Leola you tell me about one day. Is that how I greet her?"

"Nah, you can just take off your hat and say wassup. That's how the old gangstas do it."

"Then I'll write that down somewhere, yes," he says. His joy makes the brick on my chest sit a little lighter. Moms always said laughter is its own kind of medicine. I'd love for everyone here to meet everyone back home. I mean, we family. But those are dreams floating on the wind, make-believe at this point.

"I was just going over things with Bri. I'm trying to find a spell to restore our people's magic," I say.

Bati and Jhamal share a glance.

"The Chancellor is coming, don't get it twisted," I say. "This really needs to be our first priority."

"Very good, then," Bati says. "Dreams of our people fully wielding magic again have always been just that. Dreams. But if it is as you say, a way, I have no doubt the Ancestors will lead you to it, and us through it." He bows his head. But because it's Bati and I know he's cool, I don't bite my tongue.

"Please, don't do that. The bowing thing. We're homies, Bati. It's just me, Rue." I throw an arm over his shoulder.

"Well, we shall see, then," he says, his tone heavy. "I came to pass word the time for Kowana Yechi is nigh." His eyes flick to Jhamal.

I elephant ear a page, and Bri winces, muttering, "Use a bookmark," under her breath.

"Sorry, didn't think to pack those," I tease, folding the book I was poring over closed. It's the last one in the stack from the trunks, and so far, nothing promising. I tap my foot, thinking. What could I have missed? Where else could we look? Bri slides into the convo with her gadget bag snapped closed and shouldered like she's ready to go somewhere. "Do you have any other books anywhere?"

Bati purses his lips in thought. "The eurostarum had some, but those are more historical. Things I've written over the years. Nothing helpful, I fear."

She might be on to something. There's got to be a book somewhere on this island with a comprehensive list of spells. Oh, man. That's it.

"There was Totsi's Texts," I say. "That bookstore. She had all sorts of books." Once for Magical Anatomy class, I needed to learn about the varying uses of pig blood, and she had an entire section in her store on blood magic, curses, and uses. Prohibited ones, too. Those were usually locked away in a trunk disguised as a coffee table, plant, or something. But I learned my first few spells from her shelves."

"Ah! She did," Bri says, nodding.

"Did you read the ones in the back of the store?" I ask. "In that private room?" Totsi always had me post up in the back so no one passing by the storefront would spot the only brown girl in the whole City, skipping class no less.

"There was a private room?"

"Yeah, you know, past the history section."

She shakes her head.

"Well, still, you saw she had books on everything."

"She did. The only store like it. She had stuff I couldn't find at the library. I'd never seen anything like it anywhere. Most in the mythology and lore section. I mean, who knew they were actual history books?!"

I remember seeing books about the island before it was colonized, mythology. But they were streaked in red, stamped prohibited. Totsi's had multiple copies. There could be something there. If the book's not here . . . my best chance is getting to Totsi's to find the spell I need.

"But you can't be thinking of going there," Bri says, as if she can read my plotting mind. "Venturing out there, back into the Central District is a death wish, Rue."

I glimpse Jhamal before turning to Bati. He isn't going to like this. "Are you sure you don't have *anything* else here? We cleared the trunk."

Bati swirls the white hair on his chin. "No, other than what I gave you both earlier, I'm afraid." He taps his lips. "Oh, I do have one rather old one tucked away. We have a little time before the sky hangs the moon. If you'd like to look, I can take you both."

"Bri, would you mind going? I need to talk to Jhamal." I have to tell him my plan. He's literally held me up all these months, it's the least I could do.

"Yeah, of course," Bri says. "If Bati doesn't mind."

"Very well. We go, then." Bati bows himself out, gesturing for Bri to follow, and they shuffle off out of my room. Jhamal's hand works its way up to my shoulder, pressing circles into the tension buried there as the door creaks closed. It feels good, but I pull away from him.

"What?"

I sigh, pacing a few turns of the room.

"Jelani?" His tone tightens.

"Listen," I say. "You're not going to like this."

He studies me.

"If I can't find anything in the books here, I'm going to go back up there into the Central District. To Totsi's."

"Rue—"

"Alone."

"I go with you."

"And let everyone here kill one another? You missed it earlier, but Shaun and Kai were about to take each other's heads off."

"Agh. Shaun is . . . strong, a clear thinker, but when his passion gets the best of him . . . Beerchi, we . . ."

"You can't possibly think fighting Kai is the way this needs to go. He was out of line. I'm not defending her, either, she's got mad attitude. I'm just saying we can't be fighting each other like this."

"That is one way to look at it. You do not know Kai."

"And I guess you do?" I hate the way the jealousy breaks through. That's not me. That's not who I am.

"Rue, you will not."

"Bruh, that's not up to you. Time is not on our side. I have a plan that gets us fighting, together." I tuck the only book I haven't finished under my arm. "Let's get upstairs, after the Kowana Yachee . . ."

"Yeh-chi."

"Kowana *Yechi*, I'll tell everyone my plan to prepare for the fight to come. I don't want them thinking I'm going off on my own. I'm in this. All of us. Together. But this is the way. Fighting, together. I'm sure of it."

He sighs.

"Everyone's magic restored will be something they want." It's our only chance, really. The strategy wheels are turning.

A vein at his jaw pulses and he looks away.

"They'll have to get behind this. This will work, Jhamal." I face him. "Look, I know you don't like this because of how dangerous it is up there."

"And you *just* got strong again, Jelani. . . . This is madness. We need time and planning and a leader. A council of leaders, reconnaissance. This should be done carefully. You said yourself we move as a unit, we move together!"

The last time we moved together, they were unprotected. I'm not letting that happen again. We will move together once their magic is restored.

"Yes, but I'm the only one who can do this. It takes magic to access magic." He stands close to me, so close, his stare burns my skin.

"I do not like this." His breath is warm on my forehead, and the ire in his eyes draws me in.

"I'm frustrated too."

Silence.

It's him who needs comfort now. I don't want to muddy the water, get his hopes up. . . . *But, he is scared, hurting.* I reach for his hand and the lines in his face disappear. The boy he is underneath all the armor smiles back at me. He's iron, ferocious, but like me, a storm within. I lace my fingers more tightly between his, careful to keep our bodies from touching. It's all this fractured version of myself can offer him right now. I hope it's enough.

His chest sinks at my touch, his chin falls. It's such a little thing, but it says everything I've struggled to put into words. I do care about him. I squeeze. I do wish we could get back to where we were. But how? In this midst of all this? As broken as the world is right now? *As broken as I am.*

"Waiting only gives the Chancellor more time to root us out," I say. "I don't see a way around this."

He holds my hand to his chest in silence. It's hard, firm, strong, just like him. But his lips don't move. From the few things I remember about the battlefield, fear like this didn't sit on his expression. It didn't either when we were locked in the cell and he thought it was the end. And even when we were running for our lives escaping prison, his jaw was not set this way. I've only seen Jhamal truly scared once, when he laced my skin back together. When he thought I might die.

"I am going to find a way to raise the Ancestors from the dead," I say, trying to assure him. "They will fix this for us."

He meets my gaze, his wide with shock. But, he nods, and just like that he's miles away.

I make him press his forehead to mine. "Thanks for having my back."

"You are my Queen. I will always be in your corner." He reaches to kiss my hand. And though I shouldn't, I let him.

CHAPTER ELEVEN

JHAMAL AND I MOVE back down the narrow hall toward where Kowana Yechi will be held. The hall glows orange in the firelight, the fissures hardly distinguishable in the darkness.

"So how does it work exactly? The decorum, I mean." Last thing I wanna do is not know what I'm walking into or give offense. I've done enough of that; I'm trying to bond with my people, not keep pissing them off.

"There's time for people to address everyone. After the meeting." There is more he wants to say, but he presses his lips closed.

"Okay, I'll wait for the right time to speak. And how does it go?"

"Each clan nominates a tribe member, who then must accept. Then everyone casts their votes. It can get interesting, actually. There's no guarantee people will vote for their own clansman. It's one thing to consider someone a brother; it's another entirely to believe they're fit to rule over you."

"And the leader is then . . . ?" I ask as we round a stone corner. His face shines in the firelight.

"Crowned. There's usually a formal coronation, but there's no time for that now. I would guess the leader will form a war council as the first matter of business."

"Sounds like you know a lot about this. Maybe you should volunteer."

"You cannot volunteer. Humility is a leader's greatest strength."

"Well, maybe I'll nominate you." I elbow him, playfully, but he doesn't laugh.

The crowd outside the meeting room is stoic. Moonlight twinkles from a crack in the ceiling, glinting off their armor, and a crowd funnels into the doorway. Everyone's decked out and my scuffed Air Maxes look extra dirty. "I look like a scrub up in here next to them."

"A what?"

"Nothing."

He hands me a chest plate of armor. It's fairly dinged up, one-shouldered and scuffed. It looks like it used to be all gold, but now it's mostly black with gold left only on the tips. "It's all we have."

I reach but hesitate. The Yakanna don their armor with such pride. Is it right to put it on without their blessing? Somehow it just feels wrong. "I'll be alright, but thanks."

"At least hold on to it for when you go out there."

The way he says "out there" lets me know he's not at all behind my decision. I take the breastplate from him, and it's much lighter than I'd imagined. "Thanks."

I settle in a corner and fold open one last spell book just to be sure I'm not taking unnecessary risks. But my gut says what I'm looking for isn't here. I fold over a page and read through spells to fuse elements together, recipes for potions that regrow damaged limbs. An anti-aging potion that regenerates cells. Nothing on raising the dead. Or restoring magic, for that matter.

Kai and her girls are already settled in a corner around one of the long tables. Their faces are done up, streaked with gold paint. Their braids have been redone, tied up with gold twine and bells. Kai wears a ring on her finger that hooks to her wrist and up her arm. She looks like a goddess. What I imagine Mother Yakanna herself must have looked like. And she's a direct descendant from the Mother's bloodline, Jhamal had said. *She* looks like a leader. *She* checks the boxes.

I tug at the strand at my neck. Kai just wants to make the Ancestors proud. The way I hope Moms is smiling down at me. The tinge of empathy dissolves when she glances at me and her eyes fall to the mail in my hand. Her lips thin. Her girls huddle around her. Zora's countenance cracks a smile ever so slightly when our eyes meet.

The center of the room has a long staff lying down the center with flowers at each end. These are red blooms with tiny berries inside. Along the staff are three empty bowls—one for each clan's nomination. Jhamal sulks off to talk with Shaun and several Beerchi.

I flip through the pages of the text. "Seventy-Eight Uses of Parsnip." "Healing Properties of the Plinor River." Nothing useful. Bells chime when Bati enters. They ring from his hair. His ivory robes are tied at the waist and a hood covers most of his face. Several of his brothers, dressed similarly, are behind him. They sit at a far table, clustered together, eyes flicking in my direction. Bati moves toward the center and a voice bellows from the back of the room.

"Who puts themselves forward to conduct this Kowana Yechi?" someone says.

"I do." Bati bows his head. "A humble servant of Deolekkis. With truth and integrity, we cast our votes fairly and submit to the victor with loyalty as is the Ghizoni way."

"Aye!" the crowd shouts to a chorus of fists pounding the tables.

"Beerchi." He picks up a bowl that I thought was empty and out comes a folded note of paper. "Your nomination." He reads the paper. "Shauntom Naikae."

Shaun stands, surrounded by his coquella cloaked in fur. Like the Yakanna, they are all much more decked out than earlier. The furs clasped across them are hooked with a golden broach in the shape of a bear claw. Where he wore one ring before, he wears several now. From what I ran across in one of these books, the rings are passed down through the generations from Beerchi leaders before him. Each ring represents a decisive victory won. The Beerchi were nomadic people before settling on this island, and with them they brought warrior prowess and tactical wisdom. I don't know which would be a better leader. Kai is fierce too. Though Jhamal's side comments about her do give me pause. Right now, I think Shaun has my vote.

"Shauntom Naikae, descendant of Mishon Ide Beerchi, Father of Might of Ghizon," Bati begins. "You are being presented to the Ancestors and this assembly to be considered Kowana, King of our People, to represent our interests, preserve our people, culture, and traditions, and trailblaze our future. Do you accept this nomination?"

"Aye." Shaun pats his chest.

"Yakanna." Bati picks a folded note of paper from another bowl. "Your nomination. Kainese Mene." Was it even a question who they would nominate? Kai runs those girls.

She steps forward. I try to finish skimming the book, prepare to explain why raising the Ancestors should be where we focus next, but I can't look away. Kai's a ball of anticipation and Shaun's never looked more fierce. *Maybe I'll vote for Kai?*

"Kainese Mene, descendant of Mother Moi Ike Yakanna, Warrior Goddess of Ghizon," Bati says. "You are being presented to the Ancestors and this assembly to be considered Kowana, Queen of our People, to represent our interests, preserve our people, culture, and traditions, and trailblaze our future. Do you accept this nomination?"

"I do," she says. Her girls hiss and goosebumps dance up my skin. Bati moves to the third bowl, for his own clan, with a quick glance at his brothers. He pulls out a piece of paper and his eyes settle on me.

"Rue Jelani Akintola . . ."

Whispers erupt like a swarm of locusts. My heart beats out my chest.

Jhamal leans into my ear for a whisper. "They will not all be won over to your side easily, but they will come around."

"My side? I don't have a side. We all want the same thing: to see the Chancellor brought to his knees."

"Yes, but the how . . ."

"I don't know, but this ain't it. Did you have anything to do with this?"

Bati bangs his staff, trying to quiet the chatter. This is an apparent surprise to everyone, and from the thin smiles, most aren't happy about it.

"How will they ever believe you can lead them if you don't?" Jhamal says low.

"Jhamal, lead them?! I don't want to *lead* them, I just want us to remember who the real enemy is. And fight *him*. Fighting and leading aren't the same thing, Jhamal."

"What is a leader, but a person who fights for what they believe in?"

I sigh, exasperated. I don't know what to say to that, so I scan the room. I don't even know which clan my father was from. Surely that's a basic expectation of someone elected to lead them.

The crowd has quieted some and I stand because I feel like I'm supposed to. My knees threaten to falter. I don't want to be disrespectful, but there's no way . . . no . . . not me. Kai's eyes narrow, daggers of death at Jhamal. Is this what she's been acting shady with me about? *Does she think I knew this was happening?* Her gaze moves to me and it's as cold as ice. *Okay, so yes, clearly.*

"Now that we've all settled," Bati goes on, and the swell of voices simmer. "As I was saying, Rue Jelani Akintola, of descendant Mother Ike Yakanna *and* Mishon Ide Beerchi . . ."

Wait, what?

Aasim was Beerchi? But his mother Yakanna? Not only do I have a clan . . . I share heritage between them both?

Oh my god.

Kai's contempt of me makes even more sense. Like I'm a threat to her. No wonder Shaun hasn't looked at me once since saying hello. They think I'm a threat to their claims. I wish they realized I'm not their competitor. But they don't see it that way. Not now. Not with so much at stake. Kai's eyes flick to Jhamal and her nostrils flare.

My stomach is in my throat.

"No," I say, before Bati can even form the question. The silence screams and I dig a nail into my palm. "No, I don't accept. I-I . . . this is not . . ." My palms sweat. I'm speaking out of turn. Both Kai and Shaun accepted their nomination, but a part of them, a huge part

I'd guess, wants to be named Kowana. *I don't!* I can't have everyone looking at me for all the answers. I'm not cut out for that. Last time I tried . . .

Screams fill my ears and the battlefield plays on repeat in my head. *No. Never again.*

"No," I repeat. "I do not accept."

Shaun spits. "To be nominated is a great honor and high duty. You think this is a game?"

"N-no. I— You saw what happened out there. I'm not cut out for . . ." I hug the book I'm holding.

Bati's eyes flick between Jhamal and me. They planned this. The two of them. And Jhamal didn't tell me a word about it. Is that what he was busy orchestrating while Shaun and Kai were at each other's throats? He said he'd always support me. This isn't what I thought he meant.

"She does not take the Ancestors' tradition seriously," Shaun growls. "She does not even know the way. Look at the Gray she had us bury. Look at the way she makes a mockery of things."

I blow out a quick breath. "No, Shaun, listen. I . . ."

"She is not fit to lead. Magic or not. Her name should be struck from the record. The last time she fought the Chancellor for us, it amounted to more dead."

His words echo in my head, stoking my insecurity.

"She is a liability." He slides his thumb under his throat. "Pw'nijkizka. Na! Kizka, na!"

A liability? Really? I'm trying, doing my best. I *belong* here. Flames erupt from my fingers, but I snuff them out, but not before catching Shaun flinch.

"I'm not here trying to tell y'all what to do. I knew nothing of this."

"Lies," one of the Yakanna hisses.

"I swear."

Jhamal sits and says nothing, and I could scream.

"I'm not interested in being anybody's Queen." I move to the center of the room and every eye sticks to me. "All I wanted was to get y'all to see that we can't destroy ourselves from the inside out. I get being proud of where we from. I feel that hard. But they trying to kill us out there, because our entire existence is a threat to this backward-ass world they've built. They stole our magic, they've cut our numbers down. Right now, instead of taking each other's heads off, having a pissing contest, we should be reaching the Ancestors."

All chatter ceases. The silence stills me.

"Rue, do you mean . . ." Bati pulls his hood off." Magic beyond the grave? Reaching out to the dead?"

"I've felt the Ancestors before. They can feel me. I'm sure of it. They *gave* us magic, so it only makes sense that they can fix this. They can restore it."

Bati fidgets, his eyes bugging out of his head. "That sort of magic has never been done. It's quite dangerous from what I understand and only used in the direst circumstances."

"No disrespect, Bati. Nothing but love for you, but this situation is pretty fucking dire."

"This is improper." Shaun bangs the ground with his staff. "Bati, if your brothers' nominee doesn't accept, choose another or voting begins between Kainese and me. She shouldn't even be speaking at this length during the ceremony. She knows nothing."

Bati holds up a hand. "I'm the arbiter of this ceremony. I'll allow it." He turns to me. "Jelani, this is very rare, dangerous magic you seek to do. What is it exactly that you propose?"

I set down the book, which I've realized is useless. "We can't win without all of us wielding magic again. I can't save us by myself."

Shaun scoffs. "She admits it herself; she cannot save us. I am so sick at how we dance around the Ancestors' Chosen One. It's pathetic. What has she done but kill more of us?"

"Coquella, enough," Jhamal says from the shadows, gaze fixed on Shaun. "Your point has been made. Jelani has the floor right now."

"You stand with this girl because—"

"Watch it." Jhamal stands, adoration for me etched into his set jaw. Warmth flickers inside me and I move closer to him, letting my arm brush his. But I'ma chew his ass out for this, though. Just wait.

Kai folds her arms, pursing her lips. "She is right. The infighting has to stop."

I am? I mean, I think I am. But she thinks I am? I blink. The Yakannas' gaze follow her like a magnet. Only Zora's gaze flutters between us. Maybe there's hope for Kai and me. She's full of pride. Strong. A lot like me.

"I don't wanna disrespect anyone," I say. "I'm sorry for everything. Trust me, you couldn't possibly think less of me than I do of myself right now. I feel terrible."

Jhamal reaches for me, but I have to do this on my own feet. I turn to Bati.

"I'm honored that you'd think me worthy, but, Bati, that ain't me." I move toward the door. "Y'all figure out what you need to. I'm going back out there to find a way to reach the Ancestors and get everyone's magic restored." That's what we need right now. "The Ancestors will fix this." *Not me.*

I don't look back as I leave, but stares burn my skin.

Bri's back in the room when I get there, swimming in a bed of metal and wires.

"How'd it go?"

"We're leaving. Pack your bag."

"Huh?"

"Bri, we gotta get to Totsi's. We've found nothing here. A spell to reach the Ancestors is what we need."

"Central District is a war zone. That boy we found killed wasn't the only one, I'm sure."

"I know that, Bri. But what do we do when shit seems impossible?"

She stuffs her gadgets in her bag reluctantly. "We make a way."

"Exactly. And besides, maybe you'll get to put some of your contraptions to work."

"I feel like you're mocking me, but I'm going to go with it."

I wink at her and she shoulders her bag. "I appreciate all this," I say. "You're in deep now."

"I'd have it no other way."

I reach for the door to open it, but it swings open before I can touch it. Jhamal stands with Kai and Zora at his back. A tuft of white hair in the backdrop says Bati is back there somewhere too. I step back, letting them all inside.

"I'm going. You can't stop me," I start.

"Oh, I know," Jhamal says with more exasperation than I like.

"Jelani," Bati says. "I did not mean for you to feel like we were doing anything to deceive you. I would never—"

"I get it. I have all this power from the Ancestors so it makes you think y'all should follow me. But that's not my lane. I'm not cut out for all that. I don't even make the right decisions half the time. All I can do is improve from where I failed before. Fighting solo won't work. We need the Ancestors' help. That's what it is. So, I'm going."

"I am thankful you are not upset with me, dear one. I promised your father . . ." He exhales and it's heavy. "I promised him I would look after you like my own daughter. You understand?"

"I do." I squeeze his hand, and Jhamal steps next to me.

"Reconsider, please. Let me go with you." Heaviness weighs down his expression. I get he's worried. Shit, I'm worried too. But we gotta do what we gotta do.

"Kowana Yechi is halted until you return," he says. "I worked out with Kai and Shaun that one from each of their clans would go with you. That way we are unified, like we talked about." He gestures. "Zora, if you would have her."

She dips her chin when I meet her eyes.

"And me," Jhamal says.

I sigh and find myself searching his eyes. Eyes that watched and cared for me. Made sure I ate. They swim with adoration. Respect. He sees in me what I still can't find in myself.

"Is that a yes?" he asks.

His care is why I'm standing here in one piece. I can't pretend that doesn't matter. I can't pretend that when panic claws me, my eyes don't instinctively look for him. That his warmth, though I push it away, is as much a part of me as my own shadow. If Kai and Shaun have forged temporary peace, could it hurt to have Jhamal and Zora out there with me? Better chance we'll come out of this shit alive.

"Okay," I say, and he tries to hide his smirk, but I don't miss his beautiful cheeks pushing up under those onyx eyes. Zora moves to my side. Silence hangs there a moment, all eyes on Kai, as she's the only one who hasn't spoken.

"It is true then, we share blood," she says before casting her gaze to the floor. "Yakanna's spirit lives in you. I knew it. I could sense it. I . . ." She meets my eyes, hers tilted at the corners, heavy with something. Is that regret? "Zora is my most trusted saisa. She is the purest Yakanna the good Mother put on this earth. Keep her close. Danger awaits you out there, Jelani. There are thousands clamoring for your death." She shoves a piece of Yakanna armor at me, the one I'd left behind. "It would be smart to have some Ghizoni gold on you. It's not that soft metal from where you're from. It's an element forged by the Ancestors, who were gifted it from the gods themselves. It's tougher than steel."

"Thank you."

Kai parts her lips to say something else but turns to leave instead.

"All set then," I say. "Get some rest. We leave at dusk."

Trying to get to sleep is a joke; my mind goes nonstop. I curl up on the thin cot with the books Bri and I went through. She's snoring. Jhamal's in the corner, somehow sleeping while sitting straight up. I thumb through the texts again, more to keep my hands busy than anything.

Sleep must have overtaken me because I wake with Jhamal standing over me. I nudge Bri with an elbow. She grunts.

"Let's go."

Outside, storm clouds rumble, rain whipping around us between strikes of lightning. I'm careful to skirt the barbed wire around the opening to the underground lair as I latch my armor on. Zora helps me situate it just right.

"We ready?" I ask, snapping the last hook on my side.

"I am," Zora says, rising from her knees, dusting off her clothes.

"I'd wished for a better omen on the day we set out," Jhamal says, gazing at the sky with trepidation stamped on his face.

"We don't get to choose the days we fight," I say. "They choose us. The only thing we can do is be ready."

Jhamal and Zora set off first and I go behind them.

"Wait." Bri's brows are furrowed as she rummages through her pack, a loud buzzing sound going off inside it. She plucks out a familiar wristband lit up with an orange light.

"Take this, *please*. It's been going off like nonstop since we came from underground." She hands me her watch, and 183 missed messages from Julius pop up on its face. I glance at Jhamal up ahead before slipping it in my pocket.

CHAPTER TWELVE

THE OUTSIDE AIR IS thick like a blanket. The sky fades to pink with a dusky golden hue. And the crumbled cluster of buildings that used to liven with hustle and bustle, the Central District, is a dot to the west.

We walk in a line; Zora's gaze is narrowed, focused. Jhamal walks beside her, and they talk about something that deepens the lines on their faces. We could have transported to our destination, but it's too big of a risk populating somewhere without knowing who or what is already there. So, walking it is. Bri is beside me, tying up her blond hair into a bun as if she's preparing for some epic battle. Totsi's is on Market Street in the Commercial District of Ghizon, or what's left of it.

"It's a solid few hours at least," I say to Bri. I know because back in East Row, I walked that far home from the library when I missed the last bus once.

"At least." She reshoulders her bag and walks, her stare dead ahead. She hates being out here, seeing it all over again. No one wants to see their home destroyed. I get that. Tiny droplets fall from the sky, cold on my skin. I swipe up on the watch for what feels like forever.

Julius: Aye, it's been a minute, you good?

Julius: Rue?

Julius: Yo my shit is PACKED. Come through, foreal.

Julius: Fam, a nigga starting to bug out. Say something, pls

Julius: Lmk you aight or something.

Julius: RUE!

Julius: I checked on T and Ms. Leola. They good. They wanted to know if you was aight and I said I didn't know.

Julius: This shit fuckin with me, man . . . say something. The three little dots . . . a read receipt . . . something.

Me: Hey! Sorry.

Before my message even delivers, three dots pop up on the screen and my watch vibrates nonstop.

Julius: I'MA

Julius: WHOOP

Julius: YO

Julius: ASS

Julius: FOR NOT SAYING SHIT TILL NOW.

Me: Sorry, I'm okay. Got caught up. But I'm out. You seen Tasha? She okay? Ms. Leola? The crew?

Julius: Oh, crap. You aight? Yeah, everybody is good. Tasha's been bugging. Not gone lie. You was supposed to bring me with you.

The rain falls harder. I wonder if I can get a signal out of here somehow to call Tash. I make a note to ask Bri about that when we get back tomorrow.

Me: Hey, tell Tasha I'm okay. Tell her I'm almost done here and I'll be there soon.

Julius: Bet. I'm still down to come through. I ride with you, fam.

My finger hovers over the keypad a moment. Then I tuck my watch away. Can't risk it getting damaged in the rain. It's my only tie to home. It vibrates again, but the gray skies darken so low, I have to squint, and rumbles roll in the distance.

"Who's that?" Jhamal falls back to walk beside me.

"Oh, just checking on things back home. I've been gone so long, you know."

"Everything okay?"

"I think so. They're just worried."

His hand brushes mine and I savor it. Bri and Zora are up ahead. The perimeter of the District is a collage of boarded and broken windows, steam rising from puddles, and stacks of broken concrete. The world dims with each block, the fading sun eerie as it glows against bleak desolation. I step over a fracture in the pavement and gesture for Zora and Bri to stick close to the walls of the buildings, or what's left of them.

Wind whistles, tugging at my clothes as we round a corner. Dicee's shop sign creaks in the wind.

"This way." I point toward an intersection that shortcuts through the old dorm quad to the Market Street. I used to skip out on class and cut this way to get to Totsi's to get lost in some *real* books. The rain slacks. My pocket vibrates and I slip my watch out.

Julius: So, we just gon' do the silent thing again or . . . ?

A smirk tugs at my lips and Jhamal looks over his shoulder at me. My stomach does something weird.

Me: I'm here lol

Me: Listen, some stuff went down and I can't leave right now. But I'm okay and my bad for having you worried.

"Everything good?" Jhamal's expression is more curious this time.

"I'm trying to see." My fingers work furiously over the watch face, keeping an eye out as we make our way across another intersection.

Me: And thanks for checking on the fam. You a real one for that, you know. Let me know what's up with T when you can.

Julius: I'ma hold you down, always

I put the watch on my arm so I don't slip up and miss another message. There's no shortage of broken awnings and trash blowing through the streets. Shells of buildings, broken windows. A distinct feeling I'm being watched slinks over me, but I spot nothing beyond the scent of smoke in the air.

"Do you think—" I turn to Jhamal.

"Ah!"

The scream sears my nerves and there's Bri shouting, fiery arrows heading straight for her. She ducks and they whoosh over her head.

"Run," I yell, rushing over. "Take cover."

She tugs on her leg with her hands, but her foot seems resolved to stay put. "The ground—i-it's like glue or something. I-I can't move."

"Pull the shoe off, genius." I pull her arm over my shoulder and she slips her foot out of her shoe before we take off running. Another incendiary blaze flies past. Heat washes over my back, sizzling my nerves. I dart one direction, then the next, zigging and zagging, trying to shake the arrows, which are chasing me like there's a target on my back. I pull Bri along and look for Jhamal, but in the chaos I don't spot him. I let Bri go and skirt a corner and she hops off. But the arrows follow me, zipping around the building at my back. An arrow slams into the storefront, its sign going up in flames. My shirt tugs and something stings my side. Another arrow zips past.

"Zora," I yell. "Do you see the direction they're coming from?"

She shakes her head but hurries off to investigate.

Arrows fly toward us, one then another, in succession, their fiery glow reflecting off puddles on the ground. The air is thick with their heat. I motion for Bri, then shove us sideways as a cluster of magic shoots past. They spin in the air before heading right back toward us. *Were we followed?*

I run, dragging Bri toward a raised dumpster, ducking underneath it. The air is foul, but I swallow the urge to hurl. An arrow slams into the metal can we've turned into a shield.

"Every move we make, the arrows twist to follow."

Bri pants beside me, gulping down air, but doesn't utter a word. Flames zip past in her bright blue eyes. I peek from beneath the wooden platform, our cover.

"The arrows. They must sense movement," I say. "What kind of magic does that?"

"Uhm, uhm." Bri's bangs are glued to her forehead and her hands shake as she shoves some gadget back in her bag. "I . . . uhm . . . okay, think."

"Breathe and think. I have you." I grab her face, forcing her to look at me when the wooden legs to the platform catch fire. We pull ourselves out and run, another arrow hot on our tail. It's like being chased by the sun. Jhamal bounds over, his shield at our back.

"Down." We scrunch together tight on the pavement behind the golden barrier attached to his arm. Fire slams into it, but snuffs out.

"It's chasing me," I tell him. "Or all of us . . . I don't know."

We look at Bri, but her expression is frozen with fear. We need better cover. On all sides. The streets are a pile of nothing but for an overturned commercial transport vehicle.

"There!" I point and we dart that way. "Come on, help me push!"

Jhamal pushes on the vehicle to try to turn it so we can get in. Metal groans.

"*R'ski ya!*" I thrust and the car rolls. "Inside, now." Arrows rain like a hailstorm, coming faster and more at once, slamming into the roof of the car, the windows spiderwebs of growing cracks at each jab. It's so hot, I can't feel my skin. "Bri, anything you can think of? A magic that behaves like this?"

"Uhm . . . uhm . . ." She's never been under pressure like this.

I get it. But, damn, I need her to get the fuck with it. "BRI!"

"More are coming," Jhamal says, head peeking above his shield. "The shooters must be nearby."

The back door of the vehicle opens and a smoky haze follows Zora inside. Flames slam into the door as it clicks shut.

"I couldn't find anyone," she says, her face lined with disappointment, like she's let us down. Or herself down. Or both, maybe.

"It's okay," I say. "We've got this." Somehow. Someway.

"I did notice that the arrows are shooting from an upstairs window in a taller building. But no one is there. I-I looked . . . I looked everywhere."

"A trap." Bri swallows, panting. "It's a trap. They've booby-trapped this area, a-and looks like I stepped on the trigger." Her shoe. That's why it wouldn't move? She inhales a big breath and lets it out slow. "I'm sorry I froze, Rue. I'm—"

Zora scoffs. "So, what needs to be done?"

Jhamal flashes her a look that says *be nice*. But she ignores him, too.

Fire knocks overhead.

Think, Rue. "Okay . . . magic is energy," I say.

"Yes." Bri nods.

"Someone's commanded their magic to take fire arrow form. And when triggered, follow the target, right?"

"Yep."

"But how?"

"Uhm, the magic could be bewitched to cling to like-energy like a magnet would? Maybe it senses any other magic and seeks it out?"

"No, because you wouldn't trigger that, Bri. You don't have onyx anymore. I would have. It *was* seeking though. . . ." *But seeking what . . . ?*

The vehicle rattles.

"Oh my god, heat! It was seeking heat."

Zora's eyes flicker with recognition. "And the heat we're generating by all four of us hiding in here"—she coughs into her arm—"means those arrows are not going to let up."

"We have to get out," Jhamal says. "It'll burn us all to a crisp."

"Then the only way to get it off of us is to give it a hotter source to chase," Bri starts.

But I'm out of the car before I hear the rest of what she is saying. I spot a boarded-up furniture shop with a glass sign. RICKY'S, it reads, the letters glitching on the screen.

"Sorry, business owner person, but I have to," I whisper, conjuring flames in my palm. Fire spins in my hands like a turbine and I pull my palms apart. "Forezo."

The blaze swells in my grip, my face burning in its heat. Jhamal shouts but I tune him out, focusing on holding the flames there, best I can. But it's like trying to grasp a cyclone. Whistling somewhere behind me makes me whip around. A flaming arrow tip sails past the car with Bri and Zora in it, pummeling straight toward me. *It's working.* I plant my feet. *Wait for it.* Its blinding glow is all I see. The arrow grows larger, and larger, sensing the incendiary vortex in my hands.

One . . .

I force my eyes to stay open.

Two . . .

I'm blinded. Everything's orange, glowing.

Three . . .

I heave my ball of fire at the building nearby and throw myself down, my head banging the pavement. Intense heat brushes my back as the arrow zips past, slamming into the building.

Boom.

I curl in a ball, my head throbbing. *Boom boom!* Someone's yelling when something heavy sets on my back.

"Not yet, Jelani," Zora says, on top of me, arms barred around me so I can't get up. "Stay down."

The building is up in flames, black billowing above us like clouds. I try to move under Zora's weight. "If . . . you'd . . ." I grunt, "let me up, I could . . ." I manage to rotate and raise my hands. "Poi y'ska," A transparent barrier hardens between us and the burning building.

I exhale.

Zora exhales, too, releasing me.

"You okay?" I ask.

"I'm good." She stands, dusting herself off.

The flames recede and I break the spell. "You sure? You could have been killed putting yourself over me like that."

"I am here to see this mission all the way through. Whatever it takes." She tugs at her sleeves.

I sigh. "No one's dying for me."

"Kai told me to look out for you. And I intend to."

She said that? I guess knowing we share blood did matter to her after all. Despite her sourness.

"Jelani, you hold the only remnants of our Ancestors' power in your arms," Jhamal says. "That matters. It matters to all of us."

I don't deserve special treatment. Me, who almost got them killed more than once. I should be the one sacrificing to protect *them*.

"If there's any way we can truly restore the Ancestors' magic," Zora goes on. "That's something we all want. But we need your magic to do it. So of course we're going to protect it—you—at all costs."

I don't like it, but I get it.

Bri climbs out the car window, comes over to us, and offers a hand to Zora to help her up. But she doesn't take it. Bri apologizes again, but I assure her we've all frozen before.

"That trap was set for someone with magic," I say.

"And it was very advanced," Bri says. "Heat seeking magic isn't something I've ever seen done. Only heard of it anecdotally, which is why I didn't think of it first."

"I've never seen anything like it," Zora says.

"The only person capable of that advanced level of magic is—"

"The Chancellor," I say as an eeriness moves over me. I peer in every direction but find only an audience of broken windows and crumbled buildings. I hug around myself, trying to make sense of the shadows between and inside them. *He is watching. Somehow . . .*

"We need to get off these streets. And soon."

Bri shoulders her bag, Zora tucks her weapon under her arm, Jhamal sturdies his shield, and we take off in a full sprint.

CHAPTER THIRTEEN

THE MOON GLOWS OVERHEAD and my thighs ache. We can't be far off now.

Bri is still shook, dragging behind us. She used some purple potion to make a duplicate of her shoe, so she can at least walk normally again. She's not even looking in her bag anymore, just eyes straight ahead like she's seen a ghost. I take it she's never been shot at before. I want to tell her to find that *oomph* she had when she followed my captors after my arrest.

A herd of cats scatter when we cross the next intersection. We segue under Rosh Bridge and head up Creets Walk. One of the dormitory towers is up ahead. It used to be two towers connected by a bridge over a courtyard, but only one tower still stands, and a huge chunk of it is missing. The lush green that used to sit below where I'd fold over my spell book or eat lunch outside is a sandbox of glass shards and broken stone.

"We really should stop soon, for a minute," Zora says.

"For what?"

She looks at me but says nothing. I try to read her pressed lips, but she's otherwise stoic. What does she think of me? I wonder. She's been much nicer than Kai. But she keeps to herself.

"We used to study over there," I say to her, pointing to the quad courtyard, an abandoned field of rotting trees and overturned benches.

"Learn anything good?" she asks, her expression twisted with sarcasm. "Oh wait . . . the Chancellor knows nothing about the magic he purports as his own." Her jaw pulses and it's the Yakanna in her that shines now.

"My daddy never trusted him," I say to her. The way the Chancellor had stormed into their village with magic he'd unearthed just felt too convenient. "Everyone was so sick, I remember Aasim explaining." But they knew whatever magic he'd had must have been stolen. So they pretended to entertain his offer. Then fled.

"My grandmother died of the Sickness," Zora says, pushing her lip sideways. "She was very young. My mother said she used to take her to pick kaeli berries each morning. That she'd planned the most beautiful turning out—you know, when a girl becomes a woman."

"Oh, like a sweet sixteen?"

"Uh, sure. But this happens at fourteen. Well, in my GraMemi's day it did. I never had a turning out. I grew up inside a mountain. The history of my people are stories on the lips of our Elders. For me, they are dreams, pictures in my head, the way I imagine it. That is a childhood I will never know."

"I'm sorry, Zora. How much he took from you." I see my father's face. "And from me, too."

"The tales say this island was ours," she says. "It is almost make-believe, you know?"

I want to tell her it's gon' be real. That our people ain't gon' be forced to live this way, broken and in secret. That we will bloom on this island like kaeli flowers once did. But my words are wind. After everything I've done, every way I've failed, the only words she needs are actions.

The silence hangs between Zora and me as we stick to the perimeter, getting closer to Totsi's. I'm careful to avoid walking in wide-open spaces. The Chancellor's watchtower of an office is a dot up ahead at the far end of the Central District. I grit my teeth and press into the wall nearest us, sliding along its edge. It's too far for him to see us, but if he's up there, I don't want to take any chances.

Jhamal falls in step with us and heat blossoms in me. In gratitude and something else I'm not ready to give words to. "Thanks for everything earlier. I'm really glad you came."

He smiles, then winks. I hide my grin.

I check for Bri. She's still to herself, quiet. As we walk, I pause every few moments, listening. We pass the Binding Ward, where onyx was attached to my skin before I knew I didn't need that stolen toy. Before I knew the Ancestors' magic lived in these cuffs and in me. It's a heap of wreckage and something in me twists with joy. So many lies. Everything he built here was mortared in deception. Brick upon brick.

There's so much carnage. Those fighting the Chancellor must be coordinated. Buildings tall and crumbled, the Justice Ward is a hollowed-out shell of a building. This is highly organized retaliation. Definitely not just some angry rioters. Smoke rises from a hill in the distance, from a residential neighborhood.

"Is that . . . ?"

Bri shakes her head. "But my neighborhood is not that far from there."

The Chancellor clearly has plenty on his side, too. And they fight dirty. Burning people's homes? That's low as shit. Bri chews her lip. I don't know what to say that I haven't already said, so I squeeze her hand. I think of Tasha, Bri's little brothers. How she must be worried about her family.

"Hey, I meant to ask . . . any way I can use this watch to call Tasha?"

She shakes her head. "I only put that coding into your watch. Which you left with Julius. Sorry, Rue."

"It's okay." Thankfully, Julius can check on things for me. But Bri . . . she has no way to know if the next neighborhood burned will be hers. "Bri, I'm sorry. I know this is a lot."

"Stop apologizing. I chose to be out here in this fight with you. When the tyrant falls from his pedestal, we all win. This is my fight too." She walks on ahead, and there's nothing I can say. She's right. The side of right isn't hazy. There is no neutrality anymore. You're either supporting the tyrant or fighting to see him fall.

We keep moving through a thicket silence. Other than a few strays, the occasional rustle in the brush, there's nothing out here. No Patrol patrolling. No Dwegini or Zruki anywhere. I wrap around myself, the cool breeze chilly on my damp skin. The Capital is a dead zone . . . and yet somehow it feels like hundreds are watching.

"How do you put up with her?" asks Zora, who has stuck even closer by my side since the fire trap. "I do not understand. She is so clumsy, and her head is always in her bag of rocks. And for what?"

I snort and Zora smirks, but inside, my stomach flops like a fish. The unity on this island is tenuous at best. Is it foolish to hope we can coexist somehow?

"There's some really useful stuff in that bag though . . . usually," I say, skirting a crack in the pavement. "She grows on you. Give it time."

"No, thank you." Zora resituates the ring in her nose and tugs at her armor, wiggling to adjust its fit. "You can have her."

Closer now, I can see the bits of jade are painted in ornate patterns, but the gold itself sparkles with a green undertone as if crushed gems were dusted over its surface. She still wears the rings and bells from Kowana Yechi; her left ear is adorned with seven thin gold loops, one in her nose and a gold band up her left arm. Her right arm, in fact her entire right side, is bare of any adornment.

"The armor the Yakanna wear is real dope looking. So beautiful." I tug at the breastplate that's like a steel blanket wrapped around my chest. "I mean . . . as far as armor goes . . . not like I have a lot of experience with it or anything."

"I think you have a lot of experience that matters more than most of us." She glances at my gilded arms. "Did it hurt?"

"Oh my god, yes! Like lava searing into your skin."

She shudders. "Well, worth it, no?"

"Very much."

I study her. She's a flame, lethal, but I'm drawn to her like I've known her for years. Is that our Yakanna bond? "I notice you only wear things on your left. Everything on your right is bare. Is that intentional?"

"You are very observant." She takes off a bell from her hair and a few loops from her ear and hands them to me to look at closely. "You think a lot more than you speak."

The rings are surprisingly heavy. Solid Ghizoni gold. And the tiniest patterns are etched into their sparkling surface. "Well . . . I wasn't always that way. I learned the hard way. A work in progress, really."

"And you wear humility like a crown."

My cheeks burn and I don't know what to say, so I just look away.

"And yes, Jelani. Mother Yakanna believed the heart is forged with two cavities, the right filled with fear and the left side filled with love. If you are standing on the very edge of a mountain's edge, are you more captivated by the love of the view or the fear of falling?"

"Falling. I hate heights."

"And fear commands most of us more than love. But love is much more powerful." She touches the gold band on her arm, tracing it with her fingers. "We adorn the left side, the side of the heart that is filled with love, as a reminder to hold love above all things. It is most precious, more lethal than poison, more powerful than the darkest magic." Her armor glints in the sunlight. Like Kai, she holds her chin up . . . just naturally.

"It's odd to hear you talk about something so . . . I don't know. The Yakanna are so fearless."

"I've seen the same in you. You fight with such passion."

"Losing isn't a privilege I can afford."

"Well, love is a powerful fuel too. It can destroy life or give it," she says. "It must be handled with intention. It is fragile."

"Like glass."

"Like a bomb." Her composure cracks ever so slightly, her eyes tilting downward, but I don't miss it. She loves someone . . . and she loves them dangerously deep. "The only thing I fear, Jelani, is the loss of love. And the threat of that loss makes me fight without fear."

We walk the next half a block in silence and I'm grateful for it, because the conversation was beginning to make my stomach do flips. But just as we round another corner, she turns to me again.

"What do you fear, Jelani?"

I meet her eyes and find a challenge there. My parents' faces trickle through my memory. I search for words but only find the ones bobbing on the surface. And that's not what she's asking. So I let the silence hang there.

I check on Bri behind us and she's content with her gadgets, oblivious to Zora's irritation with her. And for now, I'd like to keep it that way. Last thing we need is more reasons for us to divide. Unity is our greatest strength against the Chancellor. I glimpse at the sky; a sliver of the moon peeks behind clouds.

"Zora, what do you know about what's out here?" I ask.

She doesn't bring up my skirt of her question, and I'm grateful for it. Instead, she inhales deep, closing her eyes. "Can you smell them? They are watching."

I smell burning. Smoke folds upward into the clouds in the distance. All the people who lived here have to still be here somewhere. With so much unknown lurking around every corner, darkness is a cloak, a friend to everyone. The night's probably full of mothers clutching their babies, people walking in shadows because that's where they feel safest. For as desolate as the streets are right here, there are pockets where it's popping, I bet, and not in a good way.

"Who is 'they'?" Bri asks, catching up to us.

"The Grays who intend to see the Chancellor rise back to his previous power," she says, tucking a twine of gold behind her ear. "They call themselves Loyalists," she answers, looking at me instead of Bri. "And I fear the Chancellor has even more supporters than it appears. The cover of night is when many come out of their homes, hiding behind costumes and masks to terrorize whoever dare speak against the Chancellor."

The thought of having neighbors and friends that smile at me every day, pretend to be on the side of right in this fight, only to slip out at night and burn homes in the name of the Chancellor, makes me boil with rage.

The leather glove on Zora's forearm slips, revealing scratches slashed all over her skin. "Plainclothes Patrol are rumored to have joined them too." She tugs her sleeves back up. "You can't really tell where anyone's loyalty lies just by looking." She barely glances at Bri, but I don't miss it.

Questions bite at my lips, but I don't want to make her feel some kind of way. Like, why she wears gloves and how she knows all this. She's been so helpful. I don't want her to misunderstand, think I doubt her, so I keep my nosiness to myself.

"Do you know which neighborhoods they've left untouched?" Bri asks. A chorus of howls somewhere far away pierce the air. Zora halts, sticks out her javelin to stop us in our tracks, and presses a finger to her lips.

"I . . . ," I start.

But Zora gestures for me to wait. Jhamal catches up to us. The howls morph into growls, then a whimper. Then silence. Zora removes her stick.

"Mother Ike said your ears can see better than your eyes sometimes," she says. "With their numbers, if we are ambushed unawares, it could be the difference between life and death."

I conjure a ball of light into my palm and squeeze its warmth when my watch vibrates. Jhamal peeks over my shoulder. I walk a few steps ahead of him before reading.

Julius: Hello? So, do I need to pack shower shoes or?

Me: LOL. I won't disappear again. But I'm literally in the middle of looking for a really important thing so I might be in and out. I'ma scoop you though. Promise.

Eventually. I'm in no hurry to put someone else who's important to me in harm's way, even if I did give him my word.

Julius: You know I watch a lot of spy 007 type shit. I could help you find whatever. If you'd *finally* come get me . . . 🙄

Me: 😄 I can't yet.

Julius: You smiling foreal, ain't you?

Me: Ye . . .

Delete. Delete. Delete.

Me: Maybe.

I look for Jhamal and a twinge of guilt shifts in me. He looks exhausted. I picture his face hovering over me, the times he woke me to make sure I ate, the way he sticks beside me now, so stubbornly. *Julius is a friend. That is all.*

"You need rest," I say.

"You are one to talk." He pulls a hair out of my face, holding his thumb there, stroking my cheek. I pull my face away instinctively. His lips turn in disappointment.

"We will rest when this is over," he says, his gaze now straight ahead, hard. "Like we've never rested before." And just like that he reminds me that he is so much of who I am. *Or . . . who I used to be.* I walk closer to him, letting my arm graze his, and he tries to hide his smirk.

"I'm sorry."

He raises a brow, looking at me.

"For pushing you away. I'm trying. You deserve . . ."

"Jelani, I waited my entire life to feel like this. What is another day, week?"

His adoration wraps around me and I bask in it, my conscience needling at me. I don't deserve him. For all he is to our people. The way he embodies everything the Ghizoni stand for, the Ancestors must be so proud. How could I ever be worthy of him? How could I ever redeem myself enough after what I've done to not flinch at his touch?

He isn't perfect, my conscience whispers as his conspiring with Bati to put my name forward flickers through my memory. A wave of irritation rushes through me. But the moment between us right now is a balm to my raging storm. I'll talk to him about it some other time. This moment is more comfort than I've felt . . . *let* myself feel . . . in a long time. And I'd like to sit in it a bit longer if I can.

For the next several blocks, we walk in silence, but close, so close I can feel his hand brush mine. And I make sure to keep it there, hoping he feels whatever this is I have for him that I can't seem to give words to.

The eeriness of being watched doesn't fade as the sky's darkness deepens. If those watching are indeed plainclothed Loyalists, like Zora'd described. . . why won't they just attack? Could that be who the lab guy was? My mind floats back to the fractured moments and I search for remnants of memories, holes that might be ready to fill. Bri'd said it would come back in pieces. But nothing new is there.

A vehicle hums in the distance and I move ahead of all the others.

Zora must sense the weirdness too because she stalks the next corner before we round it. Tires skid across pavement and I shove us into an alleyway just as a line of armored trucks roll by, only to screech to a stop up ahead. The Ghizon emblem with the Chancellor's face is plastered on a truck's side. Tarps are draped across the back of the truck lift and men dressed in plain clothes—Loyalists—unload a large crate.

"Wait here," I say, and Jhamal's fingers graze my wrist. "I just want to get a bit closer."

"We need to get to Totsi's, not bother with poking a hornet's nest," Jhamal whispers.

"Bati had no intel on the Chancellor's whereabouts or what he's up to. I'm not missing this chance." I creep along the stone alleyway to the very edge, just enough so I can peek around the corner.

A Patrolman unlatches the top of the crate and wheels it between two buildings, before hopping back in the truck and driving off. I motion for everyone, and my hand connects with Zora.

"Oh, sorry. I didn't realize you were behind me."

"I didn't want you to." She winks. If she's saying I would have told her to stay back like I did Jhamal, she's right. I'm just not trying to put any of them in harm's way.

"What do you think it is?" she asks.

The alleyway where they set the delivery is between a smoke shop and a boarded-up beauty boutique. With the vehicle out of sight, I peer 'round the corner for a better glimpse. The ground level of the alleyway is lined with the back doors to several shops. Up above, wide windows. One is open with a red sheet blowing in the wind.

This is a drop. Someone's waiting for this package.

Someone's here.

I press a finger to my lips, the hair on my neck standing. I point at the window, then at the box. Zora's brows furrow, but understanding hardens her expression when a door in the alley creaks open. We tuck out of sight around the corner and listen. Footsteps. Wood creaks. Breath hangs in my chest like a scythe.

I peek around the corner and the someone is alone, hovering over the box. His head is shaved on one side, an *L* branded into his scalp. The same *L* as on the palm of the boy we buried. Swooped bangs hang over his face and he looks like he hasn't slept in months.

He gazes around and I snatch myself back, hiding around the corner. *Still, Rue. Be still.* Metal scraping against itself says he's opening the box and didn't see me. I try to let out a breath, but even the thought of breathing cuts deeper than a knife.

I dare another peek. He's chest deep in the box, pulling out a metal contraption with both hands.

The Loyalist studies buttons on the device as if he's trying to figure out how to turn it on. He taps something red, and metal pinchers snap at the machine's sides.

"Maybe it's a trap?" I whisper to Zora, the feeling returning to my fingers. "The Chancellor could be working with this band of whoever they are to set traps all over the City to catch me."

"Like the fire arrows."

"Yes." It's the only thing that makes sense.

Zora's eyes meet mine and in hers is a question: What do we do?

"If we can get our hands on that trap or, better yet, him . . . maybe we could find out more about the Chancellor's plans?" I raise my eyebrows in question. What does she think of this idea? Is it dumb?

But she nods, then falls behind me, pressing her bare shoulder to my back as if to say she's ready. She moves with me in one motion. I signal for the others.

"Bri, stand by to disassemble the trap if he manages to activate it somehow."

"Jhamal, Zora, and I will take him dead on. Hang out over here." I point to a parallel alleyway. "If he gets away, he'll assume it's just the two of us and run this way thinking it's clear."

He nods, but the way he purses his lips lets me know he thinks this is a waste of time. Sure, we could keep going, but information is a powerful weapon and we could use more of those right now.

Hinges creak and metal clangs around the corner as the Loyalist struggles to work a metal latch on the contraption.

Images of my prison cell creaking open cut into me in a flash. I suck in a breath, the memory playing on repeat. *I'm thrown inside the cell by rough hands. I reach for his weapon, my magic, something, but my arms are bricks beside me. The prison door slams closed and I grip the cold bars of the cell. My magic stills inside me. My knees are weak underneath me and I look for Jhamal. Two men in white coats drag him out of sight. What are they doing to him? I slide down the walls of my cage. What have I done?*

I gasp and steady myself on the wall beside me. Jhamal never mentioned seeing guys in a lab coat. That they'd dragged him. That they'd hurt him. Why didn't he mention that? I mean, I guess, why would he want to relive that, regurgitating to me? How does that help us? *He's* been through so much already.

"Rue?" Zora blinks at me. "Are you okay? You went glassy eyed on me for a moment."

"I'm fine," I say, shoving away the memories trying to choke me. "Let's hurry."

I round the corner with Zora, hands held high, ready to block whatever curses he throws at us. He glances between us and the device.

He smashes a red button on the device then bolts. Zora and I take off after him, away from the device, which could be some kind of bomb for all I know. We chase him down the far end of the alley, spilling out into the street. *This* I didn't expect. No fight, not even one spell? What kind of followers is the Chancellor recruiting? I glance back at Bri, who is hovering over the device with careful hands.

"No, get back!" I yell.

"It's not explosive," she shouts, smoothing her hands along its side like she's looking for something.

We round on the Loyalist.

"Get away from me!" He glances in both directions, but we have him T-boned in an intersection. Jhamal emerges from the alleyway behind him. Cornered, his eyes widen.

"Bri," I shout, but she's already tinkering with the metal contraption.

"They'll be here any minute; you better run," the Loyalist says. It comes out as a threat, but his hands are shaking. I step closer and he steps back.

"Uh, Rue," Bri yells. "Not a bomb, but still urgent."

I glance at Bri, but the machine is no less activated than it was a moment ago. A light glows on its side and lasers shoot out its top.

"This thing has a homing device," she says. "He's not wrong. We have minutes to shut it down before it alerts their people that we're here."

We'd be outnumbered AF. *Shit.* The Loyalist is covered in sweat. "You better not touch me. O-or . . ."

"How long have you been working for the Chancellor?" I ask.

He slicks a hand over the branded *L* on his head.

"I'm not telling you anything." He looks both ways, and I summon my magic. It crackles between my fingers. "Answer the question."

I step toward him again and his eyes glow with fear. He backs up, bumping into Jhamal's chest. He twists the Loyalist's arms behind him and he howls. I grab him by the collar and take him back to the trap.

"Shut it off."

He fidgets with the wires, but more lasers shoot from the device, scanning in every direction. Red light blinds me a second. Pinchers snap in my direction, but I move out of the way.

"Faster!" I shove him. His hands work over the device and it shudders a moment, then the red light goes off as it powers down.

I exhale.

"N-now let me go."

"For a foot soldier for the Chancellor, you sure are scared."

He chews his lip.

"What do we do with him?" Zora asks.

"He's going to tell me what I want to know, then we'll decide." I reach for him and he holds his hands up, flinching, his sleeves rolling down. His wrists . . . I push up his sleeve. No onyx. Where there would be onyx is the X-shaped scar of someone never Bound, someone . . . magicless.

"You're Macazi?" The magicless are in league with the Chancellor's followers now? They're murdering Macazi all over this City, they've treated them like shit for generations. Make it make sense.

I look to Bri and she shrugs. "No idea. I didn't even know he'd amassed a following of Loyalists, let alone that he'd recruit Macazi."

"I'm sure the Macazi would be shocked too," I say, "to learn one of their own is playing both sides."

The Loyalist's eyes dart between us.

"Explain yourself," I say.

"I'm not saying anything. I-if you're going to kill me, so be it." He folds his arms but he stinks of fear. Brave when it counts. It's almost admirable.

"What were you going to do with that trap?"

"I do what I'm told. If anything will be said about me, it'll be that I follow through."

Jhamal unsheathes his blade. "Jelani, we've wasted enough time on this. He's a pawn. Useless."

The Loyalist's eyes flicker with something I recognize: determination. *He knows plenty. And I'm going to get it out of him.*

"Don't kill him. He goes with us."

"Rue, Macazi don't have the best reputation," Bri whispers to me. "I mean, they're not trusted with magic for a reason."

"I said, he is going with us."

Zora pulls the binding tied to the Loyalist's wrists; moonlight shines bright overhead. My feet ache. Totsi's is literally no more than a couple of blocks away, from what I remember, but we might need to make camp somewhere if we don't find it soon.

"You did good back there." Jhamal brushes up against me, our hands dangling next to one another. His pinky finger reaches for mine. That alleyway would have been trickier without him and Zora. I'm *really* grateful he pushed to come with.

"You gassing me up?" I eye his finger, dangling there for me to take it.

"I do not know what that means. I just admire how you handled it."

"Well . . . thanks." I hook my finger onto his and try to ignore the somersaults my insides are doing. He smiles at me and my cheeks burn so hot I can't help but smile back.

"I still do not think it is worth our time, but he fears you," he goes on while we walk, basically holding hands. *What am I doing?*

"And if he lives to tell this story, everyone he retells it to will fear you too. And that's what you want. Good job."

"As long as I get the information I need out of him, I don't really care if he fears me."

He tsks. "Ah, but you should care."

A gust of wind rushes around us, and I let our conversation blow away with it. This is a sweet moment and I don't want to ruin it. For several moments we walk in silence. Bri glances at the hostage a few times then at me.

"We could have pulled some good coding out of it to help us find out more about its origin," she says to me, still unhappy about leaving the deactivated trap. "Like, who made it exactly. How they plan to use it."

"Bri, we went over this. We can't lug it with us."

She huffs a sigh. "I mean, yeah. I don't know." She slows her pace, digging in her bag, and Jhamal walks so close he could be a part of me. Every few moments our bodies touch, and I wonder if he feels the adrenaline pumping through me.

"Couldn't have done this today without y'all. Foreal."

"Together." His cheeks push up under his eyes, which could outshine the starriest sky.

"Together," I echo, my heart beating so loud when a patch of birds take flight, I'm convinced it's my nerves that did it. I gulp, folding my hand more properly in his, taking the leap needling at me. He squeezes, holding on as if letting my fingers go would be the worst thing in the world. The way he clings to me makes me want to squeeze back . . . because . . . because . . .

I gaze up at the sky remembering the pain of losing my father. The way I loved him and yet he slipped from my fingers after it was too late. The way Bri broods over conversations she hasn't had with her parents, her little brothers, and not knowing if, or rather, when, she will again. The way Titube might have not told her mother goodbye before she last saw her. Time ticks and I feel it on my very skin.

I squeeze Jhamal's hand. Because somewhere deep down, I guess I want to believe I'm worth clinging to.

We walk for several minutes, the silence hanging between us, and the bone I haven't picked with Jhamal prickles through my mind. *Do I say something . . . right now?* I chew my lip.

"You know I never got in your ass like I should have about you and Bati plotting behind my back to nominate me as Queen."

He chuckles.

"I'm foreal," I say, trying to keep the moment light, sweet.

"Jelani, it was meant with the utmost respect."

"But you should have told me what you were thinking, right? In that cell, all those months, we kept nothing from each other. I told you about my Moms. Where I grew up. You told me about growing up in Yiyo. I thought we were better than that."

"I knew if I told you, you would not like it."

I let go of his fingers. "So, you do it anyway?"

He sighs. "I am sorry. That is what I should have said. I am sorry I did not tell you."

"Thank you." I cling to him again. If we're going to do this, whatever this is, we have to be on the same page. "If you know anything about me, you know that's not my lane. Like, not even close."

"Forgive me, but I will always disagree." It should be flattering but it's more irritating. I get he sees it as a high honor, but every time he looks at me, I can see right through him—the crown he wishes was on my head.

"You know, sometimes I wonder whether you think I'd make a good Queen because of who I am or because of who you want me to be." It slips out and I regret it immediately. My moment of vulnerability has me looking for a fight. Some reason to retreat, like a turtle in its shell.

He shifts, stunned, mouth open like I've wounded him.

"Rue, how could you . . ." His head drops. "My Memi, you remember her?"

"Of course, I do." In prison, he would hold me when I had nightmares. My hands would shake and he'd trace circles on my forehead, telling me stories she'd told him.

"Memi would remind me of who I am, who I would be," he'd explained. "And so too, I tell you, Jelani. You are my Queen."

Yeah, he calls me that but I thought he meant it in jest. Still, the sweetness of his intentions smooths my sharp edges. "I don't mean that how it sounds. I just . . . want to be sure you see me, all of me, the scars, the mess."

"Jelani." He faces me and we stop. "How could you say it? I see all you are. Sometimes I think I see more in you than you see in yourself."

The honesty in his eyes makes me pull tighter to him. His arm is hard against me, as iron willed as his determination. I love that about him—how he is a mirror to my strength. I could whoop his ass, but, like, if we squared up, it would be an even match. And he'd have it no other way. We fit together. Make each other stronger. Like we did in that cell. Like we're doing out here now.

And yet . . . My thumb brushes the back of his hand in my grasp. On this topic, I've never felt more divided from him.

I study my feet. How do I make him understand? There are parts of who I am he's never seen. Pieces of me rooted in ways he doesn't quite grasp. I was an entire person with a life before I even realized I'm Ghizoni. And I guess he doesn't know that Rue. I squeeze his hand, hoping he gets how badly I want him to. How badly I hope we can get there.

"Tell me, my Queen. What is it? What is it really?"

"Jhamal, I don't half do things. If I'm going in, I'm going all the way in. Moms always said working twice as hard is just what it takes for people from where I'm from. A-and taking on something *that* big, with my heart not in it, is . . . a recipe for failure. And haven't I failed us enough?" *I have to do what I know. It's who I am. That has to be enough.*

"No," he mutters to himself, his jaw set in that way he does. "I do not see this as a problem like you say. There is nothing you cannot do, Jelani."

That's not exactly what I said, but okay. In his world, I am the answer. The Chosen.

He stares as if he can see right through me. "I will not see you any other way. I cannot." He throws an arm over my shoulder, pulling me in to him. I bite back my retort. He means no harm and he wouldn't understand anyway. I swipe up on my watch.

Me: Jue, any word on T?

CHAPTER FOURTEEN

A BLOCK FROM TOTIS'S, I squint through the dim light at the street ahead of us blockaded by a collapsed building.

"Totsi's is on the other side of this pile of rubble." But to get there we have to traipse through desecrated building.

Bri has her gadget with the suction cup at the end and holds it out in front of her. "Can we transport to the other side?" Bri asks.

"Without knowing what's on the other side for sure . . . not a good idea."

"It's obviously another trap," Jhamal says, inspecting the structure before gazing around.

"You feel it too?" I ask. "Something lurking."

"I don't like this," Zora says. "Going in there with no idea of what's inside."

The hostage whose hands are tethered looks in our direction.

"Yes?" I say. But he says nothing. He's probably got all sorts of songs he could sing. But how do I get it out of him? The Chancellor would probably use torture. That's not me. I sigh. I'll think of something.

"And you're sure there is no way around?" Jhamal asks.

Bri waves her device in the air. "None."

The pile of lacquered walls, concrete, and glass that was once a stately structure lies in the middle of a street like a present on a doorstep we're meant to find.

"We go through."

Everyone nods, silent. Our hostage fidgets.

"Wait!" Bri digs in her bag and pulls out a container with pills and a vial of green liquid. "Before we go in there, take this." She hands me a pill and vial, then offers the same to Zora. But Zora doesn't even acknowledge her.

"Just in case things go poorly," Bri says. "This potion will make any wounds you sustain heal quicker. It's usually a paste, but I dried it out to powder form. More versatile that way."

I want to say, "Where was that when we were being chased with fire arrows?" But I swallow it back down and let my friend make it. Glad she's at least more composed this time. I sniff the potion, and mintiness stings my nose, my sinuses opening wide. I drop the pill in the vial and the potion fizzes like a hot soda can that's been shaken up. I tip my head back and drink. It's sweet with a note of tang, like wildflower honey, but with an acidic burn going down.

"Gross, I know. But it'll help." Bri offers the potion to Zora again.

Her expression is steel. "I do not need your tricks."

"Zora, if Bri says it'll work, it'll work."

"I do not know her to trust her. And judging from earlier . . ." She shakes her head and looks away.

Bri purses her lips, but says nothing, takes her own swig of the potion, and stuffs the rest away.

"She might change her mind," I whisper to her.

She snatches up her suction-cup gadget and holds it out like a flashlight. "I won't freeze like that again."

"Bri—"

"Just let me be mad at myself, okay? I need to get it together. Be harder on myself." She presses a button on top of the gadget and a blue light blares. "I'm ready."

The storm clouds have stopped crying, but they hover above, gloomy and foreboding. A ball of light thrashes in my hands as I step inside the fallen structure. The ground glows blue in the light from my magic. I scan, watching out for booby-trapped hot spots like the one Bri stepped on. Maybe there was a subtle mark on the ground and she missed it.

Jhamal and Zora are on my left, Bri on my right, and around us is a maze of concrete walls dotted with rods of steel stuck out at odd angles. Faint light shines up ahead through the broken building like a beacon. I point, then press a finger to my lips. I walk as softly as I can, easing each breath out, darkness growing thicker than the humidity. The walls groan and I conjure energy in my empty hand too.

"Maybe this is just a fallen building?" Bri asks. Her gadget light is swirling but not going off. "Not another trap?"

It's definitely a trap. The question is why the Chancellor's laying traps, watching from his tower, sending Loyalists after us this way instead of fighting us head-on.

The building shifts, metal rustled by strong winds groans, and chills skitter up my skin.

Clang.

My breath is tight in my chest, and the hostage, being dragged by Zora, backs into me. I steady him on his feet. We survey each direction, Zora with her javelin out.

"They are definitely here," she whispers.

Loyalists. My shoulders cinch.

"Do not panic," Zora says. "That is the most formidable foe."

We stalk over piles of rock, around metal sheeting. I step on something sticky and the hem of my pants is red. A pungent smell curls my nose, but I shove down the urge to hurl and keep moving. If darkness is their cover, it will be ours, too.

We stumble upon a fractured wall and our path is blockaded. The curtain of concrete has a hole in the center, only big enough for one of us to squeeze through at a time.

"I'll go first," Jhamal and Zora say at the same time, stepping forward.

"No, I will." This is a death trap. "If whatever is on the other side of that wall is magic, I'll need to face it. You can follow right after me. The hostage goes last. Keep him safe." *I'm not done with him.*

Questions hang on their lips, but they don't disagree.

Bri waves her gadget around the opening in the rock and the blue light flashes faster. "I silenced the beeping," she whispers, and I can hear the pride in her tone. "Magic or someone with magic is on the other side. I'm sure of it." Bri's gadget only confirms my suspicions.

"There has to be another way," Jhamal says. "Blow it open!"

Steel beams run the length of the stone box around us. Blowing a hole in the wall wouldn't work. This place could come crumbling down on top of us. I have to go through this narrow opening, alone . . . and first.

"Bri, do you have any sort of tracker in that bag of yours?"

I hear quiet jumbling and she presses something cold into my hands. "It's sticky. Just toss it and it should stick on contact."

"When I come through, if things go . . . bad . . . track whoever is over there and root them out."

"Jelani, let me," Jhamal says.

"No, you come through last with Zora and the hostage. Bri behind me, with anything in that bag that might be of use in hand and ready, you understand?"

She nods.

I pull myself up into the crevice, my arms screeching as my cuff scratches the rock. I shove my upper body through first and the hole is more like a short tunnel. Whoever or whatever is on the other side knows I'm coming. If they didn't hear our whispers, they definitely hear the hammer in my chest.

I lug my body forward until I reach the end of the tunnel. Footsteps echo in the distance. I scurry to my feet and conjure a ball of energy, tightening my grip on the tracker. There's no one here. I close my eyes to open my ears, like Z said, but the footsteps are gone.

I scan the ground, careful where I put each foot. No marks or anything obvious. I walk a little farther and spot a glowing box. It's small and metal. I step closer and am warmed in a gust of heat radiating off it. I stuff the tracker away and squat, an odd sensation wrapping around me. Something isn't right.

I fire streams of magic at the box to see if it's armed. But it just glows brighter.

"Perdch yee'me." The destroy spell shoots from my fingertips and I brace for the shatter, but the box doesn't even crack. What kind of sorcery is this? My arms are boiling, but I lock my elbows and say the spell again, more forcefully this time. My magic, a string of light, fizzes between me and the curious box like a tether.

"Rue?" Bri's voice is muffled, and I tell myself to turn around, but the orange box captivates. I can't tear my eyes away.

"Go back," I say in my head, but my lips don't move. I'm drawn to it like a magnet. Everything is heavy and thick, and sounds are dull. I blink, but my body moves in a wave like I'm underwater.

Look away. My neck stiffens. I can't. *Look away!*

The light.

The box.

It's all I see.

Closer. I step or am pulled or something. Light crackles from my fingertips, streaming to its metal edge. I'm close, so close. Warmer than before. *Touch it.* I lick my lips in anticipation.

Take it.

Hold it.

Desire whispers to me and my fingers brush its lid and tingle. Words are a haze. A muffled voice behind me speaks.

A tickling sensation coats my hand and skitters up my arm. Sound reason breaks through the spell. *Move away, Rue!* My feet don't answer.

I'm fixated, stuck, frozen, when a gush of something washes over me. My wrists teeter from hot to cold, like my magic is short-circuiting. Everything's woozy and panic flutters through me, my knees feeling wobbly. I try to shout but my lips won't open, like I'm in a nightmare I'm desperately trying to wake from.

I try to tug my magic away, but it's leashed to the box, siphoning inside it in a funnel. My knees buckle completely. I hit the ground hard, pain shooting up my legs. I try to lift my arm, to scurry myself away, but everything is heavy, so heavy. I burn all over and spot the edge of my cuff peeling away from my skin.

This box is sucking the . . . life . . . no, the *magic* . . . out of me.

I summon whatever fragment of strength I find to pull away, but the box's power lies on me like a blanket of steel. Breathing is a fight. I dig. I can't die here. I can't, not like this. My parents, they . . . My throat tightens. What will happen to the rest of them? Everything I did for East Row, would the Chancellor retaliate, go wreak havoc there? I can't.

"*You've fought bigger battles before,*" a voice whispers to me, and I go cold all over, the hair on my neck standing. "*. . . And you won.*"

Something shifts. My cuffs surge with intense heat, the coldness completely gone. My magic . . . it's answering, overpowering . . . winning. I cling to that feeling and pull at any and everything I feel until the spell breaks. A shudder rolls through me, then a crack, like a mountain of pressure breaking through a dam.

I stumble backward as far away as I can from the magic-sucking box. Someone helps me up and I pant for my breath. Bri is beside me, her gadget suctioning a vortex of matter from the box. She taps the light on top and yanks. The swirl of matter shudders and a final gush of magic slips into Bri's device. She closes a door on it with a triumphant smile.

"Rue, are you okay?" she asks.

I steady myself on my feet and my fingers instinctively reach for the edge of my cuff that was peeling away. It lies flat, flush with my skin, and I sigh in relief. "I'm okay, I think. Something, someone . . . whispered to me. I—"

"Huh?"

"I don't know. But that thing wanted my magic!"

"It wanted more than your magic," Zora says. "But Bri was quick to recognize how it worked and her Ingostro thing was able to overpower it." They share a look. "Good work, Bri." Zora helps her get the gadget into her bag, and I glare at the spot I was just pinned to, trying to make sense of what just happened. I thought the fire arrows were trying to kill me back there . . . maybe they wanted to injure me, maim me, so I couldn't move. The box in the alleyway we deactivated before we saw what it could really do. But it had a homing device to notify them. Maybe—I gasp. The realization slaps.

"These traps aren't trying to kill me." The hole in the concrete so only one person could go through. The fact that no one is out here trying to challenge me one-on-one. I pull the hostage up on his feet. The fear of death is in his eyes.

"That's not his plan, is it?"

His lip trembles.

"Answer me! The Chancellor couldn't pry my magic out of me. So he's trying to provoke me to use it, so he can steal it? That's his plan?"

The hostage studies his feet, then nods.

Bri's mouth falls open. "Oh my! I-I need to take a closer look at what type of magic that was, but I have it all stored here." She presses her red frames to her nose. "I'm going to figure out how it works, and also where it came from. That was very powerful magic, and whoever made it will definitely need replenishing or they're done for."

"Replenishing?" I ask. "You mean their onyx stones won't work? Like they've used up all their magic?"

"Yep. The Chancellor does Replenishments every five or six

years. If you use all you have before then, you're just out of luck. But the magic the Chancellor deposits is so highly concentrated, it lasts forever. My parents are old, and they've only been replenished *once*."

I study my gilded arms. That's why so much power lives in these cuffs. They were an ancient relic that the Ancestors stored their power within. And then, when the Elders were forced to flee to Yiyo, they, too, added their power to it. These things are good for an eon at least.

"Someone clearly put all they had in that box, hoping it would drain me."

"There is probably a pretty bounty on your head for that kind of handiwork," Jhamal says.

"Yep," Bri says, snapping her bag closed. "And my guess is whoever made this box is *completely* weakened."

Weakened, meaning . . . they couldn't have gotten away easily.

"Could they still be here?"

"Likely," Bri says. "They'd probably be too weak to even walk for some time."

"Find them," I say, and Zora whips out her javelin, dashing out of sight. Jhamal and Bri stay with the hostage as I jet off, searching, shaking off the spook from earlier, when shoes squeak somewhere.

"I hear you!"

I catch a glimpse of spiked hair with red tips and shoot a stream of magic in that direction. But I miss.

"You're surrounded. You can't outrun us."

He pivots to run in another direction but comes face-to-face with the point of Zora's spear.

"Please!" He falls to his knees, hands behind his head. "Don't hurt me." The onyx on his wrist is depressed, sunken in. Bri was right, he's powerless. I pull him up by his collar and notice the *L* on his chest painted red. We drag him back to the group where the others are. He looks between us all and his gaze settles on the hostage, with a flicker of recognition.

"Grag, that you?" he says.

"He's a Loyalist," Zora spits.

"I . . . ," the hostage starts.

"Tell them, Grag, tell them I'm decent. Tell them not to hurt me. Please?"

"I'll ask the questions," I say. "You former Patrol or something?"

He says nothing.

"Jelani has addressed you, open your mouth and speak or I will open it for you," Jhamal says, and Zora presses her dagger tip under the man's chin.

"Use that tongue or lose it," she says.

"N-no, not Patrol. Dwegini. Grag, tell 'em."

But Grag just looks away. Bri pats down the Dwegini and pulls a key card out of his pocket. Much like the one Kai found on the Breakfast Lady to free us from our cell.

Phiz Cielo

Dwegini

Head Researcher

Magical Molecular Anatomy and Thermodynamics

"Carrying identification?" I say. "He's an amateur."

Tears stream down his cheeks. "I-I . . . the money. There's no work anymore. The labs are all closed. I j-just wanted the money. My family, I need . . ."

Zora hits him in the back of the head and his head bobs. "Tie him up. We should get out of here."

I nod in agreement, stream a coil of light from my fingertips, and rope it around his hands.

"Twixame," I say, pointing at his lips, and they snap closed. He wiggles them but they're glued shut.

"Bri, sedate him, give him a memory sweep, and let's go." I turn to the others. "We're leaving him here." *I have no use for him.*

Phiz's eyes grow as Bri pries his lips open and pours a honey-colored liquid down his throat. His expression dulls and he slow-blinks.

"He'll be drowsy for a bit, then he'll come out of it completely confused as to how he got here."

"It's for the best," Grag mutters.

"Excuse me?" I ask.

"I . . . just, he . . . it's good you didn't keep him as a hostage. He's very lower level, hardly knows anything. He'd probably be more of a liability."

I narrow my eyes at him. Is that a lie? And if not, why would he help us?

"We have to go," Jhamal says. I give Grag one more glance before we snake our way back toward the exit of this death trap of a building and follow the moonlight.

"You sure you're okay?" Zora asks me.

"I think so. I'd never felt anything like that before, my magic leaving my body . . . it was . . . I felt so weak."

Images of my cuffs being pulled away from my body sludge

through my memory. *I burn all over as they slice.* My breath quickens. *Long eyelashes in a lab coat's face is clearer this time. He smiles as he pries. I scream. Everything goes black. Something warm is pressed to my lips and I swallow. It burns my throat.* I gasp for air. *I'm cold all over like my blood, or my power, or something is draining out of me. Someone yells. My knees give way underneath me.*

My pulse races and Jhamal squeezes my hand. "You okay? Breathe."

Five . . . four . . . three . . . two . . . one.

"You're not in there anymore. You're here, with me. You hear me?" Jhamal squeezes my hand again and this time I squeeze back. "I-I'm okay. Th-thanks." I shake off the haunting memory and force out a breath.

Zora and Bri are immersed in a conversation as I slip the gold rings and bell Zora gave me out of my pocket. I hook the rings on my left ear and affix the bell in my hair, on the left side. I need all the power I can get. I cycle through the same thoughts over and over, assuring myself we're on the cusp of victory.

But a worry keeps needling at me: If the Chancellor wants me out here, getting caught in his traps to steal my magic . . . did I escape from prison or did he let me go?

CHAPTER FIFTEEN

TOTSI'S TINY BOOKSHOP IS just up ahead. It's a lone square building with stores on either side. Moonlight lights the road ahead. Only then do I realize Jhamal's injured. He wraps a shred of fabric around his limb and ties it with his teeth.

"Is it deep?"

"Just sliced it on that jagged rock we came through. It is fine," he says, but his next step is a limp.

Zora pulls Grag, who is also bleeding, closer. Bri dabs his wound with a paste and he winces.

"You're alright," Grag says matter-of-factly.

"What'd you say?" I couldn't have heard him correctly. Is he trying to play us? Play friendly? I'm not stupid.

"You, all of you, are alright. The Chancellor would have killed me by now if I was his hostage, but you made sure I got through that trap and now . . ." He gestures at Bri.

"Yeah, well. I still intend to know what you know. I'm not letting you go until you come up off it."

"The fact that you're thinking of letting me go at all says a lot about you."

"Aye, enough of this talking," Jhamal huffs. "Either cough up some information or sit down and be quiet." He leans into me. "His tongue flips in his mouth like a trickster. He wants to appeal to you. Flatter you."

"You think I'd fall for some shit like that, Mal?" I ask.

He purses his lips. "No, but still."

"You were saying?" I say to the hostage.

Bri finishes and stands. He rolls down his pant leg.

"Listen, my name's Grag. I used to know Phiz, the guy we left back there, but not in the way you think."

"You were both first in line to sign up to be one of his Loyalists is what it looks like to me," I say. Jhamal folds his arms.

"No." He points at the *L* carved into his head. "This is my protection."

I wrinkle my nose.

"What I mean is, Loyalists see this and without question no one checks my wrists. They assume I'm one of them, a former Patrol or someone in his camp. The Chancellor isn't recruiting Macazi. He hates us. This is part of my disguise to infiltrate *them* on the Macazis' behalf. I've been making the Loyalists think I'm one of them but feeding that intel to my people." He smirks. "We're not some band of vagrants. We are well organized. I've been studying how to fly under the radar my whole life."

"So why didn't you . . ."

"Say something? I didn't know you were trustworthy. We hear things, you know? With Loyalists, I've heard all sorts of things about you. How you're a plague on our island and it's the Chancellor's calling from the gods to root you out. How you're cruel and stupid. How your presence will put everyone at risk of a resurgence in the Sickness."

My mouth falls open.

"You'd be surprised at the stuff he feeds his following and they just eat it up. Either way, I wanted to size you up for myself."

I stand taller. "I see. Well, how do I know what you're saying is true, now? You're clearly good at getting others to trust you."

"Look, I don't want anything from you. Matter of fact, I knew that was a trap we were walking into. I was waiting for you to forget about me, a chance to get away. But you made a point to ensure I got through okay, and even told her to make sure of it. I'm coming clean so you know I don't wish you any harm. The Loyalists trust me. They drop traps and I arm them. Then I feed that information to my people so they know what places to avoid. I had to activate the trap in the alley, you see? They'd have gotten suspicious if they didn't see it activated on their end." He shoves his bangs out of his face, and I can better see the scar on his head. It's puckered and red, like hot iron seared it to his flesh. If that's not commitment to going undercover, I don't know what is.

"Look, I've got this whole area mapped. This is my section. I can show you where all the traps are if you have a map?"

Jhamal shifts on his feet. Zora and Bri both leer at me. *Uhhh.* Trust him?

"Well . . . ?" I ask the others. Everyone should have a say in this.

"I mean, I do have a map," Bri says, pulling out a folded sheet of paper.

"I guess it cannot hurt," Zora says.

"It's a consensus, then." Well, almost. Jhamal has said nothing.

"Look, one other thing. I know the big guy doesn't trust me. But you should know, they're planning a big strike to some underground lair in the eastern quadrant of the Web. Over by KoKo Beans Gift Shop."

Jhamal's and my eyes meet. That's near where our people are hiding.

"Eh," Jhamal butts in. "What sort of strike? Did they say when?"

"All I know is, they've found something or someone they've been looking for and the plan was to smoke it out. Get down there, see what's what. But then you escaped from prison, and, well, that's sort of taken over the priority for now."

They've discovered something? It's gotta be the place everyone went into hiding. That bit of news appears to warm Jhamal up some. He thanks him.

"Thanks for everything," I say to Grag. "You're free to go."

"What?" Grag asks.

"Look, if you're making the Chancellor's life harder, I'm not gonna stop you. Thank the Macazi when you see them."

"N-no way, really?" The creases around his eyes take years off his appearance. He reminds me of Tasha, caught in the crosshairs of a war that truly has nothing to do with him. "My mom has been worried sick, I'm sure. I give her her medicine every afternoon. It's our thing."

"Go to her. Show Bri the spots on the map. Then bounce. Maybe we'll link again under different circumstances."

He blinks for several moments before he's engrossed in the map with Bri.

"You didn't have to do that," Jhamal says.

"No, but I thought about what you said. If he is truly working undercover for the Macazi, maybe they'll learn they have nothing to fear from us." Allies won't hurt us in the fight ahead.

"And if he's not? If he's really the Chancellor's pawn."

My gut says it's not true, but I've weighed that eventuality as well. "Then everyone he knows will know I could have killed him but didn't. They will underestimate me, think me naive, weak. And perhaps not prepare as diligently as they could." I meet his stare and pride glints there. "But we will be ready."

His lips curl in a smile and I study them, remembering the way they felt on me. Could feel . . . if I . . . We're closer somehow and reckless thoughts zip through my mind, courage welling in me. I could kiss him. I could do it. But Zora joins us, and I put some distance between him and me. I don't want to be all hugged up in a PDA way. That's rude.

"This news of the Chancellor knowing where our people are is a problem," she says.

"We need to warn them," Jhamal says.

"Totsi's is right there," I say, pointing. "We can't turn back now. One of you should go back and warn them."

They nod in agreement, but neither makes a move.

"Zora," Jhamal says, "Kai is probably worried sick without you. It should be you."

"Nice try. I gave my word to Kai. My charge is to keep an eye on Jelani and this mission to ensure its success. It should be you. Shaun's a hothead. He could use you there to help simmer him."

"She's not wrong." I turn to Jhamal and our fingers snap to each other's like magnets. "In case Bati has had a time keeping everyone from each other's throats, perhaps it should be you?"

"Is this about that person you keep texting on your watch?"

"Jhamal, what? No." I hadn't even realized he was watching that hard. "Julius is checking on things back home for me. That's all. He's, like, one of my best friends."

"I will do this because you ask me. Not because I want to."

Zora, sensing it's a private moment, slinks off to observe the conversation with Bri and Grag.

"So that's it then?" Jhamal wraps his arms around me, and I'm reminded of the comfort he gave me in that cell. The comfort I'm about to lose.

"Every time we separate, someone else dies." His jaw clenches. "Do not let it be you." His thumb brushes my lips. He's not wrong. So much destruction. So much death.

"I will be back with a way to reach the Ancestors. I promise you."

"Don't promise me. Promise yourself. If I've learned anything from you, Jelani, it is that whatever you set your mind to do, whatever you promise yourself you will stand for, you do it." His lip trembles, but he forces out his words. Trying to appear strong in that way he does. "So, do not fail yourself. Do not worry about failing me or any of us." He brings my hand to his chest. "It is impossible for me to see you any more radiantly than I do."

I don't have words that would ease this ache. I get it, I do. But I see no other way. So I press my lips to his, hoping he feels everything I've wanted but struggled to say.

"Okay," I breathe, breaking the kiss. "Let's do this. Be together. I want to try."

His lips melt into mine and heat fills me. His hand travels to my waist and he grips me firmly, pulling me into him, like I'm oxygen and he's been starved of air. I come up for a breath, taking in all of him. Holding on to the sweetness of a moment that has nothing to do with war or destruction. Wishing life were less complicated and I could sit with him by the oceanside instead of in a cell. Sleep next to him under the stars instead of on a cave floor. Wishing I could be the love he deserves. I kiss him once more, tasting sweat on his lips, his stubbornness, strength. And I deepen the kiss, savoring everything that shines about him, everything that's a mirror of myself. We pull apart and his lips are swollen from my eagerness.

He cups my cheek. "Since we met, it feels like at every turn the world tries to take you from me." His hand falls from my face and he turns away. But I don't miss the way he swipes under his eye.

"Look at me." I make him face me, and the iron resolve that was just there has cracked. I see him now, the way I saw him working over my wounds in that cell, with such care in his touch. My Jhamal. Armored to the world, but inside, fluffy, delicate, and sweet. I smooth a thumb at the tear he tried to hide.

"I will not die," I say, hoping it's true.

He takes my hand and kisses my fingertips. "Then we have already won." He shoulders his weapon and tightens the bandage on his wound. He turns to go.

Part of me goes with him.

CHAPTER SIXTEEN

TOTSI'S SHOP'S DOORS ARE barricaded shut and blackened all over. Moonlight glints on the glass windows, webbed with cracks and charred as if someone took a blowtorch to them. Faraway voices ricochet off the abandoned buildings like bullets.

"What happened here?"

Grag shrugs, but his lips twist in curiosity. He offered to accompany us to Totsi's since he, too, was going that way. I'm still watching him closely with side-eyes, though the intel he gave so far seems legit.

Zora sets down on her knees, palms up, like she's been known to do. Her lips move a mile a minute, but her whispers are too low to hear. I look at Bri and she shrugs.

"We should have started this journey properly or stopped a long time ago," Zora says, hopping up. "Thankfully, the Ancestors are gracious."

Prayer? Is that what she's been doing?

She kicks her weapon up from the ground, catching it with her hand. She twirls it on her finger, and it thrums to a stop at Grag's throat. "I'm watching you."

He gulps.

"I swear, I've told it true."

"Then why do you linger? Why aren't you running to see your Memi or whoever it is you say misses you so bad?" Zora's suspicions stoke a fire in me. I've wondered the same, but if he is telling the truth, he has valuable information. We could use that if he trusts us. I cup her wrist and lean in for a whisper.

"I am skeptical too. But my grandmother used to say that you catch more flies with honey than you do with salt."

She nods in agreement and relaxes her weapon.

My wrist vibrates. Glass crunches under my feet and I push the door handle, but it doesn't budge. Blasting this door off its hinges with my magic would make too much noise.

"Bri, anything?" I ask.

She nods, moving toward the entrance. Zora's head is on the swivel.

"Give me a few." Bri rummages through her bag at the door, and I swipe up on my watch. Maybe it's news about Tasha?

Julius: T said she thinks she wants a dog. But her daddy 'nem ain't having it. And random—I was thinking about that time we rolled through Rickey D's for a milkshake during 3rd period and you just HAD to go inside and use the restroom. You remember?

I snort laughing, and Zora cuts a sharp glance at me. I hang over my watch arm, savoring the remnants of home, comfort, for the brief moment I can.

Me: OMG I'm still scarred! I told you we shouldn't have skipped that day.

Julius: How was I supposed know Ms. Thomas and Mr. White was dipping out during 3rd period too for they own lil "milkshake" sesh in the Rickey D's restroom.

Me: OMG STAHP! 🤮

Julius: I ain't had a Rickey D's milkshake since.

Bri grunts and something clicks. "Got it. Rue?"

"Coming!" I say.

Me: Same. Ruined it for me. Tell Tasha I might be able to sell Ms. Leola on a small dog. Gtg!

I hurry through the opened door and stop dead in my tracks. Totsi's bookshelves lie in piles, toppled over, the stuffing out of her couches is in heaps, and the door to the back room where I used to hang is ripped off its hinges. Books are ripped apart, scorched in mounds all over the floor.

"If you ever find you've nowhere else to go, you come here to these books and find yourself." Totsi's words from the last time I was here rattle through my memory.

"Uhhh," Bri says. "Rue?"

"Who would do this?" The words leave my lips in a whisper, more shock than secret.

Bri runs her gadget down the wall. "This place has remnants of a protection enchantment. Whoever did this likely tried but couldn't destroy this place. Not entirely."

"Protection? It doesn't look like it worked very well."

A red letter *L* is spray painted into the walls—or what's left of them. Across the room is Totsi's counter and her register sits untouched. Behind it, Bri is blinking, staring at the floor. I hurry over, past piles of burned books, and gasp.

"Oh, shit!"

A pool of sticky red something is on the floor and my insides hover in the back of my throat. Bri rakes her hands through her hair and Zora pops up beside us. She slicks up the red with two fingers and brings it to her nose.

"It is fresh. Someone was just here."

My anger boils and I turn to Grag. "You said this way was safe. Where is she?"

"I don't even know who—"

"Liar!" I point at the letter graffitied on the wall. "That's the Loyalists' mark, isn't it?"

"Y-yes, i-it is their symbol."

"She ran a *book*store! Why did they hurt her? Where is she?"

"I-I don't know. Sh-she must have been marked."

Zora's blade finds his throat.

"You're not talking enough. Explain."

"Th-there's a-a list. Th-the Chancellor h-has a list of who he'd like to see gotten rid of. I-I swear, everything I said is true. I'm not the enemy. The Chancellor drops a name, s-someone gets it."

"Someone who?"

"I-I don't know. One of the higher-ups. I-I'm not in *that* deep with their group. And besides, I stuck to traps. He keeps his inner circle tight. The person is then tracked down and either brought in or . . ." He gulps, his eyes falling to the blood staining the ground, and I remember the wailing in the prison and the floors of cells we didn't even have time to check in our haste to get out of there.

So much death. Sick to my stomach, I hug myself and pace in a circle, blowing out a slow breath. *Calm. And think.* What is the

Chancellor after? Besides my Ancestors' relics seared into my wrists. What else is he trying to do?

I spot Grag's eyes darting around the shop.

"No offense, but wait outside," I say.

He parts his lips to rebut, but Zora tightens her grip on her rod. He disappears through the glass doors.

Death is pungent in the air. They were looking for something or destroying something. Or both. But I can't puzzle out the Chancellor right now. Tears sting my eyes. She was so good to me. The only place I had that was safe. That I knew I could go. The last time I saw her she put a tem tem pastry in my hand and saved me from being snatched. I sigh, but the weight of the world still feels like it sits squarely on me.

I need to find this spell book. Every minute that ticks, he gets an edge to find us before we can raise the Ancestors from the dead. We need solutions and *soon*.

I search through the back room where I used to hide out and read, but it's a pile of overturned storage bins and stained walls. Nothing of use. I step over shreds of pages ripped from their spines, burned. So many ashes. I pick up a partially intact book and scan.

Pictures of fists clasped, wrapped in threads of blood, catch my eye.

Blood oaths, unbreakable, punishable by death.

What secrets are you trying to erase, Chancellor? I glimpse Grag outside the windows. He could have left but hasn't, because that would make him look guilty, I gather. And for whatever reason, he's determined to make us trust him.

Zora's hand is warm on mine.

"What else has he not told us, you think?" I ask.

"Mother Yakanna says identify the opponent's vulnerability and use it. Watch me." We meet him outside and she squats in front of him. He tries to shrink.

"Do you sleep alone?"

"Huh?"

"The bed at night when you are safe at home. Do you share it with anyone?"

"M-my sisters and I all bunk together because of space."

"Ah, and what side do you sleep on? By the door, protecting them as they sleep? Or like a coward on the inside, hoping they protect you?"

"I-I . . ."

"Let me ask you, who is there to protect them now?"

He stops breathing.

"Jelani is not your enemy unless you make her so. It is your choice. If there is *any*thing else you know . . . sharing it would be a show of good faith."

"Uh . . . uhm . . . ," he stumbles over his words. "Okay, so, the Loyalists, they meet in the Web. But not the Chancellor. He keeps a distance for plausible deniability, I guess. This bookstore was at the top of the hit list, a high-priority item . . . when the City started coming apart. But he didn't say why. So, a lot of guys took it on, hoping to get in good with him. This shop owner probably had twenty or more trying to get to her first, cash in the prize the Chancellor promised. That's all I know. I swear."

Zora winks at me. "Very good."

"Nicely done," I say. "I bet you regret not leaving when you could have."

He smiles nervously.

"Get out of here, Grag," I say. "Before I change my mind."

He stumbles up and backs away, bowing in thanks before booking it down the street. Back inside, Bri's lifted blood samples from the floor and is stuffing them in a vial in her bag.

"What are you . . . ," I start when a familiar locked closet door catches my eye. I rush over, remembering the costume trunks and prohibited books Totsi kept in there. The closet's wood panels are polished, untouched. I grip the knob on the door, and it burns.

"Shit."

Zora's at my back. "What is in there?"

"I don't know, but look around: It's the only thing in here not burned. No doubt they tried to." That must be what's enchanted for protection. I grip the handle again and whisper, "Quitzi." The door warms and my magic moves through me, my fingers tingling. Like . . . like it's searching me? Deciding if I should be let in? The lock jiggles, then clicks open.

Inside the closet is like a trip back in time; a tower of trunks etched with filigree in varying colors sit one on top of another. A hook with a ring of odd-shaped keys hangs on the inside wall. I pull the top trunk off and toss Bri the keys.

"Help me get these open."

Bri and Zora work as I pull the rest of the trunks out.

"Six . . . seven . . ." I lug another onto the floor, this one with a cluster of locks. Totsi's voice is a ghost in my memory. "They will pay for what they did to her," I say under my breath, tugging at the locks.

"Costumes in this one." Bri pulls out a neatly folded stack of black costumes covered in golden-tipped scales.

"Nothing in this one." Zora holds up a hollow trunk with blue swirls painted on its side.

But my eyes are fixed on the curious trunk with the bouquet of locks. I tug at one and insert a key from the giant ring. I twist left, then right, but it doesn't give. I try another. This one turns left, then clicks. But when the lock swings open, another lock appears on the cluster.

Huh?

I try another lock and successfully unlock it and several others. But as each opens another new lock appears. I work through the enchantment, opening them all, and each time one less reappears as the others eventually disappear. Until the only one left is a star-shaped one. I cup it in my hand, studying its odd opening. It doesn't have a keyhole. Instead, it has a glass square like a fingerprint scanner. I press my thumb to it and it warms. Then it vanishes, my hand closing around air.

A second later the entire chain and bouquet of locks dissolves into dust.

"Whatever's in here must've been extremely important to Totsi," Bri says.

And . . . something she wanted me to find.

The trunk creaks as I ease it open, and a cloud of dust scratches my throat. I fan the air and find a thin bone and two gold coins inside. *This can't be all that's in here.* I feel around the bottom, sure I missed something, but all that's in the trunk are the three small items.

"What is it?" Bri turns the bone in her hand. "Is it . . . human?"

"I mean, I don't know," I say, suddenly creeped out. "It's thin and light. I dissected a fetal pig in science once and the bones were really dense and thick. So, yes?"

"Bones are the currency of death," Zora says, bringing it to her nose. "It is not human."

I shudder and shove the coins and bone in my pocket. The last trunk in the closet is wedged in the farthest corner and a tug on its handle does nothing.

"Help me with this, will you?"

The three of us grab hold.

"One . . . two . . . three!" I rear back, gritting my teeth. The handle pops off, but the trunk doesn't move, as if it's welded to the floor. "See if you can get your hands under the bottom." My fingers search for a divot, an in to slide underneath, but the trunk is flush with the floor. "How is this? . . ." The lines of the trunk blend seamlessly with the ground. As if it's . . . wait . . . part of the floor?

"Back up," I say, standing. I lift the trunk top instead of pulling. "Quitzi."

The entire floor of the closet lifts like a lid, and a wrinkly-faced woman beneath it glares at me.

"Well, you're not Totsi," she shouts as something big and blunt dents my peripheral and smacks me in the face. The world goes black.

CHAPTER SEVENTEEN

I RUB THE THROBBING SPOT on my head. My watch is a ray in the darkness. The pillow under my head is soft, and I yank myself up.

"Bri? Zora?"

Silence answers and I blink, eyes adjusting to the darkness. The bed beneath me is musty and the spot next to me is cold. I press my feet to the stone floor and blink several times, and I can see a bit clearer. Stone walls, a tall ceiling, and the telltale smell of moldy earth. I'm underground.

My heart rams in my chest and I hop up, scanning. No bars, a bed, a glass of clear liquid on a small table. I ease out a breath, my panic a flame fighting for air. There's a door and no windows but for a tiny hole in the ceiling in the room.

"Bri? Zora?" I say louder, walking around the perimeter of the room. The floor is so chilly. My foot nudges something on the floor. I scoop up my Air Maxes and slip them on. They took my shoes off? Gave me a bed? I listen for something, some sign of where I am, when my wrist shakes again. I tap it with shaky fingers.

Julius: Aye, you up?

My pulse ticks slower as I read Julius's words over and over, clinging to the only thing rooted and sure in the world right now. At least I have signal in here. Underground, it's a toss-up.

Julius: You must be sleep. I told T you said she could have three dogs. Hit me when you get up.

Julius: Okay, I know you won't get this till later, but I was thinking about that time we drove down to Galveston to go to the beach, but it rained all day. We should go back there sometime. When it's sunny.

I remember. I close my eyes and let the memory of home still my thudding heart, slow the cadence of my breath. I clutch my wristwatch tightly.

Five . . . four . . . three . . . two . . . one.

Julius had, like, ten dollars to his name. He filled up the hooptie and we hit the road. Ran out of gas when we got there. We tried doing street flows for some change. Threw his snapback on the ground upside down and everything. I did the beat and he bust the flow. In. The. Rain. We got like two dollars from some eclectic tourists before calling it quits. I ended up begging Ms. Leola to drive down and give us some money without Moms knowing. Julius's mama was livid when she woke up to go to work and her car was just gone. Jue and I was always wildin', I swear.

Me: I don't know why you told her that lie. And yeah, I remember, you thought you could build a doper sandcastle than me.

The message sends with a swish, and I savor the moment of warmth it gives me. I check my pockets, my wrists. Everything's intact, but a spot on the side of my head throbs. Whoever has me down here clearly didn't want to hurt me. I rock back and forth, the memories of the cell floor scratch at my sanity. *I'm not in there. I'm not in there anymore.* My watch buzzes and I can breathe.

Julius: Morning, sunshine. 😏 And hell yeah. Used the last of my gas money to get down there and back and I ain't even get to show yo ass up like I wanted.

Me: You wasn't gon' win, no way. So womp womp.

Julius: LOL. You good tho?

I want to tell him yes. I clutch my watch tighter. And it soothes the part of me that wants to curl up with my phone and pretend the world is not falling apart, the part of me that wants to have a normal Saturday.

Voices outside the door snatch my attention. There are two people and their tones are strained, but it's too muffled to make out what they're saying. I scooch off the bed and press against the door, listening. I close my fingers around the knob and half expect it to hurt. I twist ever so slightly and, again, I'm shocked: It turns. I slip it open ever so slightly.

Peeping between the crack, I can tell the room outside mine is a little bigger—a sitting area with a couple of seats and a splintered table. Nothing fancy. My wrist shakes. But I'm fixated on a lady pacing and another woman, the wrinkly-faced one who hit me in the head.

"Well, she should be awake any moment and I guess we'll find out," the woman in charge says.

"As you say, then." The wrinkly old woman nods, before backing out the door.

I slip the door closed and feel for some sort of light. The wall is icy and cold shudders through me. Metal . . . the walls are made of metal? My fingers close around an orb on the wall with rocks inside. I point at it.

"Forenz'o."

Nothing happens. My heart skips a beat.

I clear my throat. "Forenz'o," I say a little louder, my voice shaking.

Still nothing. Black dents the edge of my vision, my time in prison whirring through me like a dark spirit threatening to suffocate me.

"F-fo—"

The door sweeps open and light floods the room.

"I thought I heard stirring." Her dark hair is short and slick across her gray complexion. "Good morning, Rue." She moves closer, her eyes falling to my gilded arms. She lights the bowls on the wall and her blue eyes glow orange in the lamplight. She's lean, her face chiseled and jaw firm beneath a very pointy nose.

I step backward, whispering to my magic to be ready . . . just in case . . . but the heat that slinks through me snuffs out in my hands. I gape at them. It's not working.

"It's the lead. The walls are lined with it." Her fingers graze the wall. "Magic will not work down here. Down here we are equals, you and me."

I glimpse her wrists, but they are bare of onyx. Where she would have been Bound is scarred with an *X*.

"You're Macazi?"

Her lips split in a smile, but her eyes do not change. "Welcome to our home. You slept well, yes?"

I rub the sore spot on my head. The Macazi are magicless, so she can't hurt me . . . magically, that is. The knot between my shoulders eases a little. "What do you want with me?"

"I have questions. At this point, there's no issue between us."

At *this* point?

She gestures for me to sit, but I don't. I have no reason to distrust the Macazi. But I have no reason to trust them either.

"I have questions too. Where are my friends?"

She sits on the edge of my bed, probably to make me feel more at ease. But everything in her tight tone and stern stare makes me clench my fists. I don't like this. She gestures again.

"I'm standing. Answer my question."

"Me, first." She crosses one leg over the other. "What happened to Totsi?"

Of course they know each other. The way that old woman looked at me—the shock on her face when she realized I wasn't whom she'd expected—told me Totsi was protecting these people.

"I had nothing to do with her . . ." I can't finish the sentence. Saying it aloud somehow makes it more real. Last time I saw Tot, she told me I'd always have a friend at her store. Was this what she meant? They don't seem friendly. Had she known someone would come for her?

She presses her lips tight and looks away. Her shoulders hang. I move to face her, but she turns her head even farther from me. This lady isn't trying to hurt me . . . at least I don't think she is. I swallow the lump in my throat that I'm almost sure is something mixed with pride.

"Look, I found the shop like that. Last time I saw Totsi, she was smiling and fine."

Her chin falls, and pressure to fill the silence needles at me.

"I've heard Loyalists are behind it," I go on. "That the Chancellor put a hit on her."

Her lip flinches and her fingers swipe away something from her cheek. "Thanks. And your friends are fine. Both are still asleep, I believe."

"I want to see them. Now."

"You will. I promise you, they're fine. Grag told me you all were . . . alright."

Grag. He didn't clue me in to the secret trapdoor in Totsi's shop. But he apparently vouched for us? Something about him doesn't add up. Or there's a chance I'm overthinking it.

I sit on the edge of the bed, far enough away in case she tries to pop off but close enough to see that she's not tense because she's angry. She's tense because she's sad. Maybe me and this lady just started off on the wrong foot.

"Totsi was a friend to me," I say.

She nods, wiping her face with her hands before hopping up. "She had the nicest things to say about you, too." She stuffs her hands in her back pockets and gazes toward the hole in the ceiling. "My sister was always the good judge of character."

I shift in my seat. Totsi had a sister? And she knows who I am?

When I visited her shop, she'd give me space and books and time. A place to just be. And in Ghizon, that's exactly what I needed. A spot away from the stares and whispers. She'd just sit with me sometimes, lay out a few treats. She always had these lemonberry ones I loved. Anything with berries, really. At first I ain't say shit to her but "thanks." I'd just eat and read. But the more often I visited, the more we'd talk.

But now that I think about it, she never told me anything about her. She gave me the space I needed, and I filled it with *me.* Why is it so easy to do that? To take what we need before seeing anyone else? Reason 284,027,401 I'd make a shitty Queen. I never even asked her about her family, where she came from, how she happened upon opening her shop there. And now it's too late to ask her anything.

"I-I'm sorry," I say, gesturing for her name.

"Taavi."

"Taavi." I offer a hand to shake. "Nice to meet you. I'm sorry for your loss."

"Thanks." She moves to the door. "If you'll just give me a minute to compose . . ."

"Take your time." I can't do shit like this anymore. I can't have people on the periphery of my life but not take the time to really see them. Even if I am going through shit. I reach for my watch and find a couple of messages I missed from Jue.

Julius: So that's a no, then.

Julius: Fam . . . wassup?

Me: I'm not alright, actually. But I'm trying to figure this shit out. Things good with you? I haven't asked. Sorry.

It buzzes immediately.

Julius: Rue, it's me. Talk to me.

The door creaks and Taavi reenters with bright eyes and some semblance of a smile. "Sorry about that. Yes, Loyalists have been a thorn in our side for some time now. We lost one of our own just the other day. They killed him for . . ."

"Desecrating a statue of the Chancellor. I know."

She parts her lips and sits down on the bed.

"We made sure he had a proper burial."

She presses a palm to her chest.

"Everything in the world is so messed up. I'm sorry you're losing family, friends. We're losing people too."

She gives my hand a squeeze, her gaze far off.

"But I'm trying to end it, once and for all. Get rid of the Chancellor and the stolen magic he wields."

Her eyes flick in my direction.

"That's why I was in Totsi's, actually."

She leans in, unblinking, as if what I'm 'bout to say is what she's been thirsting to hear for years. "Go on."

Something inside me wiggles with nerves. How much do I tell this lady? I don't know her, know her. Not like foreal. "I'm looking for a spell book."

"We don't do any sort of, uhm . . . traditional magic stuff here, so I'm afraid I'm no help with that. Totsi was the bookish one. I'd worked hard and entered my name for Binding, but I was designated Macazi." She sighs and it's heavy "And, well, the rest is a story for another day." She brushes a deep scar on her leg.

Her faraway look dissolves and her thin lips and tight stare are back. "Listen, I won't lie to you: Everything we do here is with our survival in mind. No one's concerned about our welfare. Dwegini spit when they see us, and Zruki are only moderately better. Trade is how we . . . acquire what we need here." She taps the wall and *tings* echo through the air. "We can't risk the wrong person discovering we are down here. These walls ensure that if we're invaded, magic can't be used as a weapon against us. But lately I worry it's not enough." She meets my eyes and I go cold all over. "With the world upside down, we've been forced to leave our lair more often. The more we leave, the more we risk exposure. I have heard of a veil of protection that lies over this island, making it undiscoverable. I'd like our home to be protected the same way." Her gaze falls to my wrists.

"What are you asking?"

She is quiet for several moments. She clasps her hands and turns. "Trade is a funny thing. When interests align with people you despise, you may find yourself at the same table."

"That sounds like a threat." I call to my magic out of stubborn habit and heat inside me rises, pulling through my arms and into my hands, but it comes out like a puff of air, fizzling out.

"Don't be hasty, Rue. I am not your enemy. But there is a hefty price on your head."

"They *killed* your sister. They *killed* your guy just the other day."

"And yet I still have thousands more to protect. Thousands no one else even cares about." A tangled web of emotion glistens in her eyes. "What would you have me do?"

"I can't give you my magic. I can't use it to protect you. No offense, I don't even know you. Depositing bits of my magic here ties me to you forever. Not only that, this magic I have is all our people have left. I can't just give it to some . . ."

"Macazi."

"No, it's not like that. I don't think less of you, trust me. This is ours. That's all. It's ours and it was given to me to protect."

"And use as you deem fit."

"Lady, I can't—"

The door clicks open. "Taavi?" The woman with the wrinkly face is back.

"Take some time, think on it." Taavi claps me on the back. "I'm sure you know what it's like to carry the weight of the world on your shoulders. I know you'll choose wisely."

The woman comes in, refusing to meet my eyes. "Sup is ready."

"Willa here will take you to eat. I'll see you after." Taavi waves and ducks out the door.

"Whenever you are ready, miss," the older woman says. "And no hard feelings for that welt on your head, I hope. I was just . . . Totsi only opens that door, you see. Then there's all the blood leaking through the ceiling overhead. I-I panicked."

I don't know what to say to her, so I gesture for her to lead the way. Following her out, I reach for the nostalgic piece of home I carry on my wrist.

Me: You ever feel like no matter what choice you make in life, somebody gets hurt?

I tap send but get an error message. The corridor we've slipped into is dark, firelight bobbing along the perimeter. No cuts in the rock, no light from the outside. I tap again, but nothing. I sigh and follow the hobbling woman down the craggy hall, deeper into this underground world of people who want me to betray my own or effectively slit my throat.

CHAPTER EIGHTEEN

THE FOOD THEY GIVE me is a pureed mash of something and a few pieces of lettuce. There's a hard bit of meat on my tray too, but I'm not touching it. The only reason I'm eating at all is because I'm starting to see double. The table I was given is in the corner of their version of a kostarum. Barbed wire lines thin, ground-level windows along the cavernous ceiling. You'd never know all this was underground without being down here.

Willa sits at one end of the table from me. I told her she could leave, that I remembered the way back to my room, but she just smiled.

I scoop another bite of the mush and swallow it in one lump, trying to avoid really tasting it. The room is packed with people snaking in line to get their food from a buffet-style setup where a lady with pink coiled hair scoops one lump after the other.

The way the line works around the room means every person has to pass by my corner and linger a second before stepping forward to get their tray. Was that intentional? Am I on display? I shove a few leaves in my mouth, and eyes stick to me like sweat. The cafeteria is so silent, I can hear ole dude a few tables away chewing. I don't know if it's my presence making it this quiet or this is just how they normally eat.

Everyone has the same scar over where their onyx should have gone. Several older ones look forlorn.

"Children . . . you need to . . . agh . . . get over here," a man with high-waters and full cheeks shouts. He skirts around my table, chasing kids, and cuts the corner a little too close, bumping into it. My watery mash spills onto my lap.

"Oh, sorry! I didn't see you there," he says to me, but his gaze is glued to my arms. "M-my apologies." He breaks his hypnotic stare in time to grab the collar of a kid darting by. "I should be going, then. Willa, good to see you and, erhm, you too, Maim."

I shove the tray aside. My stomach isn't churning anymore so that's good enough. Willa tosses me a towel and there's a basin of used trays across the room. I clean myself off and head over. Willa rises from the table too, like my shadow.

"I really can walk over there by myself."

She nods but doesn't sit. Something tells me she'll be following me regardless of what I say. Across the room there are whispers as I pass. So maybe it is me causing so much silence. I hop in line and someone taps my shoulder.

"Hi, there," he says. "You must not be from around here." He smiles like his teeth are too big for his mouth. His bushy eyebrows, brown unlike his turquoise hair, slant upward, and his expression is kind. "Joshi." He sticks out a hand and I eye it.

"Rue."

"You here to see the witch or something? We don't really get many magic types here."

"I'm sorry, what?" *Witch?* Taavi said they didn't have—how did she word it?—*traditional* magic here. . . . I shuffle on my feet. I took this lady at her word. She's hiding shit? I catch Willa eyeing me from afar. I wonder if I can squeeze some truth out of her.

"You said a witch?"

Joshi chuckles nervously, sensing my apparent confusion, wiping his brow. "I mean, er-uhm . . . uh . . . the uhm . . ." He reaches for words in the air, talking with his hands. "Th-the cleanup, yes, the clean station is here, and then if you want to wash your hands, there's a station over there. Let the spigot run a minute if you can. Gets the nasty gunk out of the water. It'll come out orange, brown, sometimes green." He titters. "But a minute will do it good, and it should run nice and clear. Just a little trick I picked up."

"Uhm. Okay, thanks." I have half a mind to ask him again about the witch comment, but he's sweating bullets like he shouldn't have said anything, so I let it go.

"No problem." He plants his hands on his hips. His fidgeting settles and his smile grows. "Anything you need, you just let me know, or Stain. . . ." He points to a dude with wide ears and sprigs for hair. This dude is friendly as hell. Talking to me all normal, like I'm not the weird oddball with gold arms, or worse, an enemy with magic.

"We're the Orientators around here," he says, his eyes glinting with pride.

Okay, so he's always friendly like this. It's odd to be actually welcomed so warmly. I gaze around, and now that I'm really looking, the stares are more curious than judgy. Behind the whispers even are mostly smiles.

"Stain," he shouts. "New girl," Joshi shouts, pointing at me as if it's not obvious. Stain waves, as bubbly as Joshi, and I toss him a chin up.

"Well, thanks for the help," I say, stepping up to the basin. I set my tray and utensil inside, then turn and come face-to-face with Willa.

"Back to the room, then?" she asks. But I don't think it's an actual question. Over my shoulder, Joshi's waving, and I chuck him deuces. Behind him is a familiar face with a beanie on his head. Grag. His collar is pulled up and his hands are shoved in his pockets. We lock eyes and he waves. He jostles around with a few folks but keeps to himself mainly. He eats alone, then slinks back out the door he came through.

I still don't know what to make of him. Whether he's infiltrating the enemy and reporting back here or the other way around. I want to believe him. But is that because his story was actually believable or because I let him go? Lying to myself serves no one. Keeping my eyes on him.

The rest of the Macazi buzz around, tidying and organizing. A whole world in motion. With the food line so long, Willa leads me around the perimeter to depart. Some of those we pass sharpen blades, fashioning metal to sticks, forging armor out of dried hide and thin sheets of lead. We pass an assembly line of people working on a giant boulder, hollowing it out with sharp tools. A man with sun-scorched Gray skin sets a stack of first-aid supplies inside the rock's hollowed center before handing it to a crew on his right. The crew bolts the bottom with planks of wood and they set it beside a stack of twenty or more others before grabbing another. The rocks would blend right in with landscaping. No one would know there's first-aid supplies inside. Smart.

I guess that's how they help whoever they're sending out there to fight against the Chancellor, people like Grag. Their operation is well organized. The toppled statues, burned buildings, the evidence that someone is giving the Chancellor a run for his money, is all here. I'd suspected it was them, but to see how intricately organized and prepared they are up close is something else.

Taavi's got a job on her hands down here. They're an entire world living under the Chancellor's nose. He killed Totsi. If he knew the Macazi were down here, even minding their own business, no doubt he'd kill them, too.

Willa moves faster down the dank corridor than I'd think even possible on her frail legs, and I hustle to catch up. The walk is short from my room to the kostarum. I crane for some semblance of how to get out of here, but the pathway just curves up ahead with no sign or indication where it leads. I wonder if Bri and Zora are down that way.

"Excuse me, can you tell me where my friends are?" I ask.

"No, dear. Just eat and back is what I was told."

Taavi had said Bri and Zora are fine. It seemed so sincere, I believed her. But she didn't mention a witch, so should I?

"I need to know where they are. Now."

The gentleness in her eyes flickers with knowing. She reaches for a pocket in her shift. I don't have to see her hand to know it's curving around metal. This woman isn't going to be taken advantage of. None of the Macazi are.

"Keep walking, dear," she says, and it's more of an order than a request.

Desperation pulls at me. For losing our footing, being pulled underground, taken off our mission. Getting trapped. *Again.* My friends being captured. A vein pulses at my jaw and the woman swallows. I could hurt this woman. Get what I want. Armed or not, I'm stronger.

My mind flickers to the Chancellor's face. The way he belittles, bleeds, and corrupts, the way he let the General play his games in East Row.

That's not who I am.

And no moment of vulnerability is going to turn me into something I'm not. That's the difference between me and the Chancellor.

The woman studies my eyes, and her chest heaves harder. A tip of metal glints from her hand as she slowly pulls a blade out of her dress. This isn't the way. Not my way.

I keep walking down the hall. "I'm just worried about them, that's all."

"I understand." Her voice cracks with relief.

My door comes into view. "Okay, well, can you at least tell me if y'all got a witch here?"

Willa stops dead in her tracks but doesn't turn around. "I-I don't know anything about that, I'm afraid, dear. Taavi can answer your questions."

She closes me in my room and locks it from the outside. I pace, triggered.

I'm not in prison. She isn't the Chancellor.

They fed me, let me sleep.

This is different.

This is . . .

I tug at my hair, forcing myself to breathe.

Five . . . four . . . three . . . two . . . one.

Taavi *is* hard to read. Could she be playing me? She doesn't know me, but her sister did, and *well.* That alone makes me want to believe Taavi's cool. But why would she lie if there's some sort of magic here? And if there is, why is it a secret?

Messages vibrate my arm, one after another, as I move closer to the hole in my ceiling. I plop on the bed and exhale.

Julius: Aight, so I remember that time your Moms was at work and you had me come over but wouldn't tell me why.

Reading "Moms" stills me.

Julius: And I took forever to get there bc I was being a dumbass. Sorry for that.

Julius: Anyway, I was holding you and when you finally fell asleep, you said something I never told you.

I remember that night. Tasha had stayed with friends, and I kept hearing noises or something in the attic.

Julius: While you was dreaming, you said you was scared to fall asleep. And you thanked me for being there. Next day you ain't remember saying shit.

Julius: I guess my point is, you ain't good at talking about shit, Rue, I know that. You keep a lot bottled up, but you don't have to do that with me. Pretend you're dreaming LOL. Tell me wassup.

The way Julius rips the veil off my mirror makes me shift in my seat.

Julius: Hellllooooo.

There's no hiding with him. He's seen too much of me. He was there when Moms got sick that one time. He stayed at the house the whole time she was at the hospital. We were broken up then, but when he got word, he came over with takeout and no questions.

He didn't leave my couch until Moms came home. When Tasha ran away, it was me and him scouring the neighborhood to find her until the cops located her the next morning. And when Moms was shot, Julius sat outside on my stoop for three days. Ms. Leola said he refused to leave. She couldn't tell him my daddy had taken me and I might not come back. So he just sat there.

Julius is family. He is East Row. He's the homie, my friend . . . the first and only person to ever love me in *that* sort of way. He's a part of me, and no matter how protected I try to keep him, he's riding with me regardless of what I say.

He knows me better than anyone. I need to see him. Really *see* him. And let him back in.

Me: Hey, I lost service.

My finger hovers over the watch. How much do I say? I chew my lip. *This is Jue.* I pull the watch off my arm and let my thumbs just go.

Me: Everything here is so messed up.

Me: I got locked up. My people broke me out. But then they started fighting each other. Like really fighting, Jue. Can you imagine East and West Row down each other's throat? Like, we family, you know?

Me: Their solution was to pick a leader and someone threw my name in the hat.

Me: Wild, right? That's soooo not my lane, you feel me? So I just left. I really need to find this spell to reach our Ancestors. My people need their magic back, Jue. So we can fight off these assholes here that took everything from us.

I wait. It's not like Julius to take a breath before texting me back.

Three dots show up on the screen then disappear. I laid it all out, now he's quiet? This shit got a delete button? Three dots again.

"*Ugh.*" I get up and pace. I hate that he knows I'm squirming now. I hate that he knows . . . I don't have shit figured out. I hate . . .

My wrist vibrates.

Julius: First off, do you get a crown? Because that shit would be dooope.

I snort. He always jokes.

Julius: Second, where yo people at, Rue? Like, who you got in your corner? Where's your Row out there?

Me: Bri's with me.

Hmmm.

Me: It's some others. But it's just not the same. I'm still getting to know everyone and everything. Reason 5189 I shouldn't be a Queen.

Julius: Look, you gotta be true to you. As much as you in a crown sounds sexy as shit.

I roll my eyes and keep reading.

Julius: You need to stay true to who you are. Your heart is pure gold. It won't lead you wrong. Trust yourself, Rue. If you trust no one else, trust you.

Rue: You have wayyyy too much faith in me.

Delete. Delete. Delete.

Rue: Okay.

The door clicks open and Taavi's there, arms folded. I snap my watch back on my arm and shake off thoughts of anything else but my goal: getting out of here with what I came for. Taavi knows more than she's letting on, and she's going to help me.

"You lied to me," I say.

"I don't know what you mean." She pulls at her ear.

"You alluded to the fact that you don't have magic here."

She flinches. "We don't. We are Macazi."

"But that's not entirely true. A half-truth is still a lie, Taavi. I need a spell and I hear you have a witch here."

"She is *not* a witch." Her jaw clenches.

"So, there is some magic here?"

She says nothing, but her nostrils flare. What is she hiding?

"You're going to take me to your witch, and if she helps me get a spell to reach my Ancestors, I'll bind a protection spell to this place."

"I . . ."

"I'm not done. One more stipulation. If remnants of my magic are going to be left here, you will be committing the Macazi to fight in the coming war on our side against the Chancellor."

Her mouth falls open, fear flickering in her eyes. "W-we are not fighters, Rue."

"And I am not your genie. This is an exchange of services because, frankly, you've lied to me once and I can't be sure you won't lie again."

"We don't have magic, how would we . . ."

"There will be graves to be dug, armor prepared, wounds stitched, potions mixed, there will be plenty for your people to do. Put bodies on the line, then I know you'll shake out on my side of things. We win, your people survive."

"You have no idea what you're asking."

That may be true, but she hasn't said this witch or whoever *can't* get me the spell I need, which means she probably can. And that's not an opportunity I can afford to lose right now.

"They won't like this. I promised them safety."

"And you promised me you didn't wish me ill, and yet you're ready to turn me over to Loyalists if I don't deposit bits of my magic here. You do realize me being out here preparing to fight them might be the only thing keeping y'all alive? Do you see that? Some temporary barter with them still kills you in the end."

It's a bluff. I don't know the Chancellor's intentions with them, but from where I'm standing right now, Taavi is my opponent and her fear is her vulnerability, flames I want to stoke.

A tear streams down her cheek. "Hasn't my family been through enough?" she mutters under her breath.

"Agree, Taavi. You have no better option."

Silence hangs there, and a part of me twists with guilt. I know what is to feel like the world is depending on you. Like you hold it up with your own two hands, and if you so much as take a breath wrong, the entire thing will come crashing down. But I glue my lips shut. If things go my way, they'll be safe in the long run.

"Fine." Her glare turns to steel. "I hope you know what you're doing."

"Take me to her then. The witch."

"Don't call her that to her face. She's not a witch. She's a Seer, and she only takes payment in gold and blood."

CHAPTER NINETEEN

TAAVI CARRIES AN ORB in her hand and leads me down jagged stairs deeper into their lair. We are surrounded by lead walls, dotted with glowing glass balls, flames dancing within them. Her face glows orange in the light, and from time to time her eyes dart at my arms.

We shuffle down steep steps, and I squint for the next place to put my foot. I lean into the wall, trying to get better footing, but it's slippery, so it doesn't help. The sounds of the Macazi are a faint whisper in the distance. There's no one down here, no one but the Seer.

My heart thuds in my chest, but the jingle of Taavi's keys drown out the sound. A Seer that people refer to as a witch? I'd only known Seers to be myths, legend. In Totsi's shop, there were stories of such, but I never assumed they were real. I slick the sweat from my brow as the stairs curve in a spiral.

"Watch your step here. There's a loose one."

I step over the wiggly landing. The stairwell ends at a door bolted with metal bars across it, chains, and a cluster of locks.

"Hold this," she says, handing me the orb.

I take it, watching carefully as she fumbles through her keys.

She passes the same ones several times, her hands jittery. I swallow. What am I walking into?

She stops on the right key and takes a deep breath before putting it in the first of several keyholes. "When she is finished . . . you can just bang on the door."

"You're not coming in with me?" I tap my watch, but it's barely distinguishable in the darkness.

"No." She says something else under her breath, but I can't make it out. The next several moments are her sticking keys in all sorts of locks. She turns a dial on one, then twists a lever on another. She shoves odd-shaped keys into a variety of lock holes, and once each clicks, she pulls hard on the door handle.

"Help me with this, will you?" I pull back with her, and the lead door creaks as it opens, revealing another door behind it. This one wooden. My fingers graze the door and heat tingles my fingers. Someone groans behind it.

"She knows we're here. Are you ready?"

I nod.

"Good, because my mother hates waiting." She pushes open the door and shoves me hard into the chilled darkness. I tumble forward inside.

"Your mother?" I turn, but the door slams shut and with it light disappears. I hug around myself and I feel whispers of my magic. It hums in my skin. The walls aren't made of lead in here. That's why they keep two layers of doors and so many locks between the Seer and them, I guess. Magic tickles my insides, moving through me, unsettled and restless. But I don't move. Something pins me in place. I don't know if it's some sort of dark magic . . . or fear.

"Come closer," a voice drips in the darkness. It echoes as if it's coming from the walls themselves.

I peer around but only see black. "Who's there? Sh-show yourself," I say, conjuring a ball of fire.

Her words crawl all over me, resounding in my head. "I can smell the fear on you like musk. Come closer."

I don't know if it's the lull in her voice, the ominous way it booms over me, or some type of magic luring me, but when I tell my feet to stay still, they betray me and take a step. "Where are you? Show your face at least."

Blue flames erupt up ahead, blossoming upward, splitting the darkness. The heat draws me closer. "I still can't see you."

"Because you're not truly looking."

Zora's advice slinks through my memory, and I close my eyes.

"Closeeerrr," she breathes, and I realize it's coming from above me. I step closer to the flames to better see the rocky walls glowing an eerie green. I scan the ceiling. Drizzles of stringy white hair are dangling above the fire and I follow them to a face, sharp and sunken, skin hanging off the bone. The woman lies on a bed of stone hovering magically above the flame.

She sniffs the air. "There is a cost to my company. Make a request and pay me. Or I feed you to the flames." She cackles and her laugh ricochets. Then she folds over the edge, peering at me again. "A child?" His brows twist. "Come closer so I can see you."

"I—"

She curls a finger at me and the square of floor beneath my feet buckles, detaching from the ground and rising in the air. Up it climbs with me on top until I'm above the flames on her level. The platform beneath me halts. Blue flames swarm beneath us, licking the bottom of her stone bed, its edges so jagged, she couldn't get off there if she wanted to without grave injury to herself.

Our eyes meet, and for a moment she looks as shocked as I am. She stares at my arms.

"Jelani?"

She knows my name. I scoot away from her as much as I can on my island of stone. How does she know my name?

She pulls herself up to a sitting position. Stringy hair is a curtain around her face and a nest in her lap. I squint in the darkness and make out thin lips, a nose that is the same as Taavi's, pointy. Her watery eyes are swallowed by a million creases.

"Y-you were Totsi's mother," I say, the words spilling out before I can hold them in.

She convulses, a wail ripping from her throat in a cry of pain as a single tear runs down her cheek. "Do not speak her name," she says, her fingernails digging into the stone. She shudders in pain and flicks away the tear.

It hurts her?

Crying . . . feeling . . . remembering hurts her?

What an awful way to live. What sort of cursed existence is this? Empathy wells up in me, but I don't know this woman. Perhaps she's more sinister than she's letting on? Why else would Taavi keep her locked away here like this? Pity mixes with my fear; I sit to be eye level with her.

The Seer rolls her neck; her pallid flesh is slick with sweat. The thin shift she's wearing is tearing at the seams. Questions about her daughter, about how she got this way, about why she's kept locked up like this, sit on my lips, but I swallow them.

She studies me with a narrowed expression. "Make your request, Jelani." Her words are raspy.

I snuff out the fireball in my hand and clear my throat. "I need to know if there's a way for me to talk to my Ancestors."

Between her curtain of hair, I faintly make out a few broken teeth as her lips split in the faintest hint of a smile. It doesn't seem to cause her any pain, which is a relief.

She reaches across the thin void between us and sets a cold, bony hand on my forehead. The world goes black. I am heavy. All over. I try to inhale but can't. *What in the . . .*

"Ssssh." She presses harder, holding her hand there for a moment like she's checking my temperature. But my head feels like it might explode. Then her fingers break contact and I gasp as she comes back in focus.

"Your intentions are as pure as your heart." Her pupils are tiny dots and she stares at me, but somehow *in*to me. "But death does not flinch at the tenderhearted, Jelani. Death does not flinch ever. When it comes time, you must not flinch either."

Huh? "I . . . okay . . . so, is there a spell I use? Or?"

"Yes, yes, there are words that you can mutter to pierce the grave." She opens her palm, licking her lips.

Gold and blood.

"Uhhh." I gulp, patting my pockets, and find a lump. I pull out the bone and one of the two gold coins.

The Seer's eyes smile. "Yes, yes, that'll do."

Sickness swirls in my insides. Taavi had no idea I had a way to pay this woman. She had no idea I'd make it out of here alive, and locked me in. But Totsi, her sister, must have known I'd come for answers. She had to have left that bone and gold for me to find. She had to have wanted me to ask her mother questions and get answers. It's the only thing that makes sense.

I hand the bone and a single coin over. She bites the coin before tucking it in her bosom and drops the bone to the hungry flames below. They gush, crackling in response, the room glowing brighter.

Her eyes roll around in their sockets and her lips part. "A drizzle of jpango sap." She speaks in short breaths, as if each syllable pains her. "A loc of hair from an Elder . . . a-and . . ." She grunts. "A loc of hair from an enemy." She shudders. "Take them to your Ancestors' grave when the moon is high *and* the skies are heavy with sorrow. Chant 'u'shaka wesee' three times with your hands dug into the dirt where their spirit lives. They will come."

An Elder? But the Elders are all dead. And my enemy? The Chancellor? How will I ever . . . Cold sweat beads down my neck. "A-and what if it doesn't work? Wh-what if I can't do it the way you said. I—" I'd wished the answer would be simpler. "The Ancestors have to fix this, you understand? I need something that feels doable. How am I supposed to . . ."

"Mmph," she grunts, trying to push something out. "There is coming a—" Her lips snap shut.

"A what?" I lean so close, I can smell her rancid breath. "Tell me! There is coming a what?"

She holds out her hand, but all I have left is one coin. No bone, no blood.

Unless . . .

I suck in a breath. *Here goes nothing.* I bite down and rub my palm hard on the rugged edge of her stone bed. It burns. Blood puckers out the puncture on my hand and the Seer tilts her head in satisfaction, pointing to the fire. I hold my hand over the edge of the stone platform, and blood drips into the blue flame beneath. I hand her my last coin and she smiles.

"There is coming a what?" I ask.

"There is a coming a great betrayal, child."

Her words pierce like a dagger and I gasp.

"Trust is a dangerous thing," she goes on. "Someone you trust has already betrayed you. But they are only the first."

My throat tightens. "Who?" I squeeze out. "Tell me who!"

She holds out her hand.

"I have nothing else. No more gold. Only blood." The rings in my hair are tiny, nowhere near the amount of gold as the coin. And even if it were enough, giving her those feels . . . wrong.

"Well, then. I have given you what you've paid for." She eases herself back down on her stone pillow, gritting her teeth as if it hurts her. "Leave me now. I must rest."

As I turn my back on her, fingers as cold as death wrap around my arm. "Understand me," she whispers, her gaze racy. I try to pull away, but her grip is ironclad. "They *will* betray you, Jelani." She shoves each word out like it's a fight. "And you will not see it coming."

My platform begins its descent, and her death grip slips from my arm, but her eyes burn into me. My bones throb all over like I'm being pierced with a thousand needles.

"At least tell me who has already betrayed me!" I shout again, but the fire is out and it's so dark, I can't see my hand in front of my face. My platform eases into place in the ground with a shudder, and I barrel toward the door. I bang on it with my fists and Taavi pulls it open.

"Did you get what you need?" she asks.

I ignite a flame on my fingertip and hold it to her throat. "Get me out of here."

CHAPTER TWENTY

TRUST NO ONE.

It's not a foreign concept, but I'd be lying if the Seer's words didn't shake me. I'm careful about who I let in my bubble. It took Jhamal months in that cell to get me to open up about what happened to Moms and Tash. And he's never done anything to me. Once people wriggle their way in, something shifts, and it's impossible to get rid of them. So I keep the list short.

The fire at Taavi's throat snuffs out the minute we step into the lead-lined hall, and she quickly leads me back up the stairs without a word. I play the Seer's face over in my head. Something about her living there locked away doesn't sit right with me. She's the only one with magic here. She's different, powerful, but she's kept away from everything and everyone like a prisoner.

I flick side-eyes at Taavi, noting the way she walks. Her back is straight, chin up, and her hands don't shake. Whatever she was worried about is a thing of the past, done. But I don't care how chill and compliant she seems right now; it's not lost on me that she put me in there not knowing whether I'd be able to make it out.

"Why didn't you tell me the Seer was your mother?"

"And have you look at me the way you're looking at me now? No, thanks."

"You put me in there without knowing if I could pay her. She could have killed me."

She stops at the top of the stairs. "First, I know my sister. If you are half the person she said you were, your magic could overpower my mother's. And second, if Totsi sent you, I knew she'd prepare you."

"So just lucky me I stumbled upon the bone and gold coins. You're not making the best case for me trusting you."

She stops walking. "I told you from the beginning, everything we do here is with our survival in mind. If you were who you claimed to be, who Totsi believed you to be, I knew you'd make it out of there. And if you weren't . . ." She walks again and I follow.

I don't like it.

But I can't help but respect it.

The hall is a cloud of chatter as Macazi stuff blankets and food rations in backpacks with wide-eyed stares. Some have blades made from broken wood and sharp metal tucked into their pant legs.

"I've had them grab things to make camp," Taavi says over her shoulder. "We'll feed and water ourselves. And we have things to sleep on."

"Wait, *we?*"

She stops and turns to me. "I'm not letting you take the bulk of our strongest people without me. I'm sorry, I just don't trust that easily."

Meeting her eyes is like staring into a distorted mirror.

"I feel that," I say. "Neither do I."

We keep moving down the hall, and I spot Joshi filling a carton for a young girl who can't be any older than Tasha. Her head's shaved and she wears a hard expression that's resolute as much as it is riddled with angst.

"I'll see you up there," he says.

I paint on a smile and give Joshi a chin up.

"Many of the younger ones were born here," Taavi says. "They've never even seen the Outside. The older ones though, they remember."

The guilt wedged inside sprouts roots. Taavi couldn't have been more right: Most of these people aren't combat fighters. Their magic is trickery, cunning, wit. We need the extra hands, but I can't send these folks to slaughter. If they're in my charge, I can't let anything happen to them. They have good reason to hate the Chancellor too. We are on the same team even if I did have to use intimidation to get them on our side. But they *will* come out of this alive. I'll make sure of it.

"The ones we leave here will truly need your magic," she says. I don't like hearing her talk about my magic. But this is where we are.

"I gave you my word and I'ma keep it," I say.

Why is she even bringing that up? She doubting I'm going to do what I said? We traipse down the hall past the room I slept in and up through Totsi's closet. Zora and Bri are sitting back-to-back on the floor, Bri's nose is in a book, and Zora is running the tip of her blade against a stone.

"Rue! You're okay." Bri hops up and throws her arms around me.

Zora lets out a huge breath in relief. "So good to see you, Jelani." She clamps a hand on my shoulder, tugging up on her gloves as they slip down.

"But Bri kept reminding me that you could handle yourself. And that I shouldn't worry. You would make—"

"A way," I say. "Yes."

Bri is beaming, and the Seer's words prick me, slinking through my head like a snake.

Could it be Bri who is gonna betray me? Could it be her who already has?

"I'll call for everyone to come up," Taavi says, and I nod, despite Zora's and Bri's wrinkled expressions. Taavi takes off, and I catch them up on everything that happened while below: the Macazi I met, how frail they are as a people, the Seer giving me the spell, and my agreement with Taavi to deposit a bit of magic here for their protection in exchange for their allyship.

I leave out the Seer's warning of betrayal.

That, I'm not telling anyone.

Bri's brow dents deeper the longer I talk, and Zora's nostrils are flaring. They aren't happy with this plan, and I know why. I get it, but this is the only way.

"Go ahead." I gesture at Bri. "I can hear your brain going a thousand miles per hour. I'm listening."

"Rue, I mean, I'm an outsider here, so feel free to toss my opinion out the window, seriously. But . . ." She leans in, whispering. "The *Macazi*? They've got nothing. They have nothing to lose. I can't even imagine what sort of pent-up anger they have. . . ."

"Toward the *Chancellor*. The enemy of my enemy, Bri, is my friend. We have no reason to not like them. What have they done to anyone?"

"Well, I remember once, my dad had come home from the mines, and he'd saved up just enough coin to grab some dongyas from the sweetshop. He paid the vendor, got his order, turned his back, and it was *gone*. Just gone! Some Maca had snuck up and stolen it right under his nose. Dad saw them getting away, but there was nothing he could do at that point. They're fast runners, apparently. Like, who does that?!"

"People who are hungry."

She sighs, exasperated. "I'm just saying we have no reason *to* trust them, either. They live in alleyways and in shadows, stealing to . . ."

"*Feed* themselves."

She sighs again, this time pinching the bridge of her nose. "The Macazi aren't magical. How can they even help?"

"Bri?"

"Yes?"

"You're doing that thing again."

"What?"

"Where you sound really privileged and selfish."

She opens her mouth, then closes it. Only to open and close it again.

"Maybe marinate on that for a bit?"

She turns pink and nods.

I turn to Zora, burying my annoyance with how quickly Bri can pop off and show me no matter how tight we are, there's still dissonance. It's like she can only "get it" *so* much. Because at the end of the day, she's Zruki. She was given magic, raised in a world where she was not at the tip-top of society, but still valued, trusted. Told she mattered.

The Macazi don't have that. They were literally told and shown the opposite. Their people are carted off to community housing, tests are run on them from what I heard. That has to garner some empathy. That has to at least crack the walls of how she sees the world.

And what about my people, the Ghizoni? We got even less than the Macazi. We got nothing. Not life. Not freedom. Not a choice. None of that. Does she only ride with me on getting the Ghizoni magic back because I explained it to her? That's not gon' work. She has to fully reshape those glasses sitting on her nose. She has to get it *herself*.

She's sitting in the corner with a book, her cheeks the color of a beet. I go over and squeeze her shoulder just so she knows we're good. She tugs her lips sideways in an embarrassed smile.

"I realize her coming around is a process, but damn, being her only Ghizoni friend is exhausting at times," I say under my breath to Zora, stepping out of Bri's earshot.

She smirks. "A wise person once told me to give it time. She grows on you."

"Oh, ha ha. Is that right?"

"Taavi put us up in the same room so I was forced to get to know her better. She does take a bit of getting used to, but I can see why she is a friend."

"Well, good. So, tell me your thoughts," I say. "I want to hear what you think."

"I mean, I am no ruler or anything. . . ."

"No, of course. Neither am I. We just have to do the best we can with what we have in that moment. I have the spell now and I gave her my word."

"Well, I am thinking that it is perhaps a risk. We have no

guarantee she will keep her word. We do not know where her loyalties lie."

Trust no one.

"She wants to protect her people, I believe that."

"Yes, but the seed of good intentions can still sprout a poisonous bloom."

"But, it seems . . ."

"Things are often not what they seem, Jelani. I mean that with the most respect."

She isn't wrong. And I like that she tells me the truth, fully. Boldly. That's the kind of people I like to ride with. I glimpse a pile of scorched book covers and the wheels start turning.

"What if we make her seal it with a blood oath? That'll make sure she keeps her word."

"Graka eyo," she says, folding her gloved arms around herself. "I like it. Punishable by death. Requires two people and a witness. Clever, Jelani."

"Bet." As much as I understand Taavi's plight, I don't completely trust her. "Do you know the spell?" I ask.

"I-I do . . ." Bri's tone is tentative and Zora and I turn her way. "I'm sorry," she says. "I'm realizing most of anything I've heard about the Macazi has always been what my family's told me, and how our world deals with them. But when I sat there and thought about everything that's happened while they kept Zora and me here, they were the kindest people. They have very little and yet they fed us, let us bathe. They gave us their leader's own quarters, so we were comfortable. I'm . . . I'm sorry. I've internalized all sorts of muck over the years, apparently. And that's my work to do, not yours. I regret what I said about the Macazi. It was despicable and wrong. Again, I-I'm sorry."

"What did you say about us?" Taavi's voice cuts the air like a blade. Behind her, her people funnel out the trapdoor on the floor.

"Nothing," I say. "I need to talk with you, Taavi. We need to amend our agreement."

The Macazi form around her, bags shouldered, water cartons dangling at their sides, eyes darting from her to me and back to her.

"What kind of amendment?"

"One to ensure you don't break your word."

I found the spell book again easy enough and skimmed it. Taavi and I stand inches from each other. With no time or real place for privacy, the Macazi are an audience around us. Zora is so close, I can feel her breath on my neck.

I don't know how the rest of my people are going to feel about me doing this. Allying with the Macazi. They're magicless Grays, but they're Grays still. Who am I to make a decision for them? I can practically hear Shaun saying it now. But I can't please everyone. This is the situation we're in, and this is the only way out of here. Besides, extra bodies to help in the fight against the Chancellor only makes sense. They're coordinated and strategic from what I've seen. This alliance makes sense.

A sea of eyes stare back at me and I swallow. Only thing I didn't count on is becoming responsible for more people, making decisions for more people. *Leading,* even though it's temporary.

Bri clears her throat, and I realize everyone is waiting on me with bated breath. I take a quick glance at the page she is holding open.

"Your hand," I say, and Taavi holds out her palm. Zora pricks it and out pops a bubble of red. "Now we . . ."

"Lock hands," Zora says just as I spot it in the text. Taavi and I intertwine our arms, gripping hands. Her blood is slick between our palms, the wound dripping.

"Repeat after me," I say. "Yoi kimza ya nochka."

"Y-yoi kimza ya nochka," Taavi says, her chest rising and falling so hard, I half expect to hear her heartbeat in my ears.

"With this blood I vow," Zora translates, and whispers erupt from the crowd.

"Mwas stafa lo yeeze ya Macazi li kis," I say.

"Mwas stafa lo yeeze ya Macazi li kis," she echoes, darting a glance around.

"To honor my word that I and the Macazi will fight with you."

"Mish Deolekkis m'joma a Macazi a meh."

"Mish Deolekkis m'joma a Macazi a meh."

"I welcome the Ancestors' judgment upon me."

"Ya lis."

"Ya lis."

"For life."

"O'nah vez."

"O'nah vez."

"Only broken in death."

"Iz naya mo'lo'neesh a grazka."

I squeeze her hand and a string of red streams out of our grip, coiling around our arms, like a bloody rope. Once, twice, three times, it wraps, stinging my skin. Taavi is silent.

"I seal this promise with my blood," Zora translates. "You must say the last part!"

Taavi chews her lip then shoves the words out. "I-Iz naya mo'lo'neesh a grazka."

The stream of blood swirling around our arms flickers gold and tightens its coil like a snake.

"Ah!" Taavi winces.

The gold snaps, dissolving into dust. We untangle our arms and Bri tucks the book away. But I gesture for her to give it to me.

"Is it done?" Taavi asks, rubbing her arm, which is now covered in cuts where the blood coil touched.

"It is," I say, rubbing my arm. There are no scrapes on my arm or scratches on my metal.

"It only scars the person held by the oath," Zora says.

Ah. Okay.

"Good," Taavi says. "So we're on the same page now. Make the Chancellor answer for all the ill he's done."

Oh, he's going to more than answer. "Something like that," I say. "I'm going to go over the plan with everyone. Then you'll take me back down so I can deposit the protection spell."

"Thank you." Taavi smooths something from under her eye. "Really, thank you so much, Rue." She gestures for her people to form up, and a hundred bodies, maybe more, shuffle to their feet. I review the route we're going to take. The truth of this world, how hidden it was, shudders through me. Every time I went to Totsi's, sitting there reading for hours, helping Totsi put away her books at the end of a long day . . . and there was this entire *world* down below. So many haven't even seen the outside.

"We'll leave at dark. The cover of night can only help."

Heads nod.

"Bri, get your gadgets to scan for magic ready. Zora, you will follow behind. I want our eyes on either end."

"Good plan, Jelani," Zora says.

"You feel better now, Z?" I ask in a whisper to her.

"Yes, much. If she breaks her word, she'll reap death upon herself. And it's Zora."

"I like Z."

"But it's Zora."

"What is it with y'all not liking me shortening your names?" I nudge her shoulder playfully.

She smirks. "A name is important. Every letter is intentional, has meaning, a piece that makes up the whole. Saying it fully is a way to show respect."

"Aah, okay, I feel you. Understood." I gesture at the crowd. "Keep an eye on things. I'll be down there to deposit the spell. If it takes more than fifteen minutes, come after me. Alone."

"Still don't fully trust them, huh?"

The Seer's words echo in my head. "I trust no one."

"Wise, Jelani."

It's a lie. There is one. If I can trust no one else, I know I can trust him. And having him by my side here is long overdue. With the Seer's prophecy, I need someone next to me I *know* beyond a doubt has my back. I flick up on my watch and my fingers are lightning fast.

Me: Gimme about fifteen. I'm coming to get you.

• • •

Taavi and I head back down through the trapdoor and into their lair. I read while we walk, checking for how to imbue an object with magic.

"The lead goes through this entire place, right?"

"Yes, except for that one area . . . where . . ."

Her mother. I clench my jaw. The way she handles her just doesn't feel right, witch or Seer or whatever she is. It doesn't sit well with me. They're family!

I run a finger down the page.

Find the weakest spot of the object, usually at one end, and say the spell.

The weakest spot is definitely the cellar where she keeps the Seer. "Take me to where the lead stops, at your mother's wooden door."

We head back down the winding corridor. I read the spell three times as we walk to be sure, chanting the words in my head. Enunciation is key, and I don't wanna screw this up.

Taavi still rubs her arms. "Do you know how long it will hurt?"

"I don't. Never did a blood oath before."

We stop at the bottom. I press the wall and shudder with a chill.

"How thick is this? Must have taken a long time to get it down here like this."

"We have Totsi to thank for that. She used spells to melt down the lead into sheets. Then she magicked them to be weightless. My guys did the rest. Once the Chancellor got wind of large amounts of lead going missing, she was looked into and placed on restriction. That's when I knew she'd never be able to help us using magic again. It was too risky. And Imbuing spells are expressly prohibited."

"I remember." Saw that on, like, day one of trying out my magic. That rule is plastered everywhere. And how hypocritical when

Imbuing is precisely how the Chancellor fills onyx with magic. Of course he wouldn't want anyone toying with that spell. He knows its power.

"If they suspected Totsi anymore and came looking, we feared they'd find us." She pats the wall. "In many ways this was her life's greatest accomplishment, preparing this place for us. Protecting us." She looks away, and I hear the faintest shuffle behind the door. The Seer knows we're here.

"Well, I'm going to Imbue this lead lining your walls with a protection charm that'll absorb anything fired at it." I practice the chant to myself a few more times.

"Open her cell."

She does. I touch the edge of the metal door where it meets the wood, careful to get out of the lead-lined corridor so my magic can move freely. "And you're sure this metal is continuous throughout the whole place?"

"It is, yes."

I glance at the page once more then tuck the book under my arm, summoning warmth to my fingertips and pulling it through to my hands.

"Qis smaj y'pa," I say, pointing, and a stream of light stretches from my fingertip to the cold metal. It glows and blinding orange light ripples like a wave down the walls, up the stairs, and out of sight. Everything pulses brightly for a moment, then flickers out.

"I think it's done."

"Y-you think? We have to be sure."

I touch the lead wall. It's warm to the touch. "There's definitely magic in there. But for good measure . . . stand back."

"What are you going to do?"

"The only way to know if it'll withstand an attack is if I attack it. Consider it quality assurance."

Taavi covers her eyes. I dig deep for my magic, draw my arms back, and thrust. Energy pools and my arms gleam. Magic gushes from my hands, slamming into the wall with a *clang*. The spot where my magic hit the wall glows, pulsing, and the ground trembles. Dust rains from overhead, but the walls hold, and the glowing spot dims before fading out.

"It works!"

"H-how do you know?"

"Because that was a destruction spell. I told my magic to combust whatever it touches."

Her eyes bulge and I wink.

"O-okay, well, at least it works well." She swallows then exhales. "Is that it, then? W-we ready to go?"

"Almost," I say. "Get your mother; she's coming with us."

CHAPTER TWENTY-ONE

BACK IN EAST ROW, Julius was waiting for me outside his house, shirtless, in a floral zip-up hoodie, a fedora, and a thick gold chain around his neck. I didn't even know hoodies came in Hawaiian print. Also, this ain't some tropical vacation. But I let him make it.

He's been waiting for months, ever since I sat on Mom's stoop and locked hands with him. Ever since he saw everything that transpired here. What to say or do when things get in a pinch always comes so easy to him. And it'll be good to have someone else keep their eyes and ears open, see who is playing me two-faced.

I'd had him hold on to me tight as I mumbled the transport spell, and we vanished.

Now, in Totsi's Texts, Zora and Taavi are giving him side-eyes and he's throwin' 'em right back. The remnants of the sun glows like an ember outside, and there are so many bodies inside the bookstore, you'd think someone had the heater on blast. We're almost ready to go . . . if I can smooth over these awkward intros.

"These your friends or what?" he asks.

"Yeah. You remember Bri."

She waves.

"And this is Zora and Taavi."

Julius sticks out a hand, but no one takes it.

"Nice to meet you," Taavi says, giving his wardrobe a once-over, eyes pausing at his wrists.

"He's from back home," I say, trying to answer silent questions and chip away at the tension. We're all wary of outsiders, I get it. But Julius isn't an outsider, he's part of me.

"Yep, no magic." He holds up his hands. But it's not until his sleeves slide down, revealing his bare wrists, that Taavi's curiosity appears satisfied.

"Bri, can you give him a Defense Boost potion to help in case he gets caught up?"

"I can handle mine, shawty," he says, but I flash him a look that says I wasn't asking.

Bri hands him the potion and he guzzles it down, grimacing at the taste.

"Well, now that everyone knows everyone, we can get going." I turn to Jue. "Stick at my side at all times." I don't think anyone would try to hurt him, but just in case.

"Aight, fam," he says. "Just . . . I'm here to look out for you. So, whatever you need." He reaches to throw an arm around my shoulder, but I think of Jhamal and pull away before he can. Don't want to give him the wrong impression. He's my best friend. *Friend.* And I need him here as that right now. For counsel, to vent, keep eyes out. Zora's stare burns my back as I head to the front of the store with Julius in tow.

"Neat rows, please," I say. "The frailer travelers on the inside."

Bodies shuffle, metal clanging, as people tuck in tight, canisters bumping against weapons. Chatter sprinkles throughout the place, and

I spot the girl with the shaved head. Her cheekbones sit high, dark eyes perched on soft cheeks. She's too young to have even been designated. She must be one of the ones Taavi mentioned who was born here.

The girl clenches her jaw and I feel her fire. A familiar one. The world outside the bubble she's lived in is completely unknown to her. The way it works, the dangers that lurk, are all things she's been taught. But now she's marching into it. The difference between reading about war in my history textbook in Ms. Apple's class and actually facing the General head-on. I have half a mind to tell her to stay here, but if she's anything like me, those words will fall on deaf ears.

"Keep a close eye on that one for me," I tell Julius, pointing. "I want her protected at all costs."

"She young, ain't she?"

"Sometimes it's the ones we underestimate who are the most dangerous. She's a fire hungry to burn, but we need to control her fury, or she could hurt herself or others in the process."

"Yo, who are you?" He holds his chin with a pinch, all dramatic like. "This glow up is real, fam. I can already see the crown—"

I elbow. "Shut it with that. It's not a joke to them, really."

"Okay, okay, sorry." He rubs the spot I nabbed.

"I don't want to be insensitive or offend anyone, you know?"

"I feel that. You a whole boss, though." He reaches for my hand and I let him. "Respect." He squeezes, and I hold there a second without thinking. I snap to my senses and pull away.

The route we used to get to Totsi's would require us to go back through that fallen building and that's not going to work. Even if we don't run into a trap, going through that hole one by one would take forever. So we venture around the District, which will make the route much longer, but hopefully safer.

We dip out of Totsi's, our footsteps echoing like a drumbeat on the pavement. I cringe at every step, because it feels like we're super loud, like someone-going-through-the-kitchen-cabinets-while-you-sleep loud. Running into any traps out here would be detrimental. With this many people, we're an easy target. Maybe we can make camp in one of the underground tunnel access points around the City. Zora's got them mapped from the time the Yakanna spent trying to find which led to the Capital. It's not a perfect plan. But it's the one I got.

The road T-bones into an intersection, and all eyes are on me to decide which way we go.

"We could go that way," Grag says as if he can hear my mind tinkering. Taavi insisted he come along. "There's a passageway behind Boul Street, near Cresus Circle, where all the . . ."

"Jewelry shops, yeah, I know the way. And you're sure it's safer?"

"Sure as I can be. I missed the last briefing meetup since I just hooked back up with Taavi and the group."

Do I trust him? Not entirely. But his life is on the line out here too. "Thanks."

I brief Zora and Bri on the plan, and they both seem good with it. Taavi defers to Grag, and we set in that direction. Bri, Jue, and I walk near the front. He's taken another dose of Defense Boost just in case. I also gave him one of Bri's gadgets that works like a stun gun.

Taavi is a few steps behind us and her mother's on a cart with wheels being pushed by a Macazi. She can walk, but she's very weak and very slow. So after Taavi had argued me down that her mother had no business going with us—and me not budging at all on the topic (because *who* leaves their mother living like that!?)—Taavi came up with the cart as a solution. It's how they move around large amounts of goods underground. And the Seer is so petite, she fits right in. I don't like that it'll slow us down immensely. But I wasn't leaving her behind. She has some sort of magic, she knows things, and I want her by my side.

"Give her some water," Taavi says to someone as if she can read my thoughts. I slow up to walk beside her.

"There's food, too, if she's hungry."

Taavi cuts a glance at me. "She eats at sunrise and dusk."

I mean, there were definitely days back home a syrup sammich for dinner was about all I ate, but that wasn't because we *had* food. "Uhhh . . . because?"

She purses her lips. "*Because* she doesn't have much of an appetite the rest of the day."

"And—"

"Look, she's my mother, alright? I'll handle making sure she's okay." She reshoulders her bag. "Worse than Totsi, I swear," she says under her breath.

"I mean, you keep her locked away like a prisoner. She's lonely, can't you tell?"

"I don't have to explain myself to you. She is my mother and that wasn't part of our agreement. Drop it."

There's that steel resolve she had when we first met.

"She's your mom, but she's rolling with me. Make sure she has everything she needs. I'm not asking."

And there's mine.

"You don't know her," Taavi says as I walk faster to catch back up with Bri and Julius. "Don't be so quick to make assumptions about her. She's done terrible things."

Something about her tone doesn't sit right with me, but I keep walking. Their relationship is a tangled web of emotions . . . clearly.

Crack.

The ground buckles beneath my feet, a rift zigzagging toward me, and I freeze. Screams ring out from the masses behind me.

Crack.

A trap.

Shit.

The ground shakes again and pops spark like someone dropped a firecracker next to my foot. *What in the—* Heat rises through my shoes like the pops or whatever are burning holes in my soles. I inspect the rubber and steam rises off it. *Oh my god!*

"What's happening?" someone screeches. *Crack. Crack.* Lights pop all over the pavement with every step we take like we've stumbled on a magical land mine.

The sounds of screaming and howls of pain scratch my ears.

Zora's words prick my memory. "*Panic is the first enemy. Patience is my greatest weapon.*" I dip in my stance like she showed me, hands at the ready, searching for some indication of who or what is doing this.

"Hot," someone shouts. "It's burning me!"

People scatter in circles, clinging to one another. Their gazes sweep in my direction, then Taavi's, then back to me.

"Hold still, let me just . . ." I light my fingers and fan the ground, searching for some sign of how the trap works. That's when I see it. A grid of silver energy runs along the ground like someone laid a giant cross-link chain fence made of live wire across it.

I spot Bri and cup my hands around my mouth. "The magic is heat driven. It's melting anything on-site." She nods and I say a prayer she doesn't freeze this time.

I step on a spot where two grid lines meet and it crackles, my foot stinging like I've stepped on a flame. Burnt rubber stings my nose.

"Where the wires intersect is the most lethal spot," I shout, hoping someone hears me. Hoping it helps somehow. I look out ahead, and as far as I can see, the chain extends.

"Taavi!" I peer in every direction, but it's pure chaos, people running in every direction, into one another, pops of energy biting their heels. "Don't step on where the lines meet." I demonstrate, planting my foot between the lines, instead of on them. No pops. "Between!" I gesture, trying to shout above the screams. Short of a levitating spell, which I don't actually know, I can't think of a way to fix this with magic. Everyone has to pipe down and listen.

If panic is the enemy, we're losing.

People barrel into one another, trying to run past one another, outrun the grid. Joshi stumbles on something or someone and tumbles to the ground. He writhes in pain, the chain wires searing through his clothes.

"Joshi!" I rush over, careful to plant each step in the space between the lines. I pull him up, but he's covered in burns. "The lines, keep your feet between the lines." He nods, panting, and points. I turn to find another trampled by the others. "Everybody, listen!" My voice is raw in my throat, but I throw it as loud and big as I can. "Keep your feet *off* the lines. They burn hotter each time they make contact."

"My face. I can't see!"

People are hardly listening. Ears don't work the same amid panic. I spot Bri standing still, her feet twisted around each other, her hands out like she's trying hard to balance. Zora's next to her, balanced on one foot to avoid the other touching a hot spot. Her spear tip is on the ground and her lips are a thin line.

I hurry over. "Bri, Zora, I need you all to find the end of this chain. It goes as far as I can see to the west. But check how far it stretches on either side."

They nod.

"And look out for any eyes, anyone behind this mess."

Bri takes a tentative step. Zora stabs the ground with her javelin to rear herself in the air and leaps over several squares at a time. She stabs, leaps again, and lands with the litheness of a panther, so poised.

"Wait up," Bri says, hopscotching between the live wires of magic tic-tac-toed along the ground. "Zora, wait for me!"

Julius is straddling two feisty streams of magic crackling between his feet. "You did not tell me this was going to involve screwing up my Js. That was not in the travel memo, Rue."

The soles of my shoes look like chewed bubble gum, and my heel is practically on the pavement. "It's getting hotter, we have to move. Now!"

Some heads nod, brows cinched, and I can practically *hear* their thoughts asking, "Which way, Rue?"

Uhm. We can't go west, we can't go back, so that leaves north and south. Bri and Zora went south, so that's the way we'll go.

I point. "That way!"

The masses move in that direction in a wave, pops crackling at their feet to a chorus of screaming. This is a nightmare. I dig my nail into my palm. Find an opening, Zora, find something. I glance behind me, north, the opposite way I just told everyone to go, and it leads to a tree line. I squint but can't tell if the chain stops at the edge of the forest or keeps going. Could that have been the better way? *Shit, I don't know!*

"Ahhhh!" I spin and find the wheels on the Seer's cart melting into a puddle of bubbling metal on the street. *Oh my god!*

I run.

Julius spots her too. "Shit, man!" He hightails it to the Seer like the track star he was in high school, scooping her up from her cart before I even make it to her.

"Run!"

We sprint. My lungs cry for breath and I urge Julius to go faster, praying we reach the end soon. The cries of pain become white noise and I keep my eyes ahead, focused, running as fast as I can. I glance backward and Taavi is stepping over one stream of energy, then the next. She's far too slow. With the way the ground is heating, she'll boil before making it to the end.

I fall back to run beside her. "Come on. Left, right, left, right, left, right," I say. "Get the coordination down. We gotta move quick."

"Left, right," she says, her feet hesitating. "Right, no, left."

I loop my arm around hers and hold her tight to my side, showing her the motion, as if we're running the obstacle tire course at school. She plants her next foot firmer and the switching comes more naturally. Her coordination improves at lightning speed as I chant with her.

"That's it. Now go! As fast as you can. Get out of here." I turn back once more, with the distinct feeling something's off.

The girl.

Where's the girl with the shaved head? It's a ton of us, but I'd expect to spot her. She's the only kid in the bunch.

I spot the tiniest blip in the distance. There she is, ankle deep in some hole in the street, wincing. I rush over. "It's okay. Arm over my shoulder."

She holds on tight and I wiggle her ankle, which is turned in the complete wrong direction, out of the hole. She bites down, her nails digging into my back, but she doesn't utter a sound.

"Almost." I yank again; the smell of my flesh burns my nose. Her foot gives. I pull her up over my shoulder in a fireman's carry and take off in the direction of everyone else.

When I catch up with them, the group has outrun the trap. They sit pressed against the side of a building at least a mile from where we triggered the trap. A mile of running scared. Bodies hang over one another, panting, worn-out. Shoes are in pieces; heels are calloused and bloody. I walk, wincing with each step. At least I can walk. Many are struggling to stand.

"It looks like the trap was set for one point five square kilometers radius," Bri says, studying a round gadget in her bag. "North would have gotten us out of the hot zone much quicker."

Her words cut like a dagger. She sets a hand on my shoulder. "You couldn't have known. Seriously." She tucks away the device and is latching her bag when Zora comes up. Her leg is bleeding, and her feet are covered in blisters.

"There's an access point to the Web this way," she says. "We should get off the streets as soon as we can. Traveling underground is probably safer."

I nod in agreement, tucking away my shame.

CHAPTER TWENTY-TWO

TAAVI STICKS CLOSE BY, rounding up her people. Our group is slow, limping. Joshi's pants are a shredded memory of what they used to be. The little girl's ankle is probably sprained, but the fire in her eyes still flickers there. The Macazi are haggard, tired, terrified, but there's some semblance of relief there too. The relief that comes with fighting beside someone for the first time. Understanding that you actually can rely on each other. That you actually are a team. I failed them by having us go south . . . but no one died, so I try to hold my chin up. But it falls.

We stick to the rural edge of the city, where we pass little shops and convenience stores. All closed or abandoned. Much less burning. The targets seem more selective out here near the island's edge. Field and grass stretch out ahead of us, and in the distance, the moonlight glistens on choppy ocean waves. Bri keeps glancing toward the city, toward her neighborhood.

"If you want to leave, go check on your parents, let them know you're okay, Bri, you can." She'd been locked up too, for so long. I'm sure they're panicked.

"My dad would try to make me stay," she says. "And I'm here to finish this with you. Ride or death."

I squeeze her arm in gratitude. The loyalty runs deep. I wonder where they've fallen in the war. Zruki are loyal. Is her family running out at night, burning homes? If they are, would Bri even want to know that? The way she bites her lip, I'm sure there are many reasons she doesn't want to go home. Not right now. Not until this war is done.

Voices and a chorus of boots hitting pavement cut through the silence and my heart stutters. We hurry into a parking lot outside of some sort of food place to hide out as the people get closer. There are so many of them, from the sound of it. As many as us. I gesture for the masses to hunker down, but before I can get the instruction out, they've already pressed into a patch of trees behind the store.

"Ain't seen 'em," one of the Loyalists says.

I hold in my breath.

"Tucked tail and ran, I tell you. Something about him never sat right with me. That tattoo on his head never fooled me."

Grag. They're talking about Grag.

"I don't know," the Loyalist goes on. "Kez was saying they found some Loyalist bodies back behind Boklo's. Just left there for dead. So Kez took his guys down to the track in the middle of the night, burned a whole block of Zruki units. Maybe they got Grag's folks for deserting? Zruki, wasn't he?"

"Probably, dumb enough."

They laugh.

I look for Grag, but he's out of earshot. Bri's eyes meet mine and I reach for her hand. Those houses they're laughing about burning. That's where her family lives.

The marching stops.

"You hear something?"

I freeze, squeezing Bri's trembling hand. Zora tilts her head in question at the footman marching by. I press my fingers to my lips and shake my head no. We can't fight them right here, right now. There are too many of us injured. I hate them for what they're doing. What their friends have done. But, in this moment, choosing not to fight makes us strong.

"No, did you hear something?" the guard says.

"Guess not." The marching continues, but we hold still until every sound of them has long faded. Bri hugs around herself.

"They will pay," I say.

She nods, but I can tell her hope is fracturing.

"Let's go," I say to everyone as they emerge from the trees. "We need off these streets."

We stick at the store for a few beats until we're sure the march is out of sight. Then we continue through the outskirts of the City, toward Central District. The skyline of buildings isn't what it used to be in the distance, but the Chancellor's tower is still erected in the center. It looms large, the closer we get, the later night falls. Before long we'll be in spotting distance.

"Where's the closest access point to underground?" I ask.

"About a mile up that way." Grag points.

"We can do it," Zora says.

"Shit, speak for yourself, a nigga feet is hurting." Julius nudges me, digging for a smile, but I'm a melting pot of anxiety and fear. "I'm kidding," he says, but no one breaks a smile. Eyes find me. Hundreds, it seems. *What do we do?* They're asking. They're depending on me.

"We push to the access point," I say. "Once we're underground, we rest up and head back out in the morning. I feel like I can hear their collective gulps as we trudge on.

We move through blocks of buildings, deserted parks, and rows of high-rises. Windows stare like eyes down at us, but we push, all silent. The ivory tower is closer, lights glowing on its highest floors.

"A little farther," Grag says from somewhere in the back. And in what feels like forever, Zora rounds on a brick building and we come to a circular door in the ground. I slide it aside and we hurry inside. We descend a narrow ladder, followed by a staircase that goes deeper underground. I conjure a fireball to light the way and with my free hand help each person down. I'm careful with my footing because between my throbbing feet and the ache from carrying that girl so far, twisting the wrong way feels like my insides are being wrung out like a sponge. Julius eases past me, carrying Taavi's mother in his arms.

"We should have a few on watch overnight." Zora stands in the doorway, favoring one leg. "I can take first if you want."

"You've done so much, Zora. Rest, please. Julius and I will take first watch."

She tries to come down a step but winces. I rope her arm over my shoulder, and we take one step at a time.

"Bri," I say, my voice echoing down the stairwell, but when I look up she's already beside me.

"I have a paste I can rub into the wound to help it heal faster," she says as I hand Zora off to her.

Zora nods, swallowing each wince as the two disappear down the steps. I ease the door closed up above with a grunt.

"Yo'lis," I say, and fire dances on my fingers. Not exactly a flashlight, but it works well enough for me to see each step better. I reach the bottom and find an expanse of dirt floor with a broken glass ceiling above. Cool air whistles through the ceiling towering above.

Two Macazi hover over a bed of rocks, a spark glinting between them as they try to make a fire. Others bandage one another, make pallets on the floor, and pass around the water canister. Everyone's covered in soot and scratches.

"Mosh, your brother, where is he?" Joshi asks someone wrapping his own leg.

"Over there, grabbing some water."

"Good to hear it," Joshi says, jotting something down. "Use a little salt on that, and the blond girl with the red glasses has something she can put on that to help, I think."

The man waves his hand, and I spot Bri nodding in his direction as she heads my way.

"I'll need some time before we get going in the morning to make some more of this, she says, with a glass jar in hand. "I'm running low."

"These tunnels might connect to the larger Web. We may not have to go up to the ground again. I'll see."

"That would be good," she says before weaving back through the masses, passing out pills, vials, and dollops of her minty potion.

A hand presses the small of my back and I don't have to turn around to know who it is. I'd know that touch anywhere. I meet Julius's cinched expression. His hand moves to my hip as I turn in his grasp, and his hazel eyes flicker with gold in the firelight. I should tell him to move his hand. . . .

"I got the ole lady set up comfortable," he says. "She's had water and I gave her some food. Made sure she took a bite before I walked away. Big Momma used to pull that stuff on me. Saying she gon' eat, but then not when I leave. I made sure she had a little something before I left her there."

Oh, Jue. Always looking out for the old ladies on the block. No surprise the Seer's worked in a soft spot with him too.

"Her daughter was nearby, so I think she's good," he adds.

"Thanks," I say, and my ribs poke me, sharp pangs ringing through my words. Images of Yiyo on fire, warmth down my throat, my burning arms claw at me. But I blink hard, forcing myself to stay in the present.

"You good?" He touches something on my cheek and it burns. I don't know if it's the dim light in here or knowing everyone's too busy with their own thing to be worried about me right now, but I lean into his touch. And for a moment I let my eyes close, imagining I can wish away the throb on my right side.

"Rue . . ." His words are a whisper and I smell him. He smells like a Saturday on the stoop, jamming with the homies, like a big dinner with everyone I love sitting 'round, like Ms. Leola's hug, like morning dew, fresh linen, and that wave cream he uses under his du-rag. I inhale and for a moment I don't feel the ache on my side. I don't feel anything throbbing or stinging.

"I-I just don't have time to be hurt," I say. "I can't afford injury. We're so close and yet . . . it feels so far. I *need* us to make it back."

He takes my face in his hands, making me face him. "We will, Rue."

I nod but keep silent, because giving space to any of the words dangling on my lips will break me. And right now I need to be resolute. Strong. I press my shoulders back and pull my chin up, remembering Moms's words. Julius winks at me as I pull away from him.

"I'm going to go check on the Seer, then you and me on first watch, yes?"

He rubs his hands together. "Let's do it."

Julius plants on the steps, and I make my way across the dirt pit to the corner where Taavi is. Her mother should be close by. I haven't forgotten the words she told me. The way she dug her nails into my arm to make sure I understood the gravity of the situation. In some sort of way . . . it almost feels like she's looking out for me. There's a seed of some type of loyalty there. I don't understand it. But I sense it. And where I'm from, we reciprocate loyalty ten thousand percent. I want to lay my eyes on her myself, make sure she's good.

She's sitting upright when I find her, held up by a pile of bags at her back. Her legs are thin little things sticking out from underneath a thin white shift. Her hair is pulled back into a bun. Taavi must have done that.

"The sun is not what it once was." The old woman titters to herself. "I used to love it. But it's such an ancient friend that now I'm afraid it'll burn my skin." She tucks her feet under the edge of her garment.

"We plan to move as fast as possible. And hopefully stick underground." I sit down next to her and she darts a glance in every direction.

"Are you liking being out of there?" I ask. "Where Taavi kept you, I mean."

"Like? I cannot say yet. But I knew you would take me. I have to be there, you see. I am part of this now. I've always been part of it, really."

Uneasiness coils in me. "You have to be where?"

Her hand cups mine. "This mind is a curse. Each piece in its own time. You understand?"

"I don't." I scoot closer. "Help me understand."

"It's a curse," she hisses, gripping my hand so tight I wince. But the flicker of anger or whatever it was dissolves as fast as it came, and she loosens her grip. "Tell me about the rain. I haven't felt it on my skin in so long." She rests her head back. "Tell me, child. Go on." She's a different person out of her cell. Much less frightening. Without the stone walls and her dank lair, she could be anyone's grandma.

"The rain? O-okay, uhm. Where I'm from it rains a lot. Well, the weatherman says it's going to rain all the time, but who knows if it's actually gonna happen. It's at least cloudy most days." I glance at her and her eyes are still rolled back, so I keep going. "But, uhm, here on the island we get storms, a lot."

"Warm summer rains were my favorite," she says, eyes darting behind her eyelids and a smile tugging at her lips. "We used to lie out in the rain. Come back covered in mud. Memi hated that."

"Rain and my hair don't get along. So, I'm not a fan." I laugh.

"Your hair is so beautiful. A crown." Her eyes are open now, her neck rolled in my direction.

I tilt my head, trying to see the monster, the witch Taavi described. "Can I ask a freebie?" I hold up my hands. "I have no gold. Only blood."

"I cannot tell you anything about your future without payment, that is the way it works."

"Well, it's about you. . . ."

Her nose scrunches in confusion. "Well, that is different, I suppose." She doesn't say anything else.

"What happened to you? How did you get this way?"

She sighs and her gaze is far off . . . a lifetime away. "Love is so very blind, child." She pauses and I let the silence hang there. "I loved him more than anything. He promised me the world, his loyalty, a future . . . but when he got what he wanted . . . he was gone. I was left"—she gestures at herself—"like this."

Damn. "Your partner did this to you? Whatever happened to him?"

"Oh, child." She coils a string of hair around her finger. "The man I loved died a long time ago."

"That's so messed up. And you have to just live like this?" Her telling me not to trust just anyone was deeply rooted. It was personal.

"Never love anyone or anything so much that it changes who you are, what lengths you'll go to. That is not love, child. That is fear. Fear no one."

"I don't fear the Chancellor . . . or Shaun or any of them." I dig a circle into the dirt with my finger.

"You do fear something, though." She runs a bony finger across my brow. "It hides in the lines on your face, the lilt in your tone, the way you gird yourself in armor. Not armor in the traditional sense, of course."

I press my lips close, but thoughts needle at me. Her stare, which was so eerie in the dim blue light of her prison, is now so much clearer. She's carrying much pain. I'm not afraid of her. . . . She doesn't want to hurt me. She wants to help me.

"People *died* so I could have this shot." I sigh. "And I *still* don't even remember everything from prison. The memories are just gone . . . wisps. What if there's more I can't remember? Critical pieces of what happened on the battlefield that made things shift in his favor. I-If I fail again . . . ."

"Failing is a part of it. He never understood that, either." She laughs, but it pangs with regret more than joy. "His ambition was like a poison, a rot that festered until it took over all of him and eventually killed him. He died, but now that I think on it, did he ever really live?"

"He sounds awful."

"He was gone by the time I found I was with child, twins. He knew his dealings had cursed me and yet he never came back to check on me or them, see how we fared. Tavi and Tot hated him for it. They never forgave him for what he did to me. They were convinced he must be a monster, especially Totsi. But even still . . ." She writhes in pain. "Wh-when I think of him, all I see is a man I pitied, a man I once l-loved." She shudders and I grimace, watching her stoke such toxic memories that are obviously mingled with some sort of love. "There is a part of me that I've tried to bury that still loves him. Love is stubborn like that. A stain determined to leave its mark." She gestures at herself. "Some more visible than others."

A breeze howls, cutting through the broken glass in the ceiling. "I-is there any way to undo it? Some spell or something?" I hold up my gilded arms and they glint in the moonlight. "I have a lot of power left in these. If I can help—"

She pushes my arms back into my lap, her eyes smiling. "Sweet Jelani. I should be getting some sleep soon. If we end up in the sunlight, I'll need all my strength." She chuckles, but it turns into a hacking cough. "There is one more thing I want to leave with you." She hesitates.

I sit up. "Go on."

"There *is* a way to retrieve the memories you've forgotten, but will dwelling on the past serve?"

"There's a way? How?"

"You are not hearing me."

"What if there's some spell I tried during the fight or someone I trusted that I shouldn't have or something . . . any hint of what can help me win this time, I wanna know that. So I don't make that mistake again. I can't afford any more missteps. I need to know!" My tone spikes. "Do *you* know?"

She sighs, rubbing a temple. "I do not. But there's a potion remedy for remembering i-if you insist."

"I can't pay you."

"You don't have to." She nods toward Bri, who is hooking a young man's sling in an arm.

A potion?

"But, Jelani, don't . . ."

"Thank you," I say, rushing off, wondering if there's a remembering potion, why hadn't Bri mentioned that before?

CHAPTER TWENTY-THREE

"BEFORE WE GO UP, I need a word with Bri," I tell Julius, and he nods.

She's working a bit of paste onto a stick, then smooths it on someone's arm.

"Hey, can I talk to you for a sec?"

"Sure." She tops up the jar and I pull her out of earshot.

"How come you didn't tell me there was a remembering potion?"

She blinks, several times. "Huh?"

"There's a potion that can retrieve forgotten memories, right?"

She swallows. "Yeah."

"Well? That'd be useful, wouldn't it?"

"I don't have the ingredients, so I didn't see the point." She shrugs, not quite meeting my eyes.

My stomach does a flip. She wouldn't lie . . . she wouldn't. . . . The Seer's warning clutches at my throat, and everywhere I look I swear there are eyes. *"How do we even know what she says is true? That she did not agree to help them?"* Kai's words when we'd rescued Bri float through me. I blow out a breath. It's like the world is a distorted picture that shifts every time I blink. How do I know what's true?

"But, like, I didn't even know it was an option?"

"Sorry, Rue. Yeah, I guess I could have mentioned it. I just didn't think it was a big deal since I can't do anything about it, you know?"

How could she think that? How could she think any of this isn't a big deal? I shift on my feet amid the silence.

"Rue, I didn't mean anything by it, I swear." She reshoulders her bag. "Look, I really need to get this paste to them."

"Yeah, alright. Catch you later."

Julius catches my eye, checking his watch, tapping his foot. I move toward him. Bri's reason for not telling me doesn't satisfy. But I let it go. For now.

"You good?" he asks.

"Let's just go up." Julius and I ascend the stairs. He pushes open the door a crack and peeks first, then gives me a thumbs-up. We step out and the door is silent as it eases closed.

The edge of the Central District is much more rural than the City center. The concrete landscape is a collage of tall buildings with chunks missing and others toppled over. The secluded spot where we found underground access is behind a row of abandoned warehouses. Faint smells of something metallic or soapy hang in the air, and Jue sets a blanket down. We settle on the ground, pressing ourselves back-to-back to keep watch in opposite directions.

"Anything in particular to look for?" he asks, and I can feel his heart thrumming against my back.

"Any people, sounds, lights in the sky even."

"Got it. This place is wild. Y'all got shit more lethal than guns flying from your fingertips."

"Well, it should only be flying from *our* fingertips. They're thieves."

He pulls the round of onyx from his pocket I left with him forever ago. "It's wild that all that magic can be stored in this tiny little rock." He tosses in the air, catching it. "You figure out how you're gonna get it away from the Grays?"

"Sort of." I explain how the General's onyx popped out when I fired my magic directly at it. "But for that to happen, it can't just be me. There are thousands of Grays; we need an army to take them on."

"Which is why the first thing is getting their magic back?"

"Yep."

"It's gonna be alright, Rue."

I fidget in the silence. He doesn't know that. He wants it to be true, and I appreciate the sentiment. But he doesn't know it for a fact.

"You bugging?" His tone is gentle. "Talk to me. What you worried 'bout?"

That I can't trust Bri now? That I don't know who I can trust? But that's all bobbing on the surface of the real root of it. I see my father's open-eyed stare.

"That someone else will die because of me," I say, my insecurity breaking through, cracking me like an egg. "What if I'd figured out my magic sooner? Got to the Row sooner? You know how many people would be alive if I hadn't been so stubborn before?"

"You know how many people are alive because you were? If you'd given up, Rue . . . shit. But, nah, you're too stubborn for that." He shifts the way he's sitting and we're less back-to-back now. I can make out his profile in the moonlight.

"Who you trust most?"

"You, of course, negro, ha ha."

"You shouldn't." He faces me fully and grips my shoulders. "I told you, you should trust yourself first and foremost." He grins. "And me second."

"But how do I trust myself with something like this when I've never seen no shit like this before? Jue, they wanted me to lead them. Like *lead* . . . be their *Queen.* My last name isn't Clinton. I don't have some fancy Ivy League degree. I'm not some well-studied expert on Alexander the Great or Sun Tzu's *Art of War*. I know none of that shit. I'm just me." I sigh. "Yet somehow, I got a whole damn army of Macazi following me, basically looking to me for safety. And I'm making critical missteps, Jue!"

More people relying on me isn't what I wanted. This wasn't the plan.

"The plan is to get the Ancestors to fix this." *For something of this magnitude, they're the fixers. Not me.*

I rest my head on the wall and study the specks in the sky, jealous of how they hang there with *one* job: to shine.

"When you was working that summer job at the Y, remember?"

"Yeah?"

"That boss lady told you the number of kids that could attend was like twenty or something, right?"

"Yeah, which is so dumb, because the Y is the best place in our neighborhood with stuff for kids to do when they're out of school. There are hundreds of kids that wanted up in there. Twenty?! Yeah, right."

"So you went door-to-door in the neighborhood."

I laugh because I know where this is going. We needed more volunteers or paid staff to accommodate more kids. I wasn't just gonna let them be stuck. If they needed a place to go in lieu of school, I was gonna make sure they had one. I ended up with seventy-three signatures and a hefty donation from a church in the neighborhood. By midsummer we had classes for two-hundred-something kids from East Row. They kept the program going through the year after school, too.

"Them kids ain't no different from these people here. You see a need and you fill it. That's just who you are. Even if it takes sore feet, sleepless nights. You damn near missed your SAT test for that grassroots campaigning you had going."

"Correction, I *did* miss. I had to reschedule, and you know them waivers ain't guaranteed. Moms was not happy 'bout that. But the kids . . . it was worth it."

"Rue, that's why it's hundreds of people down there riding with you. Because that heart you got"—he touches my chest—"shines through."

A bright star catches my eye. It stands out so radiantly, I hardly notice the jagged building tops and biting chill in the air. "You always know what to say. Thanks for coming through, foreal."

"Don't act like I can't throw hands," he says.

"Mhmm." Last fight I saw Jue in was in sixth grade, and he didn't get one lick in, but I'ma let him make it. He's always had to bolster himself up, make himself seem tough, so he didn't get picked on. I never dealt with that, but Tasha did. So I get it.

He sucks his teeth.

"Don't act like when you was slinging, you weren't also hiding calculus flash cards from the bruhs. The crew you was running with had you in deep, fast, because they saw how charismatic and"—I gesture—"*sagacious* you are. You got them brains, boi." I push against him.

He laughs into his fist. "Aight, facts."

"I'm just saying . . . *that's* your magic and it's okay to lean into it. So I'ma do the fighting out here. That's not why I brought you here." He says nothing for several moments. He's chewing. I can practically hear his brain whirring, digesting my protest of his obligatory masculinity. The box the world wants to put him in because he has gold teeth, a du-rag, and baggy jeans. Fuck that.

"I'm glad you're here, Jue," I say, lying against his shoulder.

"Me too."

We let the silence blanket us, feeling no need to fill it. Just sitting here with him under the stars takes me back. To the stoop. To the place where I had my bearings. A place I knew my way around. I knew how to get stuff done my way. A place that felt like my lane. Now I'm here in this new environment, playing a different ball game entirely—one for which I'm still learning the rules. I better rise to the occasion quick because I'm up to the plate.

The moon sits high and I glance at my watch and shudder.

"You chilly?" Julius takes off his hoodie, his bare skin slick under the moon, gold links dangling down his chest. "Here."

I know he's cold, but I don't argue. I slip it on. His sleeves are so big they swallow me, which makes it extra cozy. He turns toward me more so I can better fit into the nook between his jaw and shoulder, wrapping an arm around me. And I let myself breathe for just a second. Because for the first time in a long time, it feels safe to.

I drift and sleep takes me forcefully in its grip.

The hall is empty and Jhamal and I move down it. He holds a metal pole of some sort, coated and slick in red. He holds me up and I tell my knees to work, but they only half listen.

"Your magic, Jelani," he says. "We will need it. Try harder. Please." His voice cracks.

I dig, but it doesn't answer. I bite down, straining for warmth, but my arms go loose, weak and limp next to me. My magic is there, but I don't have the strength to wield it. What's happened to me? A man with eyelashes flashes in my head.

Jhamal and I come to a set of stairs lit with glowing orbs. He pokes his head out and I dig for that familiar heat. My magic flutters in me, but lifting my arms is a fight. Like the very strength has gone from my body. I try to swallow, but my throat is chalky. I dust my lips and white powder coats my fingers.

"Water," I manage. He pulls me up by the waist, and disappointment and something else I can't quite place furrow his brow.

He looks both ways. I try to remember which way we'd come. How we even got in this place to suggest something, but my mind is morning mist on a chilly winter day.

Someone somewhere screams. A hand clasps my shoulder. My arm stings, crying stripes of blood.

"*Ah!*" I sit up, gasping.

"Rue? You knocked out there."

I gulp, taking another deep breath, handing back his hoodie. Jhamal and I were trying to escape? W-we were running together, underground, before they captured us? I . . . but my magic.

"I was too weak to get out us of there. I . . ." I claw the ground.

"Rue, out of where? You okay?" He holds on to me. "Breathe. It was just a bad dream."

No, not a dream. A memory.

CHAPTER TWENTY-FOUR

THE MORNING COMES AND my neck is sore from sleeping crooked sideways. Watch had ended and Julius and I hunkered down inside to sleep. I'm still haunted by the pieces of memory coming back to me. Jhamal never mentioned us trying to get away.

I peer around at everyone waking, bandaging, sipping water from their canteens, breaking bread. We needed this moment of safety to restore our energy, catch our breath, before making the last leg of the trip.

The Seer's words flit through my mind. I should be able to get started on getting the potion to raise the ancestors today if we get in early enough, and if introducing the Macazi to the Ghizoni goes smoothly.

The morning has been quiet, everyone a bit forlorn, worried if today will be a repeat of last night. Most are yawning still, but several are passing out food or handling cleanup. The air is damp and thick with tension so palpable you could cut it with a knife. Bri's tucked in a corner, her hair strewn about, swirling a pale green liquid in a potion jar.

"You get everything you need?" I ask her.

"Think so." She sprinkles in flakes of something, and the liquid in the bottom puffs up like foam. "And one more." She drops something in, alternating between blowing on it and stirring until it thickens into a paste. She holds it up. "Perfect."

"Thanks for doing all this."

Bri spent most of the night awake from what I heard. Everyone's feet were extra raw and sore, but her paste healed the blisters almost instantly. Until she ran out. So she spent the wee hours of the morning preparing the ingredients for more. Bri really came through.

"Of course. Joshi still has a nasty welt on his arm," she says, handing me a tiny vial and a pill. "Keep that one with you. It's not much but it's something in a pinch."

"Thanks." I tuck it away. Her answer about the potion didn't satisfy, but she's busting her ass here, clearly. It feels wrong to doubt her. But the Seer's words finger the hairs on my neck. As she rushes off, I catch a glimpse of Zora strapping a weapon to her leg. Between most everyone being able to walk fairly normally and Zora's limp not as noticeable, the guilt wedged in my chest eases some.

"Just going out for prayers," Zora says. "You want to join?"

"Yes, let's."

Outside, the world aboveground is silent. Zora and I fold ourselves on the ground. She places her palms up, head back, and chants the words the same as last time, asking the Ancestors for their favor over our travels.

My hands are scratchy on the pavement, but I find a hum of quiet and make my own plea to the Ancestors, for confidence, for strength, for wisdom, for everything I could use more of. My Ghizonian isn't as sharp as hers, so I lay out my prayers in English, hoping they still hear them. We rise together and her countenance is warm, perked up. She always beams after prayers. I hope some of that optimism rubs off on me.

Zora hops up, dusting off her legs. "Sorry, if you'll excuse me." She walks in the opposite direction, fidgeting with her armor.

"I'll see you in there," I say, heading inside.

Back underground, Stain and Joshi have all the Macazi in neat rows and are checking off names. I scan for Taavi but don't see her. I haven't seen her all morning, come to think of it.

The little girl with the shaved head is at the front stuffing bits of bread into her pocket. I really need to learn her name. The spots on her ankle that should be purple in a few days are full of pallor. She looks good. Strong. *Thank you, Bri.*

"You doing alright?" I ask.

She glances both ways. "M-me?"

"Yeah, you."

"I-I'm fine. Don't worry about me, please. You have so much to . . . I'm fine."

Thick skin, this one.

Armor.

I snatch a few pieces of hard meat from a tray and pass them to her. "Back home, I used to roll up pieces of my grandmama's corn bread in a napkin and munch on it all through first period at school."

She smiles.

"Wish I had some of that to share. It's so good."

"Thank you for helping me last night," she says, finally meeting my eyes. "I don't mean to take you away from the important things you are doing."

"Looking out for you is one of the important things I'm doing."

"Well . . . thank you."

"What's your name?"

"I am Rojala."

"I'm Rue. Or Jelani, whichever."

"Nice to meet you, Rue or Jelani."

"You let me know if you need anything, alright? Whatever it is, you tell me."

She dips her chin in agreement, and I leave her to it. She could be Tasha. And instead of being at home on the couch watching SpongeBob, she's here marching with a stranger, hoping she doesn't die.

"I'ma get you that corn bread one day. I mean it."

She smiles and her eyes flicker with something I hadn't seen before in her: hope.

With everyone formed up, Julius is easing the Seer onto her cart with some sort of makeshift wheels.

"Where'd you find . . . ?"

"Two words. Nigga rig."

We bust out laughing and slap hands.

"Glad you got her rolling again," I say.

Taavi comes up, hands on the push handle of her mother's cart. She tucks a strand of her mother's hair behind her ear. "I got it. I'll be pushing my mother here on out. We all ready then?"

The Seer lays a hand on Taavi's, and I gaze in the other direction for a moment because it feels private. Something good has happened between them. Near-death experiences tend to have that effect.

"Ready?"

All nod, but Zora frowns. "Rue, we have a problem." She holds the flashing geolocation device on her armor.

"What is it?"

She lets out a huge breath. "Shaun has declared himself King. And Bati's been locked up."

I have to lock my knees to keep myself from staggering. "How do you know? What . . ."

She fingers the blinking on her armor, the same one Kai used to summon her girls when we'd escaped prison. "This is more than geolocation. It's two-way communication."

Wait, why hasn't she mentioned this capability before now? Jhamal wouldn't have had to leave. Is she . . . keeping secrets?

"I just heard from saisa Doile."

Doile? Not Kai?

I chew my lip and swallow my questions, knowing the answers wouldn't change anything. "If Shaun declared himself King and turned on Bati . . ." I tap my foot, thinking, remembering. He could have turned on others. Getting the spell ingredients is more important than ever. With magic back, our people could protect themselves from *any*one. "We need to shift our plans. I'll introduce the Macazi to everyone later. We need to get the ingredients first."

Zora nods. "What do we need?"

I skim my brain for the Seer's words. "Jpango sap."

Bri rummages around her bag and flicks out a vial of a honey-looking substance the color of eggplant. "How much? I have some."

The Seer didn't say.

"We'll try to make this work." One less thing we have to find. I take it from her. "I also need hair from the head of an Elder and one from the enemy. But the Elders are dead, soooo." I knew this would be a problem. I'd just hoped some sort of solution would've popped in my head by now. Oh, wait! "Bati is a direct descendant of the Elders, right?"

Zora nods.

"Then maybe we can use his hair? Genetically, it's gotta be similar, right?"

"I mean, maybe," Bri says, pushing her lips sideways. "But potions can be finicky. The whole reason I hadn't done that memory one for you is because it calls for an albino quello root." She plucks out a knobby purple root vegetable. "And all I have is a purple one."

Really, Bri? She could have at least tried. She must read my mind because she averts her eyes, stuffing the quello back in her bag.

"B-but I mean, sure, let's try it," she says.

"I agree, Bati is our best option for Elder DNA," Zora says. "But the enemy hair?"

"Sneaking into the Chancellor's tower to steal a hair from his head has gotta be, like, plan Z."

"Shaun," Zora says with scowl. "Taking the crown by force, breaking the agreement to conduct Kowana Yechi when everyone is back together." Her jaw flinches. "He's made himself an enemy of us all now."

She's right.

"A hair from Shaun sounds only moderately easier," Bri says, tapping her lips, probably literally calculating the difference in risk.

"It's our only shot," I say. "We've got to find Bati and catch Shaun off guard." I turn to Bri. "The Seer said to combine them on the Ancestors' grave and chant at High Moon." I point to Yiyo in the distance. It's a crumbled chunk in a bed of foliage. The taller trees rise high, knobby and twisty, unburnt. But I remember smoke rising. I remember . . . my failure. "Those were the only other steps. Bri, is there any other prep work a potion needs?"

"Nope."

A sea of eyes stare back at me. There's so many of us . . . what I have to do needles at me. I don't like the idea of splitting up, but I don't see another way. I'm responsible for them now, temporarily, but still.

"I'll get the ingredients. And since we don't know how hostile things might be, it's probably best the Macazi wait at the Ancestors' burial site in the forest outside Yiyo. I don't think taking you to meet our people, announcing this new alliance right now, is the way to go."

"I agree," Zora says.

"That's a hike," Bri says. "We're all the way in the City. But Julius and I should be able to wait at the grave site in the brush, well hidden. It's good cover. Good idea."

"Julius stays with me. But, yes, the Macazi can camp there until I get what we need and come back." I bite my lip. "I'd transport us there, but there's so many of us."

"Let me take the Macazi," Zora says. "They could run into trouble." Her eyes dart to Bri. "You go with Jelani. It's safer."

"I can show you a route that is fairly concealed," Grag says, joining the huddle, and I can feel something I'm too scared to believe is real blossoming in my chest, the same thing I saw in the little girl's eyes: hope. Maybe unity isn't a foolish dream.

"That's big," I say to Zora. "Thank you."

"We're in this together, saisa."

Saisa . . . sister.

"We should move soon," Grag says.

I survey the landscape around us; its quiet, foreboding, chilled air is salty with a promise of rain. He has a point. "It's a plan, then," I say. "Zora, what do you know about where they are keeping Bati?"

"Doile said they carted him off to the eurostarum or book room, I believe you call it. Where they keep the ancient texts. It's a locked room in the bowels of the Web, disconnected from the Ghizoni lair."

"The Web is a maze. How will I find the exact spot? Do you know which alley has the access point?"

"Yes, behind the mail-drop slot at Jud and Quake Streets, you'll see it."

I nod. There's a music shop that way. I know it pretty well.

"You'll know you're in the right spot because when you descend, it'll split into two tunnels. The eurostarum is going to be somewhere along one of those. I can't remember which one."

"Be careful," Grag warns. "You can stumble down the wrong corridor and find who knows what."

"I would leave him, as well, Jelani," Zora says, nodding at Julius.

His eyes flick to me.

"No offense," she adds.

"He sticks with me," I say. I haven't forgotten what the Seer said. Julius is my extra eyes and ears, but I still have to keep him safe. "Bri, stick close to me. And keep your gadgets at the ready."

She nods, her jaw set with determination. "I won't freeze up this time."

"And please give Jue another dose of that Defense Boost, just in case." I have no idea how that potion works or how long it takes to wear off. She digs in her bag as I turn to face a crowd of a hundred or more Macazi. Taavi's eyes are saucers, and even the Seer tries to sit up on her cart to hear what I have to say. The lines in her face suggest she knows something is awry.

"Slight change of plans. You all will take cover in the forest outside Yiyo, where we will cast a spell at High Moon." I expect an echo of groans, but see only head nods. It makes me queasy.

"Be careful with them, please," I say to Zora.

"I will. We should arrive by dusk if we hit no snags."

Yeah, if.

"The Mother would be proud." Zora squeezes my hand. "You're doing a good job."

I feign a smile. "I don't know about that, but I guess we're about to see."

CHAPTER TWENTY-FIVE

ZORA, TAAVI, AND THE Macazi disappear toward Yiyo. When they're out of sight, Jue, Bri, and I head south, toward Quake Street. Julius's hands are stuffed in his pockets, like he understands how serious this shit is, I guess. He's not even wearing his fedora anymore. Something 'bout it being impossible to keep clean. His poor shoes are still fragments of what they were, but I promised him if we make it out of here alive, I find a way to buy him some new ones.

We pass shells of homes in abandoned neighborhoods, desecrated buildings, boarded-up shops, and on the front step of a government building, a pile of bones with giant *L*s painted on them. Zora said they didn't look human, but still. The message is clear. The Loyalists intend to see the Chancellor back in power, whatever it takes.

"It's too quiet out here," Julius says.

I feel it too.

But, despite the horror and fearing we'll be discovered as we round each corner, the trip is kind. We make it within a hundred yards of Quake with no more than sore calves and feet. The area is covered in fresh-fallen debris; some rotting smell lingers in the air.

The intersection Zora'd hipped us to is on the edge of the street where Bon and his band used to sit out and play for coins. This street used to be a tapestry of music, spicy sweet smells, and bright jewel tones graffitied all over buildings. Now the colors on the walls have faded, much more than even age explains. As if Patrol took a torch to this block. How can one person be filled with so much hate? Wind whips through shutters of a building that used to ring with life.

I spot the rim of a raised door in the ground. The access point is barely distinguishable in the cracked, paved sidewalk.

"What we walking into, fam? Gimme the scoop." Julius is always cool as a cucumber, but I catch his eyes darting around, his hands tugging at the loop on his jeans.

"What, you scared?" I tease, running a palm over the ground, feeling for a hook or insert, some sort of handle.

"Never that." He rubs his hands together and I can see his muscles flex beneath his zip-up. I avert my gaze quickly. My fingers curve into a divot and I tug, lifting the door.

"Hurry." I lower myself inside the tunnel and they follow. The iron door slams into place when he slides it closed.

The labyrinth of tunnels underground is more daunting than I remember. The air hangs with dirt from the floor, like someone just rolled through. The walls are lined with fire orbs. Who keeps them lit, I wonder. The thought slithers over me and I shudder. Something tells me these passageways are well known and used.

Looming behind me are two brittle archways. Both with worn paths. Two tunnels, like Zora'd said. One glows with blue light in the orbs on the wall and the other is completely dark.

"Uhm . . . let's try this way," I say, stepping toward the blue-lit corridor.

Bri holds out her device as we stalk through the darkness. The farther we go, the more the lights dim. Julius's breath is heavy next to me. I make out his profile in the darkness, slivers of blue light sloping around his full lips, his heavyset brow. What would he say if I told him about Jhamal?

"What is it?" Julius asks. "You staring. My fade on the side fucked up or something?" He slicks a hand over the side of his hair.

"You so dumb, shut up." I pull him along. "I was just zoned out."

"What's on your mind?"

"No one."

"I said *what*. . . ." He purses his lips and my cheeks burn.

"It's no one. I mean, nothing. Can we just focus, please? We're trying to find—"

"A dirt wall." Julius peers around. "No shortage of dirt walls down here."

"A very *specific* dirt wall, thank you very much. We need to concentrate."

"You ever hear that saying about a needle in a haystack?" Julius asks Bri.

"I haven't, but that's—" She snorts laughing. "That's exactly it."

"Y'all got jokes. This was the best plan I could come up with. Y'all have any better ideas, I'm all ears."

"I'm fucking with you, fam." Jue nudges my shoulder. "But you good foreal?"

"I am." I meet his eyes and they burn into me in that way only Julius's stare can.

"You lying, but I'ma let you have that."

Thank you.

"Okay, so we might have found our needle," Bri says, swirling her gadget at a part of the wall that's chiseled and cracked. She rumbles through her bag and pulls out a disc. "Wait for it." Her tongue pokes her cheek. The disc suctions to the wall and she taps a blinking light on top. The motor on the device hums, specks of dirt flying in every direction.

BEEP!

"This wall is eighty-three point six percent less dense than the walls around us. There's a room behind here."

I'd hoped to find the door. But I can break through this wall if I need to. "We have to be sure if I'm busting through it Kool-Aid man–style."

"What is koo lay?"

"Bri," Julius starts. "So, you've never had a Kool-Cup either? Yo, we have so much to catch you up on."

Julius gets along with everyone, I swear. He the type of dude to just strike up conversation with a random person in Walmart and sit there talking for thirty minutes. I don't know if that's a Texan thing or a hood thing. But when I'm trying to get stuff done, it's annoying.

"Jue, focus. Bri, are we sure?"

"There's definitely a room of some kind here." She drags the device along the wall and walks until she's small in the distance. "And it stops around here," her voice echoes, rippling down the tunnel. "So it's a big room. What else could it be?"

I guess there's only one way to tell. "Back up." I pool my magic through me and my arms gleam, my hands heating up. I snatch the energy creeping through me and shove.

"Feey'l," I say. A ripple of light slams into the wall and it cracks, dust particles raining overhead.

"Okay . . . again." I square my shoulders and thrust. "Feey'l."

The crack stretches, zigzagging to the floor. Bri's eyes comb the ceiling. "Uh, Rue . . . be careful. I don't know how much more it can take."

I lift my hands, hoping this doesn't bring the place down on top of us.

"Hold up." Julius whips out a blade from beneath his pant leg and taps the center of the crack. He hammers the back of it with his fist, and bits of wall crumble. "That's it. Nice and easy. I used to help my uncle with house renovations on the weekends for some side cash."

Niggas be a gold mine of skills, I swear.

He taps again, chipping away at the crack, and the tiniest hole appears, a ray of light barely visible there. We listen.

"No one's there," I say, grabbing a chunk of wall. It's cold and brittle in my fingers, crumbling like cake as I toss it away. "Let's get this hole bigger."

It takes several minutes, but we pull apart the pieces of the crumbling wall enough to really see inside. It's definitely a room. Bri was right about that.

"They sealed this one with a veil," Bri says, noticing the same thing I am. "No one would ever know there was a room here because there's no door. Smart."

There are tables and storage containers everywhere. Wires hang from above, but from the hole, that's about all I can make out.

"Here, let me. My HologrifX might . . ." Bri shoves a metal sphere about the size of a golf ball through the hole in the wall and brings her wrist to her nose. Orange light from her watch slices the darkness, flickering the room into view. A hologram 3D image of the room hovers above her wrist and she rotates our view by spinning a finger.

Glass vials line the tables along the dusty walls. Flames dance in a stone bowl in the room's center, and around it hangs all sorts of metal equipment. Tongs and trays, syringes, wide glasses, aprons, and long tubes snaked in circles lie in piles all over the ground.

"This isn't a library," I say. "It's a lab. Could Bati be in there? Does it show bodies?"

"I don't know. This is my first time using this thing."

"We can't risk not knowing. I have to go in."

"I'm going with you."

"No, you stay here with Julius."

"Rue, no. I understand I could get hurt. That's part of it. It's not your job to protect everyone, least of all me. And besides, it's a lab. There could be useful stuff in there."

"I'll keep watch," Julius says. "And I'll birdcall if I hear or see anything."

"Of course." I roll my eyes.

"What?" he says. "That's how they—"

"Do it in double-o seven, I know."

Bri looks between us.

"Don't even try to understand." I pull myself through the hole, rock scraping my sides. I take Bri's hand, and she gets through easy enough. The sphere she'd dropped through the hole snaps to her feet the minute her foot touches the floor.

"Whoa, how'd you get that thing to come back to you?"

"I modeled the performance coding after the heat-seeking fire arrows we ran into. The idea is that they seek out whatever material or form of energy I set it to." She tosses the hologram ball in her hand. "So, with this, I just set it to seek out the rubber sole on my shoe, mixed it with some of my DNA. Spit, if you're curious. . . ."

"Oh my god, *gross*!"

"And voilà! This ball will snap like a magnet to any whiff of my DNA."

"That's nasty as hell. But foreal, Bri, your ability to take shit and make new shit never ceases to amaze me." I offer her a fist bump and she pounds back. "Glad you riding with me, friend."

"Ride or death."

I don't even correct her at this point.

"Jue, you good?"

"All clear out here. I'll birdcall, remember?"

If the fire weren't burning in the room's center, we wouldn't be able to see anything. Bri is already inspecting lab supplies and dropping things in her bag. She plucks leaves from a far wall, where it looks like someone planted a floor-to-ceiling garden.

"Bati?" I whisper. "You in here?"

Digits scroll across glass screens, running calculations or programs or something. I lean in and a percentage bar at the bottom is three-fourths full. Nothing about this place feels Ghizoni to me.

"Rue . . . I don't think . . ." Bri pulls out a long arrow from under a bed of wires.

I touch the end of it, and it erupts in flames. "Ouch!"

She drops it and it clangs to the ground.

"The fire arrows . . ."

Is this . . . could this be . . . ?

DONE flashes on a glass screen and a start button pulses. I bite my lip and, despite my better judgment, tap the start button. Orange light shoots like rays from the computer and a hologram of the Chancellor's face appears.

I gasp as Bri rushes over.

"You call this your best work?" Angry lines pucker around his scowled lips. "Phiz and his team can do better work than this. If you want what's been promised, you need to deliver. If Phiz gets back to me before I hear from you, Roz, the job is his. Lucky for you, he's been hard to reach." He huffs, leaning back in his chair. "The girl's evaded all our traps and her cuffs are *still* latched on tight. Those cuffs can't be removed forcibly. Trust me; I've tried."

I shut my eyes, trying to remember that exactly happening, but there's nothing there.

"We've got to get her to *use* that magic, so we can absorb it."

I knew I was right about that.

"Make me something that'll do the trick, dammit." He slaps his desk, then rubs his chin, a faraway look in his eyes. "I have one other iron in the fire that I don't think has gone detected, in case you all prove to be imbeciles. But I expect a better answer from *you* by morning! Get me a way to sift the magic from those cuffs or, so help me, I'll wipe this whole island and start fresh. Did it once, I'll do it again."

The video cuts out.

"Wipe the island? The hell does that mean?" Julius asks, startling us both. "Sorry, I was birdcalling and y'all ain't hear me, so I came up in here. It was a rat though. False alarm."

"This is a Loyalist lab, which means their headquarters isn't far," Bri says. *"You can stumble down the wrong corridor and find who knows what."* Grag's warning bristles.

"And it sounds like the Chancellor expects someone will get that message and soon. We need to get out of here."

Bri shoves a few more plants into her bag, and we rush out the hole we came through.

"What did he mean, 'Wipe the island'?" Julius asks as he shoves himself through. "He said he's done it before?"

He reaches for me and pulls me through. The tunnel air is musty and humid compared to the chilly lab space. "The Chancellor takes an elixir to keep his cells performing youthfully. He's over a hundred, but his fitness levels are like a twenty-year-old's," Bri says. "All the Patrol on the island take the same elixir, though they do die at a relatively early age, so I imagine the potency isn't the same." She taps her lip.

"So, he very well could outlive everyone here and just start again?"

"But this didn't sound like outliving. He said *wipe*."

My father's face appears in my memory like a summoned ghost. "He's talking about the Sickness."

Jue's brows meet.

"The Sickness is what killed my people before the Central District or any of this ever existed," I say, my chest a knot. "I don't know how; my father never knew the ins of outs of the how either. But he suspected the Chancellor was behind the Sickness. It cut the tribe size down by half in less than a month. No one in the village, despite being the only ones with magic, could figure out the cause of it." I gulp down the lump in my throat. "Then the Chancellor just showed up. Rode in like a white knight saying he'd unearthed his own magic."

I add air quotes to that part because he stole whatever magic he claimed to have.

"He said he could save them. He stayed in the village for days doing spells, mixing concoctions, but the Elders smelled him for the evil he was. Nothing worked, of course, because he really wanted them to die. He was only playing savior. My people were polite to him so as not to clue him in to their suspicions. But when he left, they fled. My people ran for their lives." I sniffle.

Julius works his hand into mine and I let him.

"Those that could ran into the mountain, Yiyo. And the Chancellor built this empire out here calling himself Ghizoni. Stealing even our people's name."

"I didn't know the full of it," he says. "Shit, I'm sorry, Rue."

"He's awful," Bri says. "Growing up, I just knew he had magic and he was generous and kind enough to share it with us at Designation age. The history books say nothing of Rue's people other than they died because they got sick. I could never have imagined this."

"Do we know how he passed along the Sickness?" Julius asks. "I mean, if he's got that as his plan B, we should be learning anything and everything we can about it."

"I don't," I say.

Bri shakes her head. "No idea."

Julius's fingers trace around his mouth. "Someone on this island has to remember. Had to have known about what he did. Dirty ones always have people in their pockets that they pay to keep quiet or kill. If he cursed these people like this, someone knew. Someone helped. Someone as old as him. Someone—"

Cursed . . .

I gasp, steadying myself on the wall.

Oh.

My.

God.

"I-I know who knew," I say.

"Who?"

"Taavi's mother—the Seer."

CHAPTER TWENTY-SIX

SHE HAD LOVED SOMEONE.

Could that someone be him?

It would make so much sense. Either that or it's a million coincidences. She'd said the man she loved died. She must have meant the man she fell in love with . . . before he became the mass-murdering, power-hungry dictator he is now. It's him, I know it.

How much did he tell her about what he was doing? How much did he let her see? Did he become someone else *after* they were already an item or . . . ? I try to swallow, but my throat is dry. I can't wrap my head around all these people talking out of both sides of their mouths.

"Th-there's no way she *helped* the Chancellor though, right? She's been so kind to me. Like she wants to help me, our people. And he abandoned her, so she has to hate him, right?"

Her words echo in my head. Part of her still loves him, she said. I feel sick. Is she playing me too? I've put everyone at risk, keeping the person deceiving us around. I'm failing at this leading thing . . . all over again.

"Why would she help me if she was in league with him forever ago?"

"Sounds like a guilty conscience to me," Julius says.

Bri is chewing a hole in her lip. We meet eyes and hers dart away.

"Why are you so quiet?"

"I . . . I . . . nothing."

"What do you know, Bri?"

"Nothing, really!"

"What, are you gonna betray me too, now?" I regret the words as soon as they leave my lips, but I watch for her reaction. Because I'd be lying if I said I wasn't giving side-eyes to everyone but Jue at this point.

"Rue, are you serious?" Bri's face twists in frustration.

"Rue, come on, fam," Jue says. "Walk it off. We got shit to handle."

"I just can't believe it," I say. "She's *Totsi's* mother. Totsi, who . . ." *Oh, shit.* "H-he had his *own* daughter killed?"

Pieces of the puzzle click into place. The Seer can't be on his side. She told me I'd be betrayed. Unless . . . that's because she knew first-hand? I slide down the wall and plant on the ground, raking hands through my hair.

"I looked in that woman's eyes," I say. "She is enslaved to the pain she's carrying. There's no way."

"Well, she at least knew what the Chancellor did," Julius says. "You said yourself. Don't unconvince yourself now because you don't like it." He extends a hand for me to get up and I take it. "Either way, now's not the time to dwell."

It's true. Her knowing makes sense, I can't deny that. "Maybe she knew but did nothing?" I ask, dusting the dirt from my pants.

"Still, though, being passively aware of something and doing nothing don't make you innocent," Julius says.

I'm spiraling. I don't have a way to get real answers now. "When I see her, I'm going to ask her, straight up."

I glance at Bri and she holds tension in her expression, eyes far off. It stings. "I'm sorry, Bri. I shouldn't have said that."

"It's cool," she says, but I know it's not.

I sigh. "Zora said one of the two tunnels would take us to the place they're keeping Bati. We took the wrong one. Let's get back to the access point, the dark tunnel is the one we should have taken." We set off back up the blue-lit corridor.

Julius and Bri stick behind me, no questions asked, like they know what's what. Like they trust where I'm going to lead them. Like whatever happens, they're here for it, and the guilt over my words to Bri wedges deeper. Whatever her faults, her not giving a shit isn't one of them. She's trying. In her own imperfect way. And I get that. I get that a whole lot.

The access point comes into view and the alternate tunnel we didn't take looms ahead. It's pitch-black and the hair on my neck stands. I light flames from my fingertips. No one in their right mind would walk down this way unless they needed to. The dirt on the floor is hardly disturbed, no shoe imprints, no dust in the air. I can feel it in my bones, the room where Bati is trapped is down here. We walk for what feels like miles. My thighs ache, and the tunnel twists and turns, deeper into the Web.

We spot a patch of wall that appears disturbed. I wave my hands along the walls and Bri tries her gadget again. It suctions to the wall, and while we wait for the depth reading, I try to meet her eyes, flash a smile, but she won't look at me; I feel even smaller.

"I think we've found it," she says, smoothing the device farther along the wall. It beeps, flashing a number. "There's a room here."

"If Zora's told me right, it has to be the eurostarum."

I summon my magic and energy ripples from my hands. *Crack.* It's dark, but the split in the rock zigzags to the floor. The faint sound of panting and paper rustling pricks my ears.

"Sssh." I point at Bri, then at the wall, and she already knows what I need. The sphere rolls through the hole and a hologram floats about her watch. Piles of books stacked on shelves cut into rock line the walls, and in the corner a red-orange blob—a person. *Bati.*

"Bati," I breathe.

The shuffling stops.

"Bati," I mutter again.

"Wh-who's there?" The voice is worn, crackled with age. It's him. We crumble the pieces of the wall until the hole is big enough for us to step through. Bati's coiled up in a corner, his white robe stained yellow on its end. Ammonia wafts under my nose. How could they leave him in here, treat him like this?

"Jelani," he groans as we move him, eyes darting to the door. "You must go. If Shaun finds you here . . ." His hands are dry with ash. "I cannot let anything happen to you on account of me. I promised your father."

I want to ask why he's locked up, but does it even matter at this point? Shaun can be rash. I've seen it with my own eyes.

"And I promised him things too. You're coming with us. And besides, I found a way to summon the Ancestors. I need your help."

"There is a way, you say?" He gasps, hands cupped over his mouth, as Julius helps him up. Fortunately, Bati can walk just fine. He's just stiff from being in one position for so long.

"There is a spell, but I need a hair from an Elder. Do you think yours would work?"

"Oh, Jelani, I am not sure. But take whatever you need." He uncoils his white locks.

Julius takes out his knife. "May I?"

"Go ahead."

He cuts at the root and I tuck it in my pocket. "Let's get out of here."

"What else did it call for?"

"Jpango sap and a hair from the enemy."

His eyes widen.

"I'm going to get one from Shaun."

"It is sad it has come to this, but yes, I fear you are right. A hair from Shaun will likely satisfy that ingredient. How will you do it?"

"I'm not going to kill him. He's my brother, still. Whether he sees me that way or not."

"Your Yakanna blood shines through. But Beerchi do not always think this same way. You are his direct opposition to rule."

I want to unify us, arm us, not don a crown. How can he not see that? I think of Jhamal, the only other Beerchi I know. Loyal, fierce, determined, kind, and very prideful about his heritage. But I could see glimmers of stubbornness, him forcing his way on others. Still, he's nothing like Shaun.

"We need to get Bati to the others," I say. "I'll come back to the City to get the hair from Shaun myself." I can't let anything else happen to him.

Bati takes my hands. "The Ancestors' magic from the gods was bestowed on us to bring light into this dark world. But you have a duty to protect yourself, your people, and that is never wrong. Do what you need to do." His grip is ironclad on my wrist. "Understand, he could *kill* you, child."

"Not if I don't give him the chance to."

CHAPTER TWENTY-SEVEN

THE JOURNEY TOWARD THE forest outside Yiyo *to meet Zora and the others* is silent but for the rustle of the twisted, knobby trees and an occasional chirp. We walk but don't speak. Jue makes eyes at me every once in a while, like he wants to crack a joke, but the weight of my worries must bleed into my expression, because he says nothing. Everything's riding on this spell working. And he knows it.

Yiyo is a hike. So, since our group is small and there's nothing out here, I'd transported us as close as I could to the edge of the island. The fading sun is dipping below Yiyo, and the glass Dwegini homes that used to sprinkle the mountainside are faint glimmers, shattered in some places, gone in others. We're a mile or so from the tree line, where Zora and the Macazi should be lying low.

I step over a fallen branch and the dry ground crunches under my feet. We stick to the shade as we approach where the invisible barrier around the mountain should be, the one that used to protect my people, keep their existence secret. We find what's left of the jagged barricade. The world behind it is a heap of blown-over trees and debris. It's like walking through a nightmare. I'm reliving the failure of the battle that led to my imprisonment and weakened me—isolated my people for so long, all over again.

I close my eyes and search my memories hiding in shadowed corners but find nothing. None of it makes sense. What has come back is fractured bits in my mind. Wisps. Maybe I'll never know what happened—how the world turned upside down in the span of minutes. Why the man with the eyelashes haunts me. How Jhamal and I had a chance to get away but somehow didn't.

I catch Bri looking at me, probably wondering if it's come back. I shake my head. And she turns away. And despite the guilt, I can't help but wonder if there's anything she isn't telling me. She wasn't exactly forthcoming about the memory spell.

We skirt bushes that are no more than singed twigs. Thanks to an energizing potion Bri put together, Bati isn't as slow as he should be. The foliage thickens the closer we get to the mountain, and the sky is a pastel rainbow.

"You sure you wanna go back to get Shaun's hair yourself?" she asks.

"Yes."

Julius looks at me, but there's no question in his eyes. Just understanding. Where I go, he goes. I was mainly talking to Bri. The deeper we go, the more the unburnt parts of the forest surround us, its canopy thick overhead. I press between a pair of jpango trees and let my fingers graze their smooth surface. The first time I saw these trees, my father showed them to me. I miss him. I will make him proud. In this, I will.

"There." Bri points.

Bati's head turns in that direction. I see it too. Fire. How green can these Macazi be? They can't have a fire lit out here. Just announce you're in hiding, why don't you? We creep that way.

Thrum. A knife plants in the bark inches from my face and I freeze.

"Shit!" Julius says.

Energy tingles my fingers. Bri crouches with a yelp.

Whoosh. Another knife whips by, the blade's tailwind kissing my cheek.

"Who's there?" someone says.

I know that voice. A face with a bald head peeks from behind a tree, another blade poised to toss.

"It's me, Rue."

"Rojala?"

Our eyes lock and she exhales.

"Oh, hey, sorry! Glad you made it back safely."

"How's your ankle?" I ask.

"Better. Must have just twisted it. The camp is this way." She leads us in the opposite direction of the fire. Apparently, it was a decoy. Smart. Maybe I don't give the Macazi enough credit? It makes sense; they've been living in an entire world unseen, belowground. They'd know how to play the game of misdirection. And well.

Where the Macazi are actually holed up is tucked away behind a cluster of trees. Taavi greets us, her eyes smiling. She's really relieved to see me. She takes one look at Bati and gestures to someone blended in with a brush of leaves. "Get him water and a shaded place to sit," she says.

"Thank you, child. Careful out there. Remember what I said." Bati squeezes my hand before hobbling off.

"How's your mother?" I ask Taavi when she turns back my way. Bri and Jue share a look. What did they think—I was gonna wait to get to it? No, I need answers. Now.

"Good," Taavi says. "Very good. Thank you."

"I'm glad," I say. "I need to see her. Where is she?"

She hesitates a moment, taken aback by the suddenness of my request, I assume.

"This way," she says. We follow, ducking underneath a tangle of greenery, feeling our way through a thick knot of trees that look like they've been hooked together on purpose.

"You really hunkered down well," I say. "Even had Rojala out scouting."

"What, are you surprised?" She huffs. "This is our bread and butter."

"Oh, no, not at all surprised. I'd expect nothing less from you." It's low-key shade, but if she senses it, she says nothing.

"You made it back okay!" Zora rushes our way.

"Good to see you too, Zora." Warmth churns in me at the joy in her tone. We're really in this as a unit.

"Jelani, Julius, so good to see you." She slaps a hand on my back. "How did it go?"

"It was . . . enlightening. I'll say that." I update Zora on everything, out of earshot of Taavi. I want to approach Taavi on my own about it. See how she responds—what she admits to knowing. Because if the Chancellor is indeed her father . . . there's a reason she hasn't told me.

Zora asks tens of thousands of questions, down to where the access point was and how we broke through the wall. "So, the plan is still to get the hair from Shaun and cast the spell, yes?" she asks.

"Ye . . ."

"Good, remember, the Yakanna stand with you."

Taavi clears her throat, and I remember she's waiting. Zora rushes off, catching up with Bri, and I follow Taavi through their camp.

"So, uhm, what did you want to see Mother about?" She turns to Julius before I can answer. "There's some water over there and a few bites to eat if you want."

"I'm good, right here." He shoves his hands in his pockets, sticking close to me, but gazing in the opposite direction. Giving our convo privacy, I guess, but making it clear he ain't going nowhere.

"She's just been really tired is all," Taavi says, tugging at her ear. "Out here the sun is on her skin and, well . . . it's not going well. Sh-she's eating though. And drinking lots. I made sure of that. We found her a nice, shaded spot. But this is . . . it's just a lot for her." Taavi rambles on, filling the silence, her hands fidgeting. She brushes the blood oath scars on her arm. I'm tempted to call her ass out right now for concealing that the Chancellor is her father. But this is chess, not checkers.

"I just wanna see how she's doing," I say.

"Ah, I see. Well, just try not to keep her too long. She needs her rest." Taavi leads me to her mother without another word. But she's smart. I have no doubt she read between the lines and knows something's up.

The Seer sits up when she sees me, tilting her head as if she can see through me. She narrows her eyes and cold fingers walk down my spine. I swat at my skin but there's nothing there. Just goosebumps. She sets back on the pillow of twigs and branches at her back and flaps a hand in the air at Taavi, who leaves without a word. But I can feel her hungry glare burning the back of me.

"He stays," I say, gesturing at Julius.

But the Seer closes her eyes, resting her head on the bark. Her hair is in a different style today. Taavi must be doting on her like she says. They are bonding, it seems. That has to be a good thing. I wonder what drove the wedge between them in the first place.

I search for the right words to prick the wound I'm about to open, but nothing sounds precise enough. The frustration bubbles to the surface before I can refine it into something that isn't seeping with anger. "Why didn't you tell me?"

Silence.

A creature rustles over a crinkle of leaves somewhere in the distance. I wait. Waves lap the edge of the island. Still, she says nothing. The salty ocean air is thick on my skin. Thick in my hair.

"*Why* didn't you tell me the Chancellor was the man you fell in love with?" I squat to her field of view. "Look at me."

She parts her lips to speak but sighs, twisting her dress in her hand. "If I'd told you that, it's all you would have heard. Now that you've seen so much, you cannot unsee the rest. Once you've simmered down, that is."

"You told me to trust no one. And yet between those same teeth you lied to me."

"I am not your enemy, Jelani."

"*Tuh*. I can't tell. How could you sit there and look me in my eyes the first time you met me and say nothing?"

"It doesn't work like that, Jelani. I answered the questions you'd asked. I told you to trust no one. I . . ."

"You acted like you wanted to help me!"

"I do, child." She darts a glance around. "*Sssh*. I do!"

"Why? Is this some sort of guilt you're carrying? Is that why you're trying to help me? What's in it for you?"

"No, I . . ." Her next words come out more choked, like bile she'd prefer to swallow. "What do you want to know, child? Ask." She holds out a trembling hand, grimacing, and turns her face away.

"I don't have anything to pay you!" I pace. "You *knew* what he did to my people. How could you love a man like that? You just sat and watched him poison my people? Then roll in like some wannabe white knight?"

"Enough!" She pulls herself upright. "He didn't poison them. Not exactly." She swallows. "I . . . I did."

I stagger.

What?

"Wait . . . no, you said . . ."

"Listen." She darts another glance over her shoulder. "Taavi doesn't want you knowing this. She thinks you won't have anything to do with us if you find out. But this is my doing, not hers. Hush and listen."

I can't move, her words are like quicksand.

"We fell in love when we were young. I'd never had attention from someone like him before. He was Moyechi, and they were all really brilliant with large plats of land. My mother and her people were Tuki, a clan of mostly servant women. But I was born with an affinity for potions, you see. My mother didn't believe in any of that sort of thing, so when she saw that my baubles were making strange things happen, she threw out all my things. Xire, the Chancellor, that's his real name, found me dumping my stuff at the shore. The first thing he said to me was, "Bury it instead."

"He told me that the reason the world wanted me to throw away my potions was because they made me special. Different from them. They were jealous. We buried them together and spent each night after under the stars. He told me about his family, how he'd love to let me meet them one day. But not any time soon. He always had a reason I couldn't meet his people, come to think of it. I was a servant girl, so I didn't question it. I lived for the thrill of skipping through the forest under the stars, skinny-dipping at the edge of the island by moonlight." She blushes. "I was quite a looker, though you probably can't tell it now."

I fold my legs underneath me and sit beside her.

"And then one day he came to me with boar blood or something on his hands. He told me he wanted me to dig up those potion ingredients where we buried them and try out something. We'd all known of the brown-skinned people on the island with magic. The Ghizoni tribe. But that had nothing to do with any of us. Beyond trade agreements with them, they kept to themselves. But Xire had said he heard of a new strain of magic on the island outside of the Ghizoni, and he bet if there was any truth to it, the magic would be in me."

She rests a hand on her chest. "I mean, can you imagine? Me, magical? I couldn't. And what did I know of magic? Lowly me. Potions weren't the same as magic, not really. But he was determined to see if I could concoct whatever spell he'd found out. He gave me the instructions orally over several days, and I followed them. We met in the forest. The same spot. Each day the ingredient list got more and more vile, and that's what still haunts me. I should have known. I should have known then that he was planning something terrible." A tear slips down her cheek. "He loved me at one time. I truly believe that. But he loved himself more. He's calculating and always three steps ahead, you see."

"What happened with the potion?"

She takes a deep breath, smoothing away more tears. "The night the potion was done, the last step required letting it cook in the high sun. Then again for the same time under the high moon, stirring continuously. We'd collapsed by the time it was all done. My body on top of his, sweaty despite the sea breeze. We slept there, together, under the stars. I'll spare you the details."

"Thanks."

"But it was a magical night. Not your sort of magic, but the heart kind. When I woke up, he was gone. Taavi and Totsi found their way into the world several months later. He visited me once or twice, but I never told him about the pregnancy outright. I think a part of me was afraid of what he might do. When I couldn't hide my pregnancy anymore from my family, I was forced to tell Memi whose it was. But once word started to spread across the island that the Ghizoni had contracted the Sickness, I knew he'd taken that potion and done something terrible to their water supply. The Ghizoni started to die off. In record numbers. It was"—she shakes her head—"awful. Just awful."

"A-and as the potion worked, their tribe shrank, and bits of me started to wither away too." She picks at her loose flesh, hanging from her thin arms. "My skin began to yellow. It grew blotchy and my bones would ache all over like a nest of thorns swelling inside me. I was so sick, my family thought *I* had the Sickness. But no, no, I had some backfired version of it as a punishment for brewing a potion, dabbling in a magic that was never mine to touch."

I gasp. "That's how you ended up this way? The potion cursed you?"

The horror of it skitters up my arms like nails scratching a chalkboard. He didn't care if she lived or died. Did he know she was pregnant? What kind of monster . . . ?

"Yes. And my girls hated him for it. I never lied to them about who their father was. Totsi was angry. She worked her way up through Designation and never told her father who she was for fear he'd kill her if he found out that his daughters had lived and they knew his dirty secret. Taavi didn't get Bound. The Macazi Designation gutted her. To be *his* own blood and not be suitable to be given magic cut deep. Even if he didn't know. She'd even tried to tell someone that she was his bastard by starting a rumor, but it was taken as no more than gossip. She never quite got over that. It still pains her, I think. But she's so closed off, there's no telling what's going on in that head and heart of hers."

I don't know what to say. It's her fault. It's all her fault. But not really.

"I want to be there. The moment you face him, I want to see his face as he crumbles." She squeezes my hand. "You owe me nothing. Not even a clean death. But it would mean the world if you would do that for me."

I still can't find words. Shock is stamped on Julius's face too. He looks at the Seer and back at me. Then back to her.

"It's almost dark. I should be leaving in a little bit." I need to sit with this. Digest it. Chew it up some, then spit it out. I don't know how to feel. "One more question."

"Yes?"

"Do you know how he got magic in the first place? How he filled the onyx pressed into *his* wrist?"

"I don't know for sure, Jelani. But I do believe he took some of those lovely people, your people, and forced them to Imbue onyx and fuse it to him. And maybe not just on his wrists? He had piles of it even then. I don't know what he promised them in exchange or how he made them agree to it. But I can guarantee you, once he got what he wanted from them, he got rid of them. That's what he does."

My stomach is in knots. I twist on my feet and walk as fast as I can. I need air. I'm outside and somehow, I can't breathe.

"Rue, wait up," Jue says.

"Just gimme a minute."

I keep walking and he hangs back, which I appreciate.

I'm going to rip the onyx out of the Chancellor's skin with my fingernails. I bite down and see red.

"Oh, there you are." Bri heads my way, arms full, glass *tinkling* with each step. "The Plinor River runs through here, did you know?"

"No, I . . . huh?" I blink, trying to make sense of her randomness.

"When I saw it, it gave me an idea." She presses something cold into my hand. "I'm sorry," she says, and I turn a vial of dark blue liquid in my hand.

"A potion?"

"The remembering potion. When I saw the river, it hit me. The Plinor has special properties that make it a perfect antidote for a potion gone wrong."

"Bri, slow down. What are you talking about?"

She meets my eyes, finally. "Rue, I didn't ever mean to make you doubt me. I-I should have tried this a long time ago. I hope it works. I was so scared that I'd make it incorrectly . . ."

"Oh, Bri, look, I'm sorry for what I said. I'm just . . . Nothing is as it seems lately. Every time I turn around, someone I think I can trust is someone I can't. There's so much lying."

"You have a lot you're juggling. I just want to be sure you know I'm in your corner. I'm in this, all the way. The best way I know how to be. But I'm going to keep learning how to be better at this. Ride or die."

"Oh, shit, Bri! You got it right!"

"Got what right?"

"Nothing." I squeeze her shoulder. "Thank you, friend." The moment is warm, and damn, did I need it. I turn the vial in my hands.

"I really hope it works," she says. "I found some albino quello root in that Loyalist lab, so I'm ninety-nine point ninety-seven percent sure it'll work."

"Nah, it's cool." I tuck the potion in my pocket. "I'm gonna take a little walk alone. I should be leaving soon anyway."

"Oh, okay. You sure? I can walk with you. Zora and I were going over some devices that could be useful once it comes to fighting. The geolocation device on her armor is *really* intriguing."

"Nah, y'all go ahead. I need a minute alone."

She presses a tear-shaped glass in my hands. "And here's the water from Plinor. Remember, anything goes wrong, take it within sixty seconds. Just in case!"

"Thanks."

She smiles before taking off, and I pull the memory potion back out. Its glass shines. I pull out the stopper and hold it to my lips.

Drink, Rue.

But my hand won't move. My pulse rattles like a drum. How

much more remembering can I take? Every memory haunts me, shakes my steps. For the first time in I don't know how long, I feel like I know what I'm doing. I'm *this* close to victory.

Drink.

I can't.

Seeing everything I've forgotten . . . what if, what if it's more of me screwing up? More dying because of something I've done? How do I go from that to face Shaun? How do I tell these people to follow me to the grave site? That I know what I'm doing? That they *should* be on my side? What if I see everything and . . . I don't know . . . freeze?

I trace circles on the rim of the bottle. I wish I could ask someone their opinion. But Julius and Bri are nowhere in sight. Zora's not here. And Jhamal, the one who's full of wisdom-isms, is . . . My chin hits my chest. It's all on me.

The pervasive truth digs at me, overshadowing my fear. If the Chancellor wanted me to forget so much that he poisoned me to make sure of it, that alone means it's worth remembering.

I press the glass to my lips, tilt my head back, and gulp it down.

CHAPTER TWENTY-EIGHT

*S*OMETHING SHARP DIGS INTO *my arms. Bright lights bob over me. I'm weighed down and covered in a thin shift. The battle? I strain for the sights and sounds of magic but hear only the scrape of metal. Stale air curls in my nose and I blink.*

"Where am I?" I try to sit up, but I'm heavy all over, tethered to a table with straps. Panic claws at me. "Jhamal?"

A woman in a lab coat presses me down to the chilly table at my back. "She's awake. Give her more."

Wait . . .

My heart patters faster. The battle . . . the Chancellor. I was fighting. I tug at my arms and the strap holding me to this metal table groans. A man with long lashes and kind eyes, in a white lab coat, presses something cold to my lips. Th-there was smoke and blood . . . shouting. A-and Rahk . . . Yiyo . . . The world is hazy. I blink, but it doesn't help.

"Where am I?" I ask. "Wh-what are you—"

But the way their lips twist in satisfaction tells me my words aren't making any sense. My eyes grow heavier. I crane for a view of the room. Wires, a metal door, sterile, but the walls are made of stone. I know this place . . . from Binding. Am I in the Central District? Boots walk past a small window high on the wall.

Underground. I'm . . .

I need to get back to them . . . my people . . . they . . .

I blink again and this time the space between the images is longer. Even my breath is heavy. A weight. "Jham—" The words dissolve on my tongue as everything disappears.

A grinding sound drills in the air. Familiar lights bob above me. My skin prickles against cold metal. My feet are pressed down, arms strapped. The underground lab. I'm still here? I keep still, soaking up all I can before they realize I'm awake and sedate me again.

"Have you tried the predontle vorealator?" The man with the long eyelashes speaks.

"Of course I have. What, do you think I'm stupid or something?"

I expect the second voice to be the woman, like before. But it's unfamiliar. They must rotate shifts. I concentrate on their words, careful not to move a muscle on my face. What are they doing to me?

"It was the first thing I tried. I got my research badge same year as you, Rike."

"That's all rubbish now, isn't it? Dwegini, Zruki. It's like it never mattered. Now it's just us and them." He grunts, apparently pushing something heavy. My table moves and I resist the urge to steady myself, trying to let myself rock side to side as if I'm unconscious. The lights dim a moment before glowing brighter. They're moving me . . . across the room. But why? Maybe I can get close to the door, break the straps holding me down, then bust out of here. I'd peek but it's too risky.

"Not for long. Those loyal to the true leader of the Ghizon won't falter. Have some faith. We'll make this place what it was."

The other guy says nothing and continues to work in silence. I strain to hear, even though their conversation hovers right over me.

"How's Lella doing, news of the baby and everything?"

"It's good. She's doing what she can. Never thought we'd be bringing a baby into a world like this, you know?"

"We got a good chance here though, to prove ourselves. He's giving everyone a double take. He's got to. You know what that means?"

The other man grunts, feigning curiosity.

"Means it's an opportunity to rise in the ranks. Get close to the big guy."

The other lets silence hang between them.

"Some of his own Patrol turned on him, did you know? Razing the streets of the City, rebelling against the man that gave them everything. Can you believe it?"

"It's not that black and white, Huff."

"Is for me."

They don't speak again until my table moves back through a moment of darkness. Something clamps and my arms feel heavier. I hold my breath in my chest and ease an eyelid open. A spider-looking contraption is attached to my golden arms with pinchers at the end. They set it on my arm where the cuff meets my skin.

I gasp.

Th-they're trying to pry off my cuffs!

"She's awake!"

Something stings my neck. Sleep chases me, but I'm too weak to run.

The table is cold at my back. I immediately recognize the lab's walls around me. Light hangs overhead and Jhamal's face comes into view, hovering above me. I blink. He's slick with sweat.

"Jelani, can you hear me?" He's over me, his armor flecked with red.

"I can," I try to say, but nothing comes out.

He pulls up the edge of my shirt, exposing my bare shoulder; cool air grazes my skin. He moves a needle with a tail of thread back and forth, in and out of view.

"Just hold still a bit longer." He tears something with his teeth. The ceiling thunders above us and he cuts a glance over his shoulder to the door, worry dug into his brow.

"Thank you," I mutter. More words rush through my mind, but none makes it to my lips. Everything's foggy. The door rattles on its hinges under someone's fist, and I hear it like a thunderstorm in my head. Jhamal's hands move faster. He pants and I want to grab him, tell him it's going to be okay. Somehow. I don't like seeing him like this. Scared. But every time I glimpse his face, I see bloody armor on the ground. My pulse spikes, my breath quickening. What have I done?!

I try to muster words; panic clenches my throat. The smell of the smoke, the wails and cries from Yiyo.

"Jelani? Can you hear me?"

"Hurry up!" a voice says from the corner.

"I'm hurrying," Jhamal says. "She has to live if this is going to work."

"They are coming." The guard glances over his shoulder.

"Jhamal?" Finally, words come out. "I . . . I . . . Yiyo, the battle. The smoke. What have I done!?"

"Sssh! They will hear you." He pulls at the straps holding me down.

"I . . . I . . . I sent hundreds of our people to their death. I . . ."

"You said you knew how to handle her," the voice says again, and I turn for a glimpse of the man he's talking to. Tall. Gray skin. A Patrol guard?

"I do! She trusts me. Just . . . I'm almost . . ."

I look from Jhamal to the guard and try to claw my way away from them both. "Wh-who . . . ?"

Jhamal looks like he's seen a ghost.

BANG! The door bursts off its hinges.

His eyes bulge, crippled with fear.

I blink, but the world disappears.

The hair is longer on Jhamal's face than I've ever seen it. His cheeks sink in more than they once did. He switches on the lights in the lab. My eyes dart to the door, but there's no guard with him this time.

"Wh-what are you . . . a-and that man w-with you . . . l-last time." My tongue is heavy in my mouth, not having spoken in so long.

"Ssssh. They will hear you." He takes me by the shoulders and pulls me into him; his chest is warm against my cheek. He undoes the straps on my arms and turns a vial in his hands, cutting a glance over his shoulder. "Take this." He hands me a tiny glass with silver liquid. "I'm going to get you out of here this time."

"How long have I been in here?"

"Many weeks." He presses the vial into my hand.

Weeks?! The lab is quiet. Bloody shears and a spider-looking contraption is covered in specks of red. Next to it is a collection of metal instruments and bloodstained gauze. "Wh-what did they do to me? What happened?"

"What happened when?" He flinches.

I close my eyes and I can still smell the smoky air, hear the chaotic screams. "We were going to fight a-and . . . something . . . the world went black. What happened after?" I force myself upright despite it feeling like I'm breaking my bones in half and reach for my magic. A flame coils in my hand. "Jhamal, I . . . everyone . . . and Yiyo!" Panic wells up inside me and the magic in my hand glows in Jhamal's eyes.

"Take it." He nods at the vial in my hand.

I try to sit up, but I am woozy. "What is it?"

"It'll help." He unstraps my knees, cutting another glance at the door. "We have to hurry. Please."

I open the vial and smell it. "How many made it into Yiyo, how many did I . . . I . . ." But the thoughts choke me. I sent them to their death. "I . . . I . . . I."

"Most fled to the mountain as you'd said to. But the Chancellor expected that. They walked right into his trap. Our numbers are less than half. If that." His jaw clenches.

I gasp. He tips the potion into my open mouth and I can't help but swallow. I reach for him, but he steps back and I swat only air. My insides boil.

"Jhamal . . . ," I choke out, but everything burns and the world spins. His fingers let go of mine. I reach for him, but he is staring, worry written in lines on his face. The pain subsides and I try to pull myself up, but my knees don't work. My head is foggy . . . my body, weak. What did he have me drink? But the thought disappears and a million others with it. "Jhamal? What are we doing in here?

He reaches for me and the warm expression I know is finally there. "Now, let's get out of here."

I gasp.

Jhamal poisoned me.

CHAPTER TWENTY-NINE

RAGE BURNS THROUGH ME and the long journey back through the City isn't helping. Julius and I'd transported as close as we could to the City. But we still had a few blocks to go to the alleyway with the barbed wire. Julius hustles to keep up, glancing at me every few moments.

They were poking and prodding, trying to strip my magic from me, and Jhamal was helping them? His eyes bulged when he realized I saw he was colluding with Patrol. That's why he gave me that potion. That's what he wanted me to forget. But I see him now. I see him fully.

It's his fault we were kept away in that cell for so long. Not mine! Is that why Breakfast Lady was so friendly? Did they all know he was really on *their* side? Was that the plan the entire time? Gain my trust? Use me?

But why?! My eyes sting, dwelling on pointless questions. Stupid. I'm so stupid.

"What's on your mind?" Julius asks. He wasn't around when I took the potion. No one was.

"Nothing."

"So you don't wanna talk about it yet. Got it."

I nod. I don't want to even think about it, but my mind is doing what it wants. Julius tries to lighten the mood by reciting his favorite action scenes from Bond movies. He also is apparently *not* a part of the Connery-Is-the-Best-Bond Fan Club. He's a Craig fan, hands down. But after a while even that convo peters out and we just walk silently, out of respect for what we're about to do. Real talk, we could go in there to get this hair from Shaun and not come out alive.

As we round the familiar barbed wire near the access point to the Ghizoni underground lair, I turn to Julius. "We find Shaun. In and out. Just watch my back, lie low."

"F'sho," he says.

"I'm foreal, don't get caught up. I don't have you here to throw hands."

"I'ma do what I gotta do, mane, but I hear you. I gotchu."

I side-eye.

He rolls his eyes. "I got you in the way you need me to have you. The brains. I get it."

"Aight." Why doesn't Shaun have anyone on watch? I feel for the pothole-looking door in the ground. A coppery rot smell curls in my nostrils. "Wait."

"Yo, what's that—?" He smells it too.

I know that smell.

Death.

"There." He points and I can faintly make out something dark on the ground. I step closer, the stickiness brushes my kicks, staining them. Red.

No. No. No.

I follow the line of blood past the barb-covered door. It leads to a ripped robe and what could be gallons of blood. Our eyes meet.

"Stick very close to me," I say, before opening the door to the lair below. We slip down the rungs in the silence and move down the dimly lit passageway toward a stir of voices. I slip past an empty door and crack open two others. Where are the voices coming from? The corridor is drafty, but I'm dripping with sweat. The hall curves the familiar way. Dim light paints the corridor. Beds protrude from the walls, thin slivers of metal topped with blankets and stuffing. Still no sign of someone on duty. That's not smart. Even I know that. The air is a mix of snores and people tossing in their sleep. Every several feet we pass a door like the one to the room where Bri and I had pored over spell books before leaving here. No indication anything's even off.

"I badee, ya lilo," a low voice says.

I freeze, but it's just someone mumbling in their sleep. We tiptoe past, and something brushes my thigh. I jump. *Shit!* But it's a hand dangling over the bedside. I scoot aside and pick up the pace. The hall opens up and snakes in opposite directions. Julius looks at me and I can hear the question in his head. *Which way?*

The rooms, from what I recall, are off to the left. We hang a left and I can feel Julius's breathing at my back. This hallway isn't lined with beds, just glass domes around flames pressed into the gritty walls.

"He should be somewhere down here," I whisper, and Julius nods.

Creak.

My heart stammers in my chest and I yank Julius beside me, back to the wall, in shadow. Voices swell. I look but don't see anyone. A door creaks open and the sliver of light cuts a slice out of the hallway. I creep closer, trying to make sense of the voices. They are whispered and . . . familiar.

"How long must I wait?" someone says, her voice sharp but high.

"I don't know," Jhamal's voice is tight, laced with panic.

"That's ole dude, ain't it?" Julius asks, but I shush him. I can't see who's talking but I'd know that voice anywhere.

"Just don't be rash," Jhamal says, uneasiness in his tone, like each word makes him nauseous. Just hearing him makes my heart beat faster—raises my temperature.

"You'd said you'd keep her close," the girl says with biting irritation, "but she's off gallivanting around the island."

She . . . ?

Me?

"To find the spell," he says. "Reaching the Ancestors, we agree, is the priority."

"Yes, if only your fellow Beerchi saw it that way. She will complete the spell here, yes?"

That matter-of-fact tone. Is that . . . ?

I lean for a better view. Jhamal is leaning back on the edge of a table. I grit my teeth, anger coursing through me. He's the last person I wanted to see. Kai is in front of him, turning a blade in her hands. Her armor is in a clump on the ground. The thin robe she's wearing is dark green and sheer in parts. She's much less chiseled without her armor, soft around the edges even. And very, very beautiful.

"Yes," he says, pacing the room. "She will come back soon. I'm sure of it. You haven't told me why the spell is so important to you. It seems personal."

"The Chancellor is coming. We need to be ready. That is all. Shaun is also still a problem." She tosses her dagger and it lands in the table Jhamal's leaning on less than a finger space from his hand and I gasp. He doesn't even flinch.

Kai darts a glance in my direction. I hide behind the door, holding my lungs full of air. Julius's eyes are saucers, but he doesn't move either.

For a moment, nothing. Then her voice cuts the silence.

"I will do it tonight." She plucks her dagger from the wall, brushing Jhamal as she passes . . . on purpose. "Once he's taken care of, the Beerchi will fall in line, come around to our side of things."

Our side?

"You *will* be crowned, relax."

Jhamal is doing all this for her . . . not the Chancellor?

"But, let me handle Shaun," Jhamal says.

"You will kill him, yes?"

"Yes, but it needs to look like an accident. I want to get Bati released from that cell first, too."

I can hear the eye roll in her voice. "It's hardly a cell. It's practically a library. Doesn't he love to read?" She laughs as her fingers play on Jhamal's chest. He doesn't pull away, and though it shouldn't after seeing what he's done, something inside me twitches with heat.

"My point is that assassination will only flame the fire." He folds his arms. "Shaun declaring himself King was a mistake, I agree. But we must not be hasty."

"He *killed* my Doile!"

I swallow a gasp. The blood. Aboveground. I clamp a hand over my mouth.

"He is a monster!" Kai pushes Jhamal against the wall with her body. He lets her and I bite down.

Footsteps echo down the corridor and my heart jumps. My head says keep moving, find Shaun, ignore them. For now. Raising the Ancestors is the priority. But the returned memory is a stoked fire and seeing him has doused it in gasoline.

I rush at the door and whip it open.

"Rue," Julius says, but it's too late. The sting of Jhamal's betrayal and now this catches fire and I burn. I burn all over. I burn in the parts of me I'd buried.

Kai gasps. She's shifted to Jhamal's bed, legs curled one over the other, her robe hanging off one shoulder. Jhamal's beside her, his shirt wide open.

"Jelani," Jhamal says, moving away from her. "Wh-what are you doing here? I-I mean, when did you get back?" He reaches for me, but I step back.

"It's not how it looks." Jhamal swallows, stepping toward me. Julius steps forward too.

"You think that's why I'm here?" I huff a laugh. "I shouldn't be surprised. Add it to the list."

"Clearly." Kai pulls her shift into place, and something inside me snaps. Magic streams from my fingertips and slams into Jhamal's chest. He flies backward, pinned against the wall. I hold him there; my magic, strands of burning white light, claw at the edge of his throat.

"I'm sure it's exactly how it looks. I'm seeing clearly for the first time. But no, that's not why I'm here."

"No. Hear me out," he says.

"I'm listening, but you ain't saying shit!"

He parts his lips to speak but says nothing for several moments. "Jelani, I tried. You *know* me." His eyes dart in Kai's direction. "Come to Kai's side. Join us."

"Us."

"Jelani. My . . ."

My Queen, he was going to say, but he stops.

"Join you? I can't even look at you."

"You said she didn't want the crown," Kai says. "Looks like she does."

"This isn't about a crown, Kai. If that's what this is about for you, take it. I don't want a crown. This is about honoring our Ancestors by keeping us alive. Moi Ike Yakanna herself—"

"*Don't* speak to me like you know more about the Mother than me."

"Shut up." I fling a sticky spell at her lips. "Feey'l." I shove the air and she falls to sitting position. "You're a disgrace to the Mother herself."

I turn back to Jhamal. "I remember everything. The Patrol you were colluding with. The potion you fed me to weaken me and make me forget. So I'd be trapped in prison for months. Never mind how if you'd mixed that potion even slightly wrong, it could have *killed me*."

His eyes widen.

"What's been your plan, huh? What did Patrol promise you for your betrayal? I'd bet you it's a lie. Or was it all for her?" I look at Kai. "You just wanted to keep me under your thumb so you could conspire to put her on the throne? Did I even get rescued from that cell? Or was it a part of some master plan all along?"

Kai's expression flashes with recognition.

"I . . . I . . ."

My anger burns hotter at his stuttering shock written there. How could he? How dare he? "I see you, Jhamal." Flames flicker on my fingertips and I pin him harder to the wall.

"Rue." Julius pulls at me, but I snatch my arm away.

"J-Jelani," Jhamal stammers back, my flames flickering in his eyes.

"It takes a despicable kind of monster to pretend to love."

He starts to speak, his eyes glazed with tears. From regret for what he did or regret from being caught, I don't know. Tears sting my eyes too, and one steals its way down my cheek.

"Just tell me. Was it ever real?" I ask, cutting myself deeper, just to feel something.

"Jelani—" His face is hazy behind my salty vision.

"You could've been on my side," I say, my voice cracking. I'm a wound bleeding, oozing everywhere, and I don't know how to stop it.

He cuts Kai a glance and she's sitting, a nasty smirk dancing on her lips.

"I have to stand with Kai on this, Jelani," he says, and something inside me cracks. I hold him there a little longer, pretending the words he just muttered never existed. But the longer they hang in the air, the heavier they become. I can't deny the truth anymore. The Seer predicted this betrayal. I just never in a million years thought it'd be him.

I touch his face once more before letting him go, running my fingers across the brow that sweat for me, the lines worn into creases around his eyes, the ones that sink in his cheeks. For what we had, what we once were, what I wished we would become. But my fingers feel foreign on his skin.

"I hate you," I breathe, hoping my words break him. I let him up, my magic evaporating. Kai feels around her mouth, stretching her lips. I turn my back on Jhamal; I can't look at him. Not now, not ever again. "I'm casting the spell, summoning the Ancestors. If I were you, I'd be far away when the time comes."

Crunch.

Julius's fist connects with Jhamal's cheek. "That's the least you deserve, bruh." He sneers. "You're welcome."

My insides quake, but I choke them down and rush to the door, the crack buckling, shattering what's left of me into a million pieces. Kai whispers as the door clicks shut. Outside, I hold the doorknob, its etchings digging into my skin, when Julius gently touches my shoulder.

"Rue, let it go, fam."

My heart is in my throat and some weird mix of anger and sadness sears into me. I'd be lying if I said a raw part of me isn't burning for the love I thought we had. But if Kai could steal him, he was never truly mine. Jue's right. He will get his. I shove Jhamal out of my mind. For what he's done to our people in this war. For what he's done to us.

He's dead to me.

CHAPTER THIRTY

SHAUN IS NOWHERE TO be found in the private rooms along the hall where I stumbled upon Jhamal and Kai. The hair of an enemy is the final ingredient. If I'd been thinking, I could have taken one of Jhamal's.

My insides are a knot as we scope another corridor nearby.

"Rue, you good?" Julius asks.

"I'm fine. Just thinking—" I storm ahead, turning my back to him so he can't see whatever's on my face. I don't feel like being read right now. Images of Jhamal and me wrapped around each other in that cell for so long play in my mind, and my insides ache. I try to shove them off, but they slip their way in. My blood boils. *How could he?* He said I knew him. I never knew him. Not truly.

I skim the halls and all is quiet. Everyone's asleep. Someone's patrolling sentry down here somewhere, I'm sure of it. We round another corner. The light is dim and I squint. Julius sticks close to me. The rooms are all very small, and Shaun seems like the type who would put himself up somewhere grand. Or better yet, he would cement his position with a throne or crown or something. But where? Where down here could he find a place for that?

The room where Kowana Yechi was held had a crumbled dais in

the back. It was the largest space, from what I'd seen. "Let's try this way."

Footsteps echo around the corner up ahead and I throw out an arm to stop Julius from walking. Two Beerchi with fur wrapped around their shoulders and curved blades clutched in their hands stand outside two double doors. A bear claw has been branded into the wood.

"There are two of them," I whisper to Julius. "Do you remember the way we got here?"

"Back that way. A left, down a long hall. A right and then another left and the first ladder takes you up to the ground."

"Paying attention, I see."

"I told you I be watching that double-o-seven shit."

I smirk. *Julius got jokes. Always.*

"If this goes left, take that way as fast as you can and get out of here."

He gives me side-eyes, gesturing for me to turn right on back around. Telling me he ain't leaving. Period.

I peek back around the corner. How do I get in there *without* letting Shaun know something's up? I have no choice . . . I have to fight them. My own people. I let out a huge breath and round the corner, stepping out of the shadows. The shock doesn't register at first on their faces. After a moment they reach for their blades, but their hesitation is the split second I need. The closest Beerchi heaves his over his shoulder with a grunt to swing.

"Surpizah!" A coil of light shoots from my fingertips, attaching to his mouth like a sticky bandage. He stumbles backward, the spell gelling his mouth shut. He tries to talk, but it's all muffled, his mouth zipped closed, magic fizzing on his lips. The bigger guy raises his hands to full height, his blade grazing the ceiling. He brings it down over me, but I jump out of the way and aim for his weapon.

"Feey'l!" My magic slams into his curved blade. The force of it shoves his blade backward into a notch in the wall. He yanks it out and bits of rock go flying. He swings. I twist out of the way as sharp metal whooshes past, nicking my arm. *Shit!* I stumble backward into Julius, who's swinging left and right hooks between blade swipes at his neck from the other Beerchi.

"Yo, this dude ain't playing," he says, ducking. For his lack of fighting skills, he's doing alright. The curved blade swooshes over his head. "Bruh . . ." He jumps, the blade swiping under his feet. "I just wanna . . ." The blade comes down over him. But he sidesteps and it grazes past his arm. "Talk!"

The Beerchi growls, bringing his weapon down hard. Julius pushes me out of the way, and it sticks in the ground with a thud. He tugs on the handle of his weapon with both hands, trying to free it from its wedge on the floor. Magic coils like rope from my fingers and loops around his wrists.

"Tight," I whisper, and my magic obeys, cinching. "Tighter."

My magic binds his arms together from wrist to elbow. He howls in pain as he topples over.

"Quick, get his blade," I say. Julius dashes for it. The other Beerchi claws at his bound lips before rushing at the double doors they were guarding. The door rattles under his fist.

Shit! So much for the element of surprise.

"This shit is stuck, like for real," Julius says, arm wrapped around the weapon handle, pulling. "Aghhhh!" He tugs harder. The blade gives, throwing him backward. He lands hard, but the weapon is in his hand.

"Get that smirk off your face, we ain't done," I say.

The double doors rip open and Shaun stands there, crust in his eyes. One of his guards is on the ground bound with magical rope, and the other looks as if he's about to pee his pants after seeing what my magic did to his friend. Shaun glances between them and he blinks, still in the fog of being awoken.

I rush at him, knocking him backward. Hitting him is like a bus charging a brick wall. He pulls at me, but his hand slips on my gilded arms. I latch on to his scalp and grip firmly. But before I can tug, he shoves me hard. My back slams to the ground, stabbing pain shooting up my spine.

"Bruh," Julius says. "We really gotta work on how you treat females." Julius swings and the blade is a blur of gold. Shaun leans back just in time, the blade grazes his face and tufts from his beard fall to the floor. Pain ripples through me. I bite down and drag myself over to the pile of hair. I grab a handful and exhale . . . when a giant shoe presses my fingers flat.

"Ah!"

"Get up!" Shaun tugs me up by my collar and I try to hold on to the hair but it slips between my fingers. "I should have never let you get away the first time. Reckless. You give us a bad name."

"You killed Doile," I say. "What kind of name does that give you?"

His nostrils flare. "You do not know what you speak of. *Tuh*. My name is one to be feared."

"This is not the way."

He laughs. "She thinks she knows the Ghizoni way. You know

nothing. This is not a war you can win. You showed us that already when you came here and the Chancellor all but killed you."

"And you can? You can win, Shaun?"

More fill in the hallway, summoned by the commotion. Eyes are everywhere. Yakanna, more Beerchi, several others whose expressions I can't quite read.

Shaun slaps his chest. "This is *my* way." He turns to his guard. "Let her go. Let her stand up straight, accept her place with some dignity." His men back up. I could kill him. I could shoot a flicker of magic so fast into that spot in his neck just below his ear, he'd be done for. But then what makes me any different from him?

"You may kneel, take the vow, and follow us like the rest of them," he says. "You fight well, thanks to the Ancestors' generosity. So I would give you a fitting rank among our best fighters here." He holds up his chin and he's so close. So very close I can count the beads of sweat on his brow. "Swear it."

"Rue . . . ," Julius starts, but I shoot him a glance and he closes his mouth.

"I only fight for what I believe in," I spit, and dig my thumbs into his eyes. "Surpizah," I say, before he can react.

He screams. Sticky magic seeps from my fingers. The glob of white energy pins his eyes shut. I grip his roots and yank. A scream rips from his throat. Julius grabs me by the arm, and we run, booking it like a hundred-meter dash down the hallway.

We bluster past people who stare and whisper. But no one stops us. And that's how I know Shaun's leadership will be short lived. When the Ancestors restore everyone's magic, they'll have the strength to fight and protect themselves from even him if they choose.

"Faster!" I shout to Julius, and I pound the ground as hard as I can. We round the hallway, skirting each corner, then another. The ladder up to the ground comes into view and Julius throws himself up it, climbing lightning fast.

"Back to the Yiyo?" he asks, panting.

"Yes, to the Ancestors' grave. At High Moon, we raise the dead."

CHAPTER THIRTY-ONE

THE SKY IS A stormy ocean sort of blue, stars peeking between the thick jpango leaves of the canopy as we hurry toward Yiyo. Unsure of the state of things over that way, I transported us to the very edge of the forest. But the actual mountain, which sits beside the Ancestors burial ground, is still a decent hike away.

"Aye, wait up." Julius keeps up behind me.

The time to cast the spell is when the moon is highest in the sky, so there's still a bit of time to go. I pray it works. My mind is a haze of confusion. Anger still courses through me. It's like I'm teetering on the edge of a cliff and my next move will either blow me back to solid footing or knock me off completely. I can't breathe at this altitude. I can't think.

I stop and pull the empty potion vial out of my pocket. I turn it in my hands, the truth of it searing into me all over again. I close my eyes and see Rahk, smoke billowing from Yiyo, screaming rattles 'round in my head. Jhamal pressing the poison to my lips. The Patrol he'd conspired with. Kai hugged around him.

I blow out a breath and try to shove it all out, but remnants linger. Every moment of silence, my mind fills with flashes of his betrayal.

The sour of his love. Sadness pangs through me at what I thought we had. Who I thought he was. My sadness burns into anger. I blink hard. *Out, out. Get out of my head.* This is why I don't let people in my space. Once they're in there, it's hard to get them out. Jhamal is the last thing I should be thinking about right now. And yet my mind is tethered to him. Love does that. I hate it.

"Rue?" Julius says, a silhouette between the branches. Which is ironically fitting. He's always been there, a phone call away, just out of earshot. I breathe his name and he's there. Always.

"Hey," I say.

"Hey." He tugs on my arm, turning me to him. Then he takes the empty potion vial from my fingers, turning it in his hands. "Fam . . ." His fingers graze for mine and I hook into them, to hold on tight to *some*thing I know won't leave me. My eyes sting and I hold my chin up. I won't cry. I won't. I inhale, holding it. Holding myself in one piece.

"We can talk about it." Julius presses me into his chest and I break, like a dam. "I'm sorry." His whispers warm my ear and I cry harder.

My chest aches and my knees are weak. I thought Jhamal rode for me. I thought he loved me the way I loved him. That's the most fucked-up part, assuming someone cares for you the same way you care for them. I slide down to the ground, hugging my knees.

Julius crouches too, arms roped around me. My head finds that nook, my nook, between his jaw and chest. He holds me in silence for a long minute. I savor the way he gives me space to process while being tangled around me, holding me up but not barging in. He smooths tears from my cheek, shaking his head.

When I'm ready, I sit up a bit in his grasp and I tell him. Everything. About the Seer's words of warning and my time in the cell with Jhamal. He scowls at the mention of kisses and how he played me, doting on my wounds.

"Did he ever touch you?"

"No. Not like that."

That relaxes him some. But at every mention of Jhamal, a vein in his jaw pulses. When I finish, his nostrils are flared and he's doing that thing he does when he's pissed off. "I wanna see this Jhamal dude one more time. I just wanna talk."

I shove his shoulder playfully. He knows that's not what I need from him. But his expression doesn't change.

"I just don't feel like I can trust anyone, Jue. Every time I turn around, someone's lying or speaking half-truths."

"What I tell you?"

"Trust myself. But you don't understand."

"What don't I understand? Tell me."

I sigh. "This is some next-level shit. People's lives are in my hands. Their future. Julius, I don't know what I'm doing. A-and so I surround myself with smart people. People who know what they're doing. Like Bri and Jhamal and Zora and you. And . . ."

"Stop." He rests a finger on my lips. "We not doing that. You not gon' tear yourself down like that. I remember when we first met, it was to study for math and shit, you remember?" He smirks.

"Yeah," I say. He's a wall at my back. I curl into him as he holds me.

"I was okay at Geometry. But Mr. Macey's tests were *hard* as hell. You had seen how I did on homework and thought I knew what I was doing. But like foreal, Rue, I used to study my ass off between our study sessions so you wouldn't leave my ass in the dust. I ain't want you to stop meeting with me. I had to make them grades to impress you."

"You so dumb. You had to make those grades because you *needed* those grades." I laugh. "Not become some cute . . ."

"Fine-ass."

I snort. "Okay, fine-ass . . ."

"Queen."

I flash him a look. "We don't use that word. Fine-ass girl is studying with you."

"Look, I pulled an A in Geometry because of your help. You're the smartest person I know."

Flecks of hazel in his eyes glimmer in the moonlight. The night is calling to me, but right here, wrapped up with Julius under the stars, laughing 'bout stupid shit, is medicine to my soul. A sweet quiet I've been parched for. Like . . . like all along, right here with him is where I shoulda been anyway.

"You get me," I say. "I-in a way . . . no one else does."

He smiles and my insides tingle with nerves.

"And the way you look at me, like . . . like I'm the brightest star."

"The *only* star."

"Why, though?" I ask, because I need to know. If I know what he sees in me, maybe I'll see it too. Because from where I'm standing, I'm outside my lane, trying to fix the monumental mess I've made of everything. And I'm terrified my next step will be the wrong move. What else could my people lose?

"You changed me, Rue." Now it's him who looks away, his fingers touching the corners of his eyes.

"Changed you how?"

"You always saw the best in me, you know. Even when I was hustling. You ain't like it, and told me I could and should do other things, but you never looked at me different because of it."

"Of course not. But *you* looked at you differently, too, lest we forget. You started feeling yourself, hard."

"Facts." He drops his head. "I was a jerk when that money started rolling in good. Man. And all the attention. Oh my god. All them . . ."

"Nope. Not gonna do that. Not bringing up no THOTs in my moment." Those memories are staying buried.

"*Your* moment?"

"That's what I said." I roll my neck so he knows I'm not playing.

"I like that sauce you put on it." He runs a finger down the bridge of my nose and pauses at my lips.

My everything is on fire. He stares but all I see are his lips. I remember their gentleness, their heat. The way our kiss, my first ever kiss, brought the heavens down to earth. My insides are in knots. It's been so long, *so* long, since I've felt this flicker, this flame, and let it swallow me.

"Rue, I love you."

The remnants of anything I have to keep him at a distance shatter.

"I've always loved you," he goes on. "And I'll never forgive myself for screwing up what we had. If living in your shadow is where I have to be, then I'll be here, forever. Just to be close to you, there for you, to make up for what I did." He takes my hand and holds it to his chest. "Your name is etched right here. And here . . ." He lifts his shirt and my name is in cursive across his chest. "That's never gonna change." His words sink into me.

And I let them. "I love you too, Jue."

His smile could outshine the sun. "Say it again."

"I love you," I whisper.

His breath is warm on my lips. "Rue . . ."

I suck in a breath, trembling with anticipation.

"I've waited so long to ask you this again." His cheeks push up under his eyes. "Can I kiss you?"

I lean in, pressing my lips to his as my answer, and the world disappears. His mouth melts into mine and I'm warm all over. His hands pull me deeper into him and I open my mouth wider, Julius's love wrapping around me. I've never felt safer. He tugs at my lip and nuzzles my nose. I break away for a breath and find a tear on his cheek. I kiss it away. He holds my face in his hands and we sit there, foreheads pressed together. I don't want this moment to end. I want to sit in this feeling forever.

"When this is over," I say, "i-if things go our way, it's me and you."

"Whatever happens, it's me and you," he says. "Always."

I kiss him once more before pulling away. The moon is higher.

"It'll be time soon," I say, pulling him up with me, and we set out of the forest, hand in hand. Me and Julius against the world.

CHAPTER THIRTY-TWO

THUNDERCLOUDS FLICKER OVERHEAD AS we trekked the rest of the way to the grave site. Zora, Taavi, and the Macazi are hardly noticeable tucked in and around the jpango branches and thick foliage near Yiyo.

"Everyone okay?" I ask, panting. The hike wasn't short. A few miles at least. I know because I ran one stint of cross-country. Mainly because I wanted to see Julius at practice.

"Yes," Taavi says, studying me closely. She must know I talked to her mother about the Chancellor. But she's all plastic smiles, so I say nothing.

"We haven't seen anyone else," Zora says, gaping at Shaun's hair in my hand. "That can't have been easy. The Yakanna would be very proud."

I don't know what to say, so I take the hair and stick it in my pocket with a nod. She needs to know about Kai. But now still isn't the time.

"My Ancestors' burial ground is just beyond the clearing in a dirt pit on the cliff's edge beside Yiyo. Let's get moving." I hustle toward it with Zora, Taavi, Julius, and the rest at my back. We push through the forest and the clearing around Yiyo comes into view. Yiyo's peak kisses the clouds; beside it is a stretch of unmarked dirt. I remember well the place where I touched the ground and felt my

Ancestors for the first time—where I met a certain someone as he practiced his sparring. Seems like a lifetime ago.

Julius points. "Is that . . ."

In the distance, through a part in the trees is Jhamal heading our way with Kai and the Yakanna, in full armor, beside him. Zora turns, hearing the commotion. Her weapon falls from her fingertips and she runs to them. Kai is tough as nails, but I swear I see her lip tremble. They hug tight, spinning in a circle, and her sisters wrap around them. They hold it there, swaying, chanting something. I know that feeling. That feeling of one of your own coming home again, safe, okay. Nothing like it. As angry as I am with Jhamal, and Kai, I'm happy for the rest of them.

A horn blows, and in the far distance, behind Jhamal, are flocks of men in fur, curved blades attached to their arms. Beerchi. Shaun isn't among them. It's no secret what I left to do. It's no secret what this spell will be able to do. And it says something that so many of Shaun's people showed up to see it.

"Rue," Julius says. "The moon."

The sky's black is starting to wash out to a deep shade of blue. I shove off concerns about who is watching and hurry to the grave. My people surround me, a tapestry of gray furs and gold and jade armor. Maybe . . . maybe this can finally bring us back together again? Could it be enough? My fingers shake but I exhale, trying to steady them. What if someone followed us? What if the Chancellor sees? Bri flashes me a thumbs-up, then crosses her fingers.

I bury the thoughts and kick off my shoes, stepping onto the soil where my Ancestors were buried. The very ground tingles under my feet and I fall to my knees, palms up, head back. Starting with a prayer just seems right. I search for the Seer's words, trying to remember the instructions she gave.

When the sky is heavy with sorrow . . .

"Ancestors, rain. I need rain." I dip the ends of Shaun's hair and Bati's in the jpango sap and set them in the dirt beside one another. Gray wisps of clouds roll in, and I thank the Ancestors for hearing my prayer. I sink my hands into the ground.

Chant, three times . . .

One. "U'shaka wesee," I say. The tips of my fingers tingle under the soil and my arms gleam. The Yakanna fall to their knees, except Kai. She watches with bated breath. Jhamal stares, but I focus on the dirt between my fingers.

Two. "U'shaka wesee." The dirt stirs like dust, unsettled. Something underneath the dirt touches my fingertips. I yelp but keep my hands still. *It's okay. It's a bug. It's a shift in the earth. It's definitely not dead people's fingers.* The wind picks up and dirt rises higher, swirling in a cyclone around us. Thunder clatters louder overhead and the entire world darkens, rain drizzling around us. The wind gusts sharply, trees sway, some bent all the way over.

"They are coming," someone says.

The Beerchi fall to their knees too.

Three. "U'shaka wesee." Something in the dirt pulls me tighter to it and my elbows buckle. I'm prostrate on the ground with an invisible weight on my back. The fine debris raining in the air glints in the moonlight. I squint. The dirt is not dirt but ashes of gold.

The dust shifts to the shape of a person. First an outline of one person. Then another. Until there are several figures, silhouetted in golden dust.

The Ancestors. I gasp.

Their features are faint shadows, wisps that disappear if you stare too hard or too long. Even their clothes glisten so bright, you wouldn't know the sun was hiding on the other side of the world. I sit up blinking, trying to make sense of what I'm seeing. Luscious cloaks wrap around their frames, jewels hug their knuckles, and sculpted metal rests on their nests of coiled hair. Golden stripes run down their arms, across their cheeks, and are dotted around their temples.

I reach for words, for breath, but I have neither. I'm frozen, facing my Ancestors in their full robed majesty.

"Who calls upon the Ancient Ones?" The earth trembles and the voice booms overhead like it's coming from the clouds. I try to say something, but it comes out like a squeak.

One of the robed Ancestors steps forward, sweeping her hand in an upward motion, and somehow I am standing. Dust swirls around us, a backdrop of chaos, but in the center, I, the Ancestors, the Ghizoni, stand in an eye of calm.

"Rise, Jelani."

My name.

They know my name.

Of course they know your name!

"A storm wars within this one," one of the other Ancestors says, and the one closest to me steps closer.

"Do not be afraid, Jelani."

I'm not, I want to say. But again, words escape me. Maybe I am? Maybe I'm terrified. She holds out her hand and I take it. Her skin is dust on my fingers, but grows warm the longer I hold it, skin materializing out of nothing. Where there was just the silhouette of a woman written in swirls of dusty golden haze, now is a woman in fully human form, holding my hand. Her skin is richer than the lushest valleys on the earth. Her eyes hang like jewels beneath long lashes. Her nose curves and slopes widely, like the journey of the moon around the sun. She is perfection. A bed of jewels dot a tangle of metal resting on her head. Her hair is tightly coiled, braided with gold into a high bun. I smile, thinking of Moi Ike Yakanna and just how glorious she, too, must have been.

These are *my* people.

This is who I come from.

I am part of them.

The truth of it is a weight on my chest, but in the best way.

"I do not have much time in this form, dear one," she says, her skin is deep ebony so radiant, I'm sure she gives the stars their light. "What is it you have called upon us for? Make it known."

"I . . . I . . ." I try to look around, but like a dream, nothing I tell myself to do is working. I can't take steps. I can't turn my head. I can hardly breathe. "I . . . The magic you gave me. The magic you gave our people. It has been stolen." Lightning crackles. "A-and we need you to restore it, so we can take our land back from the thieves."

The Ancestor touches her crown, easing it more upright on her head, before clasping her hands. "Jelani, I am sorry but we cannot restore the magic."

Her words knock the wind out of me. My tongue sticks to the roof of my mouth. "No, w-wait, but y-you gave it." Blood drains from me and I dig a nail into my palm. "Th-this was my plan. This was the entire plan. *Y-you* have to fix this. I . . ."

"Listen closely, because time is short." She takes my hand in hers again and it is like holding fire. "The magic we gave was a gift from the gods, woven into our blood. It flowed through us; it even fertilized the soil where our people were buried. So much so that the ground burst forth with vegetation rich in magic. We'd eat it and it would nourish our abilities even further. It helped us strengthen our control over our powers, helped us find synergy. Magic saturated our corner of this island."

I gaze at the ground; it pulses as she speaks and I can almost picture the way they lived.

"But any remnants of what used to be lie dormant, like seeds in winter."

She coils one hand over the other and a ball of onyx appears there, like the one the Grays wear. I reach for it but it's nothing more than air.

"Understand me, until *this* stolen magic"—she indicates the stone—"is removed from the traitors and returned back to the very soil it came from, there's no magic left to give."

"B-but . . ."

"You see, Jelani, the magic wasn't for *them*. It was for *us*. And the moment its purity was broken by binding to those for whom it wasn't meant, it caved in on itself. Simple self-preservation. Magic is alive. It preserves, defends. You probably feel it moving, searching, humming inside you. But as living things live, they also *die*."

I stagger, steadying myself, her words a dagger.

"Fortunate for us, our magic is not dead, not entirely . . . sleeping, more like."

Something tinges inside me and my knees feel weak.

"Magic is home in *our* people. It draws strength from *us* as we draw strength from it. And as long as it's being forcibly used by others, it will never be what it was for our people again." Her hand, fire, cups my cheek. "Jelani, you are the gifted exception. The final arrow in the quiver. But even your hands have only had a taste of what we are truly capable of. Can you move mountains? Do your fingers command the wind?"

I shake my head.

She shows me her palms. "Mine once did. Return your Ancestors' magic stored in that onyx to the earth. Let the soil soak in its richness, and it will flow fiercely through our people once again. Your heart for humanity, the rare tenacity you possess, the way you balance justice and mercy. You're the perfectly balanced blend of the best parts of my saisa and coquella, Yakanna and Beerchi."

Perfect. No, not me.

"Your perfection isn't in that you don't make mistakes, it's how you grow from them," she says, as if she can read my mind. "You have to fix this, dear one. You, Jelani. No one else. Our time is done. Trust yourself. Remember, *as* the onyx is returned, the magic will be restored."

"O-okay, b-but . . ." Wind howls so loudly it drowns out my words as she blows away like dust. I blink several times, but the sky has cleared. In moments the thunderclouds evaporate, and the sky is empty as if it were all a dream. Golden dirt is caked under my nails, so it had to be real.

"Th-they can't help. They can't—" The words choke me. I stare at everyone who is also staring at me. They all heard the Ancestors say that *I'm* the exception. It has to be *me*. My heart rams in my chest and I try to gulp down air, but I can't take it in fast enough.

I can't . . .

This can't . . .

I rake my hands through my hair and run.

CHAPTER THIRTY-THREE

RUE!"

It's Julius, but I keep charging ahead, back to the shade of the jpango trees. Away from all the eyes, expectations. This wasn't how it was supposed to go.

"Dammit, Rue, slow down. I'm supposed to be the track star."

The ground softens under my feet when I slip beneath the canopy. Moonlight hides and I can barely make out my hands in front of my face. I pause for a breath, panting. Where am I going? Where can I truly run to on this island? I press my back into a thick trunk and slide down it, hugging my knees, itching to breathe. But the forest's leaves, the blanket of darkness, this island. I claw at my neck.

"Jelani?" The voice is as small as she is. Rojala's eyes are barely visible between the branches. Leaves crunch as she makes her way to me, and I wipe my face on my sleeve.

"Hey, I didn't know you were in here. Thought everyone was out there."

"Taavi wanted me to sit with the witch. So I stayed behind. Are you okay?"

"I don't know." I regret it the moment I say it. She sits beside me rubbing a hand over her shaved head.

"I don't know either."

"What do you mean?"

"Something is strange with Taavi. Ever since we left."

I let the silence sit and she fills it, the distraction a balm to my panic. I focus on my breathing, listening.

"She trusts me and keeps me close, helping her out with things. She's very to herself. But it's like whatever I do lately, I'm doing something wrong. I got yelled at for bringing you all to camp the other night when I was supposed to be scouting.

"But you were scouting; that's how you found us."

"I know, but she wasn't happy when I just showed up with you all. Then she was asking all sorts of questions about what I'd told you. I assured her I spoke to you with only the most respect. As any of us should."

"Rojala."

"Yes?"

"I'm no one special. I'm just me, Rue."

"But that is exactly it. You are different from anyone Taavi's had dealings with before. And we've met some characters. You . . ."

"I promise you, half the time I don't know what I'm doing."

She laughs. "Me either. When I got stuck on the grid and you found me, I had been trying to dig out this thing glittering in the pavement. I swear I saw it every time we stopped for water. Just a little flicker of something silver burrowed in the ground." She digs in her pocket and drops a silver pin in my hand no bigger than a bobby pin. "But digging it out almost burned my feet off. And it's not even anything. Just some dumb piece of metal."

I turn it in my hands, then tuck it in my pocket. Her instincts, the way she questions herself. I stare at the girl, who couldn't be more different from me on the outside, and see so much of who I am within.

"You don't always have to know what you're doing," I say. "It's okay to try something and mess up. And learn from it."

"I guess." Her voice is far-off. The night's glow is barely visible on her face, but I can hear her shoulders slump in her tone.

"Everyone always looks to you for answers," she says. "More so than even Taavi now." Her tone lightens, like the thought pleases her. This girl trusts me and lord only knows what I did to deserve it.

I shift in my seat. "I just try to be true to who I am. I'm just me."

"Out here I feel like it's my chance to figure that out," she says, drawing circles in the dirt. "Show the Macazi who I can be for them."

"Don't be who they need you to be. Be who you need to be for you."

She smirks, considering.

Why is it always so much easier to give advice than take it?

"How do you know who you are?" she asks.

I sit back and take in the dregs of the night air. *That's a good question.* "I guess I think about where I came from."

She studies me for several moments. "You will make a good Queen."

"Rojala, I'm not going to rule Ghizon."

A stolen peek of moonlight darts between the branches, illuminating her tilted-eyed stare. She didn't hear the Ancestors. She wasn't out there. This is her unadulterated opinion of me too. Her conclusion grates and I pick at my skin. Thoughts of home swim in my memory. Tasha's tie-dye everything, my old bed. Moms's hug. My lip trembles. I bite it so it stops.

"If you're not going to be Queen, then who will?" she presses. "Who would be better?"

"I don't know, but . . ." Pressure builds in my head as my thoughts trail off. I hop up and Rojala startles.

Her eyes follow me. Stick to me with admiration—or maybe expectation. Or some muddled mix of the two. "Well, Queen or not, wherever you end up, I'd like to go there too."

I sigh. Her words pierce through the brick of panic to the soft center underneath. I pick a red berry from a flower on a bush. It's stubbornly attached to thick petals, but I work it off. I remember these from the Ancestors' vision before my magic came to me, when I stood on their burial ground and felt them the first time. It feels like a lifetime ago. Then, the berries were everywhere. The little boy in the vision knew them well. I mash the berry between my fingers.

"Kaeli berries," Rojala says, joining my side, plucking one into her mouth. "If they're too ripe, they're really tart. Gotta pick them just right."

The forest is a fragment of what it used to be. Red used to dot these woods like a Christmas tree. So much destruction. So much death. So much pressure. And this girl sees the fix . . . the Ancestors see the fix *in me*? This wasn't the plan. This was the opposite of the plan.

I smooth my hands on my pants, but the berry's juice lingers, like a stain, a mark, a memory of my first encounter with the Ancestors that I'm forced to remember. I rub harder but it doesn't go away.

"Jela . . ."

"Please. Just stop."

Her eyes pinch, like she's discovered a blemish on a perfect portrait. I stare back but it's more than Rojala I see. It's buried bodies and forgotten bones; it's the weight of injustice packed down under the earth, buried under generations of unresolved anger and fear. It's my father's death. My mother, bleeding out on the carpet. It's Yiyo burning.

How can I be who they want me to be if this is all I see?

Rojala stares at me in such wonder, hope dangling in her eyes, willing me to say something that pieces her world back together—something to make the entire life she's lived underground with meek provisions, the family she's lost, the pain she's suffered on this journey alone, the hope ballooning in her chest *right now* . . . believable. But I don't have those words. I don't have comfort to give her. Or myself. I'm lost. Confused. Scared. And when I feel that way, there's only one thing that ever helps. Just the thought of it makes my next breath come easier.

"I owe you some corn bread, don't I?"

She smiles and I glance over my shoulder.

"You trust me?"

She nods and I wrap my hand in hers, mutter a transport spell to East Row just as someone's hand clamps my shoulder. My magic pulls at us, the world spins, and we're gone.

Ms. Leola's is busy as usual on a Sunday. Cooking starts before the sun comes up. The kitchen smells like heaven, notes of buttery, salty something permeating the air. Julius's hand is still on my shoulder.

"You scared the shit out of me, grabbing me like that!" My heart pounds. I wrap an arm around Rojala to ground myself and exhale.

She's looking around wide-eyed, her jaw hanging open.

"You running through the forest, you had me buggin'. I had to catch your ass!" Lines wrinkle his brow. "And what are we doing here, anyway?"

"Rue, baby, that you?" Ms. Leola says, the door creaking open. "Oh my god!" She pulls me in a bear hug. I hug around her frail body, thin but iron strong. She holds my face and kisses my cheek. "I'm just . . ." She clutches her chest and turns to Jue. "And Julius." She kisses him. "You didn't say you was going for a long time. Where have y'all been? I been worried sick over here 'bout you, boy. Get on here and get something to eat." Her eyes fall to Rojala, her pale skin even grayer in the midday sun. "And what's yo name, baby?"

She looks at me and I nod. "Rojala."

"Ma'am," I say.

"Rojala, ma'am," she repeats.

"Well, we got plenty to eat and you look like you could use a bite or two. Come on now." The door slaps shut behind us, and Tasha about knocks me over. She has two cats, one in each arm. I flash Julius a look. She's a cat lady now, apparently. My sister.

"You're back!"

"Uh, not exactly," Julius says, and I elbow him. "Fam, it's a mf-ing war brewing cross the globe. What is you doing?"

He squeezes my hand then taps his watch.

I sit at the table and survey the collards, macaroni and cheese, candied yams, and smothered oxtails on the plate Ms. Leola just handed me. I exhale the tiniest breath and settle in the chair, scents of home washing over me.

Rojala, the shock scrubbed from her face, pokes a finger in

the orange mush on her plate and sticks a finger in her mouth. "Mmmmmm." Her eyes widen, creasing around the corners. "Oh, that's good."

Ms. Leola sets a wedge of sweet potato pie in front of me and sits in a chair. Her head rests on her hands. I shove food in my mouth to avoid answering the questions lingering in her eyes. The note of garlic in the collards hits just right and the season on 'em is spot-on. Not too salty with just a dash of heat. I gulp down more as Julius takes a measured bite, his eyes darting from me to Ms. Leola.

"So?" she says.

"OO?" I swallow. "I mean, so?"

"I know that look," she says, leveling her eyes at me. "You pop up without a call."

Rojala sets her fork down on her empty plate. Her eyes fall to the floor. "This is my fault."

"No! I brought you here. It's okay."

"Rue," Julius says, his tone tight. "We gotta go, fam. You know this."

Ms. Leola sets a hand on my knee, which is bouncing out of control. "I'm listening, baby."

Each breath is fragile in my chest, like if I breathe in too deep, I'll shatter into a million pieces. I just want to eat and sit and be home. Be here, in East Row, with everything I know. I hug around myself and spill. I tell Ms. Leola about everything, from the Seer's prophecy to me accusing Bri, the Yakanna, Jhamal's betrayal, the Ancestors.

"Not Sir Chocolate, he was so *fine*," Tasha says, and I slap her shoulder.

"Shut up, this is serious."

She glances at Rojala, studying her tattered shirt and smudged face and mouths, *sorry*. Julius takes another tentative bite of food. Rojala stares at me like she can't believe the words coming out of my mouth. Like she sees through me finally. Like I'm not the fearless person she'd once thought.

"So you have this big problem and you don't know how to fix it," Ms. Leola says. "So you ran here for a bite to eat?"

My cheeks burn in shame.

"Listen, baby, them folks over there said *you* gotta do it." She pokes my chest. "You. I want you to think about all that means for your Ancestors to say *you* are the one to do it. Think about what they've been through, all they've overcome. Your Ancestors on your mother's side, too. You're bred from the best stock, child. It doesn't get any more rich or capable or tenacious. Dr. King marched down them streets, dogs attacking his legs. Rosa sat on that bus, went to jail for it. Your daddy's people were chased into hiding on that island, killed off, stolen from. And yet, still . . . what Maya say?"

Heat flushes my cheeks. "I rise."

"Consider everything those Ghizoni have seen in their lives and they believe *you* are the one to lead them through it. You think they don't know what they talking about?"

"I don't know the first thing about any of this. I screw up time and time again. And now my people at each other's throats and I don't know what to do. I have no idea how we can survive this. This ain't me, Ms. Leola. It's too . . ."

"Remember when you took that trip up to Brown University with your mama?"

I nod. We ain't have extra money for a hotel or plane ticket so

Moms packed up the car and we drove it straight, slept in the car, did the tour, and drove back. It rained the whole way, but when I stepped out on that campus, the sun had chased all the clouds away. And I knew I was meant to be there.

"And you remember what you told me right there . . ." She points at the doorway. "In front of yo mama?"

Tears sting my eyes. I do. The truth of it knots me up inside. I've been here before, not literally but in so many other ways. "I-I said if that school let me in, I'd figure out how to make it there."

"You woulda been a fish out of water then, too. What you know about your people over in Ghizon?"

"That the Ghizoni name came from the God of Light when they gifted magic to my Ancestors to fill the world with good. I know the armor we wear is trimmed in ripples to mimic the ocean around our homeland. The carvings and gems embedded into the metal signify the power and richness woven into who we are." I sit up straighter. "I know we pray to the gods for favor and again always in thanks. We keep our right sides bare." I touch the ring in my hair. "To honor love and the role it plays."

Zora's face swirls in my memory. And Kai. And Shaun. And little Titube with her golden flower. And even . . . Jhamal. His face rattles through my mind like faint echoes of a gong I'm straining to hear. I'm furious with him, but love tethers us, and I'm not sure that'll ever go away. I actually think it makes me hate him more.

"I know we dance even after loss to cling to joy. I know we fight as a unit, side by side, because we are only as strong as our weakest. We cover each other, protect each other. We'd prefer to die fighting for what we believe in than live in the shadow of oppression. I know a lot, I guess. But I definitely don't have all the answers."

"You don't have to." It's Rojala who speaks this time. "It's okay to try something and mess up. And learn from it."

I grin at her parroting. Now that I think on it, I did negotiate to bring on an ally for my people. Hundreds to fight on our side. And I've kept them alive. I intercepted an electronic Loyalist transmission, and I know what the Chancellor's up to, at least somewhat. I went against the status quo when it wasn't cool to do. I secured a spell to raise the dead, for goodness' sake. I even *spoke* to my Ancestors.

I stand up from the table, my wrists catching a glint of sunlight from the window.

Ms. Leola winks. "I get it, baby. Sometimes you gotta remember where you came from, to understand the purpose in where you going."

She's so right. I've been so busy asking everyone else for answers, so busy looking to someone else to fix this, to lead. So convinced that girls from the hood don't wear crowns, I didn't realize I've been leading this entire time. Carving a path. Doing something I've never seen someone like me do before.

I *am* a leader, whether I want to be one or not.

My Ancestors' daughter.

It's who I am. Who I've always been. Who my people are.

And I, Rue from East Row, am enough to fill those shoes.

CHAPTER THIRTY-FOUR

BENEATH THE TREES OUTSIDE the Ancestors' grave site, the Macazi and Ghizoni surround me. Whispers flit like fireflies among the branches as morning sun peeks between the canopy. Thick leaves with beaded dew glitter in the light. Everyone's watching, waiting. Even Shaun leans on a timber, arms folded. I hope he's here for the right reasons.

When Jue, Rojala, and I returned, I'd found everyone still lingering over the Ancestors who'd come and gone. I told them to form up, that I had something to say. And I guess because of what's just happened, everyone wants to hear it. Almost everyone.

"Have you seen Kai?" I ask Julius, who's helping Bri fold a piece of metal for some sort of suction gadget she's messing with.

Neither she nor the Yakanna nor Jhamal are anywhere to be seen. And after the reunion Zora had with her sisters, I can only assume Zora knows now where Kai stands. And I guess where the Yakanna stand, by default. I don't like it, but the Yakanna are loyal to one another. I have to trudge forward.

"Not since we got back." His tongue pokes his cheek.

"What are you doing?"

"I'm trying to make a second one of these suction things," Bri says. "I have an idea."

Taavi's worn expression flashes between the trees and I flag her down.

"Where do you want us?" she starts, before I can even mention why I called her name.

"I need lead."

Her forehead crinkles.

"The lead you used to line your home. Where'd you get it?"

"For what? Is this a new plan? The Ancestors. I thought . . ."

"It's a slight amendment. Is there more?"

"Yes, there's plenty at a dump site on the outskirts of the Lower Central District.

"Take as many as you need and get it."

"It's really heavy."

"Just bring me what you can carry, I can expand it with a spell."

"Okay. Can I ask what it's for?"

"Why?"

"I just want to know what the plan is, is all." She doesn't meet my eyes. "And look . . . I'm sorry I didn't tell you about the Chancellor being my father. I was ashamed, if I'm honest. And I didn't want you to think less of me." Something sours on my tongue about her apology, but I swallow it down. I give her the benefit of the doubt. I get having a complicated relationship with your father and not wanting to talk about it.

"Just don't keep anything else from me and we're good." I offer a handshake and she takes it.

With Taavi off to get the lead, I face the group. "Form up, I'd like to address all of you." It wasn't coincidental that I sent Taavi off to get the lead before addressing the masses here. I'm not naive. If she can withhold info once, she can do it again. And I prefer not to take any risks with this new plan. This is my final shot. If this doesn't work, we'll all be done for. Erased.

Julius and Bri pop a squat on the ground, and Rojala sits beside them. The Seer is folded up next to a tree in the distance. Her eyes are closed, but I know she's listening. I look for jade-dotted armor one more time but don't spot any. Jhamal must be with Kai, too. Julius gives me a head nod to begin, and I dig out words I should have found a long time ago.

"Listen, I don't have all the answers and I can't pretend to." Hundreds of eyes stare back at me between the trees. Macazi, Ghizoni, Beerchi. People on this island who have watched their understanding of the world crack and crumble these past several weeks. I have to show them I can put it back together, rightly, stone upon stone.

I take a deep breath and keep going. "I-I'd hoped raising the Ancestors was the way to go, that they could fix this. And in some ways they helped. We know your magic *can* be restored, that we have to return the stolen onyx on the traitors' wrists to the earth. But it didn't fix everything. It's not what I'd envisioned would happen." I huff a breath and steady my feet. "We can't fight each other anymore. I've *been* saying that, but until we have a leader that unifies us, we'll continue to crack from the inside. I get that now. And we really need to turn our eyes outward—to *them*."

I point east, toward the Chancellor's tower, an ivory emblem in the distance. "The true enemy. So I'm asking you now to trust me. Not because I have all the answers. Not because I do everything right. But because I'm not giving up on this fight. And I have a pretty good plan this time, I think." *I hope*. "But I can't finish it without you, Bati, your wisdom. And you, Rojala, your precision with a blade. And you Bri, your gadgets. All of you. My people. My family." Jhamal's name hangs on my tongue and somewhere inside me pangs with sadness. "We rise from the ashes *together*."

I blow out a big breath.

"So, I ask you to swear your loyalty to me and I promise you, I'll make a way out of this for us or die trying. If you would have me . . . I humbly ask for the honor of serving as your Queen."

Leaves rustle under Bri, Julius, Rojala, and a few others who plant on their knees in fealty, bowing their heads. Others follow, nearly all the Macazi, Joshi flicking a tear from his cheek. The Ghizoni kneel in waves and a flutter cinches in my chest. I stand a little straighter. But the Beerchi still stand. Shaun unfolds then refolds his arms.

I swallow. "This does not have to come to blows, Shaun, please."

"I cannot honor your claim. You must prove yourself first. It is not personal, it is just the Beerchi way." He raises his blade. "I'm sure you understand."

"Final warning, Shaun. Put your blade down. Tell your men to stand with me, unified. And submit yourself for punishment for the murder of our Yakanna sister."

The crowd explodes in whispers.

"For the last time, the Yakanna girl. You do not know what you speak of. I never touched Doile. If you must know, she is my brother's effija."

Effija? Promised? Like, betrothed?

Shaun's nostrils flare, his chest rising and falling. "You do not know me to judge me. I would never touch a hair on my sister's head. Even Kai. I would fight her in combat but never end her. She is my sister. Beerchi are loyal."

"Loyal," his brothers echo.

"S-so who did this?"

"It is not honorable to accuse without proof, but if anyone touched Doile, I would bet my beard it was Kai."

Chatter erupts and my insides do flips. I want to believe better of her. But first Jhamal. Now this. . . . It doesn't look good.

"I was too quick to judge and for that I'm sorry. I won't judge Kai either until she is present and can speak for herself."

Shaun dips his chin in respect and for a glimmer of a moment I think he really sees me. Or at least sees who I believe I can be. His coquella steps forward and sets a hand on Shaun's back. The two share a look and coquella takes a knee.

"It has to be unity, brother. Somewhere in all this we've lost sight of the way. This is not who we Beerchi are." He shakes his head. "We are might and pride, but like you say, Shaun, we are *loyal*. The Ancestors have spoken. Kneel with me, brother." Shaun's coquella lays his curved blade at my feet, folds forward, bowing fully.

Words escape me. My skin tingles all over.

With one Beerchi sworn to me, the rest, one by one, follow suit, cloaks on the ground, a pile of curved gold metal at my feet. Shaun is left standing alone. He blows out a breath, shuffling on his feet for several moments. Then he slips off his rings and unlatches his cloak. His chin never dips. In fact, he raises it. He hesitates another moment but kneels.

And finally, I can breathe.

"Thank you." I dig for my voice, but I'm all shock and stutters. I've done it. I've asked them to follow me. I've vowed to lead them and they're trusting me. A crowd of silent stares wait, staring, unblinking. "The plan. O-oh, right. So, we will lure the Chancellor and his men *inside* our lair.

Let them think they found us. But the walls will be lined with lead, so their stolen magic will not work." Gasps pop like firecrackers. "But the trick is, *my* magic won't work either."

Many eyes widen in fear.

"We have the fiercest warriors on the island," I say.

"Ya!" they cry.

"Their *only* advantage is that they have magic. When we strip them of that, they are nothing. They stand no chance! So we fight them as equals. And as their onyx is removed, Bri and Julius"—Bri waves her hand and Julius throws a chin up—"will collect the onyx and get it to the grave site." I explain how the lead worked for the Macazi and heads nod in understanding. "Let's gather up and head back. It'll be too bright to be out here soon."

People jostle around me. The Seer meets my eyes. I nod at her and she smiles in return. I settle down in the dirt on my knees, palms up, in the posture of prayer and gratitude to the Ancestors. I can't leave this site without sending up a prayer for favor as we walk into what's next. Thanking them for believing in me, for pushing me to do what I didn't believe I could. Zora crosses my mind, and I think of how she used to feed me the words when I'd forget. But the words come to me easily when I reach for them this time. Some Ghizoni join me, echoing my prayers, while the Macazi wait in neat lines in silent reverence.

When the prayer is done, I catch myself looking for Jhamal when Julius's face slips into view.

"I'm proud of you," he says in earshot of Rojala and Bri, who come over too.

I squeeze his hand, all words escaping me right now. "This is only the beginning," I manage. "We still have to win this thing.

But for now, we lie low and bait them to come."

"How do we know they'll come?" Bri asks.

"Oh, they'll come." I pull the thin bobby pin from my pocket that Rojala gave me and squeeze. A red light beeps on the end of it. "It's a tracker that's been following us, reporting our location."

Rojala gasps.

"Yep, someone planted this on us, who knows how long ago."

And I'm not so sure it wasn't Jhamal.

I close in on the opening to our underground lair with everyone behind me, the Macazi, the Beerchi, Bri. Morning sun peeks at us from the west. Both directions around us are undisturbed.

"*Psssst,*" someone whispers, but I see no one.

The area is no more than barbed wire and crumbled concrete, a dumpster, and piles of broken glass. The Ghizoni and Macazi step carefully over the barbed wire and slip down the entrance. Julius handles the Seer and Joshi takes up the rear. Taavi stands aside next to a wagon full of tiny graphite-colored balls—lead.

"*Psssst.*"

Okay, I didn't imagine it that time. "You can go ahead inside, I'll meet you in there," I say, and Taavi nods, ducking inside behind the others. When the door clamps closed, I follow the direction of the sound more closely.

"Over here."

I recognize the voice when she speaks. Zora's face peeks from behind a barrel, gesturing for me to come faster. She pulls me down behind it, flashing a gaze in both directions before ducking down too. Her grip on my arm is tight.

"Listen to me, they are tracking you."

I finger the bobby pin in my pocket.

"The Chancellor knows where you are and yet he has not struck yet. Why?"

The picture of what's ahead contorts in my mind into something far more daunting than even I'd understood. If he has known where we are but hasn't attacked us head-on, it has to be because . . .

The truth of how the Chancellor's been plotting slaps. The way when we left prison we always felt like we were being watched. "He wanted us to raise the Ancestors. He wanted us to get this far." Oh my god. But how did he . . . "Wait, Kai is she . . . ?"

Her countenance cracks with desperation at the sound of Kai's name, and shivers skitter up my arm. "Listen, Jelani." Zora grips my arm, her nails digging in. Worry claws at me. I've never seen Zora like this. She glances over her shoulder.

"I don't know how the Chancellor knows. But I do know he was supposed to strike soon, but the Ancestors' being raised changed things. Something did not go according to plan and now . . ." She glances over her shoulder. "And now there's a new plan."

Fear washes over like a chill from the wind. *Could Jhamal be in league with him too? In my memory, I saw him plotting with Patrol.* My head throbs. The lies, the deception. It's so much. All of this is so much.

"What's the new plan he has? Tell me." Trepidation lives where my resolve and determination used to.

"I don't know. But Kai is reporting to the Chancellor."

My mind races through what-ifs. "No, she wouldn't. Our beef was about Shaun." *And maybe Jhamal. Maybe.*

"It does not matter if Shaun is no longer King. It was never about

Shaun." Her nails dig harder into my skin. "You do not understand, Jelani." Her eyes are glazed, and it's only then that I notice her gloves are gone. Scratches streak her arms, like magic burned her skin.

I've seen marks like this before, it confuses me. I reach to touch them, but she grabs my hand, her pulse raging through her fingertips.

"It's about the future of our people," she says. Her nostrils flare and her chest huffs. "Who would she think is best to carve out our path forward?" Her whisper is thick. "You? From some faraway place? Or her, a direct descendant of the Mother?"

"Well, I-I'd hoped we could maybe do it together or . . ."

"This war will end either us or them. And whoever wins, Kai intends to be on top. I have to go. You did not see me."

"Thank you for this, Zora." I want to ask about the other Yakanna, but how do I word that without . . . I bite my tongue.

"Saisa." She grips my shoulder.

"Saisa." I grip hers, too, trying to keep my frazzling nerves calm. If we have to fight *against* all the Yakanna . . . that could be a big-ass problem. I blow out a breath. One issue at a time.

She shifts on her feet, the location insignia on her armor glowing. "True Yakanna stand with you, Rue." She sets my hand back on my bare right shoulder. "Remember who we truly are." She rubs the scars on her arm, her eyes tilting at the corners. "Some of us had almost forgotten," she says, before running off.

An eeriness keeps me crouched there, still, watching her go. When we ran for our lives, were almost burned alive by those traps, Zora didn't flinch. A chill skitters up my arm. But here, just now, Zora was utterly terrified.

CHAPTER THIRTY-FIVE

BRI IS HUDDLED OVER her bag of gadgets, and there are actual wires coming out of her hair.

"You have a little something." I point. But she misses the joke, pressing her glasses to her nose. Sweat rolls off her brow, but she catches it with the back of her hand before pressing the thin end of a wire into an open hole in her suction gadget.

"You sure this is gonna work?" I ask.

She chews her lip, unblinking, as she braids three wires and presses them into another end. Her eyes widen and she taps a red button at the top. It lights up, flies from her fingers through the air, and snaps to my wrist with a *clink*.

"Yes!" she says. "It's the same technology I used in the HologrifX, from the heat-seeking fire arrows. You remember?"

"We almost died. I definitely remember."

"I calibrated it to suction to objects imbued with magic." A piece falls off the top and she pushes it back on. "Your cuffs, for example. The onyx!"

I'd asked her to help me brainstorm some way to collect the onyx quickly. Carving it from their wrists won't be easy or quick, but once we get it out, we need to hightail it to the grave site.

Bri'd mentioned she had an idea that just might work.

I pluck the suction gadget from my wrists and it's like pulling off a starfish.

"Bri, this is good."

She holds a matching silver ball with a handle on the end. "And I made two. One for Julius. Just need to add the handle to this one." She smiles hopefully and I squeeze her shoulder.

"I'll leave you to it, then. There's someone I need to speak to."

But she doesn't even respond, back to her hyper focus.

If the Chancellor's coming, he's going to come at night, I'd bet. To take us unawares. Little does he know, we'll be ready. I climb up and out of the lair, careful to peek first before coming out aboveground, Zora's words floating through my memory. The lead is in piles just past the barbed wire, beside the dumpster where we found Doile's blood. I touch the stone and a chill moves through me, like my fingers have been dipped in ice water. The cold creeps through my bones and my magic quivers as if it can sense the restraint the lead brings. I snatch my finger away and the cold feeling dissolves, magic pooling, warming my fingertip. This won't be easy.

I flip through a spell book for a stretching spell. The pages crinkle with each turn. How do I work with something so poisonous I can't touch it? I grab a gray lump from the cart, biting back the discomfort coiling in my chest, and set it on the ground.

"Iwi yaka," I say, aiming at it. It wiggles, then stills. I step closer and the world threatens to spin. I squat, catching myself with a hand on the pavement. My fingers trace the text in the book and I sound out the words again, straightening my back when I say it. "Iwee yakaz!"

The lead glows, rising in the air. It convulses, stretching, folding over on itself as it widens like dough being kneaded. A chill sweeps toward me and I walk quite a ways back, far enough away from its power to subdue me. It contorts into a thin sheet, about the size of a poster, then eases to the ground.

"Iwee yakaz," I say again. It pulses but doesn't move. That's as big as it's going to get.

I move closer but its toxicity is magnetic. I give it wider berth, clinging to the warmth that hums inside me. This might just work. I turn over the cart of lead and spread them out, lining them up in neat rows. My arms are heavy and ache from the weight. I try not to touch them too much, fighting off the chill as I spread them out with my fingers. When they're all laid out, I retreat until they're very small in the distance.

"Iwee yakaz," I say, pointing at the first row of chunks of lead, waving my hand in one smooth motion over it. The lead stretches to a plate and I move on to the next. It takes a while, but by the time sweat crawls down my neck, I hold my arm up blocking the sun and it's done.

I slip back underground, and the corridor is lined with bodies slipping on armor. The Macazi don't have any traditional armor, but they wear chunks of lead around their necks, dangling from their wrists, as wide circles in their ears. I keep a distance and steady my steps, feeling my magic hesitate the longer I'm near them.

"Joshi," I say as turquoise sprigs of hair appear on my peripheral. "Go on up and grab those sheets of lead I made. Take a few people with you. They're heavy. Line them up down here against the walls. Start at the entrance and focus on the common areas."

"Got it," Joshi says, snapping a strap across his chest that holds an assortment of knives, which I'd guess are made of lead. "You going to be down here while we do it?"

"Yeah, I'll have to be." I shift on my feet. The idea of being down here while the ability to use my magic slips from my fingers frankly scares the shit out of me, but I see no way around it. "Have you seen Taavi?"

"I haven't. Not since she returned with the lead."

"Find her. Tell her I need to see her. I want to talk to her before nightfall."

Joshi nods and is off.

I round a few corners between armored bodies looking for some glimpse or whisper of Taavi. I duck my head into a large room where meetings were held. Ghizoni and Macazi work in pairs to clear piles of debris stacked against the walls, making space for the lead plates. I give them a thumbs-up and keep on down the hall. Maybe she's in here? I peep into a small bedroom. Nope. Nothing. No one. *Where is she?*

I turn and bump into Julius, his expression strained. "Hey," I say.

"Ole girl and all her people are gone."

"You mean Kai?"

He nods.

"What do you mean, 'gone'?"

"I mean, there's no trace of them anywhere down here. I've looked in the room Jhamal was in, everything. No sign of them."

It crosses my mind to ask if there's any sign of Jhamal, but I shake off the question. My thoughts and him are like a moth to a flame. *Forget about him.* I link hands with Julius.

"I don't know where they could have gone."

Howling slices the air. I dart down the hall toward the sound, Julius on my heels. Dim light brushes the dirt floor and Rojala's on her knees screaming. Inches from her are legs, unmoving. Zora lies there, eyes open. I rush over, taking her hand in mine. It's still warm.

"Zora!" I press a hand to her chest. Something faint flutters there. "Zora, talk to me, please!" Tears sting my eyes. Her lips move, but I can barely make out their whisper.

"I promised her," she says. "I swore it. But I couldn't. Not after meeting you. Getting to know you." She laces her shaky fingers between mine. "My sister. I could never hurt you, Jelani. No matter what she threatened me with." She holds my hand to her bare right side and tries to speak, but the words come out a sputter, a pool of red growing beneath her.

"No, please! Zora, stay with me. Help! Can we get her help? Bri!" I pat my pockets for the jar of minty potion. I scoop all I can on my finger, tears streaming down my cheeks, and press it into her side where blood gushes. But it's like trying to mop up water from the ocean.

"More, I need . . . Bri!" I squeeze Zora's hand, sobbing harder when I see the words burned into her chest by some sort of magic.

OATHBREAKER

In her hand she clutches two jade stones. She presses them into my palm and shudders one more time. She's gone. My world darkens and anger burns through me like wildfire. I caress the scars on her arm, just like the ones I saw Taavi take when we made our agreement. Graka eyo, a blood oath. Zora took an oath to Kai, swearing to betray me? The revelation breaks over me like a wave. But she refused. And died for it.

Then it was Kai.

I gasp.

The prophecy.

Kai is who the Seer was referring to.

Which means . . . Jhamal never . . .

Boom.

The ground trembles. Something shatters. Footsteps and sniffles echo somewhere far off.

"Rue!" It's Julius.

I spot a topknot with shaved sides fleeing around a corner.

"Rue!" Julius's eyes are a web of red. "The Chancellor. He's here."

CHAPTER THIRTY-SIX

"HURRY, HELP ME TAKE her body somewhere safe!" I tug on Julius's arm, and he and Rojala help me. I rush back down the winding hall and into one of the side rooms, where we tuck Zora away. Her limp arms, the way she pulled on her gloves. How many times did she try to keep emotionally distant in order to spy on me, but just couldn't? She is gone. My sister who showed me how to fight, who gave me the bell I wear in my hair, who taught me the Ancestors' prayer. The weight of it makes me sturdy myself on the wall. Rojala's face materializes in front of me.

"Jelani? What do we do?" Rojala holds Zora's hand.

"Uh . . ." Why is the world this way? I hate it here. I blow out a breath, latching on to the urgency at hand. I blink, trying to wish away the grief, bury it, but there's so much that's built; it's like a gray cloud promising a hard rain.

"Y-you stay in here." I swallow, getting my bearings. "And stand guard over her." I can see the "but" in her eyes. But she nods, and Julius and I shut them inside. The world rumbles, shouting rings through the air.

Zora . . . I say her name, carrying her with me in every step.

I pull Julius to me. "Find Bri. Collect onyx." He's off, and I shove my way through bodies to get a glimpse of the situation. Patrolmen pour through the hole in the ceiling. Some in plain clothes, Loyalists, and others in slick uniforms with the Ghizoni emblem on their chest. No sign of the Chancellor. Yet.

One leaps from the last rung of the ladder, aiming his hands to fire magic at Joshi. He thrusts, but nothing happens. Joshi's ready. The Loyalist glares at his own wrist, thrusting his hands again in utter confusion. Joshi swings a chunk of metal and it slaps his head with a *smack*.

"Their wrists!" I shout at Joshi as bodies jostle me around. "The onyx on their . . ."

But Joshi's moved on, fighting off two Patrol who caught him off guard. I dash over, grabbing the Loyalist's limp legs. I drag him, searching for a spot to pull him aside when something slams into my back.

It's a tall fighter with a knot on her head, her right shoulder bared. Yakanna. I see Zora's face in my mind. And Doile's. My insides pang. She swipes at the men funneling through the tunnel, each dropping like flies. She swings, pivots, then jabs. And where there was one Patrol on the ground, lie three.

"Y-you came?" I say.

Her chin falls. "Zora told us everything before . . ." She pulls me to her, bringing her blade down hard behind me. Someone grunts before collapsing on the ground. "Go. Do whatever is needed. The Yakanna stand with you, Jelani." There's a note of sadness in her voice, but thirst for vengeance burns behind each syllable.

"For Zora," I say, setting a hand on her bare shoulder.

"For Zora."

I plow through the masses, dodging, throwing blows. The Chancellor's men are completely caught off guard without access to magic. My foot bumps a curved blade and I scoop it up. I look for the Beerchi who dropped it but spot none. Something shoves into me and I turn, blade up and ready. I swipe. The Loyalist sidesteps and I miss. I raise the handle again, bringing it down hard, and red splatters my shoes. He holds the place his nose just was, shrieking, and I move on to the next.

The ceiling door opens and light from outside pours in. A head peeps in, then he closes it. A blade dents my view; a lanky Patrolman hovers over me, a dagger clutched in his hand.

He's armed. They know.

The clang of metal tears at my ears, and I realize several of the last Patrol to come through carry weapons of some sort. They've caught on. *But how? No one that's come in has made it back out. Unless . . .*

Kai.

So that's why she was down here a moment ago. To tip off the Chancellor.

I grit my teeth and my blood runs hot. Patrol swings and I duck, metal whooshing over my head. Light on my feet, I bob and weave between his blows. He swipes and I slide aside into someone or something and it shoves me back. He pivots, panting. I'm wearing him down. He charges at me once more, and I hook an arm around him, using his momentum to shove him to the ground. His head bobs. I snatch his weapon and pop him in the head with it.

I drag him to the other Patrol, who's still out like a light. Two bodies, four beads of onyx. I need to get them out of this corridor and try to get this onyx out. I tug on both bodies, but it's like trying to drag a sack of bricks. I finagle one into a side room and hurry back for the other, but he's gone. *Shit!*

"I got it!!" Joshi shouts from somewhere, holding up a black ball.

"Toss it over here," Julius shouts. The bloody ball of onyx flies from Joshi's fingers through the air and Julius's gadget cups it like a catcher's mitt. A flicker of joy tugs at me but I bury it. It's too early to assume the best.

"There she is," someone shouts, and I hold my fists up, tucking my chin, ready. I look for who said it, but the corridor is a chaotic crash of bodies and metal. Blood splatters the walls and dust makes my throat itch. I blink and a figure at the end of the hall looms, staring. I blink again and his face is clearer through the haze. Broad shoulders, gold breastplate against smooth ebony smooth skin.

Jhamal.

He stares, unmoving, and emotions rush through me like waves, an expanse of chaos filling the space between us in more ways than one. The Seer's face and Zora's body float through my mind. So do he and Kai. I see him holding the potion to my lips. Everything in me that just felt strong, fractures. How does he do this to me? I part my lips to speak, but a tangle of armor obstructs my view, and just like that he's gone. And as much as I hate it . . . a piece of me I'll never get back goes with him.

My spine pinches in pain.

"Jelani, watch out!"

I hold my side. My pants are ripped and swelling with red. I lower my waistband and find my skin split.

Thankfully, the wound is not deep. I pull out the jar of minty paste and rub the remnants on the wound. It tingles, and where there was just red is smooth brown skin again. I rush down the corridor, wedging myself in the maze of people. Gray skin is in a heap on the ground, tangled around brown limbs. My insides quake with sadness, but I tuck my lip and keep going. I mutter a prayer to the Ancestors as I pass my fallen brothers and sisters. I will come back and bury them all with my two hands. Every last one of them.

"Koz mwona." *Make it so, I pray.*

A curved blade swings like a pendulum chopping down Loyalists with each swipe. The Beerchi attached to it meets my gaping stare, nodding at me. I stand a little straighter.

United.

My people. Well, most of them.

I did this.

An elbow slams my chin and I swing in response, my fist connecting with someone's cheek. I don't look to see who it is. I keep going. Kai's got to be down here spying somewhere. And with her the Chancellor.

"Jelani!" The voice is aged. The Seer is folded on one of the beds jutting from the wall, veiled by a thin curtain. Taavi sits next to her, shaking.

"What is she doing out here?" I ask her. "She should be tucked away. And where have you been?"

"I've been here, trying to find somewhere to stash her. But I've searched this place high and low and nowhere's truly hidden."

War rages in the backdrop, my ears burning from the sounds of bodies grunting and slamming the ground. Death drips in the air. I don't entirely believe her, but there's not time to press further.

"Je . . ." The Seer coughs over her words. "Jelani." She clears her throat, clamping a firm hand on my wrist. Taavi's brows cinch. The Seer's lips move, and she squirms where she sits. She's trying to tell me something, warn me? Is she fighting the curse to do it? Or has this trip finally withered her down irreparably?

"I'm listening."

"Yuh . . . puhh." She fights for words, but all that comes out are chokes. She grips her throat, shaking her head, and points to the dirt floor above us.

"Up? Aboveground? I need to go aboveground?"

She nods.

The Chancellor.

He sent his men, but like the coward he is, he's not coming down here himself. I settle back into the wall. I have to face him again. Aboveground. Where his magic is intact. My insides slosh; no matter how many times I swallow, the lump in my throat won't go down.

The Ancestors believed I could do this.

They chose me to do this.

Me, Rue from East Row.

And it's different now. Before, he stood in formation with thousands. Now many of his men lie in heaps down here on the floor. He sent them to weaken us, no doubt. But he underestimated me. I'm used to being underestimated.

If anyone's weakened by this siege attempt, it's them. Our numbers are a fraction of theirs and yet they're dropping like flies. It's just like I said—without their stolen magic, they're nothing, a footnote in a history book. If that.

I rise, but the Seer holds tight to me, pointing to herself as well.

"She wants to go too." I'd almost forgotten. "I promised her."

"Mother, that is not wise," Taavi says. "H-he's out there."

He . . . her father.

"You stay here," she says. "I-I'll go up with Jelani."

She stares at her daughter, her expression carrying the weight of something I don't fully understand. After several moments she nods in agreement, but even that seems to pain her.

"Okay, and we're leaving her with Rojala," I say to Taavi.

"Rojala? She's a . . ."

"I trust Rojala with my life."

Taavi doesn't question again and helps me carry her mother. She's a pallet of cinder blocks in my arms. I shove through the crowds, stepping over bodies until I spot the door to the room where I left Zora. Inside, Rojala is cleaning Zora's body with a damp cloth.

"You okay?"

"I am," she says. Taavi kisses her mother's forehead. She says something to her, coiling a bony finger through her daughter's hair, but it's too low for me to catch it. Taavi nods in response, but her lip quivers when she snaps back to my side.

"Barricade as much as you can against this door, anything you can find," I say to Rojala.

"I will."

Worry takes flight in me, fluttering around in my chest as I shut them inside. Taavi and I set off to find the Chancellor. Her father. I spot Julius dodging a blow at his head and clapping back with a right hook. The Loyalist folds to the ground and Julius crouches over him, pressing the suction gadget to his wrist.

"Rue," he shouts. "Look!" He pulls the gadget away and there's a tiny red scar in the Loyalist's arm where the onyx used to be.

"Oh my god." I glance at Taavi, expecting her to be blown away, too. But she's wholly distracted, pulling at her ear.

"Keep going," I tell him.

"Where you going?" he asks.

"Outside. The Chancellor's up there. He won't come in now that he knows about the lead."

"Rue, last time you faced him one-on-one . . ." He stops. He doesn't need to finish the thought, because that same worry has my chest in a knot.

"I have to, Jue," I say, realizing I've been in this moment before. Seen that expression on someone else pleading with me. It is and was honest, true. That I can't deny. Maybe at some point Jhamal did love me. Julius tucks his lip, his worry, and nods.

"Get Bri and get to the grave," I tell him. "Take all the onyx you have right now. Then come back for more."

He holds on to me, squeezing, before letting my hand go.

"I can do this," I say.

He strokes my cheek, thumb caressing my jaw. "Oh, I know. Just be careful."

"You, too." I take his hand and plant a kiss in his palm, hoping it's not our last, and go.

CHAPTER THIRTY-SEVEN

ABOVEGROUND, THE CHANCELLOR STANDS, magic fizzing in his hands, Patrol flanking his sides. Kai, slick in her gold armor, stands behind him. The breastplate she wears is new, more angular, jutting over both her shoulders. A crown with spires spread like sunrays rests on her head. Jhamal is a shadow behind her. My blood rises from a simmer to a boil. He looks right at me, through me, but I set my glare on the Chancellor.

"You're looking well these days," the Chancellor says.

I step out of the hole fully, pooling heat to my fingertips. Magic crackles in my hands and I hold my chin up. I can't let him get in my head, break my focus. Last time, I was sorely outnumbered, but up here his forces have been whittled down, thanks to our trap down below.

"The Mother doesn't smile on this treachery," I say to Kai. She flinches but doesn't respond. "And the Chancellor can't crown you on this island anyway. It's not his. Everything he has he stole. Matter of fact, everything he has, he committed genocide to get."

The Chancellor's mug reddens. "She speaks nonsense. Do not listen to her." He cuts a glance at the handful of men shrouded around him, onyx glowing on their wrists. A few glance at one another, questions wrinkling their brows. But their laser focus on me returns with a blink.

"Kai, you've done good work," the Chancellor says. "Don't let her seduce you with lies."

A smirk tugs at her lips. "It wasn't my original plan. That was spoiled . . . by someone I shouldn't have trusted."

"Someone you *loved* but killed."

This time, her lip trembles. I continue. "I'd say that's something you both have in common, but I don't think that man is capable of loving anyone but himself." This time his eyes narrow.

"The consequence of breaking a blood oath is death," Kai says. "She swore she would report to me on your position and plans at all times. She swore if you somehow raised the Ancestors and survived it, she would kill you. She broke her word. I did not kill her, her lie did."

"Blood is on your hands and you know it. For asking Zora, who loved you and served you, and would do anything for you, to be a snitch. For putting her in a position to either be loyal to the person she loves or betray her conscience. You a bitch for that. If you want to have me killed, do it yourself."

"Is that supposed to intimidate me?" She titters, dusting her shoulder and straightening her crown.

Zora's open-eyed stare flashes in my memory, her warm smile, the way she fought so fearlessly, the way she tugged on her gloves relentlessly. "You coulda shown mercy. She loved you. She was your sister . . ."

"Shut your mouth!" She spits her words like fire. "You know nothing of what you speak."

I've struck a chord. "I know why Yakanna's right sides are bare." I move as I talk, careful to keep Taavi as protected behind me as I can. She's frozen—her legs wobbling like stilts about to buckle. "I know why we wear jade in our armor. I know killing your own saisa and pinning blame on your coquella is disgusting." Her eyes widen in surprise. She glares at the Chancellor, lips tightening. He glances back at her and she presses her lips closed, nostrils flaring.

Shit.

She didn't kill Doile either. . . . The Chancellor did?

And she still stands with him?

"I know the Mother's vengeance burns as hot as her pride," I continue. "You gon' get yours for this, Kai."

"Is that a threat?"

"It's a promise."

The Chancellor moves closer to her, and Jhamal's eyes flick in his direction. "She's a liar, just trying to steal your inheritance. Can't you see? You deserve that crown. Don't let anyone tell you different." He plays to her pride because he knows something she hasn't realized: it's her weakness.

"You like using that excuse, don't you? Whispering it to people you want to manipulate? How they're special and if they'd only trust you, you could help them be great. You have a motus operandi, I'll give you that, Xire."

His face reddens. He knows I know the secret he tried to burn away when he destroyed Totsi's. The truth he scrubbed from every history class and magic book. The truth he killed and slaughtered for.

He glares at me. "You're a dead person talking." He shoots and his magic darts like arrows in my direction. I whip open my hands, whispering a spell, and a wall as transparent as glass oozes from my fingers, stretching tall in front of us. His magic slams into the barrier and fizzles out.

"Stay behind me," I say to Taavi, but she doesn't move, eyes darting between me and him, fingers pressed to her earlobe. Magic fires in my direction and I sidestep, careful to keep my barrier up, holding it like a shield. Their magic rains against me and my shield flickers.

"No!" I mutter the shield spell again . . . too late. Another assault from a cluster of daggers barrels into me and my magicked shield evaporates. His men rush at me.

"Yo lis." Fire streams from my fingers swallowing a pair of them. But more skirt the flames and keep coming. "This way!" I pull Taavi along; she's like a brick. Streams of energy fly around me, a tangled web. I dodge and twist, ducking as light zips overhead. My chest is heavy. I can't win this only playing defense.

Magic streams through the air like a missile, and I raise my arm, blocking. My cuffs glow. They absorbed the hit? *Oh, shit!*

Shock is written in lines on Patrol's face, too. They freeze and it's the second I need.

"Feey'l." I thrust and air ripples, energy rolling like waves, knocking them over like a stack of dominoes. They fall to the ground. I step over them and erect another barrier in front of Taavi and me. "Get the beads off their wrists," I say to her. "Dig it out if you have to."

Taavi's feet stick like glue. Magic gushes at us, like cords of light zipping through the air. But each attack slams into my barrier, my wrists warming. "Taavi! The onyx, now! You swore."

Their magic slams into the barrier again and I shudder, steadying my feet, pushing back. Again they fire, and I brace myself, squinting. This barrier's going to break any second, I can feel it. Their magic smashes into the wall in front of us, making tiny holes everywhere.

Fill . . . uh . . . replenish . . . I bite my lip, searching for the right fucking words. "Shee'ye ya fuste!" *That's the one!* The tiny holes fill themselves. The barrier between us glows a deeper shade of orange, thickening, strengthening itself.

"Get on the other side of that shield!" the Chancellor growls, and another pair of Patrol rush at me from either side, but I'm ready. I let the barrier spell fizzle out once they're in arm's reach. Spells form on their lips, but I snatch their collars and smack them together before they get it out. I press them together, two bodies, shoved side by side. A shield. I duck behind them just as magic from the Chancellor slams into his own men. Their shoulders shake, eyes rolling, energy buzzing through them like electricity.

The Chancellor's mouth falls open in shock. He fumes.

I shove the bodies of the limp guards to the ground and erect another shield.

"Their numbers are almost cut in half," I say over my shoulder to Taavi, who's crouched over a body pulling at its wrist, her hands shaking. "Patience makes all the difference. Exploiting their weakness. He's impatient. It's all over his face. Look at him."

The Chancellor is an angry red boil ready to pop.

Kai holds her javelin at the ready, but without magic, she's as vulnerable as our people below. Foolish she's chosen *him* for protection. Jhamal holds a shield of gold beside her, waiting, ready to protect her, I guess, and the heat in my palms burns hotter.

Clank.

The door in the ground opens and an army of fur-lined Ghizoni carrying curved lead blades piles out. "No," I want to say, but they form up beside me before I can get a word out. My magic is a wall between us and the enemy. "When this barrier buckles, we'll have seconds to fight them off."

The Beerchi nod and the barrier shudders, flickering, as a gust of fire explodes against it.

"So, it's shield down, strike, shield up," I say. "And we'll push forward as much as we can. Got it?"

"Shield down, strike, shield up, got it."

"I'll put up another as fast as I can. Ready?"

"Aim!" The Chancellor must read my mind because his men aim their arms up this time, blowing my plan to smithereens. "Fire," he commands. Magic streams from their hands, arcs in the air, and plummets from the sky, up and over my barrier.

"Mwa!" The Beerchis hook their lead blades overhead with a clang, tucking me, all of us, beneath. The streams of magic raining from the sky graze the shield above us and evaporate like steam. A Beerchi breaks from the formation. Stepping out, he swipes, and a whole line of Patrol fall.

"That's what I'm talking 'bout!" I go to slap his hand but he just grins.

"See, you do not have to think of everything yourself, Jelani. The beauty of unity, eh?"

My smile widens.

"Let me," Kai says.

With Patrol in heaps on the ground, Kai steps forward. Jhamal steps beside her. I glare at him, but he's the one who looks away this time.

"They won't follow you, Kai, no matter how pure your blood is. Because your heart is rotten. And I know my people. We tired of the bullshit."

She hisses and swipes her javelin. I jump, stumbling back as I land.

"Argh," a Beerchi brother screams, ready to charge, but I halt him with a hand.

"No, if my sister wants to square up, I'ma be the one to beat some sense into her ass."

She stabs and I jump aside, dodging. She twirls her rod across her back, over her shoulder, and brings it down overhead. I sidestep. Her metal cries, scraping against my cuffs. I study her the way Zora taught me. She's fighting from fear, not love. That's the vulnerability I have to exploit.

"Zora told me everything she knows, everything *you* taught her," I say, her blade whooshing past my cheek. My breath rattles in my chest and I keep my arms moving to stay loose. She's quick and not fucking playing around. But if she still has a heart in there somewhere, I'm going to prick it. She thrusts again, her armor catching a glint of sunlight and I'm blind. I stumble, slamming the ground, and pinching pain shoots up my spine. She jabs.

"Yo lis."

The tip of her javelin burns in the flames on my fingers. The heat climbs up the rod and she winces, dropping it like a hot potato. I'm up on my feet. She scoops her blade back up and I let her. I don't want to kill her. I don't even really want to hurt her.

We circle.

"She told me no one held the Mother in more reverence. No one prayed to the Ancestors with more diligence, no one trained harder. . . ."

"Shut up!" She flips backward and swipes.

I pivot sideways and catch the end of her rod. I yank and she stumbles forward, the crown on her head slipping. I clench her weapon in my hands and her eyes widen. I hold her there, glaring into her. A spell tiptoes through my mind, magic rushing into my hands. But the curve of her cheeks, the strength in her jaw, the tilt of her chin, even now, in this moment where I could end her, morphs into an image of the Ancestors.

They chose *me*.

For *my* reason.

For *my* way of doing things.

I can smell her, a mix of fear and desperation warring with each other. I look for her bare shoulder but realize there isn't one.

I place a hand on my right shoulder, remembering Zora's words about fighting from love versus fear. I don't want to die out here, but that's not what's keeping me on my feet. I don't fear failing my people anymore. I'm doing the best that I can. Being me. And being me is enough. I'm not standing here from fear or pride or some need to prove I can do this.

I'm standing here because I love my people too much to not.

And that fuels like nothing else.

"I will not kill you." I push off, letting her weapon go as we circle each other.

She straightens her crown but pushes too much and it leans the other way, lopsided.

"You can't want something so bad that you lose yourself getting it. You gotta remember who you are, Kai, where you come from."

"Ahhh!" She twists on her feet, her anger erupting, and throws her javelin. It streaks through the air, a blur of gold.

"Feey'l." I shove the air and the path of the arrow shifts, missing me by an inch. I step back, bumping into Taavi. Kai's weaponless, but something other than fear or anger flickers in her eyes.

"Do it!" Kai yells . . . not at me . . . but to Taavi behind me.

Jhamal's expression shifts.

I turn and am face-to-face with Taavi. Time slows, my heart thudding in my throat.

"I'm sorry," Taavi whispers, and something presses into my side. I'm cold all over like ice has been injected into my veins. I see myself shaking as if I'm being tased, but I feel nothing. I try to pull away, but I can't move. Words hang on my lips, but my mouth is stiff.

I'm weightless.

Frozen.

Paralyzed.

The metal box in Taavi's hand presses harder to my side as tears stream her cheeks. How could she do this? After all her screwups I looked past, everything I did for her people. Toxic thinking is lethal. It spreads like a cancer. Tears pool in my eyes, but I have no way to even blink to stop them.

"I hate that it had to come to this, saisa." Kai pulls out a dagger strapped to her thigh and throws it. It pummels through the air, end over tip, heading straight for my chest. I try to breathe, move, get out the way, but fear stills whatever fractured part of me there is left. I close my eyes.

This is the end. . . .

I did all I could.

Literally.

And it wasn't enough. The wind rustles the bells in my hair. But I am Ghizoni, blood of the Beerchi, brave and loyal, and blood of the Yakanna, loving and fearless. We die with honor, fighting for what we believe in, not living an oppressive lie.

I lived my truth.

And I will die for it.

I wait for death to rip through me, hoping it doesn't hurt. Hoping it means I'll get to see Moms and my daddy again.

Then brown and gold dent my peripheral.

Jhamal flings his body in front of me, knocking the metal box aside. Kai's dagger slices through him and he collapses.

Her shrill cry rips the air.

CHAPTER THIRTY-EIGHT

"JHAMAL!"

His head is cradled in my arms, blood is everywhere, soaking through my pant legs. A tangled mix of rage and sorrow rips through me. I grab a Beerchi by the wrist. "This is your brother, get him to safety. Whatever it takes."

Kai weeps on her knees, hands cupped to her face.

"Look what you've done!" The scream thunders through me, my chest heaving with anger.

Kai reaches toward him as the Beerchi carry Jhamal, who is holding his wound, wincing in pain.

"*No!* You don't get to touch him. You don't get to look at him."

"I-I just wanted to preserve us. I-I just wanted us to win. Once." She scrambles up to her feet, deep lines creasing her face, which is swollen with tears. "I loved him so much."

"Your love is poison." I aim at her and magic coils around her like a rope, binding her where she stands. She doesn't fight it. "Leave her there. She's going to watch the terror she's brought upon our people."

I swivel, taking in the chaos around me. The door to the underground is wide open and Ghizoni and Macazi are everywhere, holding lead as shields, blocking streams of magic coming from the few

Patrol left. The Chancellor aims, shooting daggers as fast as he can, but he's only one person. A Beerchi bears down on him holding a sheet of lead the width of his arms.

"Aarrrrgh!" He brings it down over the Chancellor's head. But he blocks it. They wrestle, limbs tangled, when another Beerchi swings a solid right hook and the Chancellor's head swims. He spews magic in every direction, woozy on his feet. His magic ricochets like a bullet until it hits a group of Macazi, and they topple over.

Taavi works through the crowd pressing her metal box to any Ghizoni she sees. They drop to their knees on contact, convulsing, temporarily paralyzed like I'd been. Then she binds them with rope.

"No!" I rush over and shove her out of the way, but she's made short work of it, and a dozen, maybe more, of my people are folded on the ground. She gazes up at me, but where I expect to see grit and determination in her stare, I only see pain. Her hands tremble as she stuns another's ankle as he rushes by. He falls.

"Stop it!" I pull her up by the collar and shake; the metal gadget falls from her hands and rolls away. "What's gotten into you?"

Her shoulders slump, her lip trembling, the firm defiance and confidence she used to hold in her posture is fractured, broken.

"Why would you do this?"

"He's my father, Rue. My *father*. Totsi never wanted it . . . b-but . . . I have a chance here. T-to show him . . ."

"Taavi," I sigh, but before I can get the words out, something pinches my spine and my knees hit the dirt. The Chancellor's broken free from the Beerchi and is coming after me. His magic stings my back and the spot is wet, sticky. Taavi rushes off as I pull myself up to find more of my people bound, limbs tied on the ground, their lead weapons and accessories discarded. The winds that had blown in our favor are changing course and I'm running out of steam. Their glazed gazes pierce me.

I muster as much strength as I can and fire magic at the Chancellor. Flames roll through the air from my fingertips. "Fight *me*!"

My magic catches his sleeve and he stumbles backward.

"Leave my people out of this! I'm who you want. Me. My magic. Come take it!"

He gathers both his hands when a frail voice cracks the air.

"Xiiiirrrrre!"

His pale complexion drains. He's white as a ghost.

"And *you*!" The Seer turns to Taavi, thunder booming overhead. "*You* should be ashamed of yourself." Taavi folds in on herself, weeping, and I don't even know who this woman is. Only deep regret can torture a person like that. She wore a tough mask, but in the end, she wanted what she would never be able to get from the cold-hearted Chancellor: a father who loved her.

My people struggle on shaky limbs to pull themselves to their feet, some flinch less, the stun wearing off. The Seer hobbles toward the Chancellor, using a lead stick as a cane. "I had to see your face one more time."

He doesn't move, rigid with shock or fear or something equally as potent.

"Look at me, Xire. Look at your life's work."

He blinks and I call on my magic. He's going to take her out any second, I just know it. I wait, but he stares, his hands unmoving.

"K-kitri." He gulps. "I-I thought you were dead."

"You'd *hoped* I was dead," she hisses, taking another step, her skin peeling in the direct sun. I want to go to her, to do something, but this is her moment and it's been a long time coming.

"Did he tell you all how he founded this great land?" She addresses the Loyalists, but the Macazi, the Ghizoni look up too. "How he poisoned those good people's Ancestors?"

"Well . . . I didn't technically. You did."

Lightning crackles and the world darkens. Cold droplets of rain pelt my skin.

"Do you know what happens, Xire, when you dabble in magic that wasn't meant for you?"

He steps back. "I-I made so many mistakes back then, I . . ." He's frozen with fear. I would be too if I was talking to someone I thought I'd killed.

She steps toward him. "Did you know what it would do to me?"

He licks his lips nervously. "I-I had an idea. B-but not exactly."

"It cursed me, Xire. Poisoned my blood and locked me in this rotting body forever."

He swallows and the rain falls harder.

"It gave me their pain as torture, day in and day out. Aches in my bones, nightmares; it made it impossible for me to feel affection without excruciating agony." She spits the words between gritted teeth. "It destroyed my life. *You* destroy things. It's what you do." She stands inches from him now. "I said I'd never make another potion, because of what it did." She whips out the box Taavi was using and presses it to him. His shoulders slump, hands shaking, energy paralyzing him from head to toe.

She leans in and whispers, "I *lied*." She pries his mouth open and pours a vial of liquid down his throat. He convulses and the taser disconnects. He manages to shove her aside, firing a weak stream of magic at her. Already fragile, she falls limp.

"Hurry!" I yell. "The onyx."

His men fling magic in our direction, chaos erupting again. Shards streak past and I dart sideways, missing them by the hair on my head. There are only a few of his men left, those who've picked themselves up off the ground or managed to survive and climbed up here from down below. I aim at one of them, but his arm shifts and my magic flies right past his wrist.

"The girl. Aim for the girl, her arms." The Chancellor coughs up words, choking on the poison the Seer fed him. He contorts in pain and the Seer lies unmoving. I charge in that direction when fire burns my back. Patrol shoots at me, threads of energy tethering me from every direction, all aimed at my wrists. I bite down, trying to lift my arms, but they're cement under the weight of their attack.

"She's breaking," the Chancellor shouts. "Harder! Harder now. Don't let up!"

"*Aaahhh!*" I strain to lift my arms, my everything feeling like it's on fire, but I can't.

Pops of magic spark on my periphery. My head snaps in that direction.

A Yakanna stares at her hands, eyes bulging.

Pop.

Magic crackles like electricity between her fingertips.

I gasp.

"I-I," she stutters, and jaws dangle everywhere.

Julius, Bri, they made it to the grave site! A lump swells in my throat. The Ancestors' words float through my memory. "*As the onyx is returned . . . the magic will be restored.*" She said "as"!

"Keep it steady on the girl," the Chancellor shouts. "Hold it there."

Pop.

The Yakanna yanks her arms apart. The restraints on her arms break. She stands, gaping at the Ancestors' magic pouring from her hands. "My magic!" she shouts. "I-it works!"

I nod, tears stinging my eyes, despite the pull of the Chancellor's men draining me. A Beerchi beside her is bug-eyed at the same thing happening in his own hands. Beerchi rise, snapping their restraints, freeing themselves, summoning their Ancestors' power to their fingertips.

Pop. Pop.

More stand, the Ancestors' magic returning, chains breaking, light and fire filling the air.

"Hold it on her!" The Chancellor's face reddens as his knees buckle. "The cuffs are the key!" He plants on the ground, the curse he swallowed causing his skin to bubble. "Just get . . ." He grunts. "The cuffs. Th-that's all . . . we need is the . . ."

My arms are heavy, so heavy. But if our people's magic is back, mine should be even . . . Heat creeps through me, not like the usual tickle, but something much hotter, heavier. I yank my arms away and the Patrolmen's tethers fall off. Magic, strong, like I've never felt it pools to my hands and I let it rip through me.

I raise my hands and the clouds overhead lift. I clench my fists and tug down and a rain falls harder, beating the ground. I gasp glaring at my hands, the ancestor's words tugging at me. Stronger, I'm so much stronger. I brandish an arm to the right and a line of trees rip out of the rumbling ground and tumble like thunder.

"Wh-what now?" a Loyalist shouts.

But the Chancellor can hardly answer; the curse is working its way through him and he's in the fetal position on the ground. I plant my feet firm and lift my hands, sitting in the sinking feeling in my feet, wondering just how capable I could be. Lift. Air gusts under my feet and I rise, floating above everything else. Up, up, in the air. Trees snap at the direction of my fingertips. I shove them at Loyalists in every direction. They topple over and those that don't fall, run. The Chancellor's taken root in the ground.

"Get off this island!" My voice thunders from the clouds and lightning zigzags through the sky.

Levitating above the trees, I catch a glimpse of the Chancellor's ivory tower in the Central District, far in the distance. I fill my lungs, and then I blow. The forest bends, their leaves grazing the ground under my breath. The rains fall sideways. The tower's windows shatter in a melodious chorus of chimes.

I rotate my wrist up and his entire tower detaches from the ground and lifts in the air. Faint cries from the Chancellor wailing below me scratch my ears. I shove and the block of concrete flies through the air, its shadow shading the City, before splashing in the ocean. It bobs, then sinks.

Down.

Drowned.

To be forgotten at the bottom of nowhere.

I lower myself to the ground, the world a blur of color. Bri and Julius have returned from the grave site to an army of hugs. My wrists glow like they've never glowed before when I approach the Chancellor, who's hunched over, skin wrinkling, wincing in pain. My people stand around, some staring in shock, others pulling at onyx in the perpetrators' arms. More sprouting magic, more wielding it with smiles. Their unbridled joy is palpable.

But I'm not done.

"Make him stand."

Shaun holds the Chancellor up with a single hand. I aim at his wrists. Magic streams to them and his onyx glows. He wails in pain and I urge my magic harder.

"Ah!" He squirms. I press.

The onyx on his wrists pops out. Then another oozes out from under his sleeve. Shaun's brows meet and he rips his shirt off. I gasp. The Chancellor's a grid of black beads, onyx burrowed into every part of his skin. I draw my hands together and pull. Black siphons from him to my hands like ebony rain. My arms ache, but I lock my elbows. His whole body glows, his skin a matrix of red scars. He collapses once it's done, and a pile of stones sits at my feet. Enough to bind a small army.

"We're the same, you and I, you know that," he says to me, trying to sit up. "Both strong leaders. I'm sure we could reach some sort of . . ."

"Strong? You think fighting and leading are the same thing. And you're right, sort of. But you think one guarantees the other. And it doesn't. A true leader fights for others. You fight for yourself. For power. You kill anything that gets close to you because you believe love is weakness, a liability. But I see through you, Xire. You try to exploit love in others, which says you understand it, personally." I squat to his level and make him look me in the eyes. "To let yourself love someone requires courage. And at your core, Xire, you're a coward."

I push him upright, he twitches in pain. Still, I'm not done. "Taavi, come here."

Taavi is huddled in a ball, weeping over her mother's body. She pulls herself up and walks over.

"Look at her!" I hold her in front of the Chancellor. "This is your daughter."

His eyes flicker with recognition.

"You knew," I say.

"I-I heard the rumors."

Taavi sucks in a breath.

"How could you hate her? She's done nothing to you."

He pants, haggard. The poison has sunken in his cheeks and shrouded his eyes in red. He's wasting away by the second. A tear streams his cheek. "Hate her? I've done many things I regret. But I could never hate you, Taavi."

I see through him. My anger burns hotter.

He opens his arms and Taavi looks at me for permission.

"Go ahead." I hold on to the rest of my words.

Taavi steps into the hug and the Chancellor wraps his arms around her. She sobs harder.

"That'a girl," he says. "That'a girl." He whips her around and holds her to himself like a shield, shoving a blade into her side. She screams.

"Her lung is a millimeter from my blade. I press it in deeper, she dies. I do nothing soon and she bleeds out. Let me go and . . ."

Magic flies from my fingers straight through his eye sockets. The ground beneath him buckles and he cries, clawing at his eyes. Taavi pulls herself out of his grasp, shock stamped on her face.

"He doesn't love you," I tell her. "And nothing you do can ever change that. He isn't worthy of your love." She clutches her side, and Bri grabs her, ready with a jar of minty paste in hand.

Now, I'm done.

"Why even do that? Give her a second chance?" someone mutters behind me.

"She had to see his heart for herself." I turn to face them. "Mercy isn't a weakness. Like stubbornness, you just have to know when to wield it."

CHAPTER THIRTY-NINE

I FIND JHAMAL ON A raised bed in the shade of a jpango tree, the light in his eyes dim.

I crouch beside him and he winces, trying to turn to me.

"I never meant to hurt you, Jelani. Causing you pain is the worst . . ."

"N-no, don't try to speak if it hurts." I pull him into me. Confused, sad, angry. There's so much blood, the soil is soaked.

"No, you must know. The truth of everything." He holds on tight to me. "When I came for you in that lab the first time, thanks to a Patrol I had turned my way, I realized you were so angry with yourself for what had happened, how you failed. So I looked to magic. I did not know how to brew a potion, but I studied the books. Forgetting would be best. A gift in a sort of way. I had hoped it could give you the focus and confidence to rise to all the Ancestors see in you. But when I gave it to you, you became so weak. I-I didn't know that would be a side effect. I read nothing about that in any book." He groans.

"Please, if it hurts, don't—"

"No, I need to say this." He tightens his grip on my hand. "You still remembered parts of the battle. I didn't know what to do. I'd made this whole mess trying to force what I thought should happen. Like I did with Bati, trying to get you on the throne." A tear rolls down his cheek. "I spent every day putting you back together. I was determined to make up for what I'd done, and live out my love for you, even if it killed me." He coughs, his hand slipping off his wound. It's deep and I press my hand to it as if I can make it go away.

He wraps his hand around mine. "I could have prevented this in some way. Or should've . . . I . . ."

I smooth his tear away as mine begin to flow.

"I-I'm sorry, my Queen. I struggled to see you, all of you, right in front of me, and trust you fully. Instead, I tried to take things into my own hands. It is a lesson I learned with Kai, too."

"But, Kai, I-I thought . . ."

"I would never put you in harm's way on purpose." He strokes my face. "Kai was being pressured to kill you. And I know her well. Under the right circumstances, she might have done it. I couldn't let that happen. I had to keep Kai close, so she trusted me and would tell me everything. I had to make her believe it was her I wanted. Play into her vanity. It was never true. I never touched her. She tried, but there was always an excuse I'd find." He unfolds my fingers, pressing my palm. "You see, even when I wasn't with you, you held my heart in your hand. I only kept her close, pretended to plot to murder my brother, t-to protect you." He brushes a hair out of my face. "My Queen." His words are a sputter and they break me. "She has an evil streak, that one. But there is good in her too. It was my hope she would be won over by your tender heart, your strength, wisdom."

"*Please* don't die," I beg.

He ignores me, filling the last of our time together with words he's held so long, and I cry harder.

"We're the same, you and I. In so many ways. I do not judge you for being angry with me. I would have been angry too. It is I that am sorry. I should have never taken memories from you. I should have never lied. Even for good intention. I felt it my duty to see you on that throne. But even duty can sometimes cloud vision. You trusted me and I made a mess of that." He shudders.

"N-no." I smooth the tears off my face. "I understand now. I . . ." I squeeze his fingers. "It's okay."

"I see through your armor . . . and I guess I hoped you could see through mine. It is why we are so perfect together. It's always been for you. Everything. *I* have always been for you, my Queen."

Tears stream down my face, and I kiss his forehead, his fingers, the back of his hand, wishing time would slow. Wishing I could take so many things back.

"Memi told me when I was little of a word from the Ancestors' she had received. The cuffs that would call a great warrior to our home to avenge us. I told her I was Beerchi, none braver, none more loyal. I would protect this Special One. Memi let me train every day until the moon gave way to the sun. I trained and trained before there were whispers of your footsteps on this island. I prayed to the Ancestors to give me the courage to do whatever it took to preserve their Chosen. Falling in love with you wasn't part of the plan, but it was the best part of anything I ever did."

I weep uncontrollably, face pressed against his chest.

"Jhamal." The words are raw. "I love you, too. So much. I'm sorry . . . I'm so, so sorry." I loop my fingers between his. "Hear me, I love you. I have loved you since you knit together my wounds in that cell, since you told me stories to fall asleep and nursed me back to health. Jhamal, I love you."

"You cannot hide your love for me any more than you can hide the nose on your face. It is in those tears that you cry and the way you touch my hand. I savor it all. Every moment. Every breath."

I weep, my chest a knot.

"You are my life and have been for so long." He groans in my arms and I pull him closer, pressing on his wound as hard as I can. But in seconds my hand swims in blood.

"Jhamal, no, stay with me, please." My voice cracks. "I-I can get you out of here. I . . ."

"No," he breathes. "Sssh. The last moments I have, I will look upon the sun. Smile for me, my Queen."

I sniffle and force my lips to curl; tears are salty on them.

"Please!" I cry out, turning my palms upward and looking up. "Ancestors, if you can give me anything, do anything for me in this moment, please keep his heart beating." I collapse, crying on his chest. "Please, I'm so sorry I doubted your loyalty. I'm so sorry I . . ."

"You had to protect your heart. Protecting things is your gift. It is what you do. I will leave this world loving you and you loving me. Knowing he tried to take you from this world, and I helped stop it." His eyes close and I hold on to the hum of his breath against me, growing more shallow by the second. I press him to me as if that'll save him. As if that'll make it possible to hold him here. Moments pass and I don't breathe.

He goes still in my arms, a smile painted on his lips.

And my heart bleeds.

CHAPTER FORTY

IT'S BEEN AN ENTIRE day since Jhamal died in my arms and somehow it feels like a decade. I laid awake last night replaying the stories he'd told me when we were locked up together. I remember the way he looked at me, and the entire world quiets. I hold my eyes closed, as if doing so lets me hold on to him. He had a scent about him and I would give the world if I could smell it once more. I move down the corridor and he is in every moment, every conversation, and the spaces between them.

I chew my lip and blow out a breath, steadying myself on the door outside the cell where Kai's been locked away. I have to talk to her. I'm not even sure what to say, but that doesn't absolve me of responsibility. And if I'm honest . . . she is Yakanna, my saisa, and she is hurting.

With a wave of my hand the lock on her door clicks open. I slip inside and find her hunched over a small wooden box, pulling at scraps of paper inside. She doesn't even glance in my direction. I settle in a chair in the corner. Her room is in disarray—bed toppled over, linens tangled, food bowl overturned, her grief on display. I settle into my seat, careful to honor the silence.

Her topknot is unbraided and hangs in tight coils, draping her face and back. From the bottom down she's still dressed in her armor, but her new breastplate is cracked in half, her left side exposed, bare. Smeared paint mixed with tears runs down her cheeks as she brings another scrap of paper to her face. I can faintly make out scrawly handwriting on the page. She plucks a jade from the box, drawing circles on its glassy surface before returning it. She pulls at threads on her pant leg before turning her glassy-eyed stare my way. She says nothing, but I hear her.

"I'm sorry," I say, sensing the invitation to speak. "I know you loved them both."

We sit like that until the light dims in the room, so dark I can barely make out either of us. I rotate an orb affixed to the ceiling.

"Feey'l." Flames swell in the glass and the room brightens. I skirt my chair and take a chance, sitting on the floor beside her. "Kainese, I know you didn't kill Doile. I'm not here to judge you. I'm here to listen."

Her eyelids lift and her sullen stare burns into me.

"When I was little, Memi used to say I was fearless." She glances at her bare left shoulder. "She was wrong." She stands, her hands worrying one another. "I would like to say I'd never hurt my family, that I would do anything to keep them safe, to honor the Mother, protect my people. And yet somewhere in that haze I forgot what Memi's words truly meant."

She turns to me. "Memi meant fear would not drive me, love would. And I believed that. I held on to it so tight, pressed it to my face so firmly, that I could not see anything around it. How could I? Memi's fearless daughter, blood of the Mother herself, lose footing? Never. Every step I took was so sure in the beginning."

Her fingers graze a gemmed pin on her bedside table. "When you came to this island and Jhamal was sure of who you would be, what you'd become, I accepted it. I believed you would be perfect." She smirks. "You see the irony, don't you? I thought you'd be everything I was sure I was. But as you made missteps, and people began to die, I saw the fractures in your exterior. I saw that you were not perfect, infallible. And—" She drops her head. "That is where my first misstep was. . . . I was *sure* I could never stumble the way you had. I was sure that I could do it better. I would. . . ."

A tear drips from her chin. "So when the Chancellor offered me the opportunity to lead our people in this new version of Ghizon, offering freedom and annexation and all of these golden promises, I told myself I was doing the right thing. When he told me to break you out of prison and make it look like I fought my way in, I believed misleading you was the only way to hold on to the glittered vision of the future he'd promised. I was certain the sacrifices were necessary. I am Kainese, the Mother's own. When Jhamal pressed that I should support you and I made him choose, he folded, and I took it as a sign from the Ancestors that this was the way. Funny how when we are blind we can interpret things any way that suits us. I told myself what I was doing was right. When I thought Shaun killed Doile, I told myself, 'See? I am not like him.' When I made Zora promise me"—her voice cracks and the hand at her lip trembles—"sh-she would gain your trust and tell me everything, I knew she would obey, because Zora believed if I was leading her a way, that must be *the* way. I told myself I was shepherding her like a good leader would."

She inhales a shaky breath. "And when I saw her betray that

blood oath . . . I knew the magic of the spell would slay her. But I told myself *she* did that to herself, not me." She sobs and I wrap my arms around her. She is heavy on my shoulder, weeping.

"When Jhamal jumped in front of that dagger for you . . . when I knew he'd only pretended to support me, plotting and lying to me . . ." Her eyes harden. "That is not him, Jelani. I've known him since we were small. Jhamal's heart is more pure than all our gold. So when I saw him do that . . . I-I . . ."

But she doesn't finish. She paces the room a few times before settling back on the floor. I'm not sure what to say, so I keep quiet, give her space to process.

She huffs, meeting my stare. "It sounds so naive in hindsight, doesn't it?"

"I-I mean, I'm not one to judge."

"I swear to you, Jelani, darkness creeps in like music, like an intoxicating melody playing to our own vanities. And I *danced*, Jelani. . . ." She sniffles. "I was blind to the fragility of my own humanity. That I could be driven by anger or pride. That I could be wrong, Jelani." Her shoulders shake from her crying.

"May I?" I ask, holding the edge of her armor. She nods, muffling her cry as I unstrap her breastplate. I set it on the ground and what's left are both her bare shoulders, round with muscle, and yet slender and fragile. I set my hands on her right shoulder and I take her hand and put it on mine.

"You're no more imperfect than I am, saisa. And I am sure the Mother is smiling with pride right now."

She meets my eyes.

"If I've learned anything through all this, Kai, it's that it's *these* moments, like this one right now, that define who we are. And when we mess up, because we all will, the people we keep around us hold us up through it. The goal isn't to *not* fall. . . ." I take her hands in mine. "It's to get back up."

She nods.

I smile. "Come with me. I have something I'd like your help with." She agrees and I hand her the Yakanna breastplate sitting unused in the corner. She hesitates but takes it.

"Where are we going?" she asks, latching it on.

"You'll see."

Outside, the sun beats over Yiyo. Ocean waves lap the shore, and I run my fingers through the leaves as we pass. Kai comes along hesitantly. I'd asked everyone to give us this moment with just the two of us, and I'm glad she was up for it. Jhamal lies still on the ground, and she clamps her mouth with a whimper. I loop my arm in hers.

"Forgiveness starts with yourself. Jhamal said he saw something in you." I lay my hand on her bare shoulder. "And I see it too."

She tucks her lip, nodding, as she realizes what we're about to do.

We spread his arms and legs wide.

"May I?" I ask, reaching for the armor she's wearing. Stones were what we used for the Macazi we buried, but gems are what the Ancestors used, and the only gems we have are on the Yakanna armor.

"Yes," she says, and I flicker flames from my fingertips to the edge of her armor until it starts to drip, melting. Two pieces of jade pressed into the metal plop into my hands, piping hot. I cool them then place them over Jhamal's eyes.

"Wismaja ya, Jhamal," I say, remembering what the men said during the Macazi burial. "Rest well."

Kai sings this time, and it is even more beautiful than anything I've ever heard, panged with notes of pain. Her voice cracks and I reach for her hands. She keeps going. Her last note hangs in the air like a star, and I coil one hand over the other, remembering the words my little friend whispered, and a gold bloom appears. I work my fingers around its edges and more blooms appear with each spot I touch. I place the golden bouquet in Jhamal's fingers, winding its vines around his arms. Then several around his head, like a crown. Kai sprinkles the dirt from the Ancestors' grave over his feet as I stake wooden torches every few steps around the burial site.

"The prayer is next, right?" she asks.

"Yes."

"Doilekki, mis kishaq pwana yo meh," we sing, covering him with earth. We move in sync, in silence, as saisas. When he's fully covered, Kai's magic glistens from her fingertips as we light the torches in a circle around the mound. I finish one side, she the other, and when done, we collapse with a sigh, sitting next to the mound. Tears well in my eyes and I let them. Kai smooths sadness from her cheek. "How long can we stay?"

"As long as we like."

"Jelani."

"Yes?"

"I cannot imagine a finer Ghizoni Queen."

EPILOGUE

THE CROWN RESTING ON my natural curls is lighter than I thought it'd be.

Without my coconut oil, I was trippin', worried my hair would be frizzed out. But the jpango tree makes an oil that's just as good, I've learned. My hair is fresh, tightly coiled, and luscious in the mirror. Gold spires point in every direction from my headdress, strings of jewels hanging from their tips catch the sunlight. I tilt my chin, admiring the trail of gold paint from my hairline down my face. Colorful dots encircle my temples, and I reach to touch them.

"Ah, ah," the woman who made up my face says, tucking away her tray of colors. "It's not dry yet."

Rings loop around my left ear and tiny bells dangle from my hair. White paint covers my eyebrows. I try to let my hands hang casually, but my fingers worry at one another. Silks hang from every part of me, weighing me down like a blanket. The coronation robes are layers upon layers, tucked, tied, and twisted around every part of me. I hold in a breath, an elderly Ghizoni woman pulling ribbons at my back.

"One more."

I suck it in and my ribs squeeze. I'm seriously considering changing the traditional coronation attire to jeans and a hoodie at this point. But for today, we're following tradition to the *nth* degree. I want to do it the way the Ancestors did. I want to do it right. It's the very least I could do to honor them.

"Good," she says, and I smile. I twist my torso and the fabric shifts. It's golden brocade, beaded in jade, sparkling in the firelight. I run my fingers down it and take a deep breath. It's happening. This is actually happening. We more than survived. We won.

"Chin up." Hands lay a cone-like necklace of bone around my neck, painted with swirly blue designs. "The blue is reminiscent of the ocean, Jelani." The woman presses and something snaps into place. The neckline of the dress forces my head up, but not uncomfortably. She takes my wrists and slides rings on my fingers. "And for luck." She pulls out two minted Ghizoni coins, and I blink.

"Can I see that?"

I turn the gold in my hands. My face is minted on the coin where the Chancellor's used to be. She takes them from me, a smirk playing on her lips.

"The world is changing, is it not?" She tucks the gold coins in a pouch, then stuffs them in my bust. "Titube will finish you up, then." She presses her hands together then sets them both on my bare right shoulder. "My Queen."

"Thank you so much, Lalae."

She dips her chin and disappears behind the door. There weren't many spaces inside the mountain still intact for this sort of thing, but the grandest room they could find is the one they put me in. I told them I didn't need all that, but they insisted. And tradition is very important to our people, so I kept my mouth shut from then on.

I try to take a step, but Titube holds my foot still.

"Not yet," she says, holding my foot above a pile of dust. "Okay, now."

I dip my foot in the soft pile of earth.

"Now the next one."

I dip my second foot in the pile of golden ash. My feet shine metallic from the ankle down. Titube's tiny hands work around my calves, tying golden twine. "We pray that strength from our roots would wrap around us, lift us up. That we would walk on the soil they built with pride." She loops the end of the twine at my ankle in a bow. "It is what the twine represents."

"Ah, I see."

"When the world is right again, maybe one day you can escort me to my turning out? Memi says it is when I get to wear nice robes like this one."

"It's a plan, then. I would love that."

She stands, her cheeks pushing up under her eyes. "Now you are finished, my Queen." She bows, backing away, but before she can run off, I take her by the hand.

"Would *you* escort *me* into the Kowana ceremony?"

Her eyes are moons. "You mean it? M-me?"

I nod, tucking her hand under my arm, and we depart the room as the creaky door swishes closed behind us.

The ceremony is quicker than I expect it to be. Waves lap the edge of the mountain, cool air gusting the hem of my robes. My people sit in an arc around us, done up in stripes with dotted faces. Ornaments loop in and out of their hair, and the *ting* of gold beads rings through the air with each breeze. The Ancestors' burial ground is under our feet, and the sun is almost hidden behind Yiyo's crest as I complete the last ritual of the ceremony. While I'm on my knees, Bati sets a cloak of fur across my shoulders.

"From Father Mishon Ide Beerchi," he says.

"Mwaaa!" Barks of glee erupt from the Beerchi in the crowd.

"And from the Mother Moi Ike Yakanna," Bati says. The ground rumbles under their pounding in revelry. He smiles, raising his voice above the cheer, and presses a golden javelin into my hand. "And last but certainly not least. A gift from Gahlee, me and my brothers." He hooks a beaded strand between my wrist, then my finger. It twists once on itself in an infinity pattern. He traces his fingers along it. "Leading is a never-ending battle between believing you are good enough to do it and understanding how capable you are of making a grave misstep." Bati traces the threaded symbol on his own robe, and whistles flit through the branches from his brothers. "The eternal balance of humility and pride, my Queen."

I tilt my head in a bow before rising to my feet.

"It is with the highest honor," he bellows, "I present Rue Jelani Akintola, daughter of Moi Mother Ike and Mishon Ide Beerchi, direct descendant of Aasim Ade Akintola and Naomi April Harris, daughter of East Row and *Queen* of Ghizon in her own right."

Hollers blare in my ear and the sounds of plucked strings flit through the air. Music takes over the ceremony, and somewhere garlicky onion goodness is heating up.

With the ceremony over, I slip my bare feet into my Maxes and join the dancing. I loop arms with Bati, who might look ancient but moves like he's still got it. We circle and I spin, twisting my hips, grinding to the beat. The best I can, anyway, in this gown. When my dance is done, I'm hip to hip with a Beerchi who got me looking like I can't dance compared to his moves. I sway with him, rocking to the beat until my feet are sore and my cheeks burn from grinning. I catch sight of Julius, who's trying to teach Bri how to bop. It's not going well.

"I'm going to catch my breath for a beat, if that's cool." The Beerchi dances off, looping a Yakanna around the waist.

My gaze moves to Jue and Bri in the crowd like a moth to a light. "I never properly thanked you two."

Jue squeezes my hand and Bri pulls at pieces of my fabric. "This is *actual* gold, Rue."

"It is?" I don't know why I'm surprised. I shouldn't expect anything less.

"Yeah," she says, squinting. "And you're welcome. I'm so glad it worked."

"I wish we could have seen how it went down," Jue says.

"Oh, it was ham. For a minute there I thought we were done for. What exactly happened at the grave site?"

"At first nothing," he says. "We just poured the onyx on top of the dirt and stood there looking like some dummies."

"But then Julius got down on his hands and knees and pressed the onyx into the dirt. It absorbed it. Like, sucked it right in."

"The more we pressed into the surface, the warmer the ground grew, until it was so hot, we couldn't stand on it. Well, I couldn't, anyway," Bri says.

"Yeah," I say. "As the magic started returning, the more freely our magic moved."

I catch a glimpse of Titube dancing, a crowd clapping around her. Her fingers coil and twist, flowers bloom everyplace she points. Something like fireworks pops in the air, and I hug around myself.

"All of this . . . it's just unreal." Bellied frogs croak and crickets hum in the branches. In one direction the ocean bathes in the moonlight. In the other, an abyss, a black shadow that used to be the Capital.

"What about the people who didn't stand with the Chancellor?" Julius asks. "Everyone else on the island?"

"They're still scattered out there somewhere."

"Not many," Bri says. "Their numbers are whittled way down. There's no surviving out there anymore. There's nothing to survive on. My parents and brothers are out there somewhere."

"Bri, we have to find them."

She nods. But she's right. The Central District is a deserted heap. And it will no longer be the center of the island. It was built on a lie, which means it's rotted down to the very foundation and must be rebuilt from scratch. The Ghizon I build will sit at the foot of Yiyo, among the jpango trees. The Central District will be ripped up. All of it. Even the concrete. But I'm not naive: With the history of this island, turmoil is inevitable.

"If anyone out there still toting stolen onyx ever gets the stupid idea to rise again, they'd be severely outnumbered," I say. "But I'm just gonna do me. That's all I can do."

I'm going to lead in a way I haven't seen it done before. Before, I'd felt so intimidated carving a path, being the first, doing something *this* big, because I hadn't seen anyone like me do it before. But there's freedom in that.

"Some *have* come forward," I say. Bri nods. I put her in charge of overseeing Unbinding. A hundred or so who'd been working against the Loyalists to restore peace and unity to the island came out of the woodwork, asking for community after the Chancellor had fallen. She made sure their onyx was removed and I ensured they have a place here—a way to make a living and a home.

"A Queen." Julius licks his lips, and I look away. I love his jokes, but there's a part of me still pulsing with pain. I need time. I tug my fur more squarely over my shoulders.

"Can I, uhm . . . catch up with y'all in a bit? The Council is meeting soon, so I'll see you there."

"I still don't understand how you have a Council but you're a Queen," Bri says. "Not that I'm complaining. I've never been on anything nearly as important in my life." She laughs.

"Same," Jue says, and they slap hands. Bri is slow with it, but she sort of finesses the handshake at the end. She's rough around the edges but a definite keeper.

"Well, I'll be splitting my time between East Row and here, now. And, besides, everyone's looking at me, but that doesn't mean I know everything. If I've learned anything about leading at all, it's that it involves doing more listening than speaking."

Bri, Bati, and Julius sit on the Ghizon Council. I'd considered Taavi, but she is, understandably, still piecing herself back together. She'd told me how she and her mother had been estranged for so long because of her soft spot for her father. She and Totsi butted heads for similar reasons. But this journey brought them back together, even if only for a moment, before she died. Taavi has a lot of trauma and healing to work through. Stepping down from leadership to heal is probably wise.

Funny thing about whom people see fit to lead. It isn't always the right bloodline or the right list of accolades.

It's the heart for the people.

All the people.

The first law we will sign is that magic will be wielded only by my people, the brown-skinned people on this island. The second is that everyone else will be trained in an array of science and tech talents that suit them. But they will not touch our magic ever again. Macazi will be trained too. And the classes Zruki and Dwegini are done. Now it's just us. And them. But we're going to work together to build a Ghizon we're all proud of.

I don't know if it's a perfect plan. Or that perfect even exists. But it's my plan and we're going to try it.

"Aight, I'll catch y'all later," I say.

By the time I'm out of sight of everyone, it's so dark outside, I can hardly see my hand in front of my face. I slip between branches, tugging my gown with me. It's so heavy. All of this is so heavy. I straighten, determined to better carry the weight.

When I slip out of the patch of trees, I see it. The mound of dirt encircled with gold and flames I was looking for. The place we laid Jhamal to rest. I haven't had a moment here, alone, by myself. The last time was for Kai. But this . . . this is for me.

Flames dance around the grave. I approach and its warmth stokes a tender part of me. I step through the flames and they snuff out a moment under the weight of my gown but rekindle once I'm inside the fire circle. I stare at my hands. Like my love for him, Jhamal's fire will burn forever here. This is some of the best magic I've ever done.

I sit beside the raised grave and dirt soots up the hem of my gown, but I don't care. My fingers trace the golden plaque affixed like a headstone, its words gleaming in the firelight.

JHAMAL KYNTE MALIX

NONE MORE LOYAL.

NONE MORE BRAVE.

I take off my crown, setting it beside me, and bunch up my skirt fabric to fashion a pillow. I lie down beside his headstone and trace circles in the dirt.

"I dreamed of you," I say. "It was both of us at the ceremony. You set a cloak on my shoulders and said, 'I told you so,' when they crowned me." I chuckle, wiggling to get more comfortable. "I've been thinking on what to do with Kai and Shaun. You have such wise counsel. So I thought I'd come here and just talk through it with you." I press my face to the earth and imagine his hand stroking my hair. "That sound okay?"

Wind whistles through the trees and I let my eyes close.

Sleep must've taken me because it's Julius who finds me for the Council meeting.

"How'd you know I'd be here?" I ask.

"Rue, I know you better than anyone. From everything you told me, it's clear that dude loved the shit outta you. And you loved the shit outta him." He smooths a tear from my cheek I didn't know was there. "That's gonna take some time. I get it."

"Thank you."

"Of course."

I slip my hand into his and we disappear back through the forest, my Queenly duties calling.

Six Weeks Later

Sights of East Row are just the pick-me-up I needed. I have much work to do here, too, but it's been weeks and weeks of Council meetings in Ghizon. Julius and I have been back and forth between here and Ghizon, getting started on some of that work. But what I've really been craving is a day to just sit down with Ms. Leola's pound cake and a side of mac and cheese.

I raise a fist to knock, but her door sweeps open and the room is full of people. Ms. Leola always has a packed house, but this is even more so. A banner hangs above.

WELCOME HOME, QUEEN!

"How did they . . ."

Julius cheeses.

"You . . ."

"I might've made a call."

They usher me inside, and the house smells like heaven. I'm swallowed in hugs and cheek kisses. I can't get a word in edgewise before my butt plops in a chair. The air is a congested mess of questions, and I try to answer as many as I can between bites. My stomach thanks me and I shovel in more. Notes of salty bacon pop on my taste buds. I'm warm all over when I notice Tasha sitting across from me, hand resting on her chin.

"So, like, does this make me a Princess now, or . . . ?"

I laugh. "Actually, about that." I scoop my last bite of mac and cheese from the plate. "I have something to show you."

She perks up.

"Actually, all of you." I dab the corners of my mouth and push back from the table. "Jue!" I wink at him and he already knows. The project. What we've been coming back and forth to East Row these past few weeks for. The sign goes up today, so it's time we give our peeps a peek.

"Aight, fam, this way," he says. "Everybody form a nice neat line."

Ms. Leola scoots to the front. "I'm a senior citizen, can I get the front spot?"

"You a Queen, Ms. Leola, y'all slide over." The crowd parts like the Red Sea and Ms. Leola heads up the line. I stuff a piece of corn bread in my pocket and follow the crowd out the door.

The sun is beating over the concrete in East Row.

"How far we going?" Aunt Niecey says, walking arm in arm with Ms. Leola. "You know my arthritis can't do these long walks."

"Just around the corner here." I lead us to the backside of the Row, and an old building that used to be boarded up is hugged in construction equipment. It's really amazing how far solid gold goes here. Especially when your face is on it. It's two stories tall with sweeping windows and clean lines. The ground sinks in in one spot, roped off with orange cones where an underground parking structure is going to be.

"Ooo lawd, " Cousin Neicey says. "I'll be glad when they done with whatever they building back here. Them trucks so noisy all day and night."

"The sign," I say, pointing.

"What it say now, chile?" Ms. Leola holds a hand over her brow, squinting. "You know I can't see in that sun like that. Only brought my readers." She jiggles the glasses hanging around her neck. Aunt Niecey and Cousin Keisha peer upward, squinting too.

"What's *Rooted?*" Keisha asks, pulling her neon braids over her shoulder, her lip gloss poppin'.

"It's a community center I'm building here to connect our community to our roots. Part of the work I'm doing in East Row is to make sure anyone who wants to visit Ghizon can. And anyone with ties to the Ancestors will be shown how to access and wield their magic."

There's no way I'm the only one ever with ancestry there. If the onyx warming to Julius's fingers is any indication, East Row is an untapped mine of magical people who just haven't realized it yet. And I'm not going to let access to resources or information stifle our ability to come into our power.

"Yo, the sign look so dope," Julius says. One side of the building is a solid wall of glass with windows rimmed in gold. "Rooted" is scripted in bold letters beneath the image of a jpango tree. Its leaves make up parts of the letters.

"It's looking good, isn't it?" I say.

"It is."

"Two more months and it's ready, they said. I told Bati I'd let him come see it. Promised him some of Ms. Leola's cooking, too."

"Oh, he ain't going back, then."

We laugh and I spot Cousin Keisha on her Instagram Live with the building in the background talking about "my cousin is a Queen" and she might be royalty too, so they better double tap her video.

"Keesh wild, man." Julius laughs into his fist.

"You better recognize melanated royalty," I say, smirking.

"Nah, but for real, nothing is going to be the same after this, Rue." He throws an arm over my shoulder.

"No, it won't." I lay my head on his shoulder. "And it shouldn't be."

ACKNOWLEDGMENTS

Is It Really *The End?*

Wow, the end of this duology feels like the end of an era. This book was a grind. I wrote, revised, and edited it during a pandemic, where life meant limiting time away from home, being isolated, and pretending to be okay with it. Emotionally and physically exhausted from all the protocols and sanitizing and safety measures and *stress* of worrying about loved ones. And somehow, despite it all, I was able to put together this final iteration of Rue's story.

It is my ultimate hope that this was an uplifting final chapter for my readers in this journey of self-discovery Rue has taken us on. I'm so grateful to Simon & Schuster and Denene Millner for the opportunity to give Rue this space to reach and uplift hearts. And a huge thanks to the amazing Taj Francis for the jaw-dropping cover art! It's an absolute honor to have been able to canonize this Black girl magic for Black girls like young me, my teenage sisters.

This duology, and particularly this second book, *Ashes of Gold,* is a charge to every reader who saw yourself in Rue to lift your chin and step up to the challenges ahead of you, especially those that seem too hard to face. Especially the fights we feel called to, but don't think we can win. We step up, not because we have all the answers, not because we think it'll be easy; we step up because we are purposed to. It's *who* we are: leaders, changemakers, history shakers.

Black girl, look at your history.

Black girl, know you are magic.

Consider all that your people have done and rest deep in your spirit, knowing you will do great things too. Because that is just who you are, sis.

I sincerely hope Rue's story has helped you see more in yourself than you did before. She certainly did that for me.

Thank Yous

First and foremost, I'm so thankful to God for this gift of words. I'm so grateful to my husband and children, who have sacrificed so much to allow me the time and space to string together these words.

Thank you, Mommy, Grandma, and Grandpa, for always believing. For inspiring so much of Rue's story by just being who you are. To Paige, Naomi, Auntie Regina, Rocqell, Roslyn, Uncle Chuck, Micah, Sydney, for always rooting for me. Jennifer, my ride or die, my sister, I love you, girl. To Diarra, my Brooklyn Queen, for all you see in me, the way you ride with me through thick and thin no matter what. For looping me arm in arm when we see goals too tall and being there step-by-step as we scale them all. For keeping me grounded, rooted in my faith, and ever aware of my purpose.

To Emily, my dear friend and rockstar CP: Thank you for holding me up through this. You had a front-row seat to how tough this one was, and you walked every single step with me, at the expense of your own sleep and priorities. Draft after draft. Line after line. Through a pandemic, Pitch Wars, my debut season, and just *life*. There aren't enough words to fully express just how grateful I am to you.

To Nic Stone, my birthday twin, my book mom, and my dear friend, who keeps me in line, wraps me in encouragement when I'm low, snatches me up when I need it, and always tells me the truth. Your fierce advocacy, your friendship, your heart, has left a mark on me that can never be erased. You've helped me grow as a writer, a wife, and as a woman. Thank you! And in true twin-Cancer fashion, I'm crying (and you're not, LMAO).

To Sabaa, for always encouraging me to trust myself. For listening to my wild ideas and assuring me I can chase each one. To Natalie, for always believing, cheerleading. For seeing what Rue could be from the very beginning, thank you! To Jodi, for wrapping me up in your arms and shepherding me and this book to shelves. I would not have survived bringing my second novel into the world without you! Working with you has changed my life! You're a dream come true. <3

To Jessica Lewis, for holding me up through the low moments, for listening, for feedback, for sharing your editorial brilliance with me. For always being down for a middle-of-the-night plot brainstorm session, ha ha. You're one of the most talented writers and beautiful people I've ever met. It's an honor to call you friend. <3

To Steph Jones and Tami Charles, for sisterhood and laughs. For inspiration and encouragement, distraction, a place to vent. To my tribe: the QueenSquad, for all the glass we are shattering. For big dreams and even bigger accomplishments. Kris, thank you for holding me up during debut year while I was simultaneously editing this book. I very literally would have collapsed without your help. Kelis, thank you for always being there. For seeing more in me and Rue than I could ever dream.

HUGE thanks to Jarred Amato and the entire Project Lit community! And to Rue's Crew, who shouted *loud* and *proud* for Rue from the very beginning! This book would not be so well-known without your support. Andonnia Maiben, Shelia Colón-Bagley,

Kayla Stansbury, Holly Davis, Anikka Cosgrove, Runeda Scott, Justice Hill, Ebony Williams, Bayley Pepper, Laronda McCray, Holly Hughes, Jessica Richter, Tianna Peterson, Lori Harris, Asheree Vaughn, so many of you! Thank you!

To Jessica F., for friendship and laughs, cutesy Miles Marco Polos, dinner prep chats, for listening to me cry through my how many (?) ear infections. For reading, discussing, then reading again. For everything you give and everything you are. <3 To Jessica O., for being right there with me every time I needed feedback or wanted to bounce ideas. For dedicating entire days to speed-reading. I got to know you so much more as I was drafting and editing this book, and I'm so blessed by your talented writer brain and even more by your beautiful heart.

Thank you to every single critique partner and beta reader, the Mermaids, #the21ders, the class of 2k21, YAYSquad, Mary R., Alechia, Faridah, Ayana, Alexa, Jesse Q. Sutanto, Graci Kim, Sonora, Naz, Taj, my Twitter writing community, to whom I will always and forever be indebted. To my followers on socials, educators who have brought Rue into their classrooms, bloggers, bookstagrammers, any and everyone who has ever retweeted a post, shared, or commented, thank you. Your love of Rue and all she stands for is a huge part of why her story has been shared so widely. I am so grateful for the place she holds in your heart.

And lastly, thank you, Houston, the southeast side, off Scott between Sunnyside and Third Ward, Jack Yates Lions, Cullen Bobcats, the amazing Velda Hunter. Thank you for the magic you inspire, the greatness you produce. Thank you for rearing and raising me. You shine so brightly!

It is my hope, with this author thing, I'm making you proud.

ABOUT THE AUTHOR

J. Elle is the *New York Times* bestselling author of *Wings of Ebony*. Elle has a bachelor's in journalism and an MA in educational administration and human development. She grew up in Texas, but has lived all over, from coast to coast, which she credits as inspiration for her writing. When she's not writing, the former educator can be found mentoring aspiring authors, binging reality TV, loving on her three littles, or cooking up something true to her Louisiana roots. *Ashes of Gold*, her second novel, is part two of the *Wings of Ebony* duology.